KAGEKI SHOJO!!

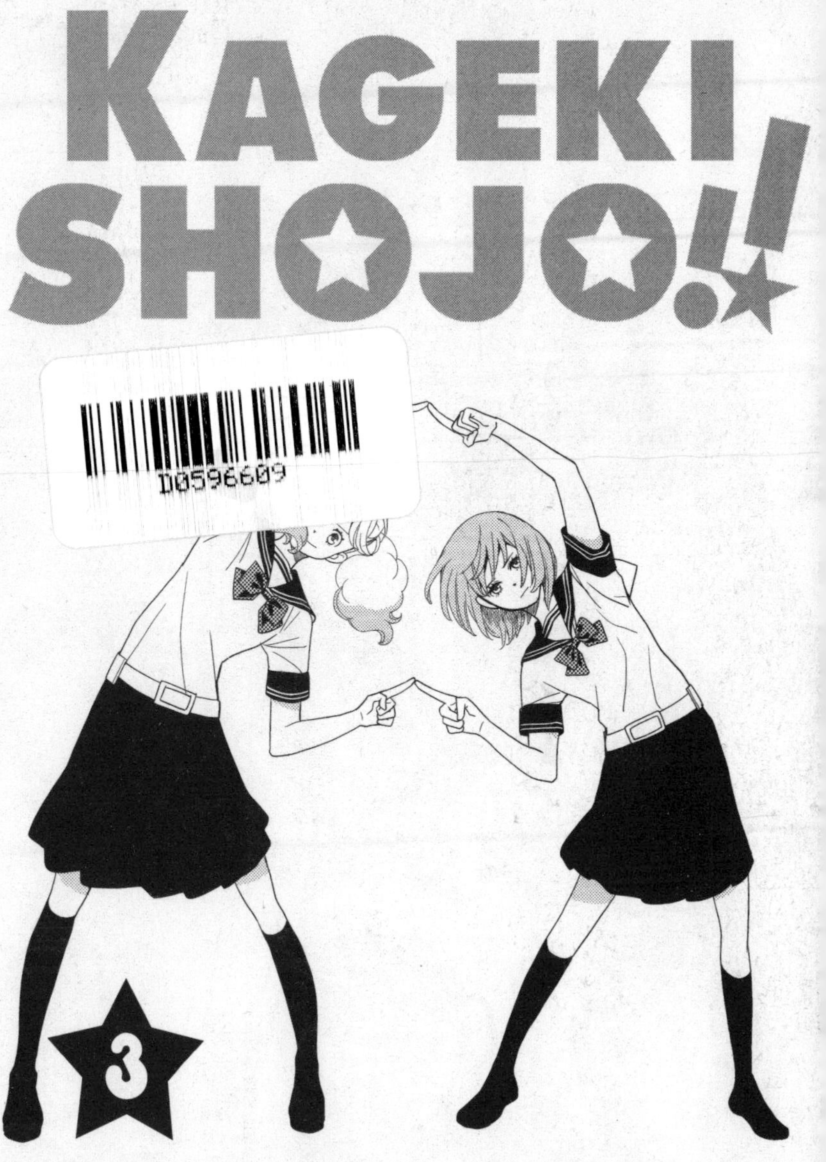

3

story & art by
Kumiko Saiki

Characters

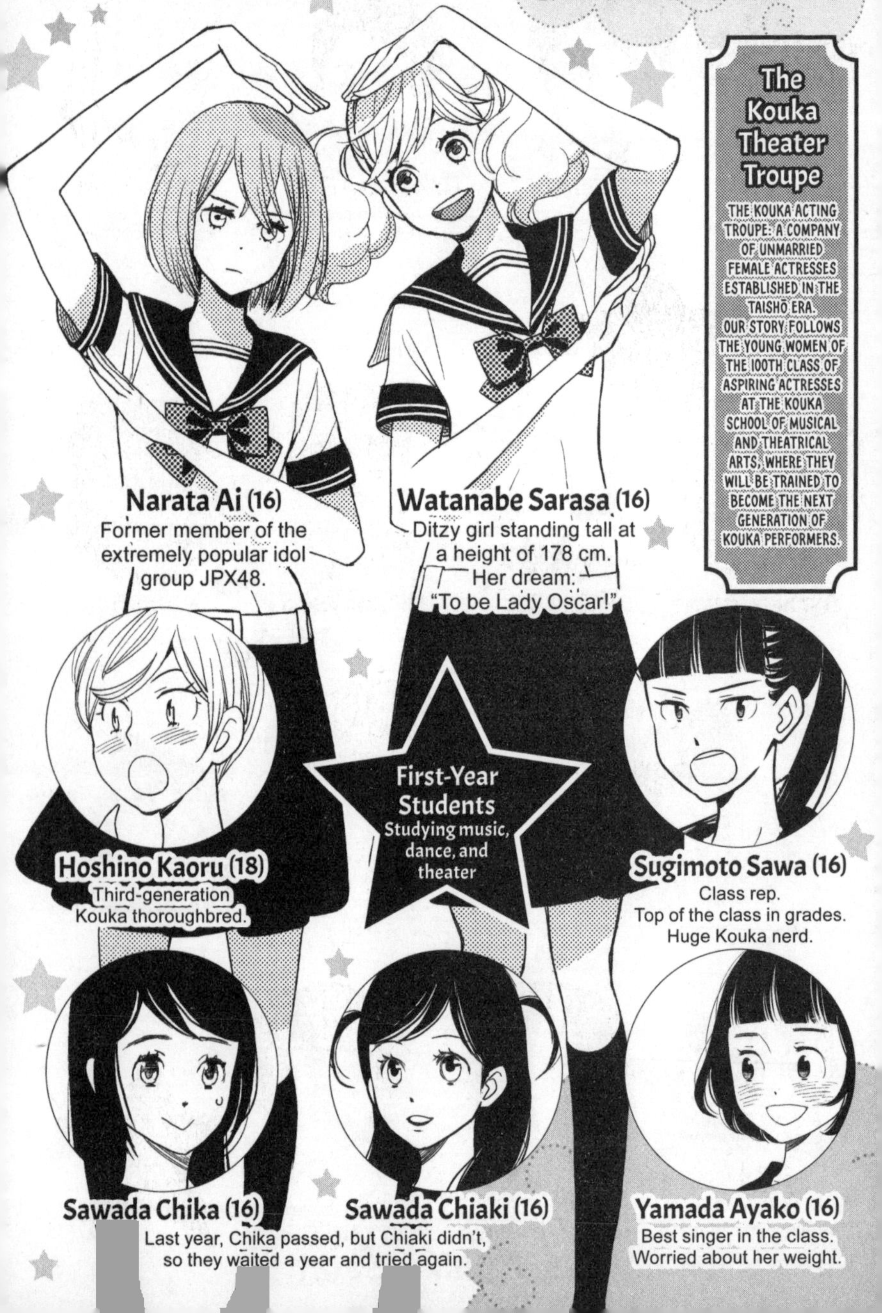
The Kouka Theater Troupe
THE KOUKA ACTING TROUPE: A COMPANY OF UNMARRIED FEMALE ACTRESSES ESTABLISHED IN THE TAISHŌ ERA. OUR STORY FOLLOWS THE YOUNG WOMEN OF THE 100TH CLASS OF ASPIRING ACTRESSES AT THE KOUKA SCHOOL OF MUSICAL AND THEATRICAL ARTS, WHERE THEY WILL BE TRAINED TO BECOME THE NEXT GENERATION OF KOUKA PERFORMERS.
Watanabe Sarasa (16)
Ditzy girl standing tall at a height of 178 cm. Her dream: "To be Lady Oscar!"
Narata Ai (16)
Former member of the extremely popular idol group JPX48.
First-Year Students
Studying music, dance, and theater
Sugimoto Sawa (16)
Class rep. Top of the class in grades. Huge Kouka nerd.
Hoshino Kaoru (18)
Third-generation Kouka thoroughbred.
Yamada Ayako (16)
Best singer in the class. Worried about her weight.
Sawada Chiaki (16)
Sawada Chika (16)
Last year, Chika passed, but Chiaki didn't, so they waited a year and tried again.

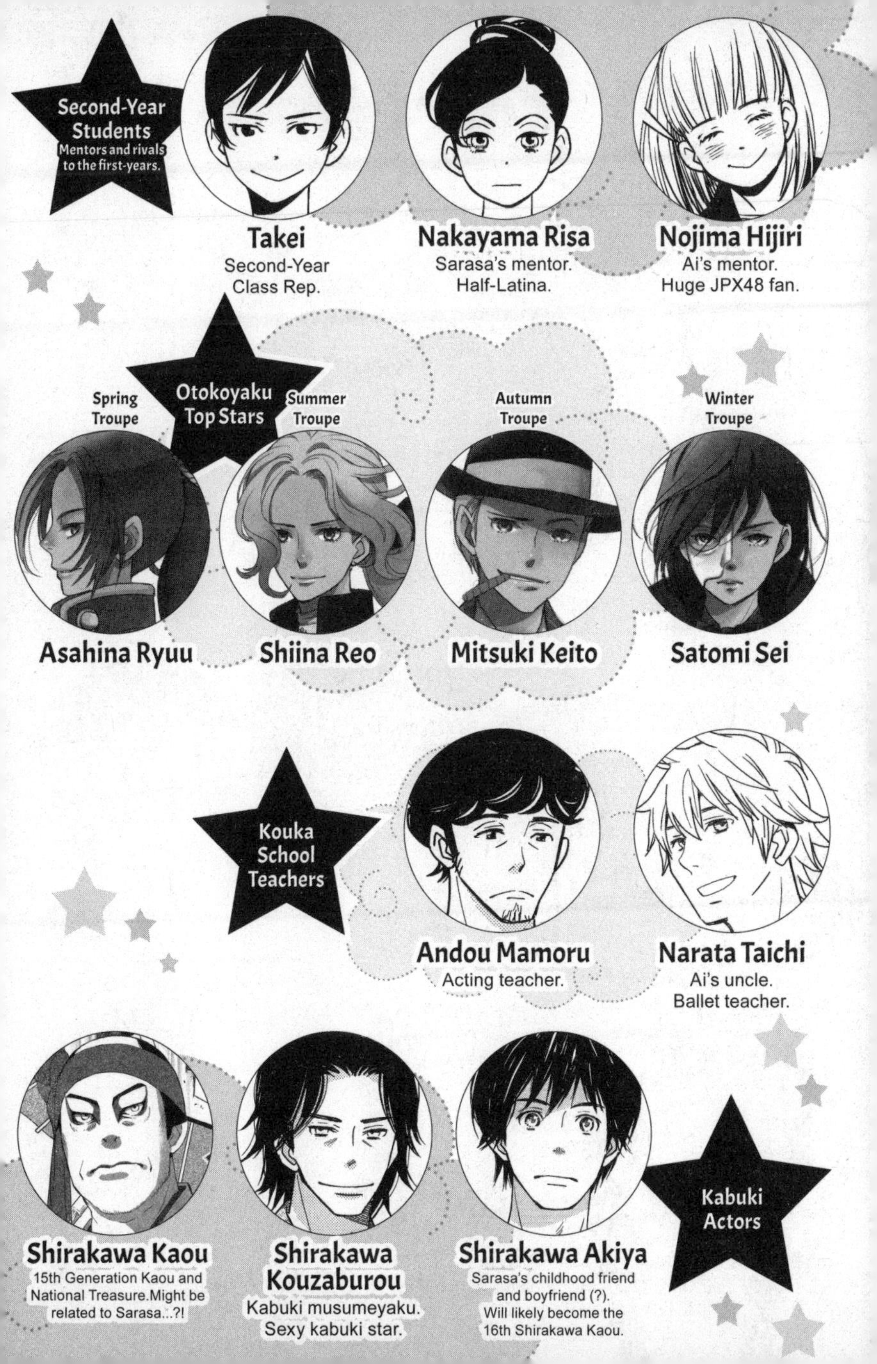

Second-Year Students
Mentors and rivals to the first-years.
Takei
Second-Year Class Rep.
Nakayama Risa
Sarasa's mentor. Half-Latina.
Nojima Hijiri
Ai's mentor. Huge JPX48 fan.
Otokoyaku Top Stars
Spring Troupe
Asahina Ryuu
Summer Troupe
Shiina Reo
Autumn Troupe
Mitsuki Keito
Winter Troupe
Satomi Sei
Kouka School Teachers
Andou Mamoru
Acting teacher.
Narata Taichi
Ai's uncle. Ballet teacher.
Shirakawa Kaou
15th Generation Kaou and National Treasure.Might be related to Sarasa...?!
Shirakawa Kouzaburou
Kabuki musumeyaku. Sexy kabuki star.
Shirakawa Akiya
Sarasa's childhood friend and boyfriend (?). Will likely become the 16th Shirakawa Kaou.
Kabuki Actors

CONTENTS

No.

Date

Kouka Troupe Terms to Know! ★

Kouka Theater Troupe
Founded a hundred years ago as a theater troupe comprised of young, unmarried women.
Split into four troupes (Spring/Summer/Autumn/Winter). Main theater is in Kobe.

Otokoyaku / Musumeyaku
Designated roles for the gender of characters actresses play. Otokoyaku actresses play male or
masculine characters, while musumeyaku actresses play female or feminine characters.

Top Star
The actress who heads her troupe. Each troupe has an otokoyaku top star and musumeyaku top star.
Top stars appear in every major production.

Kouka School of Musical and Theatrical Arts
Two-year prep school where the next stars of the Kouka Troupe are forged.
Girls can apply anytime between 9th and 12th grade!

First-Year Students vs. Second-Year Students
While first-year students primarily focus on their studies, second-year students are tasked both
with their studies and mentoring the first-year students, as well as managing their cleaning
schedule and helping them with lifestyle adjustments.

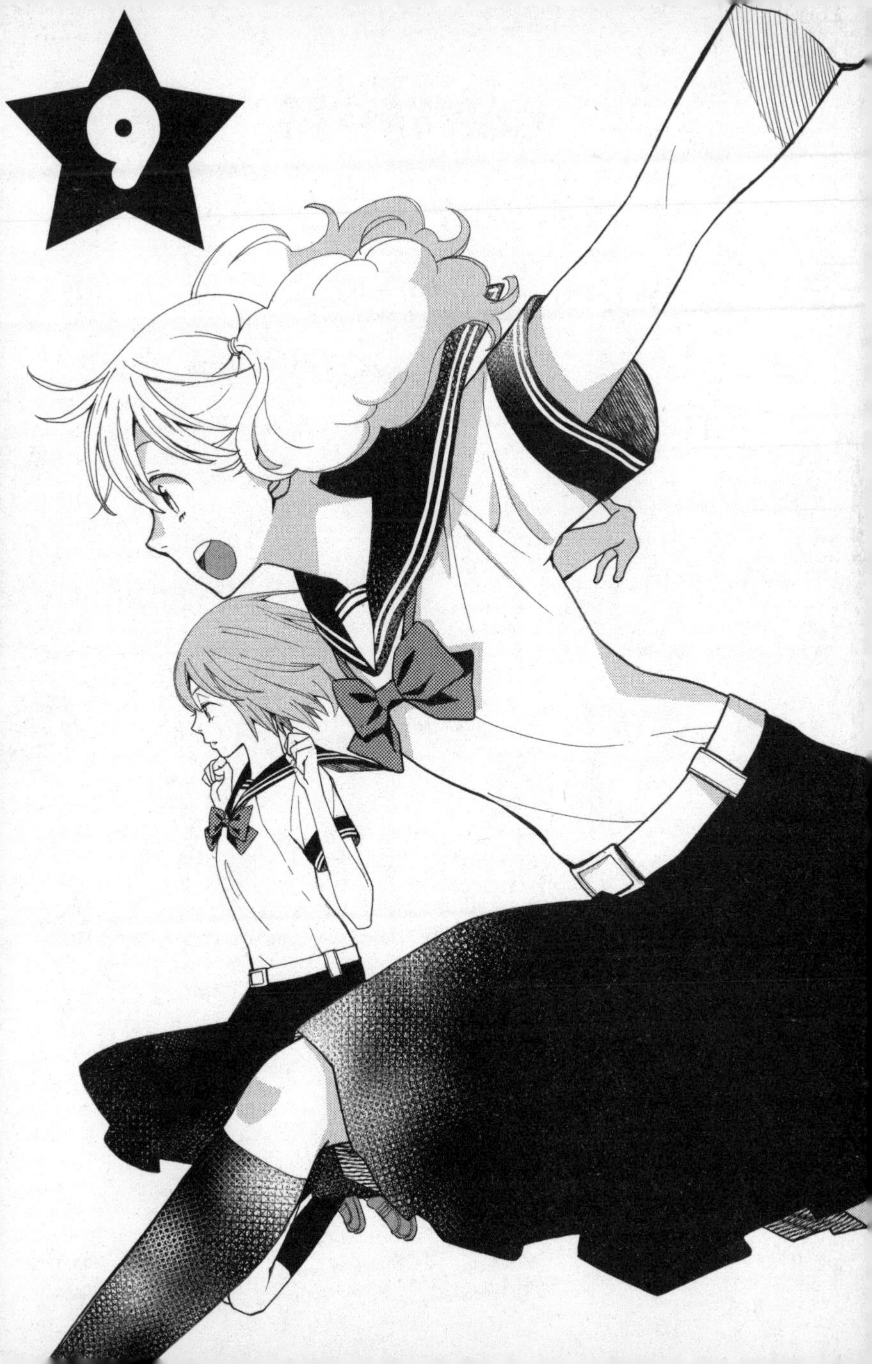
9

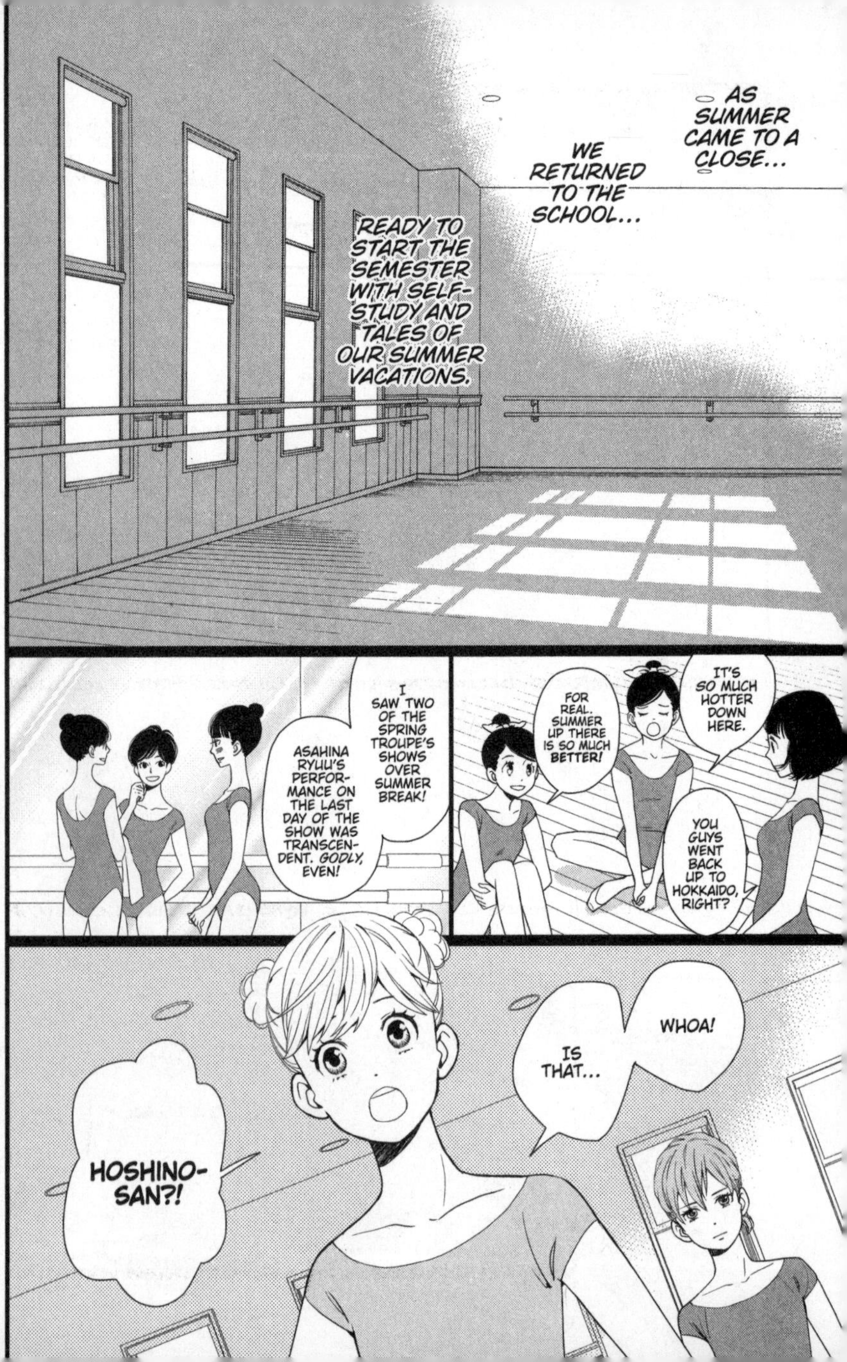
AS SUMMER CAME TO A CLOSE...
WE RETURNED TO THE SCHOOL...
READY TO START THE SEMESTER WITH SELF-STUDY AND TALES OF OUR SUMMER VACATIONS.
IT'S SO MUCH HOTTER DOWN HERE.
FOR REAL. SUMMER UP THERE IS SO MUCH BETTER!
YOU GUYS WENT BACK UP TO HOKKAIDO, RIGHT?
I SAW TWO OF THE SPRING TROUPE'S SHOWS OVER SUMMER BREAK!
ASAHINA RYUU'S PERFORMANCE ON THE LAST DAY OF THE SHOW WAS TRANSCENDENT. GODLY, EVEN!
WHOA!
IS THAT...
HOSHINO-SAN?!

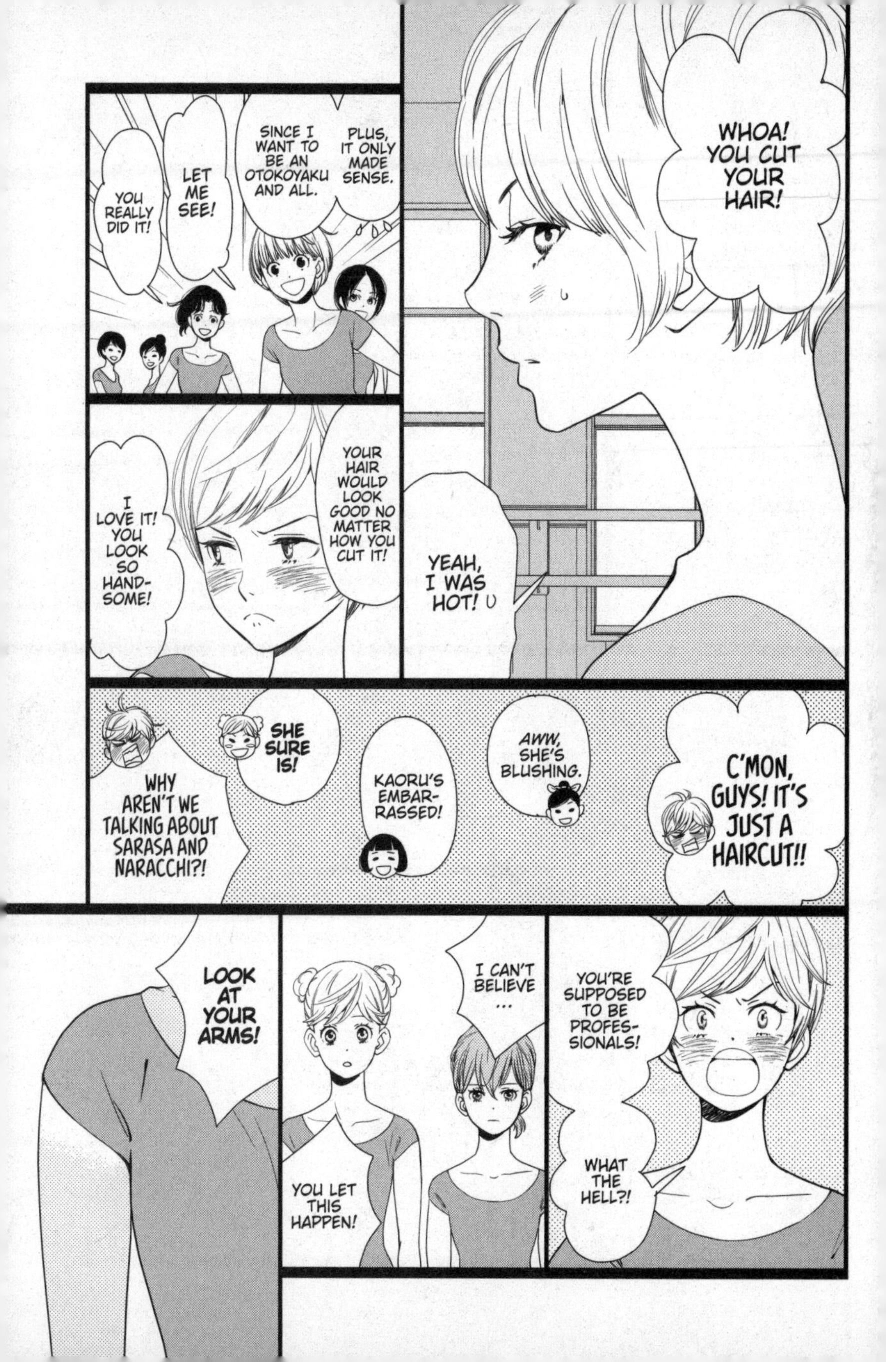
WHOA! YOU CUT YOUR HAIR!
YEAH, I WAS HOT!
SINCE I WANT TO BE AN OTOKOYAKU AND ALL.
PLUS, IT ONLY MADE SENSE.
LET ME SEE!
YOU REALLY DID IT!
YOUR HAIR WOULD LOOK GOOD NO MATTER HOW YOU CUT IT!
I LOVE IT! YOU LOOK SO HANDSOME!
C'MON, GUYS! IT'S JUST A HAIRCUT!!
AWW, SHE'S BLUSHING.
KAORU'S EMBARRASSED!
SHE SURE IS!
WHY AREN'T WE TALKING ABOUT SARASA AND NARACCHI?!
YOU'RE SUPPOSED TO BE PROFESSIONALS!
WHAT THE HELL?!
I CAN'T BELIEVE ...
YOU LET THIS HAPPEN!
LOOK AT YOUR ARMS!

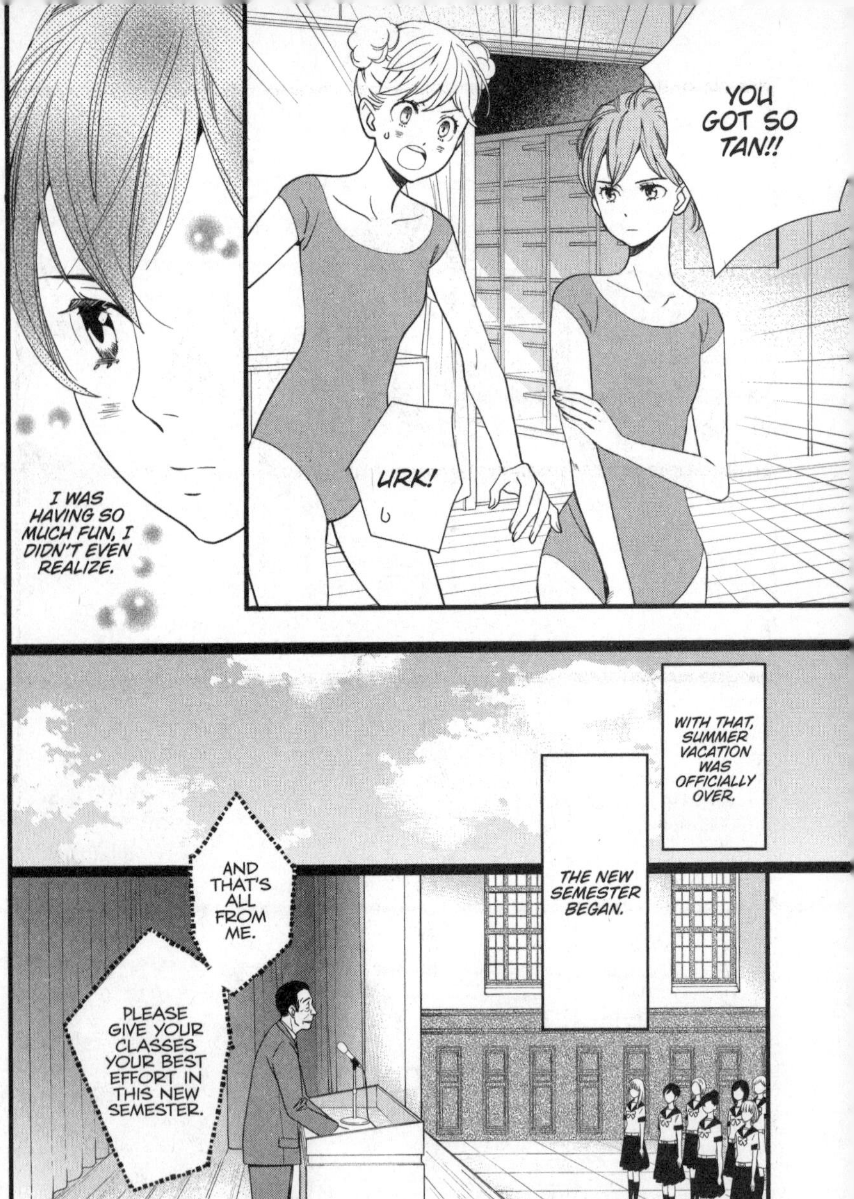
YOU GOT SO TAN!!
URK!
I WAS HAVING SO MUCH FUN, I DIDN'T EVEN REALIZE.
WITH THAT, SUMMER VACATION WAS OFFICIALLY OVER.
THE NEW SEMESTER BEGAN.
AND THAT'S ALL FROM ME.
PLEASE GIVE YOUR CLASSES YOUR BEST EFFORT IN THIS NEW SEMESTER.

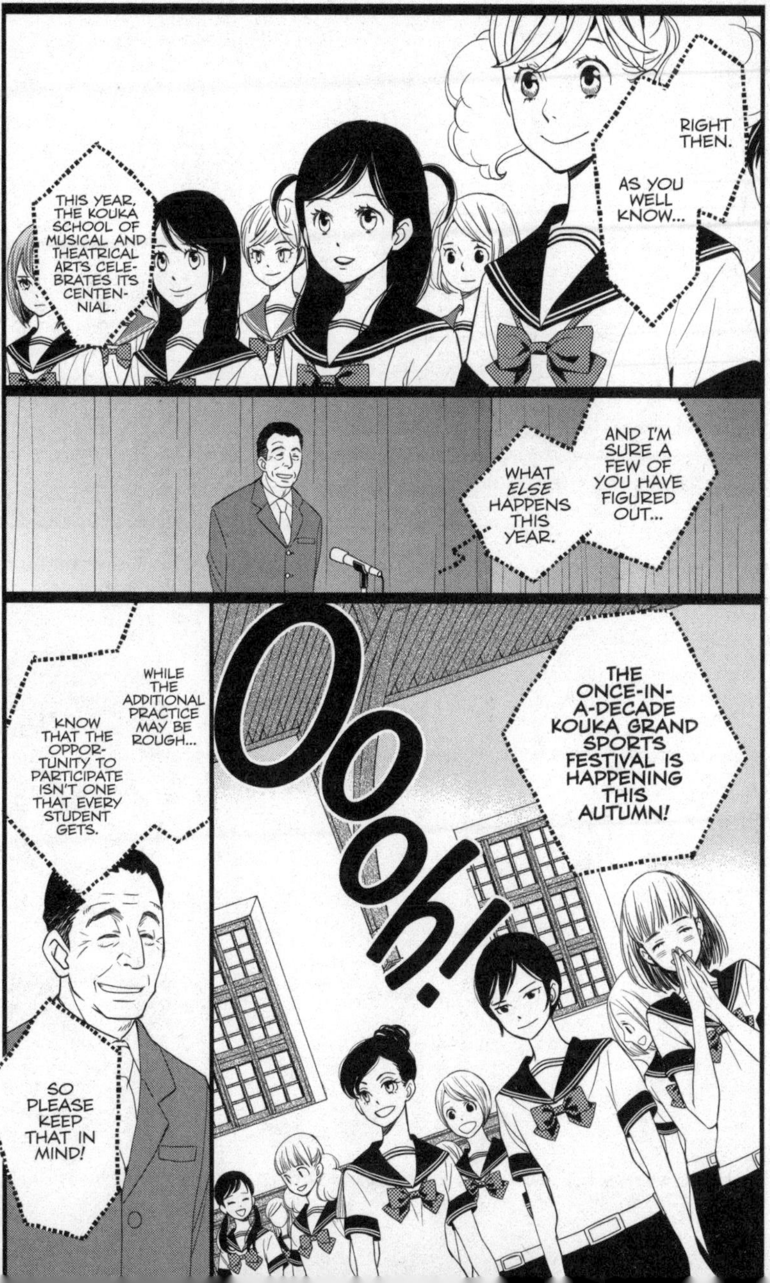
RIGHT THEN.
AS YOU WELL KNOW...
THIS YEAR, THE KOUKA SCHOOL OF MUSICAL AND THEATRICAL ARTS CELEBRATES ITS CENTENNIAL.
AND I'M SURE A FEW OF YOU HAVE FIGURED OUT...
WHAT *ELSE* HAPPENS THIS YEAR.
THE ONCE-IN-A-DECADE KOUKA GRAND SPORTS FESTIVAL IS HAPPENING THIS AUTUMN!
Oooh!!
WHILE THE ADDITIONAL PRACTICE MAY BE ROUGH...
KNOW THAT THE OPPORTUNITY TO PARTICIPATE ISN'T ONE THAT EVERY STUDENT GETS.
SO PLEASE KEEP THAT IN MIND!

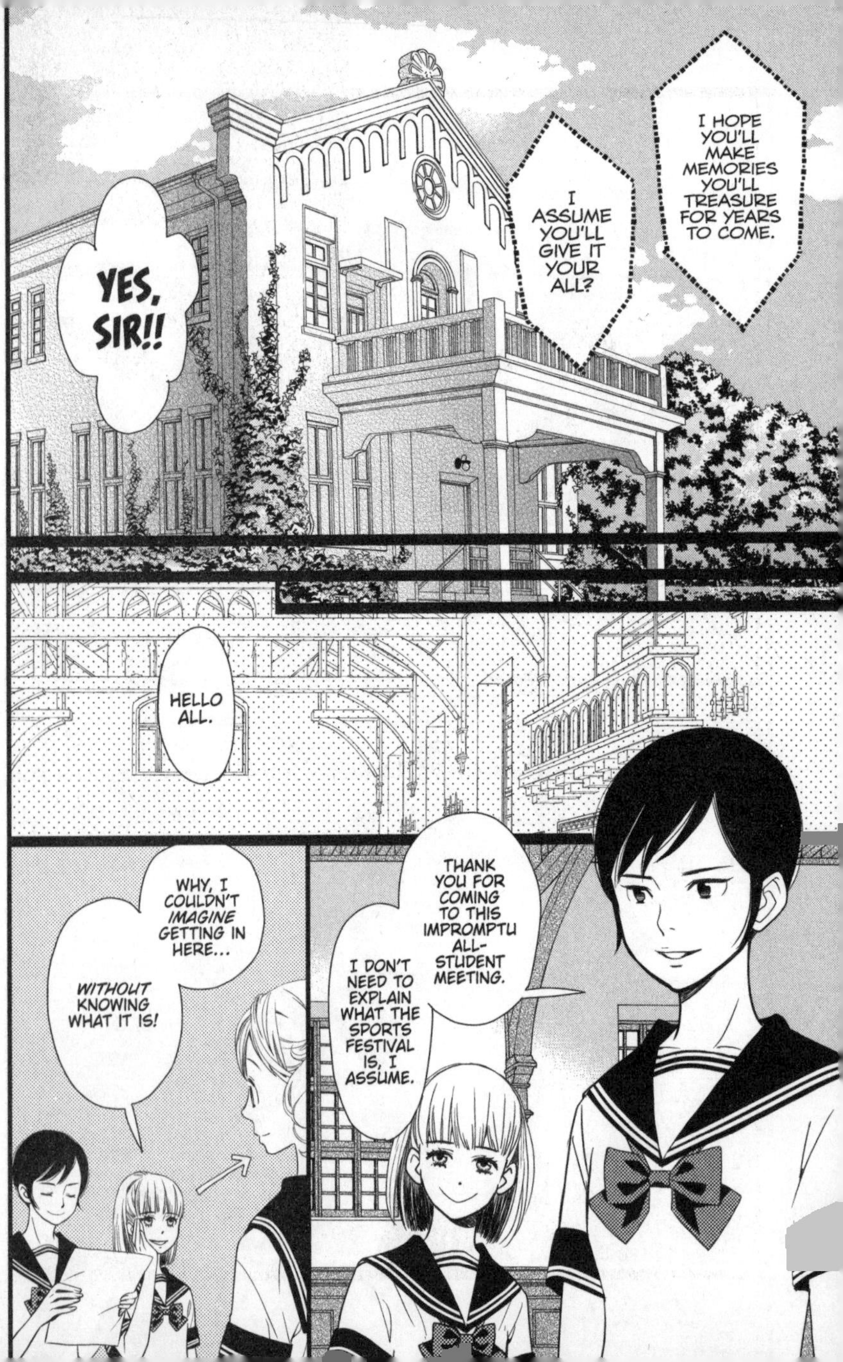
I HOPE YOU'LL MAKE MEMORIES YOU'LL TREASURE FOR YEARS TO COME.
I ASSUME YOU'LL GIVE IT YOUR ALL?
YES, SIR!!
HELLO ALL.
THANK YOU FOR COMING TO THIS IMPROMPTU ALL-STUDENT MEETING.
I DON'T NEED TO EXPLAIN WHAT THE SPORTS FESTIVAL IS, I ASSUME.
WHY, I COULDN'T *IMAGINE* GETTING IN HERE...
WITHOUT KNOWING WHAT IT IS!

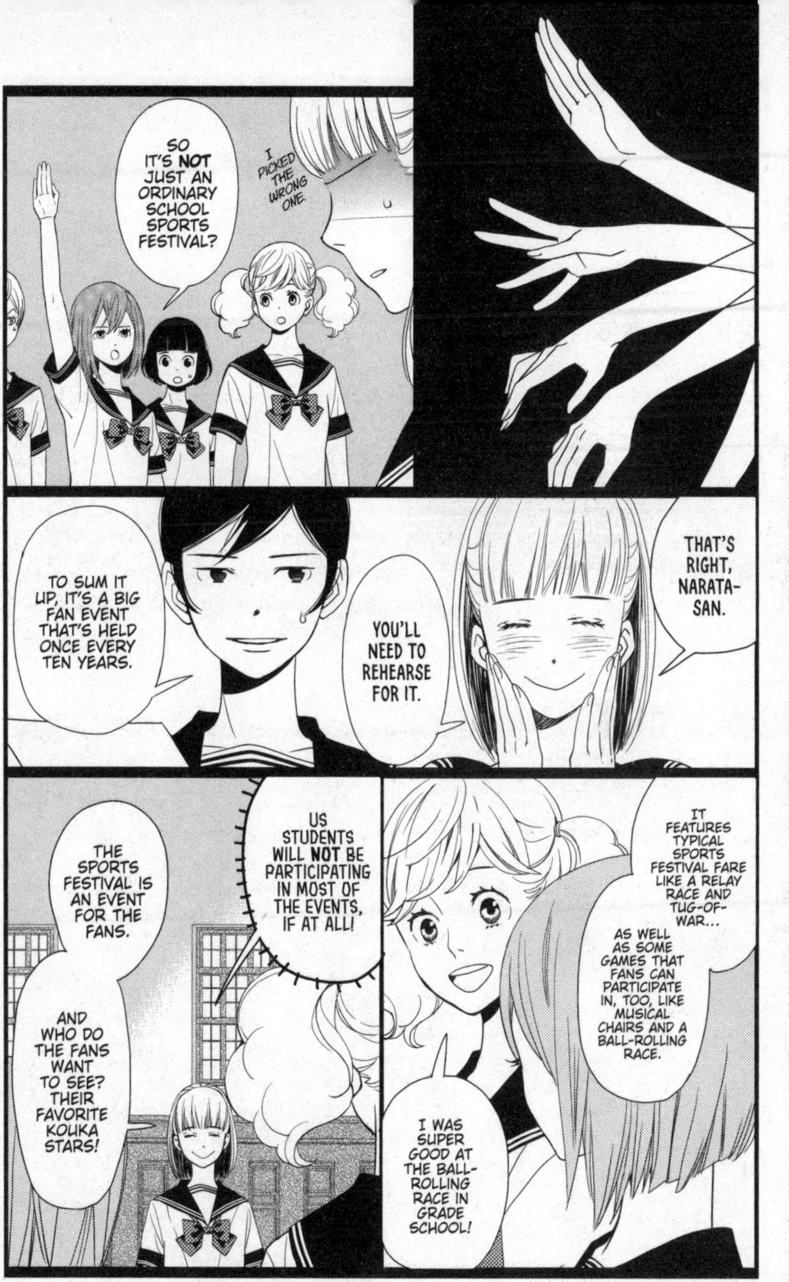
I PICKED THE WRONG ONE.
SO IT'S NOT JUST AN ORDINARY SCHOOL SPORTS FESTIVAL?
THAT'S RIGHT, NARATA-SAN.
YOU'LL NEED TO REHEARSE FOR IT.
TO SUM IT UP, IT'S A BIG FAN EVENT THAT'S HELD ONCE EVERY TEN YEARS.
IT FEATURES TYPICAL SPORTS FESTIVAL FARE LIKE A RELAY RACE AND TUG-OF-WAR...
AS WELL AS SOME GAMES THAT FANS CAN PARTICIPATE IN, TOO, LIKE MUSICAL CHAIRS AND A BALL-ROLLING RACE.
I WAS SUPER GOOD AT THE BALL-ROLLING RACE IN GRADE SCHOOL!
US STUDENTS WILL NOT BE PARTICIPATING IN MOST OF THE EVENTS, IF AT ALL!
THE SPORTS FESTIVAL IS AN EVENT FOR THE FANS.
AND WHO DO THE FANS WANT TO SEE? THEIR FAVORITE KOUKA STARS!

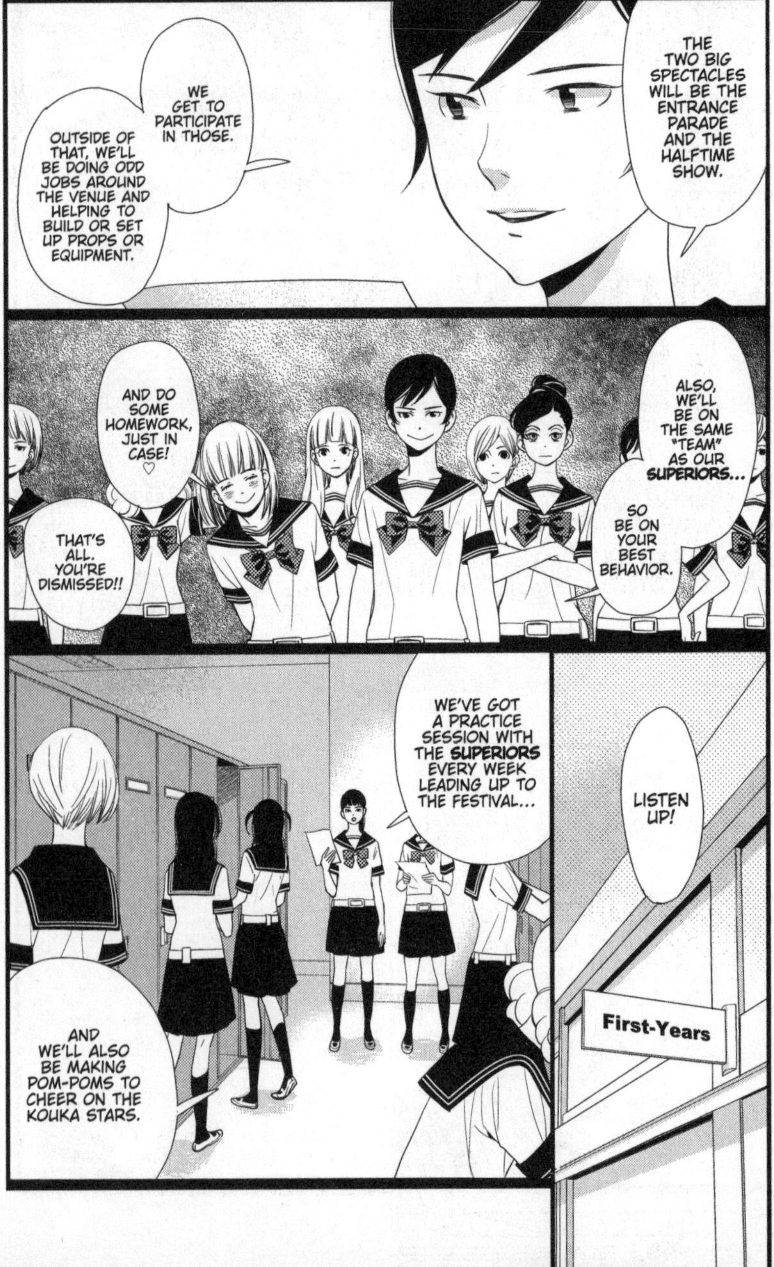
THE TWO BIG SPECTACLES WILL BE THE ENTRANCE PARADE AND THE HALFTIME SHOW.
WE GET TO PARTICIPATE IN THOSE.
OUTSIDE OF THAT, WE'LL BE DOING ODD JOBS AROUND THE VENUE AND HELPING TO BUILD OR SET UP PROPS OR EQUIPMENT.
ALSO, WE'LL BE ON THE SAME "TEAM" AS OUR **SUPERIORS...**
SO BE ON YOUR BEST BEHAVIOR.
AND DO SOME HOMEWORK, JUST IN CASE! ♡
THAT'S ALL. YOU'RE DISMISSED!!
LISTEN UP!
First-Years
WE'VE GOT A PRACTICE SESSION WITH THE **SUPERIORS** EVERY WEEK LEADING UP TO THE FESTIVAL...
AND WE'LL ALSO BE MAKING POM-POMS TO CHEER ON THE KOUKA STARS.

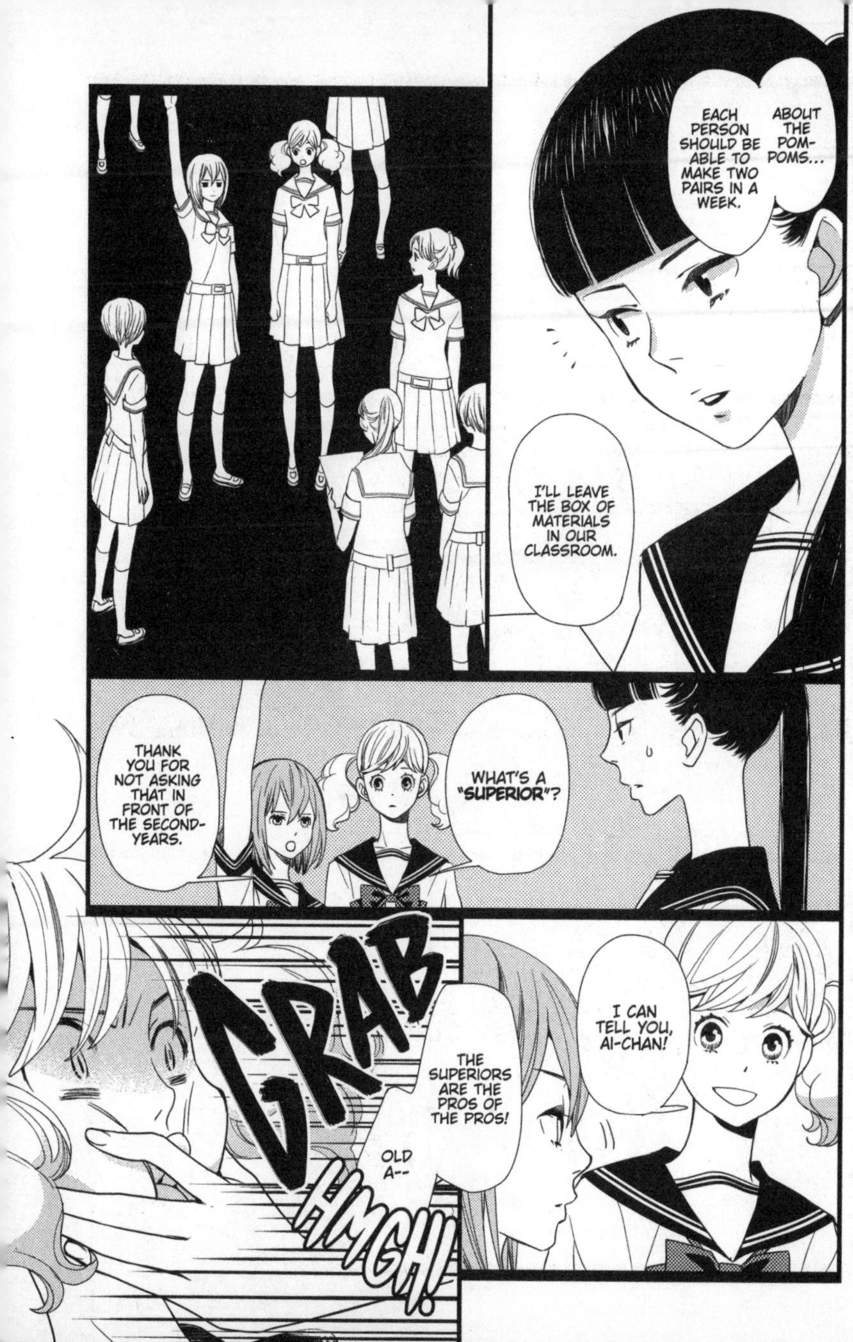
ABOUT THE POM-POMS...
EACH PERSON SHOULD BE ABLE TO MAKE TWO PAIRS IN A WEEK.
I'LL LEAVE THE BOX OF MATERIALS IN OUR CLASSROOM.
WHAT'S A "**SUPERIOR**"?
THANK YOU FOR NOT ASKING THAT IN FRONT OF THE SECOND-YEARS.
I CAN TELL YOU, AI-CHAN!
THE SUPERIORS ARE THE PROS OF THE PROS!
OLD A--
GRAB
HMGH!

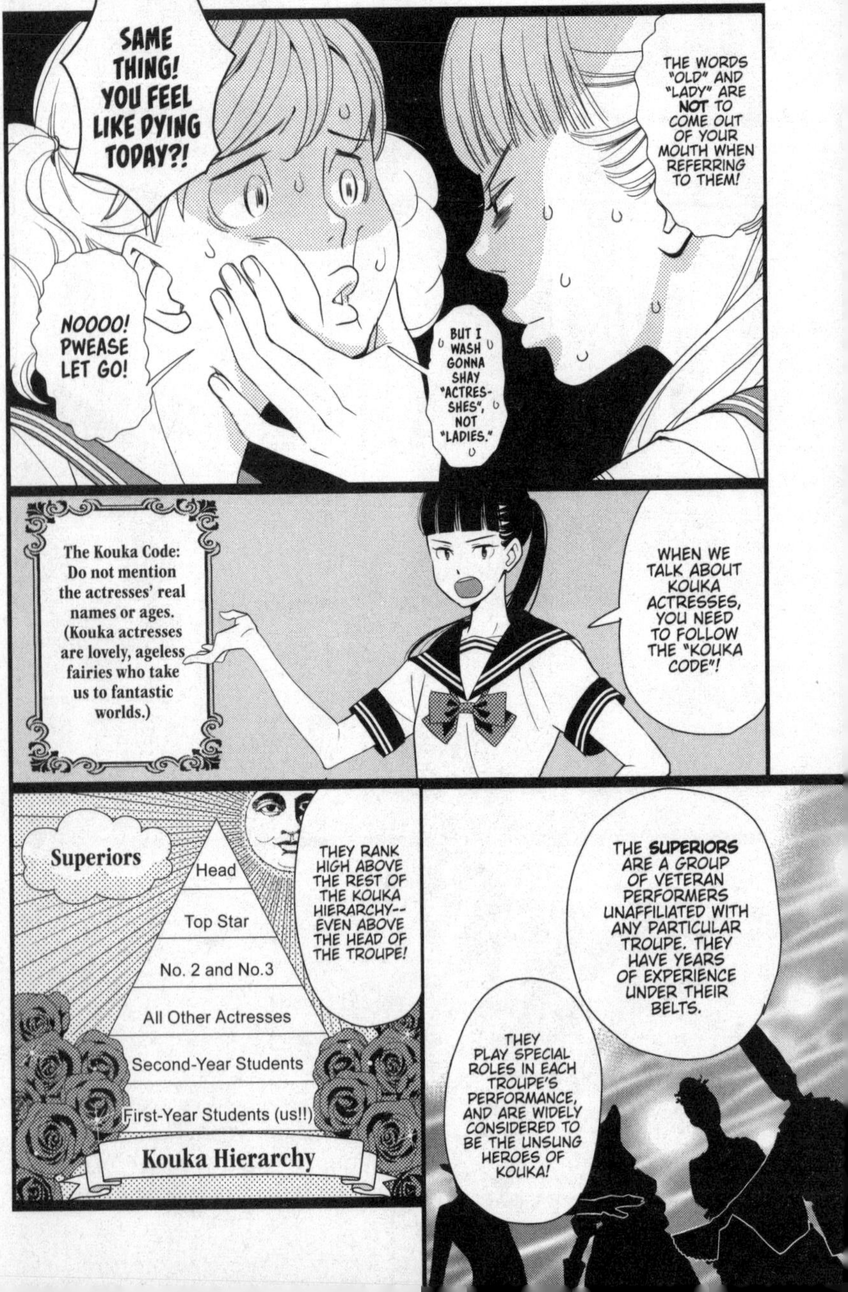
THE WORDS "OLD" AND "LADY" ARE NOT TO COME OUT OF YOUR MOUTH WHEN REFERRING TO THEM!
BUT I WASH GONNA SHAY "ACTRES-SHES", NOT "LADIES."
SAME THING! YOU FEEL LIKE DYING TODAY?!
NOOOO! PWEASE LET GO!
WHEN WE TALK ABOUT KOUKA ACTRESSES, YOU NEED TO FOLLOW THE "KOUKA CODE"!
The Kouka Code: Do not mention the actresses' real names or ages. (Kouka actresses are lovely, ageless fairies who take us to fantastic worlds.)
THE SUPERIORS ARE A GROUP OF VETERAN PERFORMERS UNAFFILIATED WITH ANY PARTICULAR TROUPE. THEY HAVE YEARS OF EXPERIENCE UNDER THEIR BELTS.
THEY PLAY SPECIAL ROLES IN EACH TROUPE'S PERFORMANCE, AND ARE WIDELY CONSIDERED TO BE THE UNSUNG HEROES OF KOUKA!
THEY RANK HIGH ABOVE THE REST OF THE KOUKA HIERARCHY-- EVEN ABOVE THE HEAD OF THE TROUPE!
Superiors
Head
Top Star
No. 2 and No.3
All Other Actresses
Second-Year Students
First-Year Students (us!!)
Kouka Hierarchy

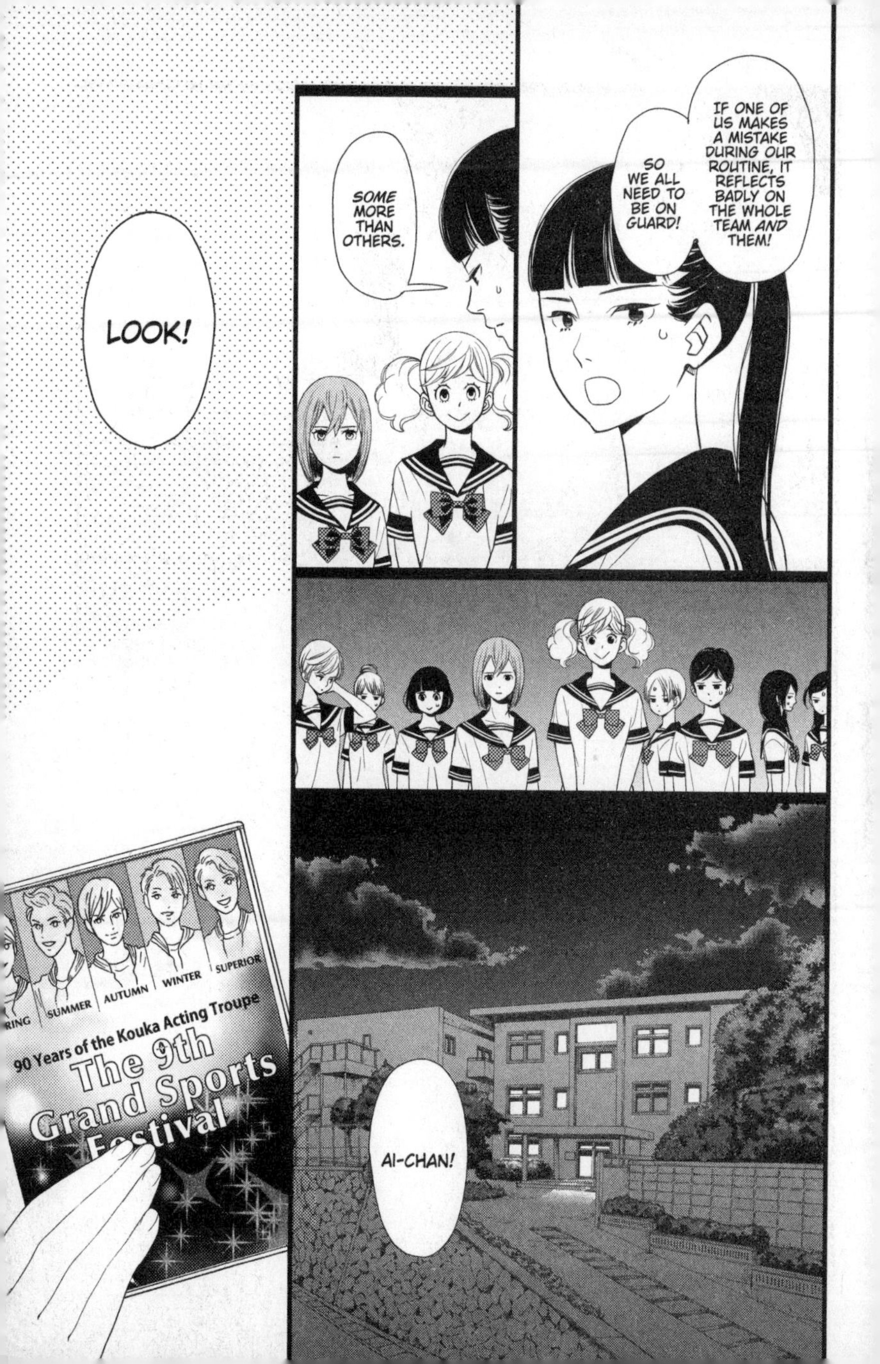
IF ONE OF US MAKES A MISTAKE DURING OUR ROUTINE, IT REFLECTS BADLY ON THE WHOLE TEAM AND THEM!
SO WE ALL NEED TO BE ON GUARD!
SOME MORE THAN OTHERS.
AI-CHAN!
LOOK!
RING
SUMMER
AUTUMN
WINTER
SUPERIOR
90 Years of the Kouka Acting Troupe
The 9th Grand Sports Festival

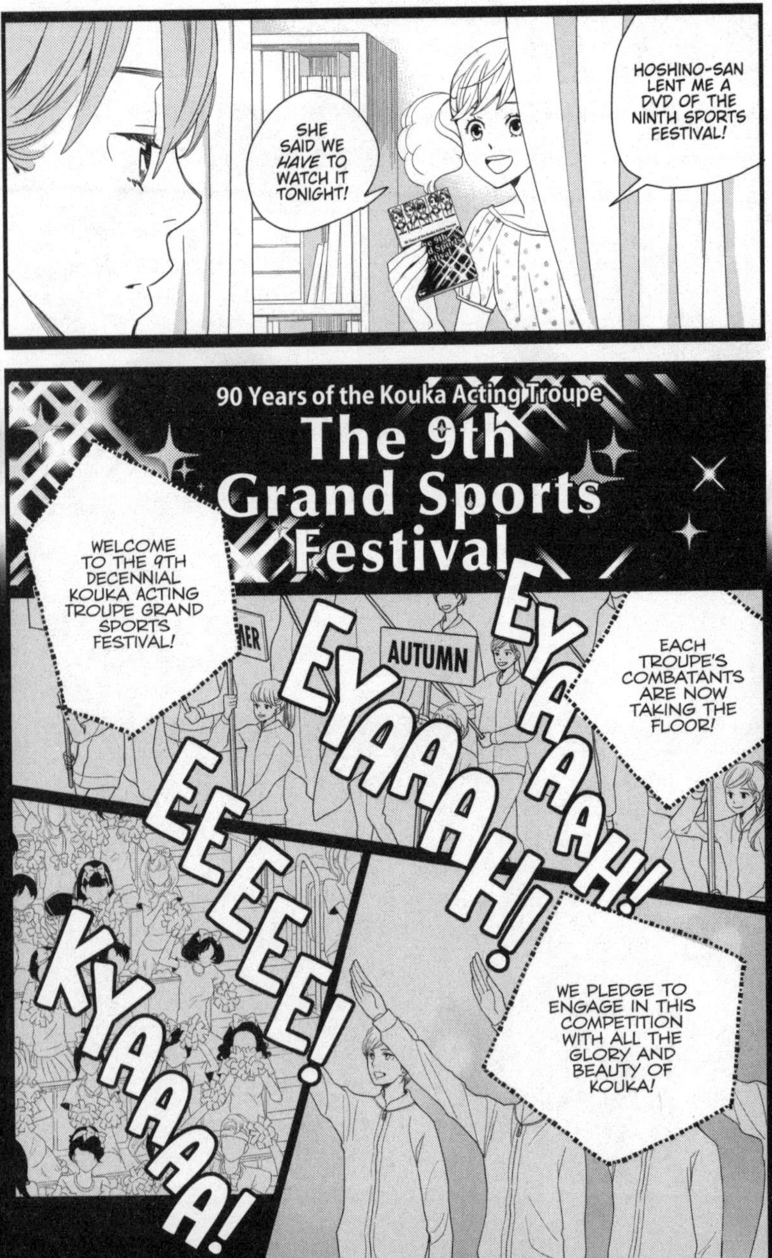
HOSHINO-SAN LENT ME A DVD OF THE NINTH SPORTS FESTIVAL!
SHE SAID WE HAVE TO WATCH IT TONIGHT!
90 Years of the Kouka Acting Troupe
The 9th Grand Sports Festival
EYAAAH!
EACH TROUPE'S COMBATANTS ARE NOW TAKING THE FLOOR!
AUTUMN
WELCOME TO THE 9TH DECENNIAL KOUKA ACTING TROUPE GRAND SPORTS FESTIVAL!
EYAAAAH!
WE PLEDGE TO ENGAGE IN THIS COMPETITION WITH ALL THE GLORY AND BEAUTY OF KOUKA!
EEEEEE!
KYAAAAA!

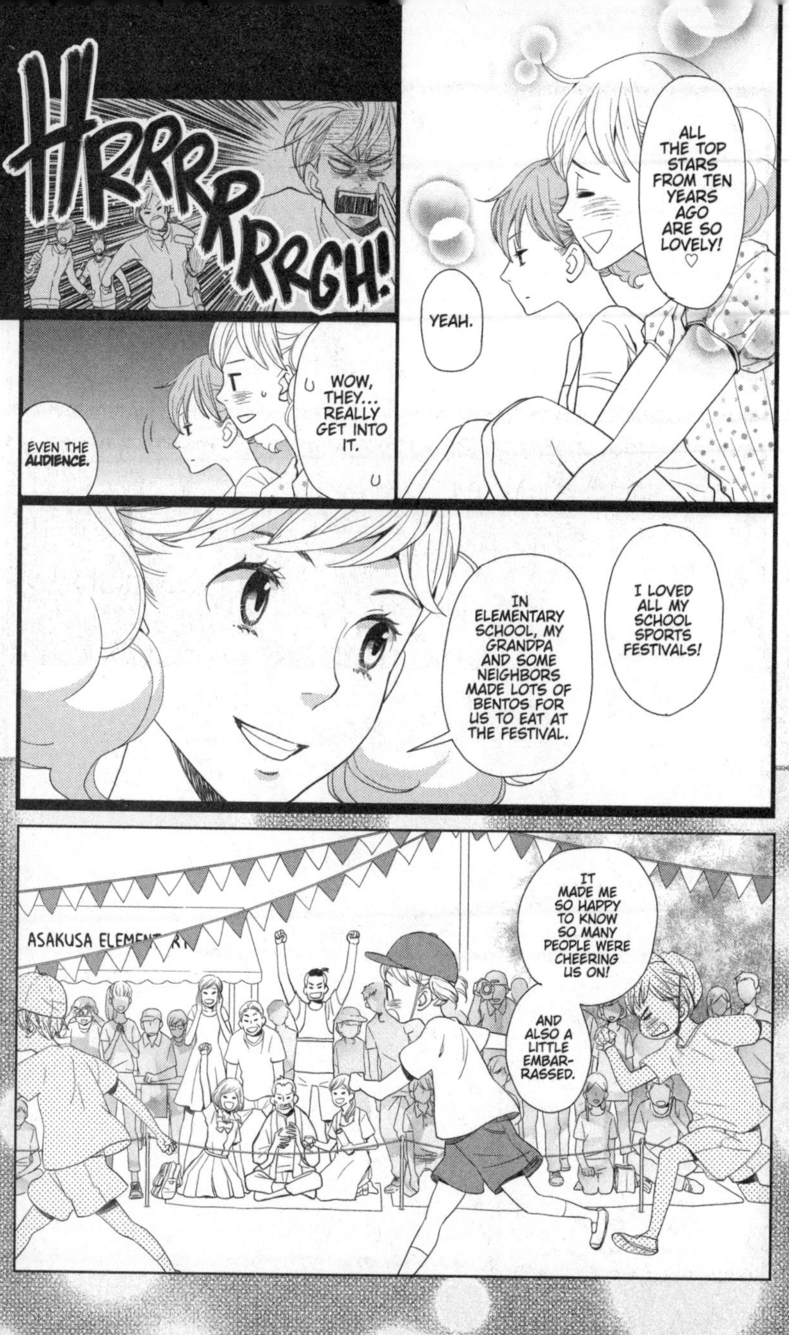
ALL THE TOP STARS FROM TEN YEARS AGO ARE SO LOVELY! ♡
YEAH.
HRRRRRRGH!
WOW, THEY... REALLY GET INTO IT.
EVEN THE AUDIENCE.
I LOVED ALL MY SCHOOL SPORTS FESTIVALS!
IN ELEMENTARY SCHOOL, MY GRANDPA AND SOME NEIGHBORS MADE LOTS OF BENTOS FOR US TO EAT AT THE FESTIVAL.
IT MADE ME SO HAPPY TO KNOW SO MANY PEOPLE WERE CHEERING US ON!
AND ALSO A LITTLE EMBARRASSED.
ASAKUSA ELEMENT

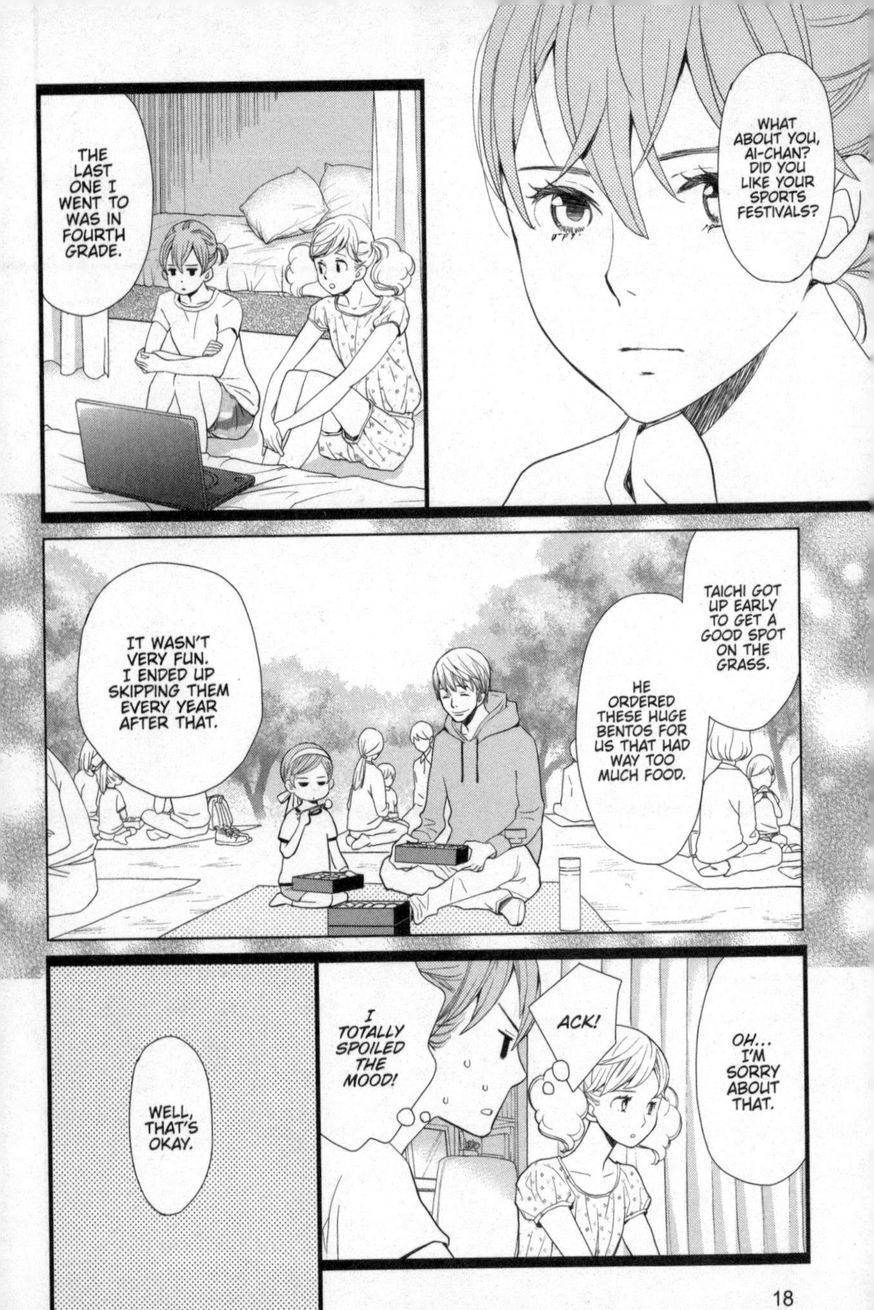
WHAT ABOUT YOU, AI-CHAN? DID YOU LIKE YOUR SPORTS FESTIVALS?
THE LAST ONE I WENT TO WAS IN FOURTH GRADE.
TAICHI GOT UP EARLY TO GET A GOOD SPOT ON THE GRASS.
HE ORDERED THESE HUGE BENTOS FOR US THAT HAD WAY TOO MUCH FOOD.
IT WASN'T VERY FUN. I ENDED UP SKIPPING THEM EVERY YEAR AFTER THAT.
OH... I'M SORRY ABOUT THAT.
ACK!
I TOTALLY SPOILED THE MOOD!
WELL, THAT'S OKAY.

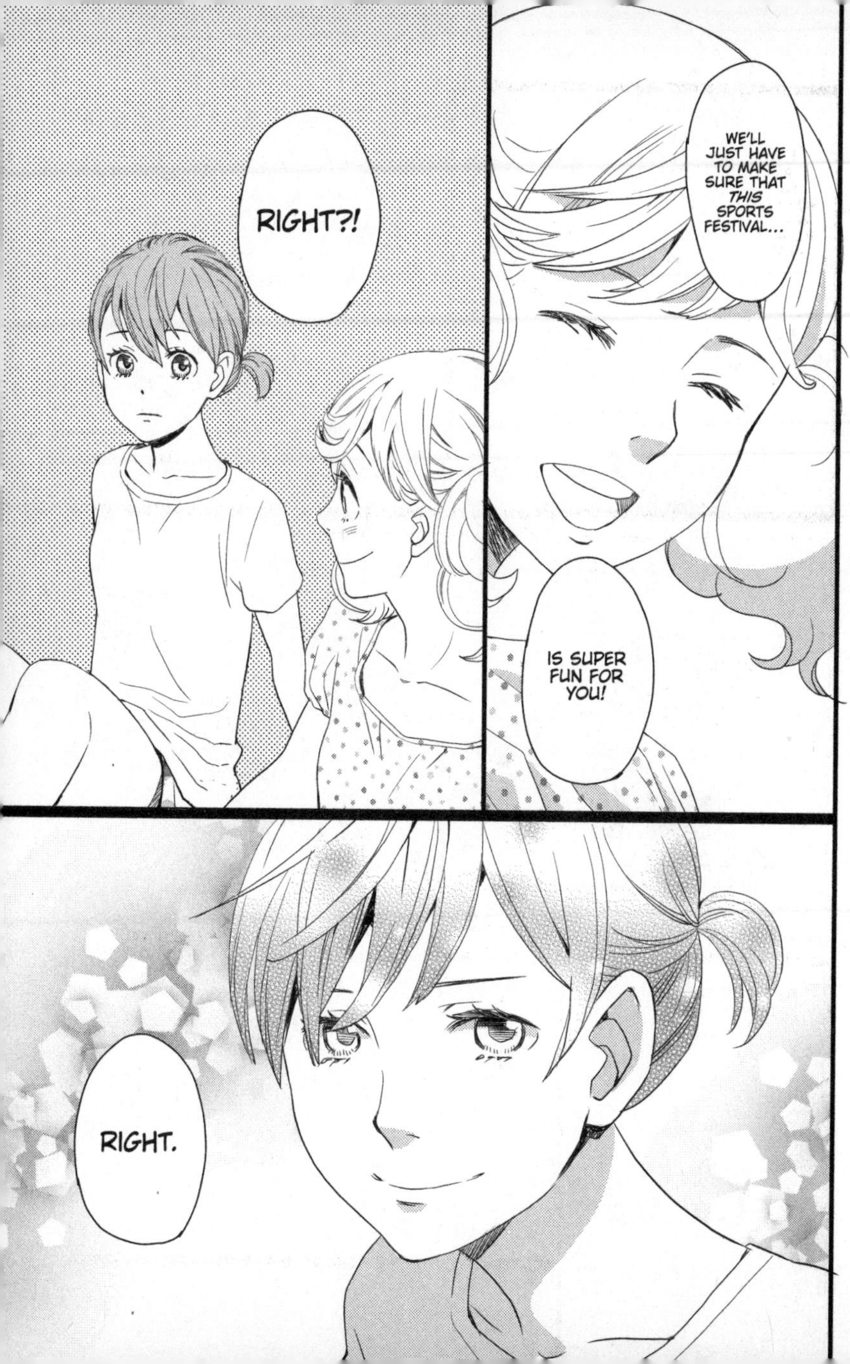
WE'LL JUST HAVE TO MAKE SURE THAT *THIS* SPORTS FESTIVAL...
IS SUPER FUN FOR YOU!
RIGHT?!
RIGHT.

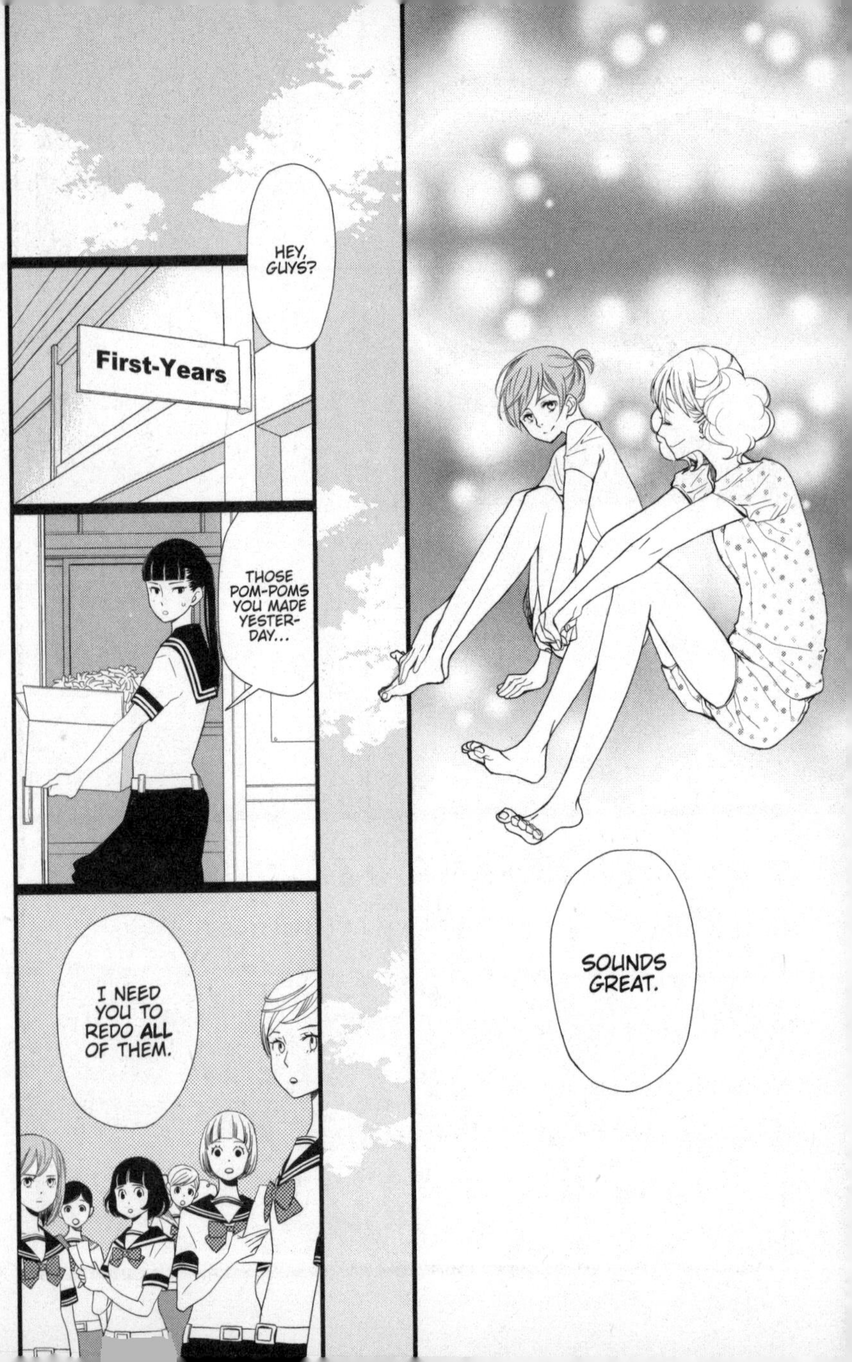
SOUNDS GREAT.
HEY, GUYS?
First-Years
THOSE POM-POMS YOU MADE YESTERDAY...
I NEED YOU TO REDO **ALL** OF THEM.

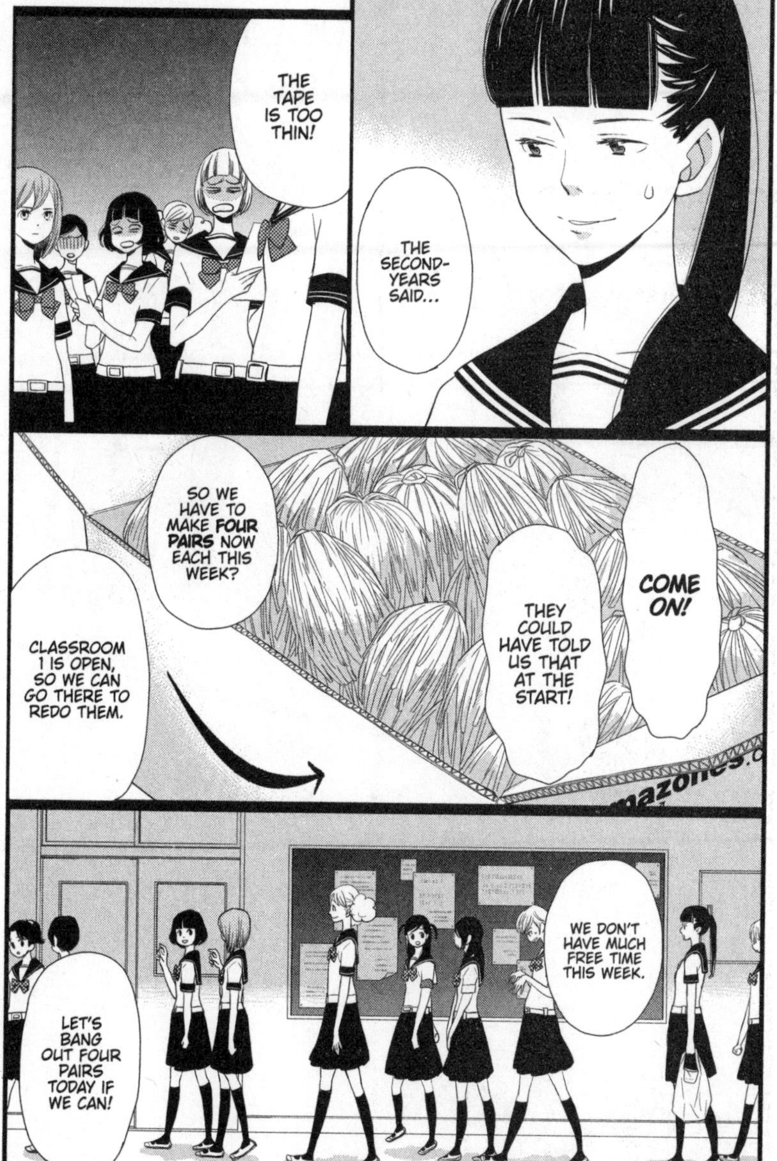
THE SECOND-YEARS SAID...
THE TAPE IS TOO THIN!
COME ON!
THEY COULD HAVE TOLD US THAT AT THE START!
SO WE HAVE TO MAKE **FOUR PAIRS** NOW EACH THIS WEEK?
CLASSROOM 1 IS OPEN, SO WE CAN GO THERE TO REDO THEM.
WE DON'T HAVE MUCH FREE TIME THIS WEEK.
LET'S BANG OUT FOUR PAIRS TODAY IF WE CAN!

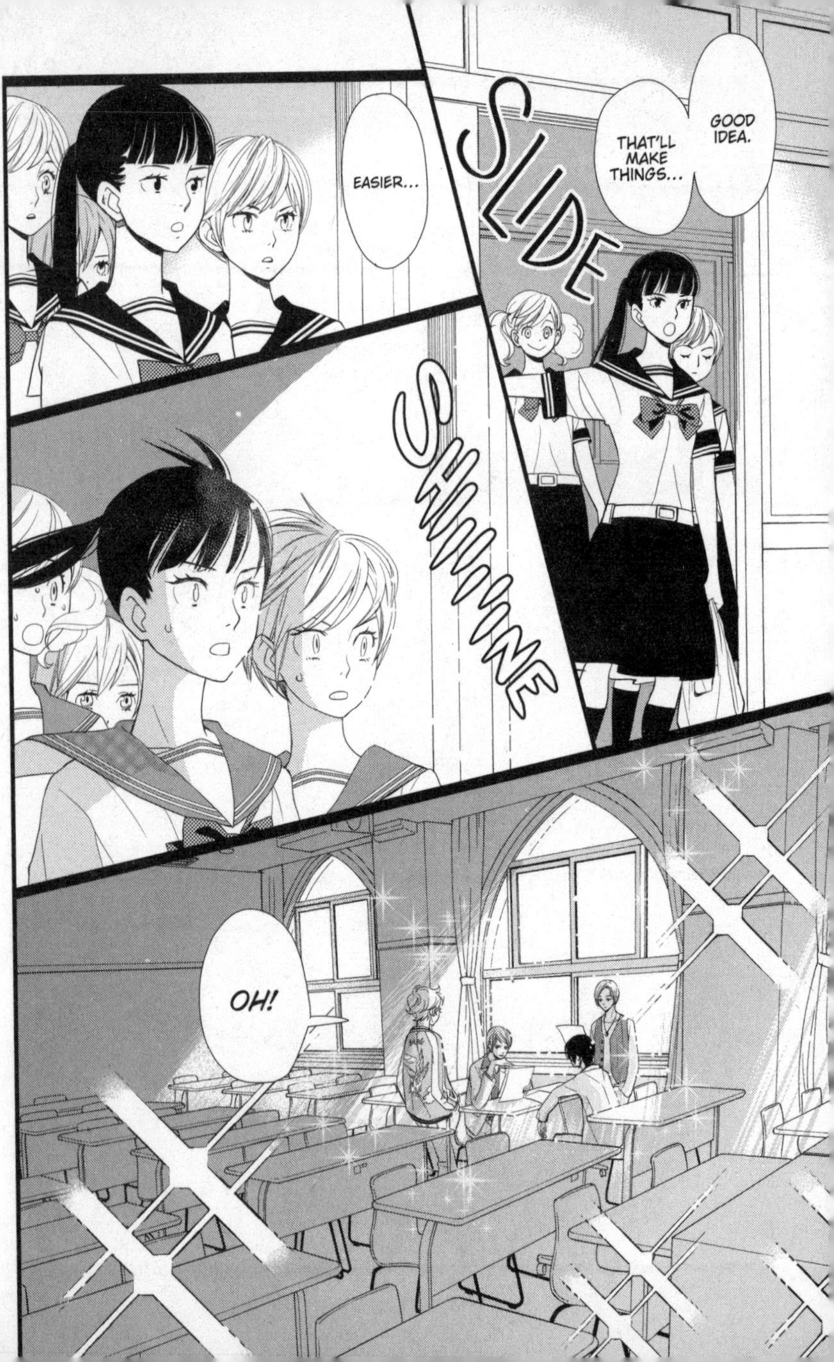
GOOD IDEA.
THAT'LL MAKE THINGS…
SLIDE
EASIER…
SHIIIINE
OH!

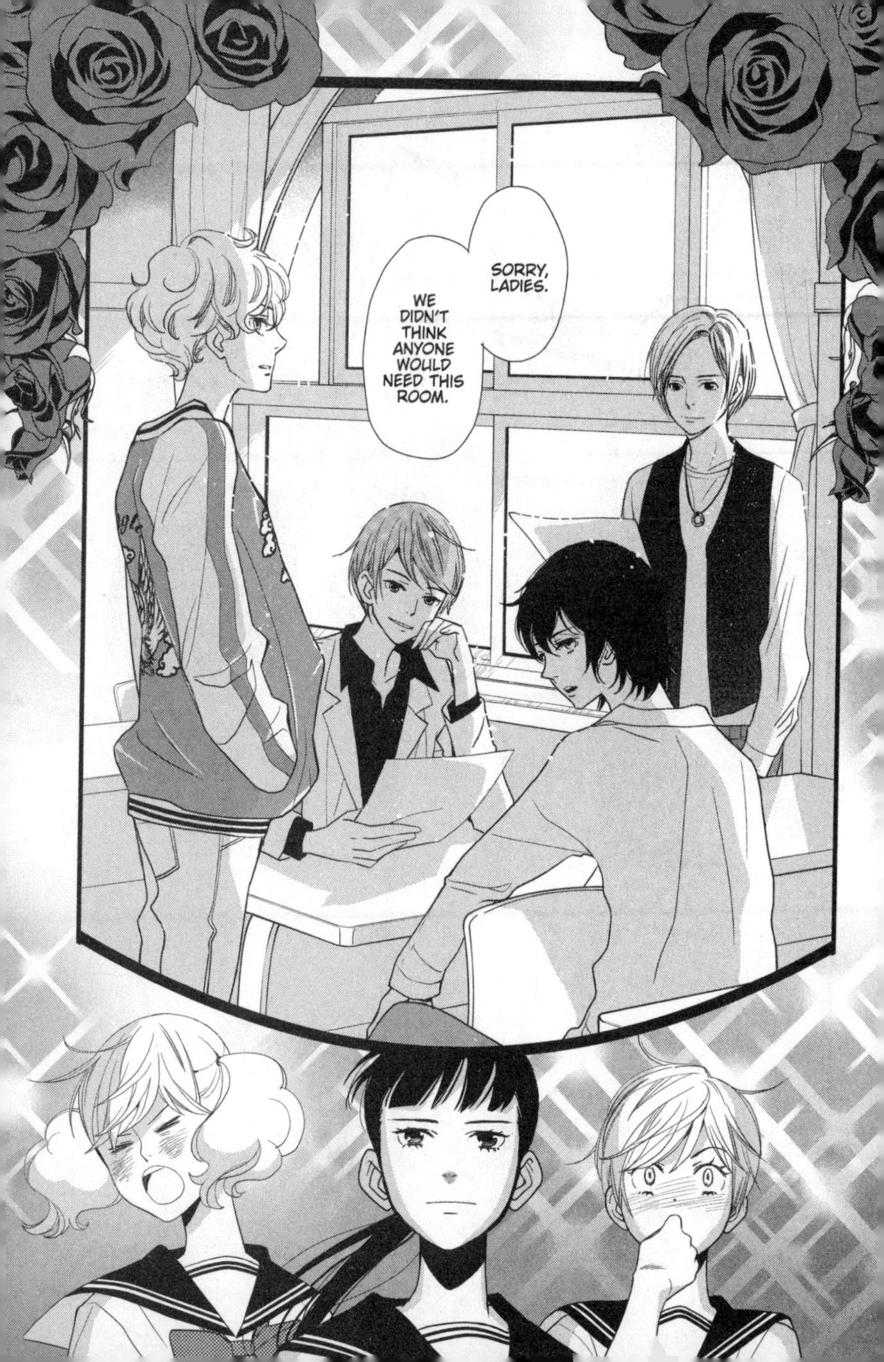
SORRY, LADIES.
WE DIDN'T THINK ANYONE WOULD NEED THIS ROOM.

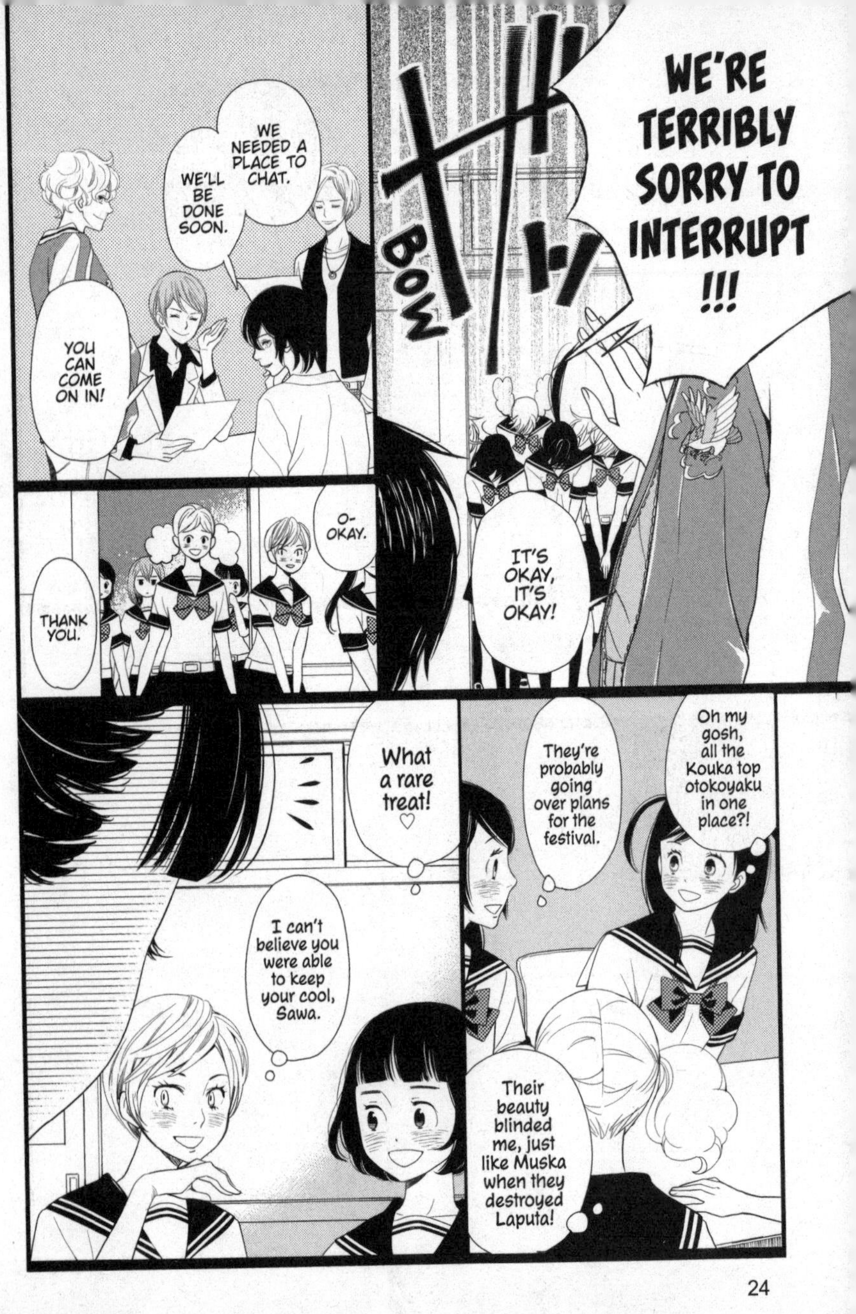
WE'RE TERRIBLY SORRY TO INTERRUPT !!!
BOW
IT'S OKAY, IT'S OKAY!
WE NEEDED A PLACE TO CHAT.
WE'LL BE DONE SOON.
YOU CAN COME ON IN!
O-OKAY.
THANK YOU.
Oh my gosh, all the Kouka top otokoyaku in one place?!
They're probably going over plans for the festival.
Their beauty blinded me, just like Muska when they destroyed Laputa!
What a rare treat! ♡
I can't believe you were able to keep your cool, Sawa.

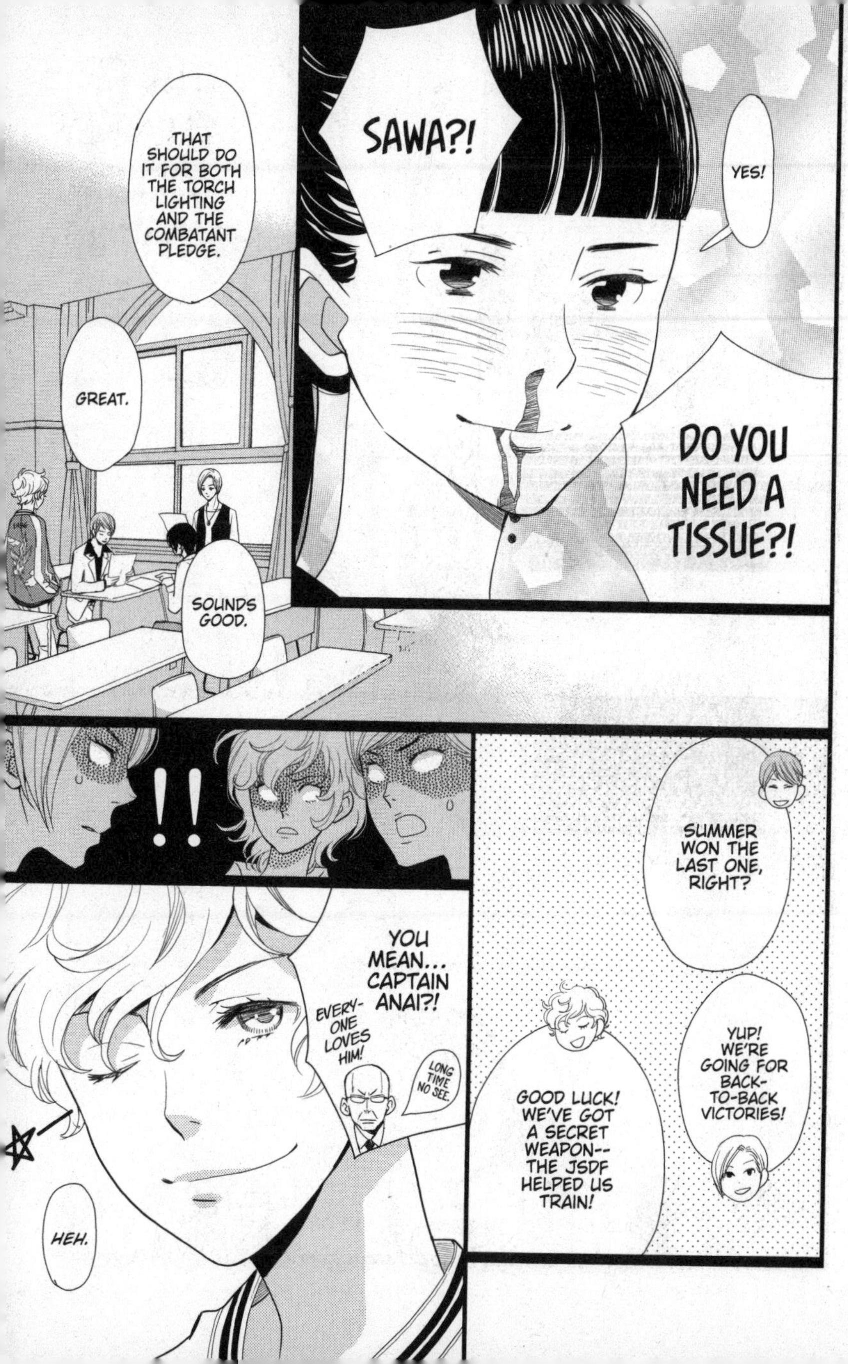
SAWA?!
YES!
DO YOU NEED A TISSUE?!
THAT SHOULD DO IT FOR BOTH THE TORCH LIGHTING AND THE COMBATANT PLEDGE.
GREAT.
SOUNDS GOOD.
SUMMER WON THE LAST ONE, RIGHT?
YUP! WE'RE GOING FOR BACK-TO-BACK VICTORIES!
GOOD LUCK! WE'VE GOT A SECRET WEAPON-- THE JSDF HELPED US TRAIN!
!!
YOU MEAN... CAPTAIN ANAI?!
EVERY-ONE LOVES HIM!
LONG TIME NO SEE.
HEH.

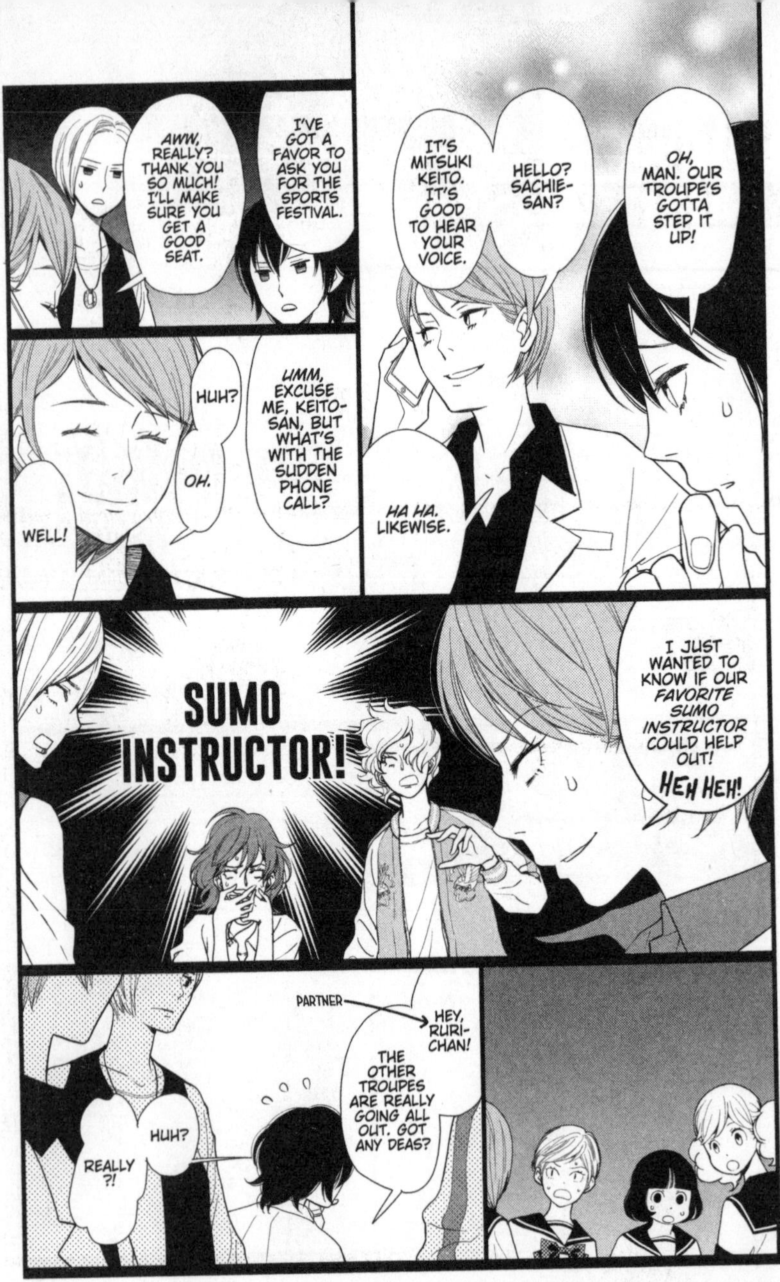
OH, MAN. OUR TROUPE'S GOTTA STEP IT UP!
HELLO? SACHIE-SAN?
IT'S MITSUKI KEITO. IT'S GOOD TO HEAR YOUR VOICE.
HA HA. LIKEWISE.
I'VE GOT A FAVOR TO ASK YOU FOR THE SPORTS FESTIVAL.
AWW, REALLY? THANK YOU SO MUCH! I'LL MAKE SURE YOU GET A GOOD SEAT.
UMM, EXCUSE ME, KEITO-SAN, BUT WHAT'S WITH THE SUDDEN PHONE CALL?
HUH?
OH.
WELL!
I JUST WANTED TO KNOW IF OUR FAVORITE SUMO INSTRUCTOR COULD HELP OUT!
HEH HEH!
SUMO INSTRUCTOR!
HEY, RURI-CHAN!
PARTNER
THE OTHER TROUPES ARE REALLY GOING ALL OUT. GOT ANY DEAS?
HUH?
REALLY ?!

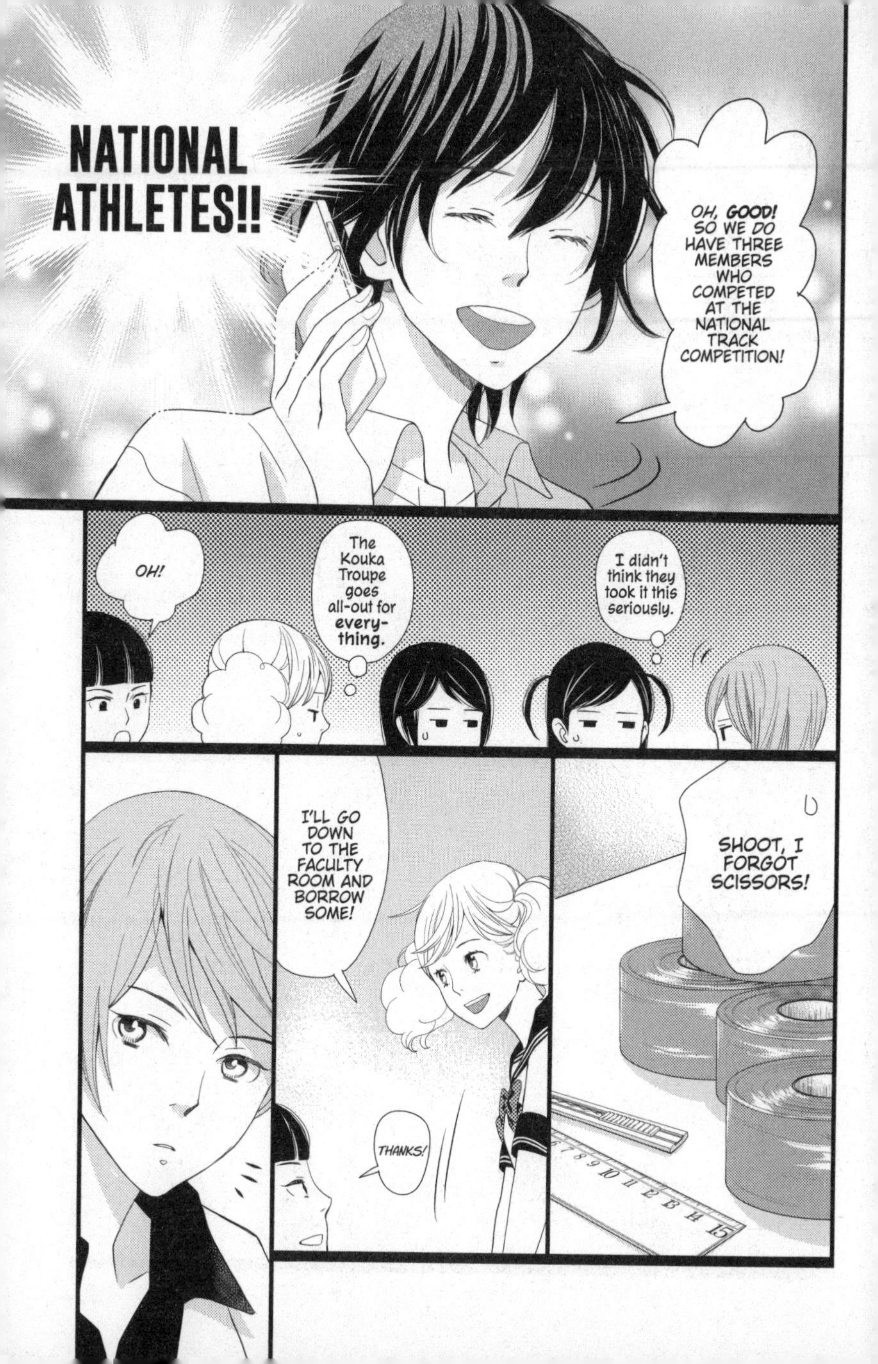
OH, GOOD! SO WE DO HAVE THREE MEMBERS WHO COMPETED AT THE NATIONAL TRACK COMPETITION!
NATIONAL ATHLETES!!
I didn't think they took it this seriously.
The Kouka Troupe goes all-out for everything.
OH!
SHOOT, I FORGOT SCISSORS!
I'LL GO DOWN TO THE FACULTY ROOM AND BORROW SOME!
THANKS!

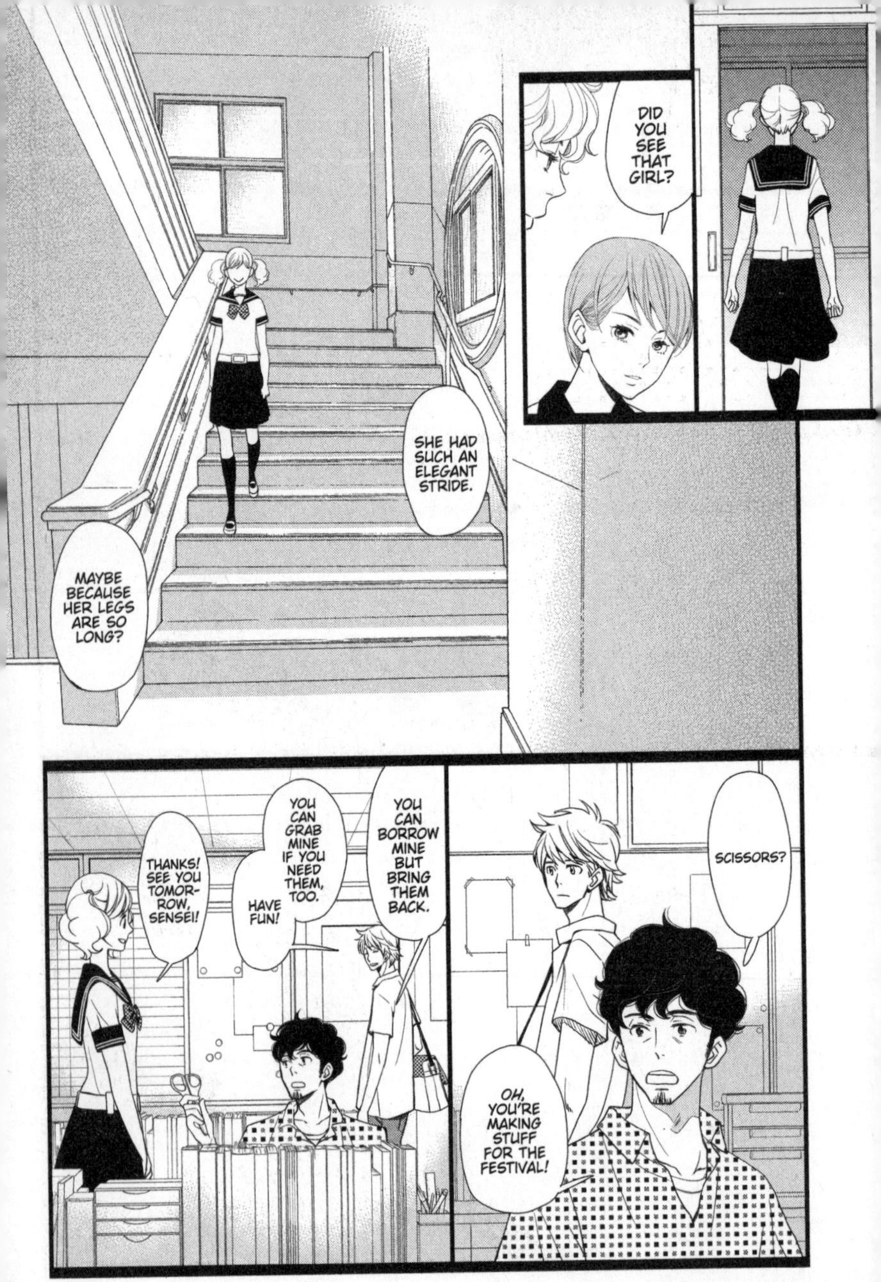
DID YOU SEE THAT GIRL?
SHE HAD SUCH AN ELEGANT STRIDE.
MAYBE BECAUSE HER LEGS ARE SO LONG?
SCISSORS?
OH, YOU'RE MAKING STUFF FOR THE FESTIVAL!
YOU CAN BORROW MINE BUT BRING THEM BACK.
YOU CAN GRAB MINE IF YOU NEED THEM, TOO.
HAVE FUN!
THANKS! SEE YOU TOMOR-ROW, SENSEI!

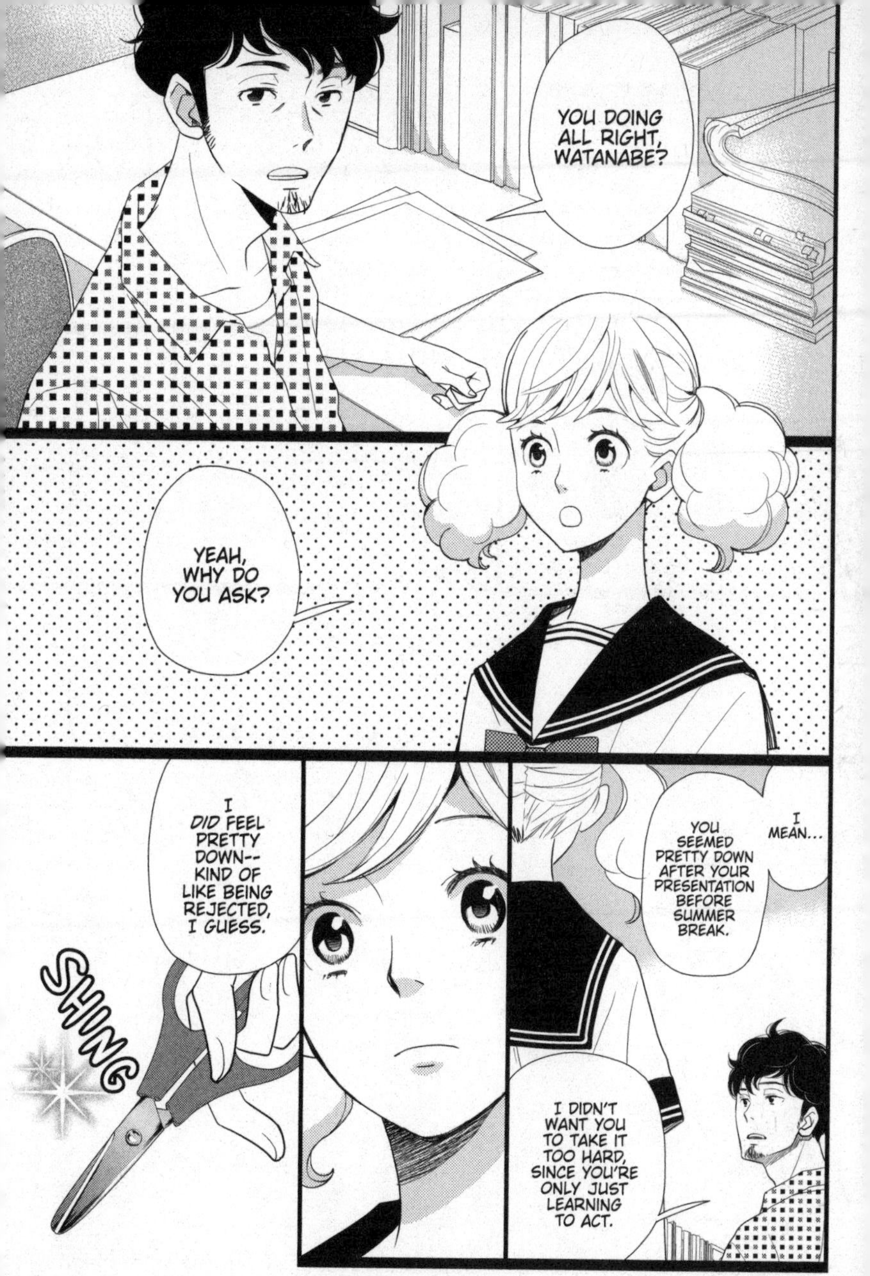
YOU DOING ALL RIGHT, WATANABE?
YEAH, WHY DO YOU ASK?
I MEAN...
YOU SEEMED PRETTY DOWN AFTER YOUR PRESENTATION BEFORE SUMMER BREAK.
I DIDN'T WANT YOU TO TAKE IT TOO HARD, SINCE YOU'RE ONLY JUST LEARNING TO ACT.
I *DID* FEEL PRETTY DOWN-- KIND OF LIKE BEING REJECTED, I GUESS.
SHING

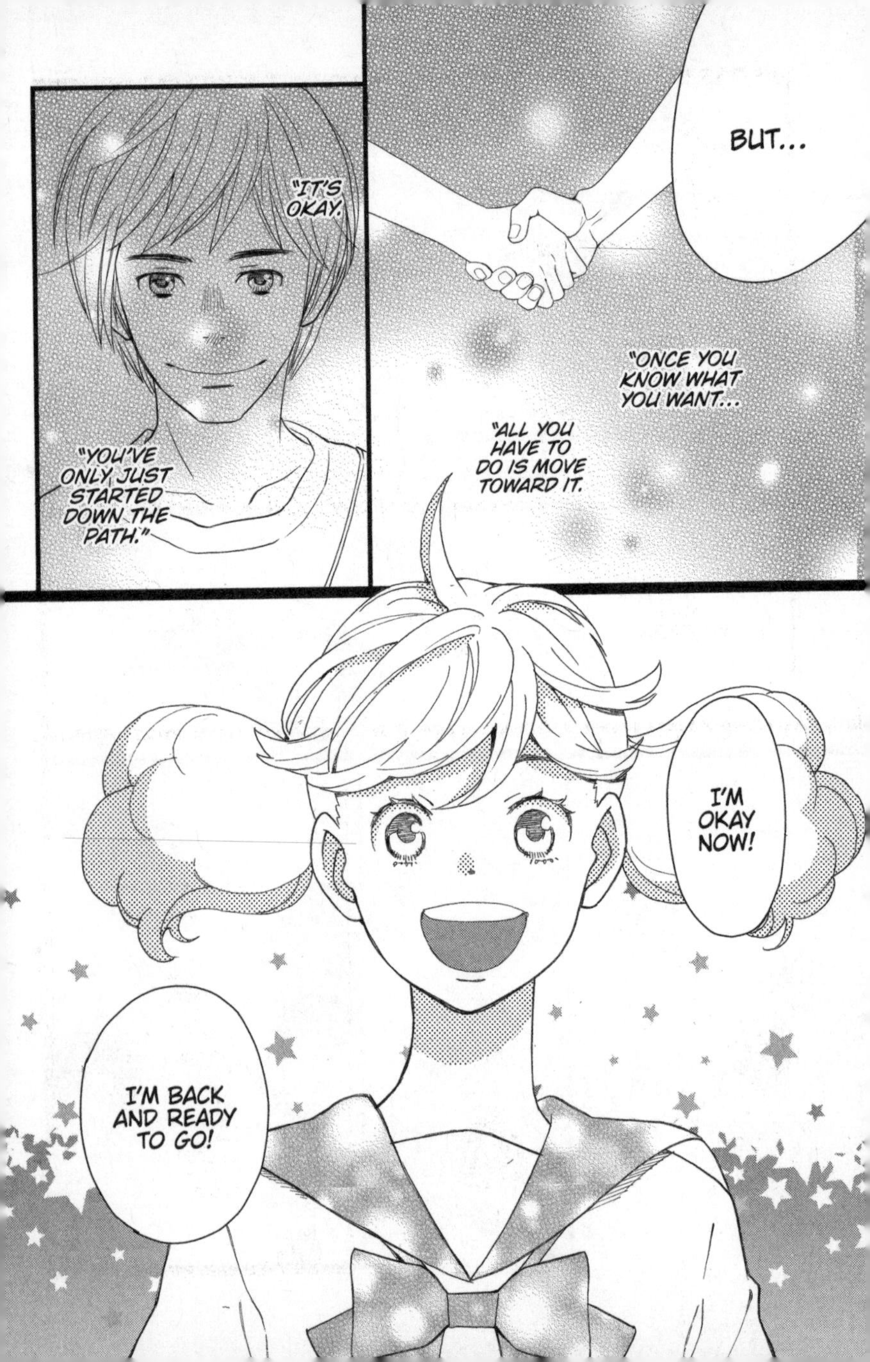
BUT...
"ONCE YOU KNOW WHAT YOU WANT...
"ALL YOU HAVE TO DO IS MOVE TOWARD IT.
"IT'S OKAY.
"YOU'VE ONLY JUST STARTED DOWN THE PATH."
I'M OKAY NOW!
I'M BACK AND READY TO GO!

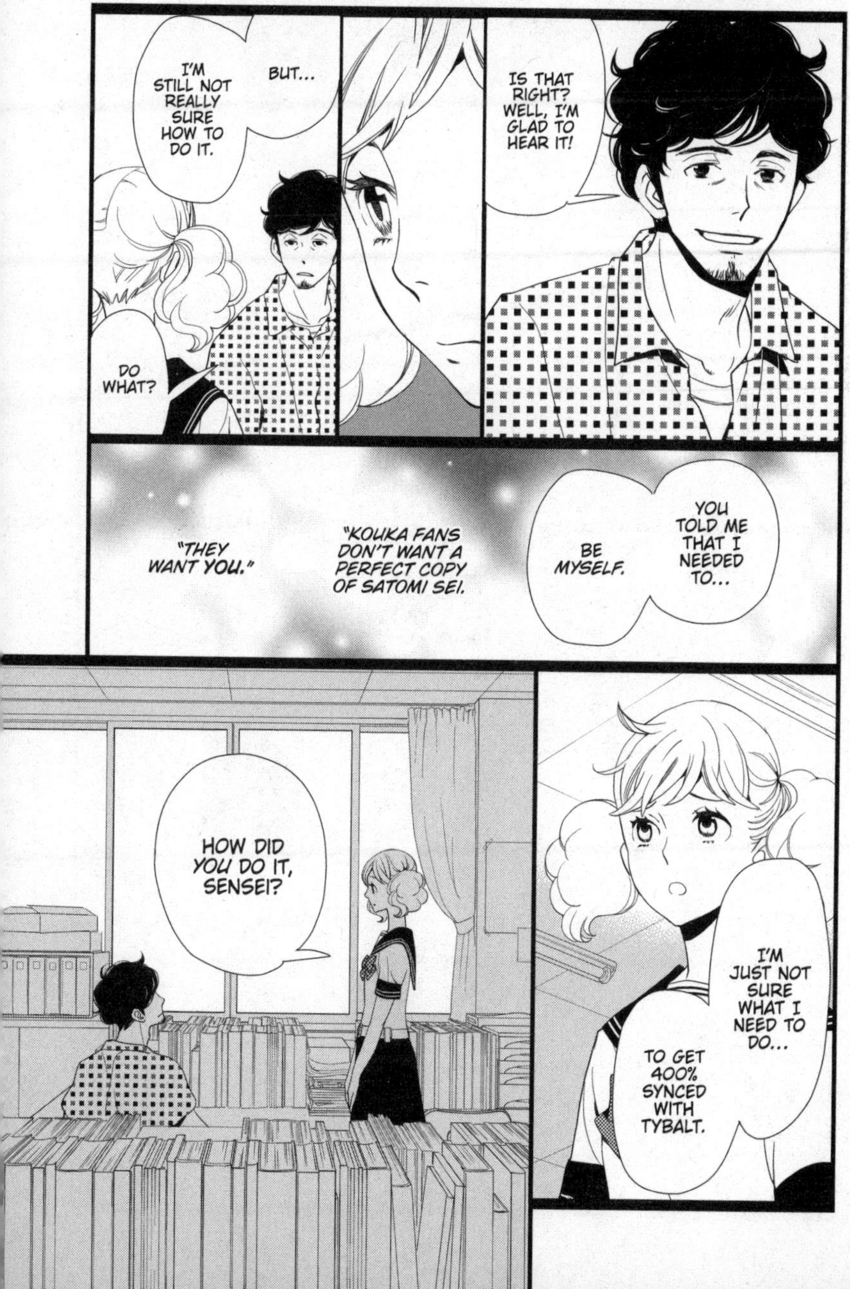
IS THAT RIGHT? WELL, I'M GLAD TO HEAR IT!
BUT...
I'M STILL NOT REALLY SURE HOW TO DO IT.
DO WHAT?
YOU TOLD ME THAT I NEEDED TO...
BE MYSELF.
"KOUKA FANS DON'T WANT A PERFECT COPY OF SATOMI SEI.
"THEY WANT YOU."
I'M JUST NOT SURE WHAT I NEED TO DO...
TO GET 400% SYNCED WITH TYBALT.
HOW DID YOU DO IT, SENSEI?

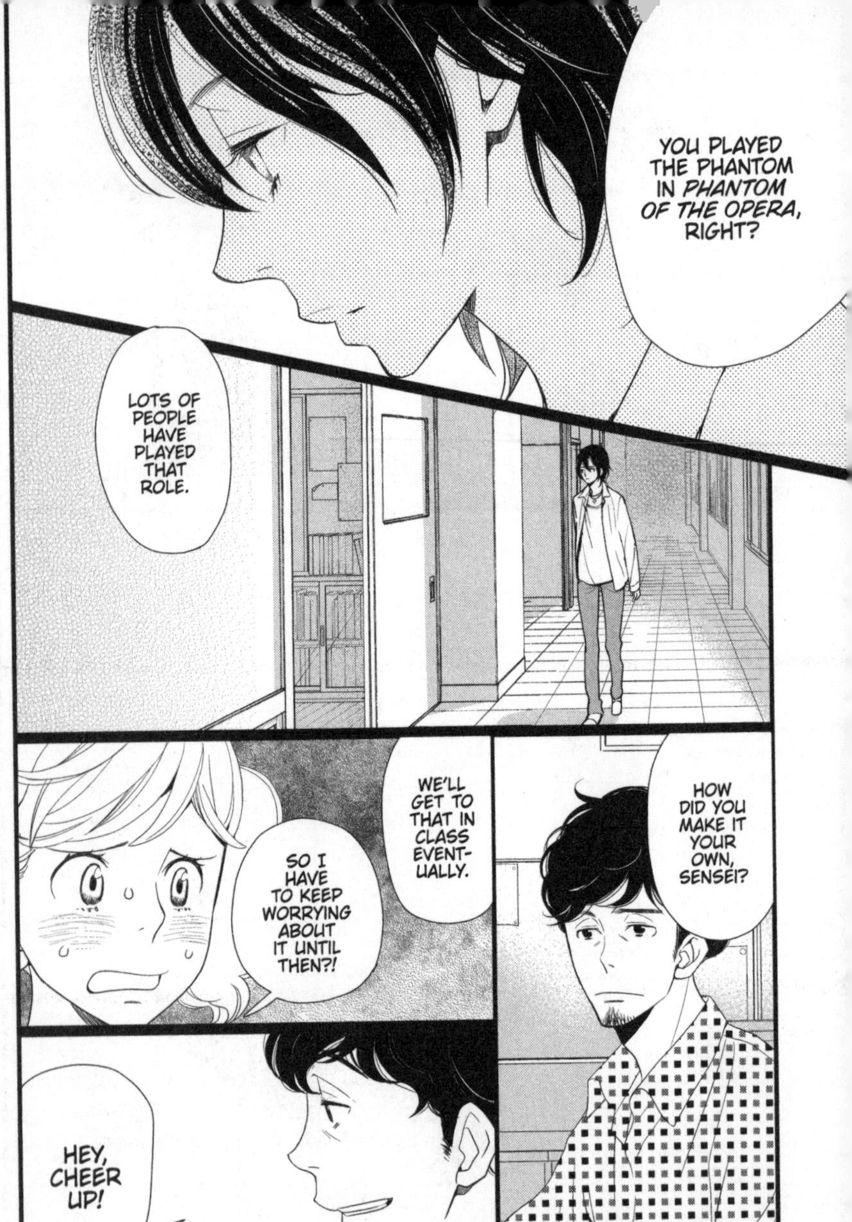
YOU PLAYED THE PHANTOM IN *PHANTOM OF THE OPERA*, RIGHT?
LOTS OF PEOPLE HAVE PLAYED THAT ROLE.
HOW DID YOU MAKE IT YOUR OWN, SENSEI?
WE'LL GET TO THAT IN CLASS EVENT-UALLY.
SO I HAVE TO KEEP WORRYING ABOUT IT UNTIL THEN?!
HEY, CHEER UP!

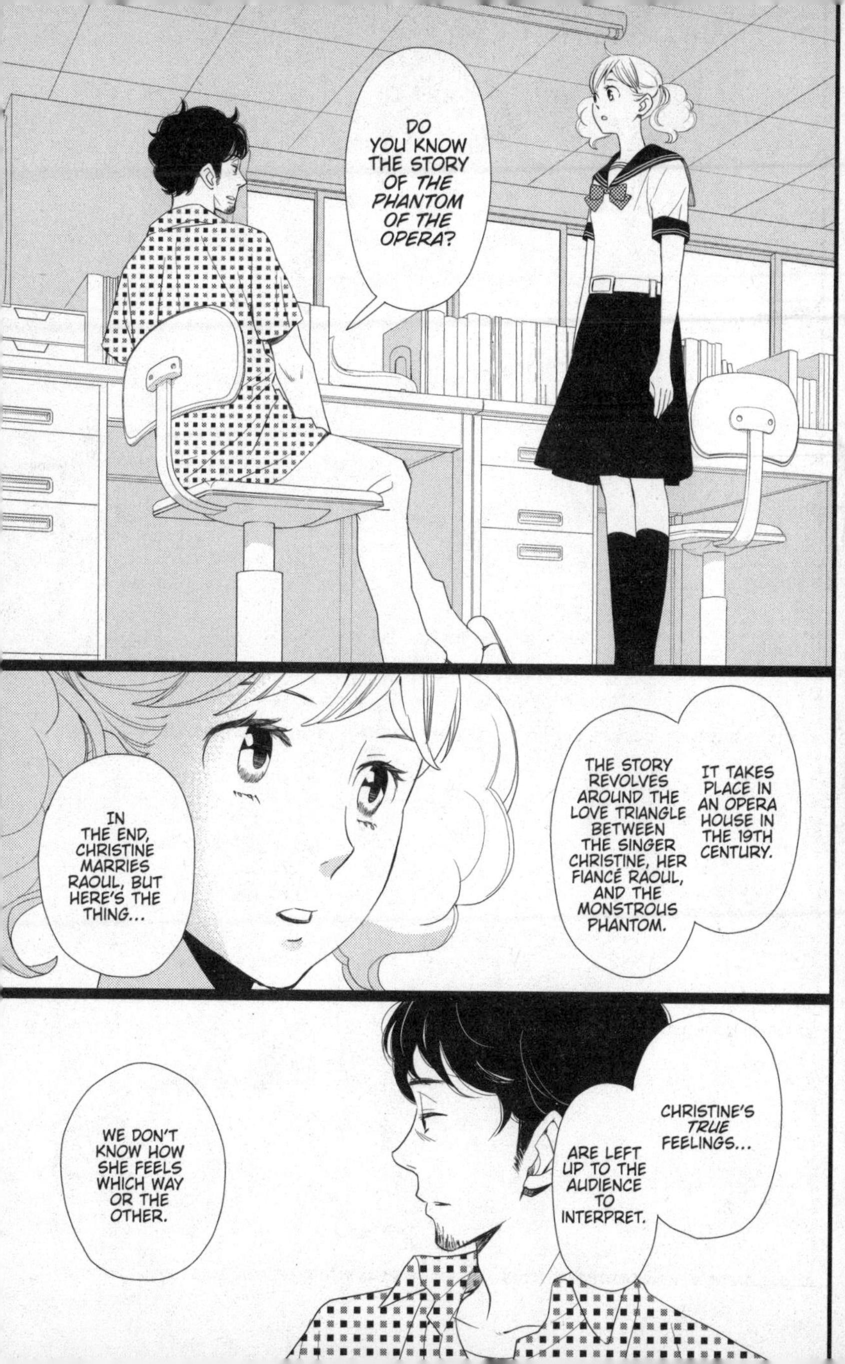
DO YOU KNOW THE STORY OF *THE PHANTOM OF THE OPERA*?
IT TAKES PLACE IN AN OPERA HOUSE IN THE 19TH CENTURY.
THE STORY REVOLVES AROUND THE LOVE TRIANGLE BETWEEN THE SINGER CHRISTINE, HER FIANCÉ RAOUL, AND THE MONSTROUS PHANTOM.
IN THE END, CHRISTINE MARRIES RAOUL, BUT HERE'S THE THING...
CHRISTINE'S *TRUE* FEELINGS...
ARE LEFT UP TO THE AUDIENCE TO INTERPRET.
WE DON'T KNOW HOW SHE FEELS WHICH WAY OR THE OTHER.

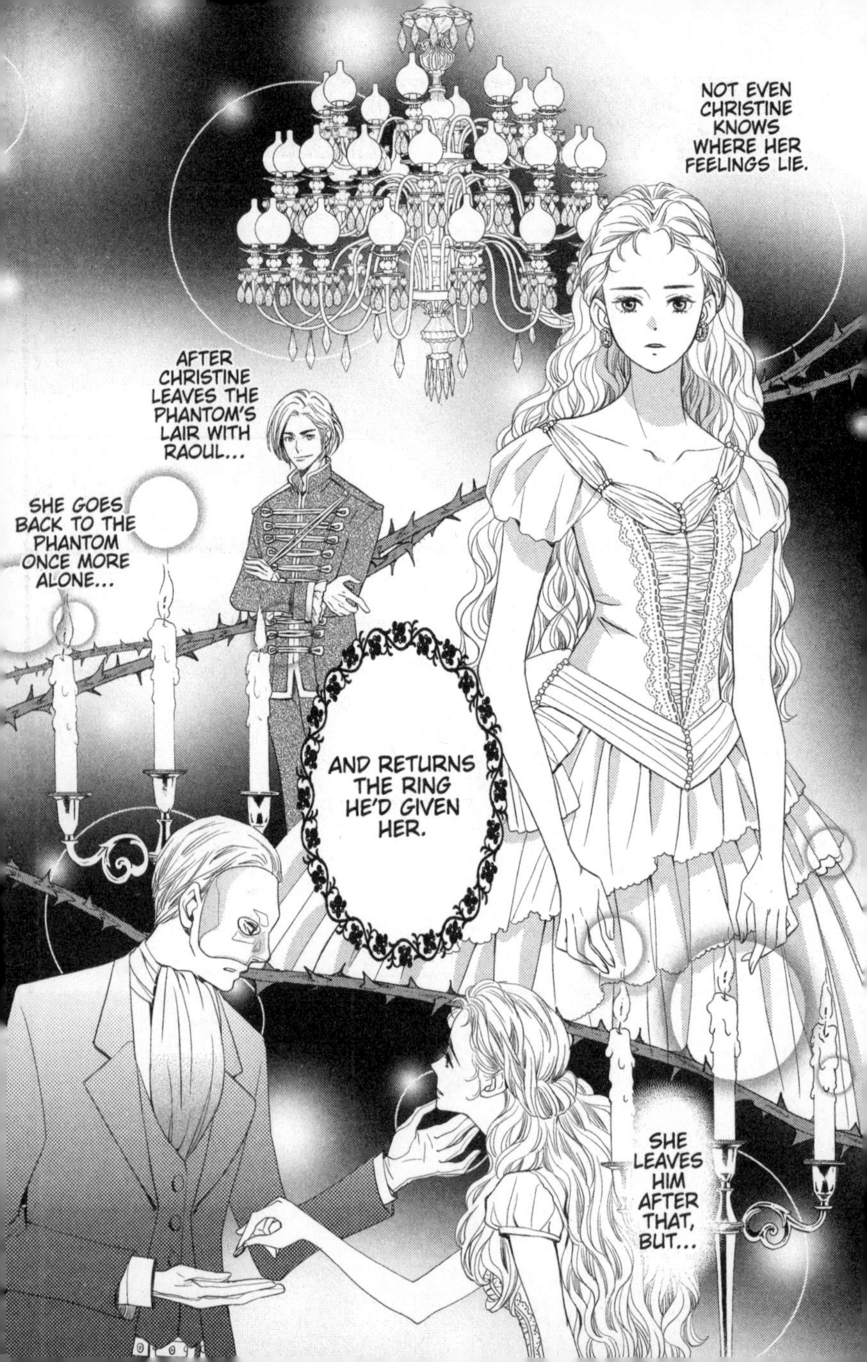
AFTER CHRISTINE LEAVES THE PHANTOM'S LAIR WITH RAOUL...
SHE GOES BACK TO THE PHANTOM ONCE MORE ALONE...
AND RETURNS THE RING HE'D GIVEN HER.
SHE LEAVES HIM AFTER THAT, BUT...
NOT EVEN CHRISTINE KNOWS WHERE HER FEELINGS LIE.

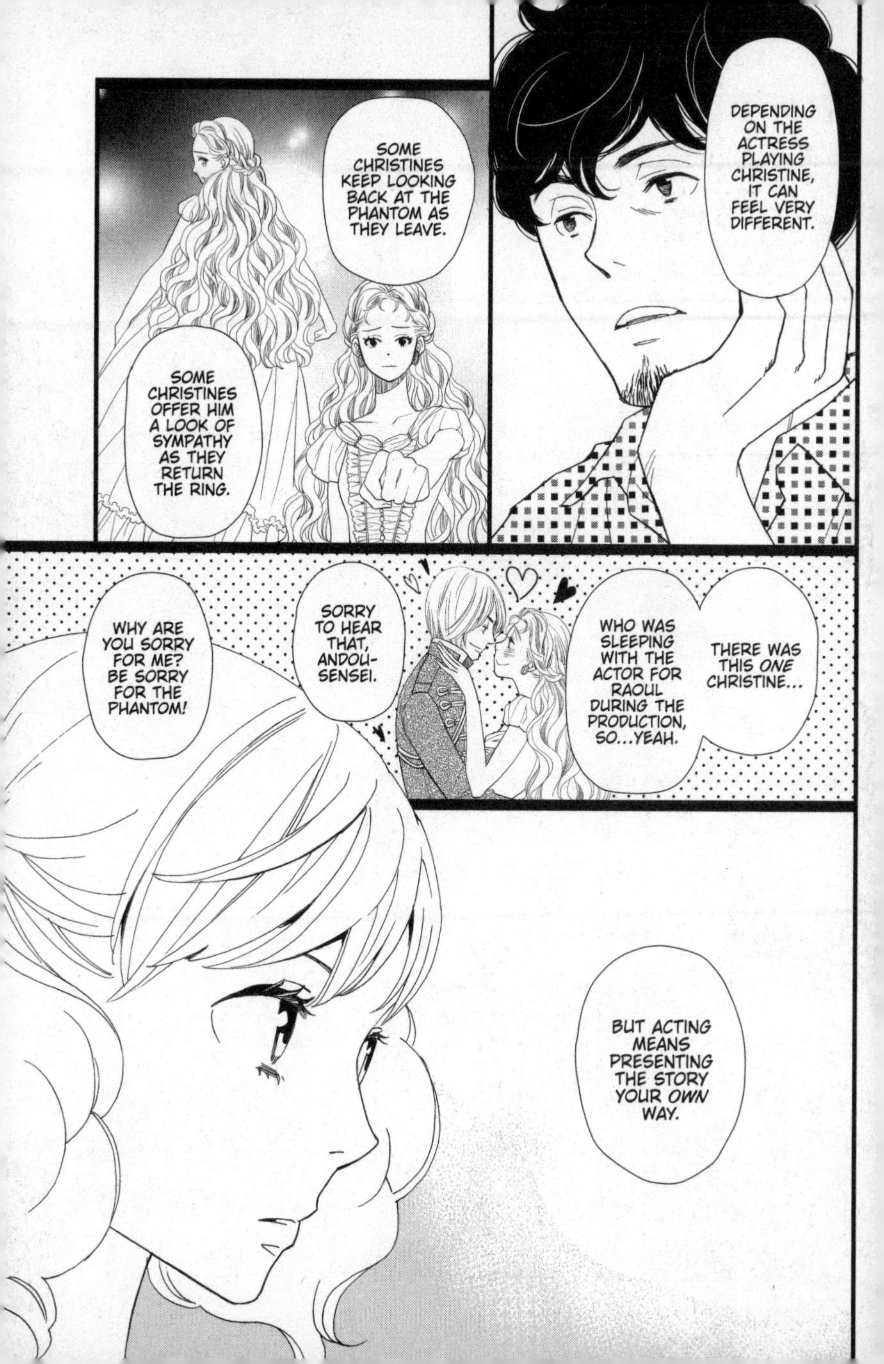
DEPENDING ON THE ACTRESS PLAYING CHRISTINE, IT CAN FEEL VERY DIFFERENT.
SOME CHRISTINES KEEP LOOKING BACK AT THE PHANTOM AS THEY LEAVE.
SOME CHRISTINES OFFER HIM A LOOK OF SYMPATHY AS THEY RETURN THE RING.
THERE WAS THIS *ONE* CHRISTINE...
WHO WAS SLEEPING WITH THE ACTOR FOR RAOUL DURING THE PRODUCTION, SO...YEAH.
SORRY TO HEAR THAT, ANDOU-SENSEI.
WHY ARE YOU SORRY FOR ME? BE SORRY FOR THE PHANTOM!
BUT ACTING MEANS PRESENTING THE STORY YOUR *OWN* WAY.

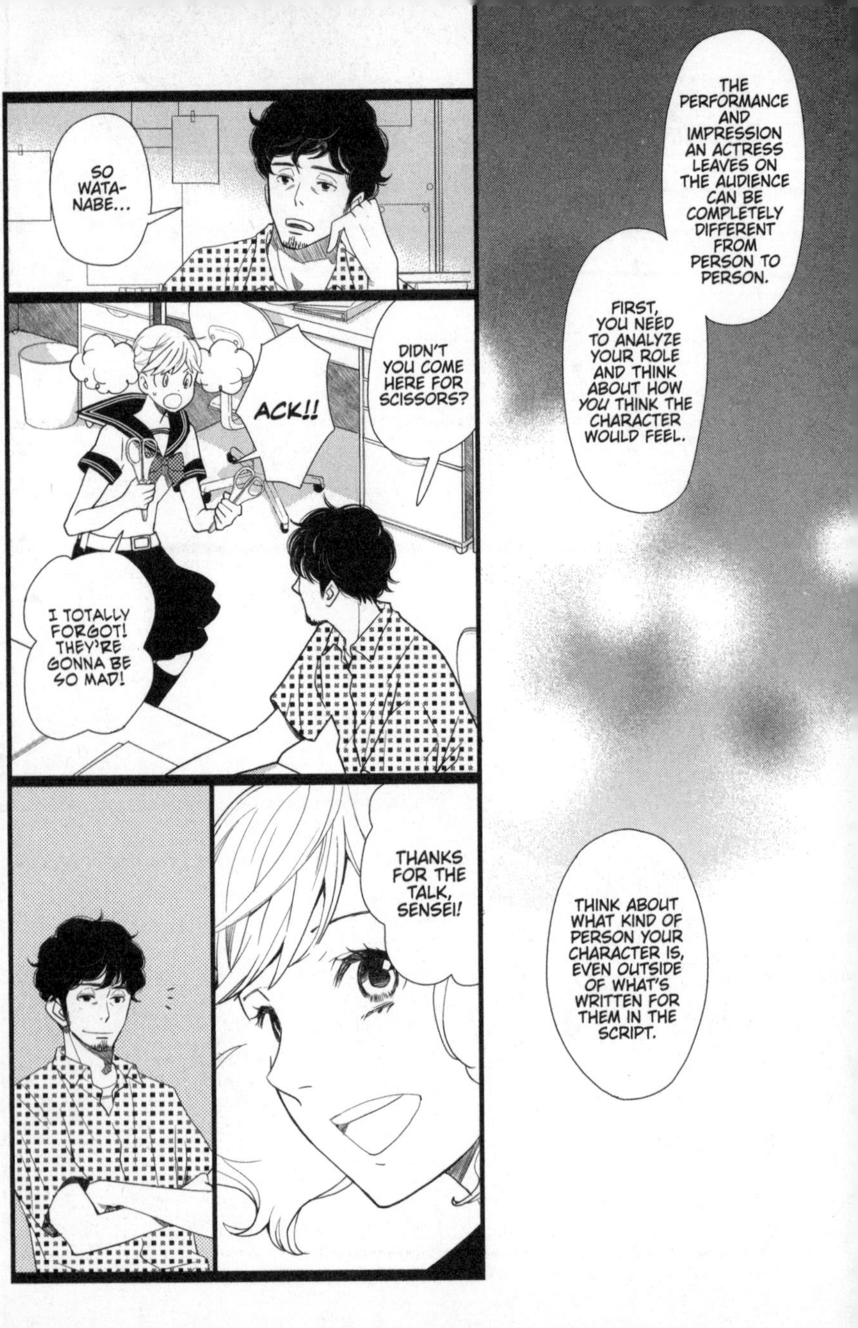
THE PERFORMANCE AND IMPRESSION AN ACTRESS LEAVES ON THE AUDIENCE CAN BE COMPLETELY DIFFERENT FROM PERSON TO PERSON.
FIRST, YOU NEED TO ANALYZE YOUR ROLE AND THINK ABOUT HOW *YOU* THINK THE CHARACTER WOULD FEEL.
THINK ABOUT WHAT KIND OF PERSON YOUR CHARACTER IS, EVEN OUTSIDE OF WHAT'S WRITTEN FOR THEM IN THE SCRIPT.
SO WATA-NABE...
DIDN'T YOU COME HERE FOR SCISSORS?
ACK!!
I TOTALLY FORGOT! THEY'RE GONNA BE SO MAD!
THANKS FOR THE TALK, SENSEI!

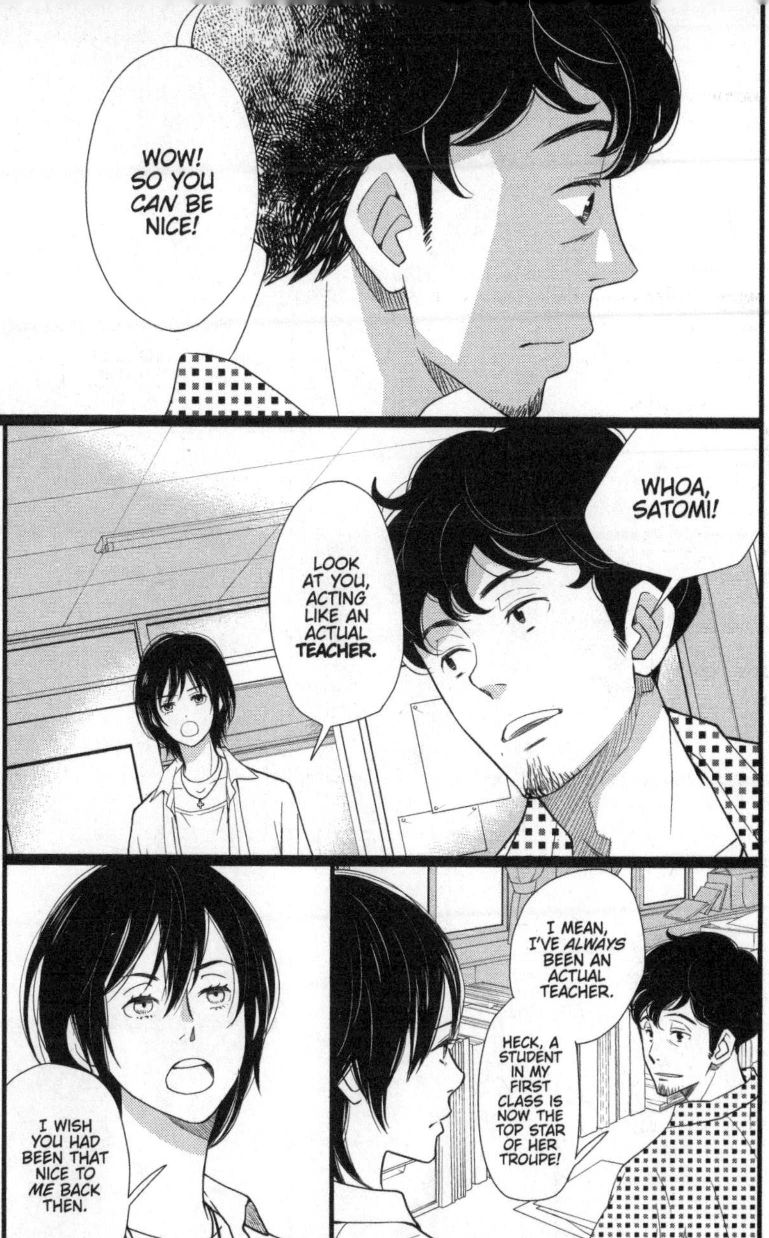
WOW! SO YOU CAN BE NICE!
WHOA, SATOMI!
LOOK AT YOU, ACTING LIKE AN ACTUAL TEACHER.
I MEAN, I'VE *ALWAYS* BEEN AN ACTUAL TEACHER.
HECK, A STUDENT IN MY FIRST CLASS IS NOW THE TOP STAR OF HER TROUPE!
I WISH YOU HAD BEEN THAT NICE TO *ME* BACK THEN.

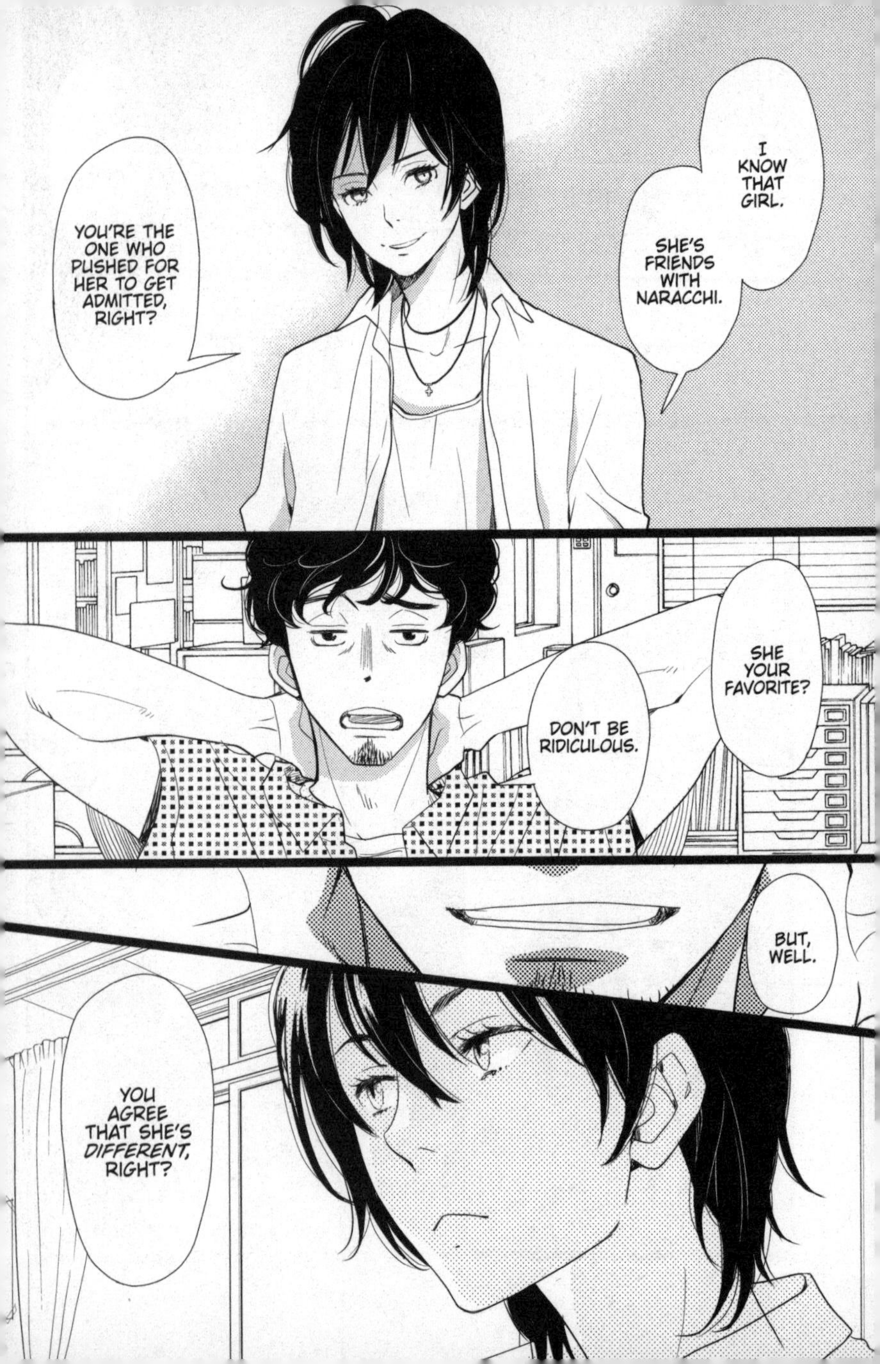
I KNOW THAT GIRL.
SHE'S FRIENDS WITH NARACCHI.
YOU'RE THE ONE WHO PUSHED FOR HER TO GET ADMITTED, RIGHT?
SHE YOUR FAVORITE?
DON'T BE RIDICULOUS.
BUT, WELL.
YOU AGREE THAT SHE'S *DIFFERENT*, RIGHT?

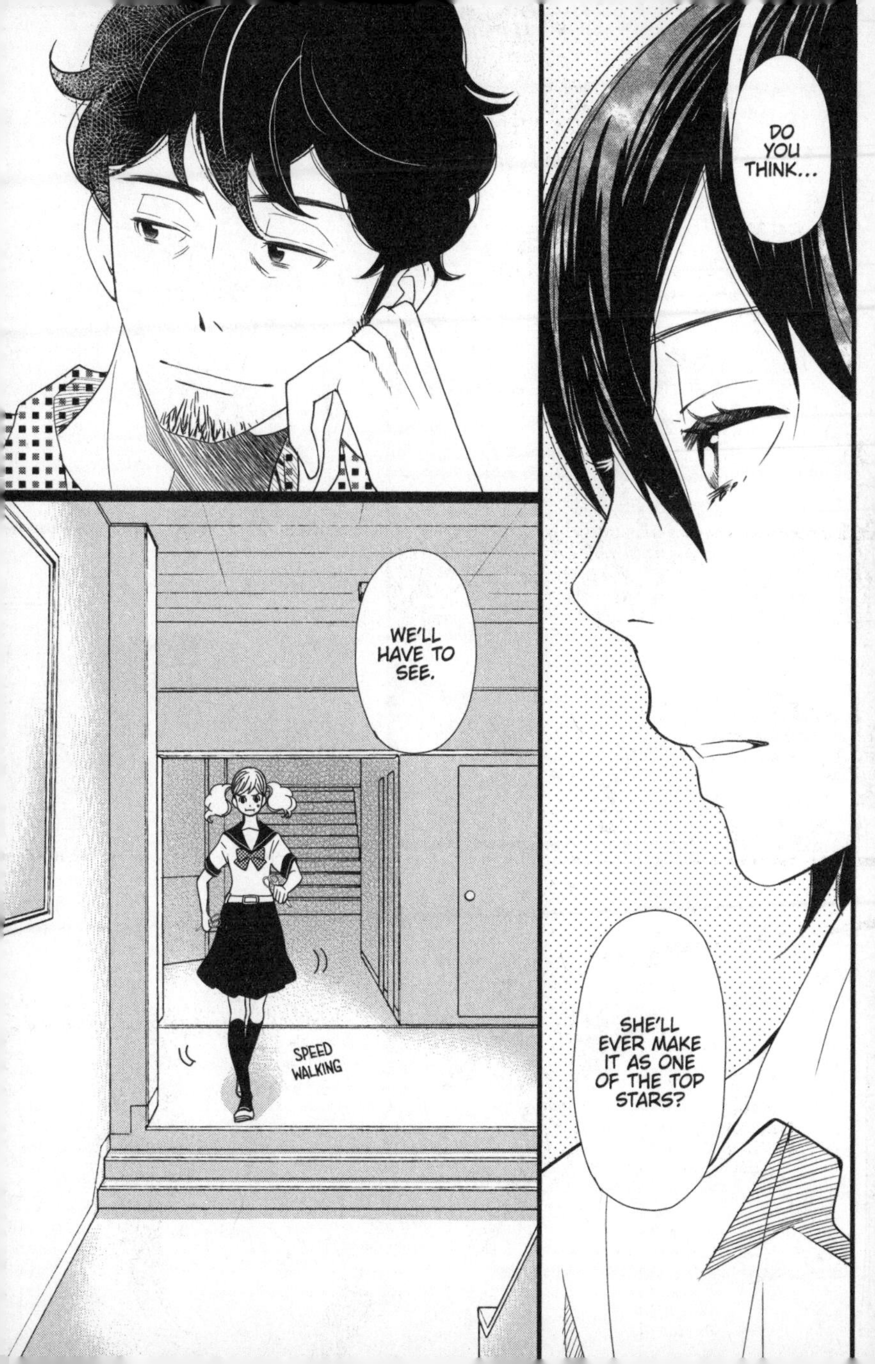
DO YOU THINK...
SHE'LL EVER MAKE IT AS ONE OF THE TOP STARS?
WE'LL HAVE TO SEE.
SPEED WALKING

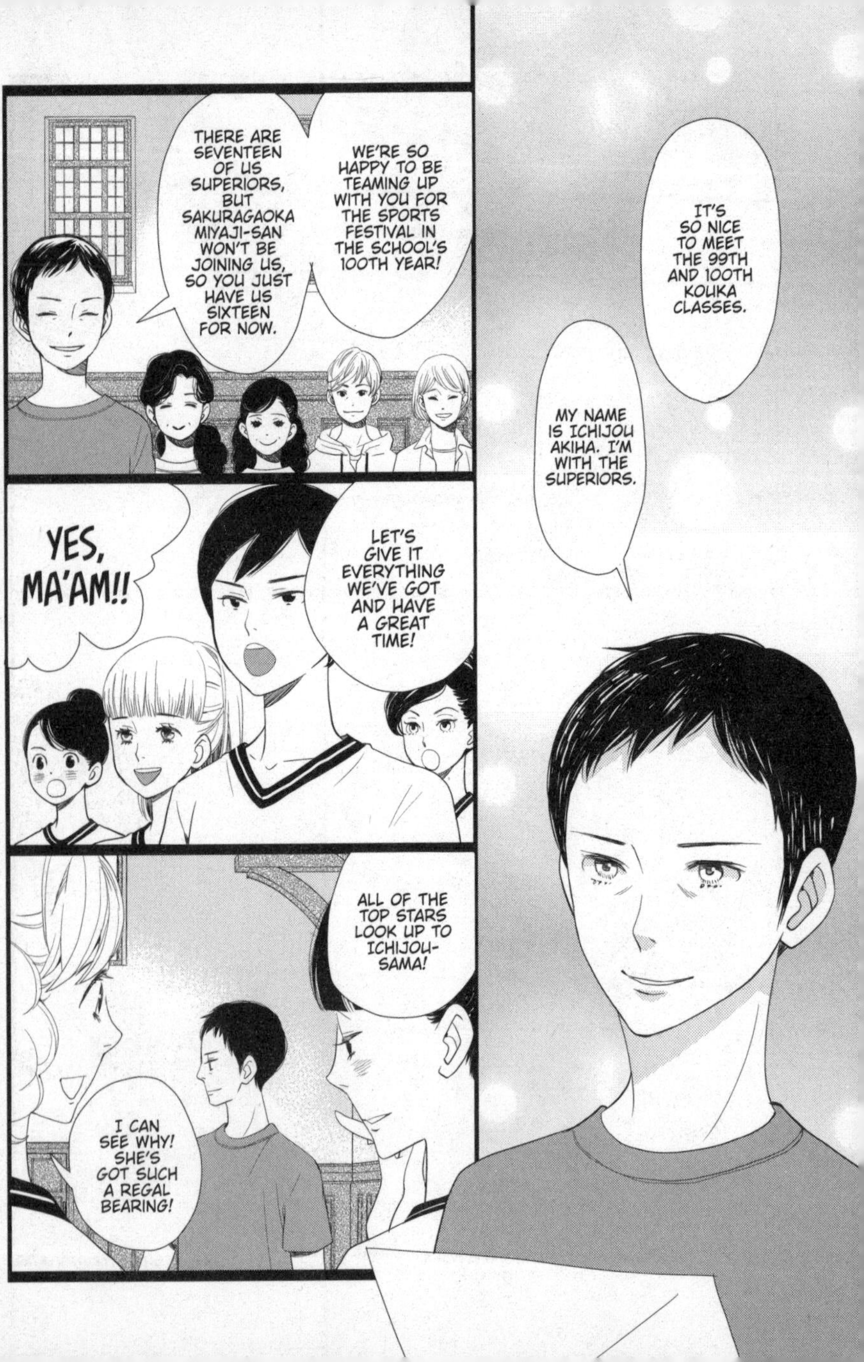
IT'S SO NICE TO MEET THE 99TH AND 100TH KOUKA CLASSES.
MY NAME IS ICHIJOU AKIHA. I'M WITH THE SUPERIORS.
WE'RE SO HAPPY TO BE TEAMING UP WITH YOU FOR THE SPORTS FESTIVAL IN THE SCHOOL'S 100TH YEAR!
THERE ARE SEVENTEEN OF US SUPERIORS, BUT SAKURAGAOKA MIYAJI-SAN WON'T BE JOINING US, SO YOU JUST HAVE US SIXTEEN FOR NOW.
LET'S GIVE IT EVERYTHING WE'VE GOT AND HAVE A GREAT TIME!
YES, MA'AM!!
ALL OF THE TOP STARS LOOK UP TO ICHIJOU-SAMA!
I CAN SEE WHY! SHE'S GOT SUCH A REGAL BEARING!

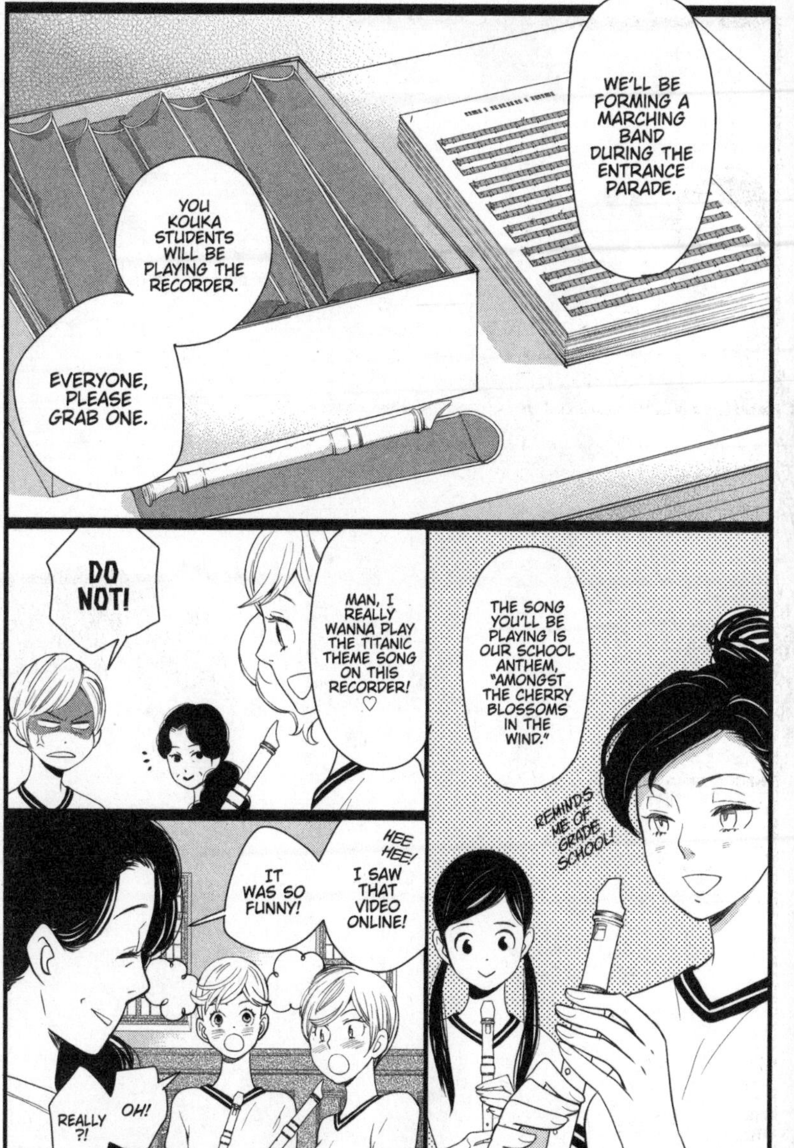
WE'LL BE FORMING A MARCHING BAND DURING THE ENTRANCE PARADE.
YOU KOUKA STUDENTS WILL BE PLAYING THE RECORDER.
EVERYONE, PLEASE GRAB ONE.
THE SONG YOU'LL BE PLAYING IS OUR SCHOOL ANTHEM, "AMONGST THE CHERRY BLOSSOMS IN THE WIND."
REMINDS ME OF GRADE SCHOOL!
MAN, I REALLY WANNA PLAY THE TITANIC THEME SONG ON THIS RECORDER! ♡
DO NOT!
HEE HEE!
I SAW THAT VIDEO ONLINE!
IT WAS SO FUNNY!
OH!
REALLY ?!

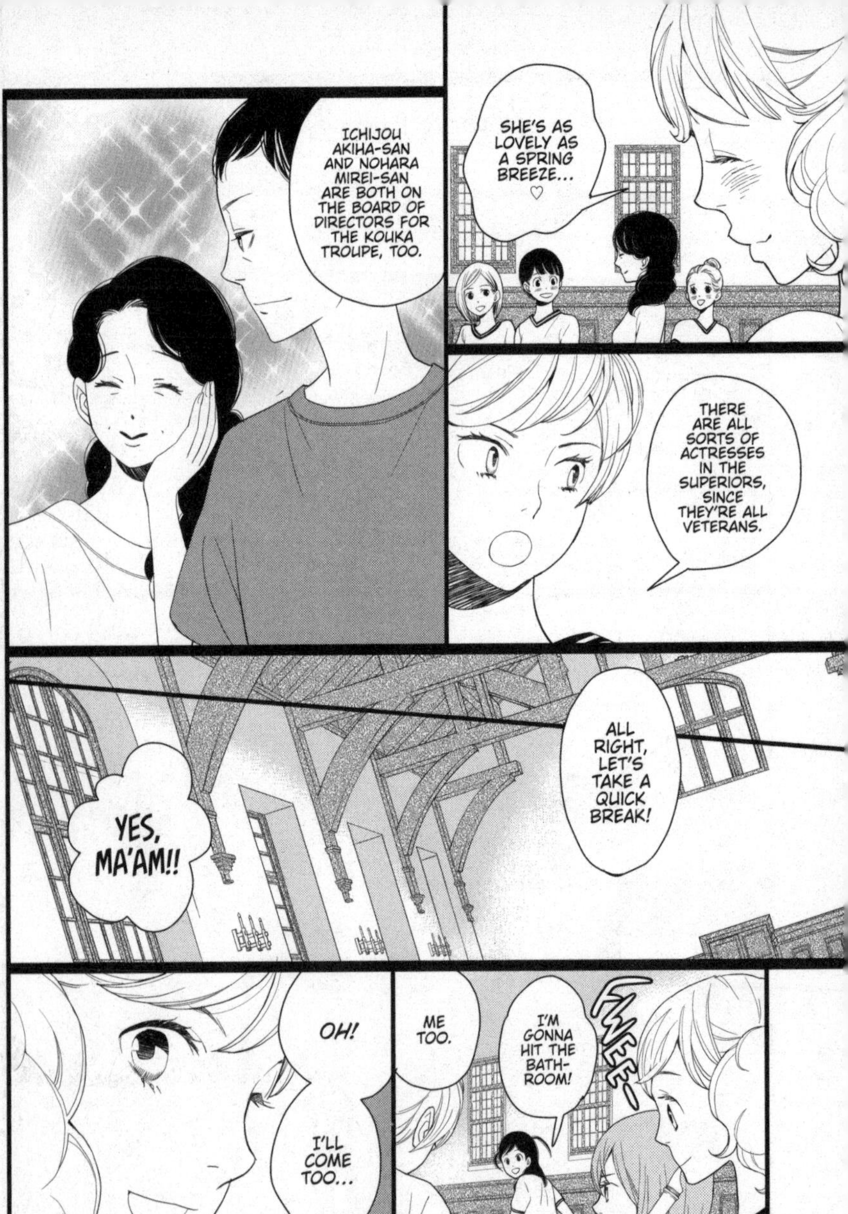
SHE'S AS LOVELY AS A SPRING BREEZE... ♡
THERE ARE ALL SORTS OF ACTRESSES IN THE SUPERIORS, SINCE THEY'RE ALL VETERANS.
ICHIJOU AKIHA-SAN AND NOHARA MIREI-SAN ARE BOTH ON THE BOARD OF DIRECTORS FOR THE KOUKA TROUPE, TOO.
ALL RIGHT, LET'S TAKE A QUICK BREAK!
YES, MA'AM!!
KWEE-
I'M GONNA HIT THE BATH-ROOM!
ME TOO.
OH!
I'LL COME TOO...

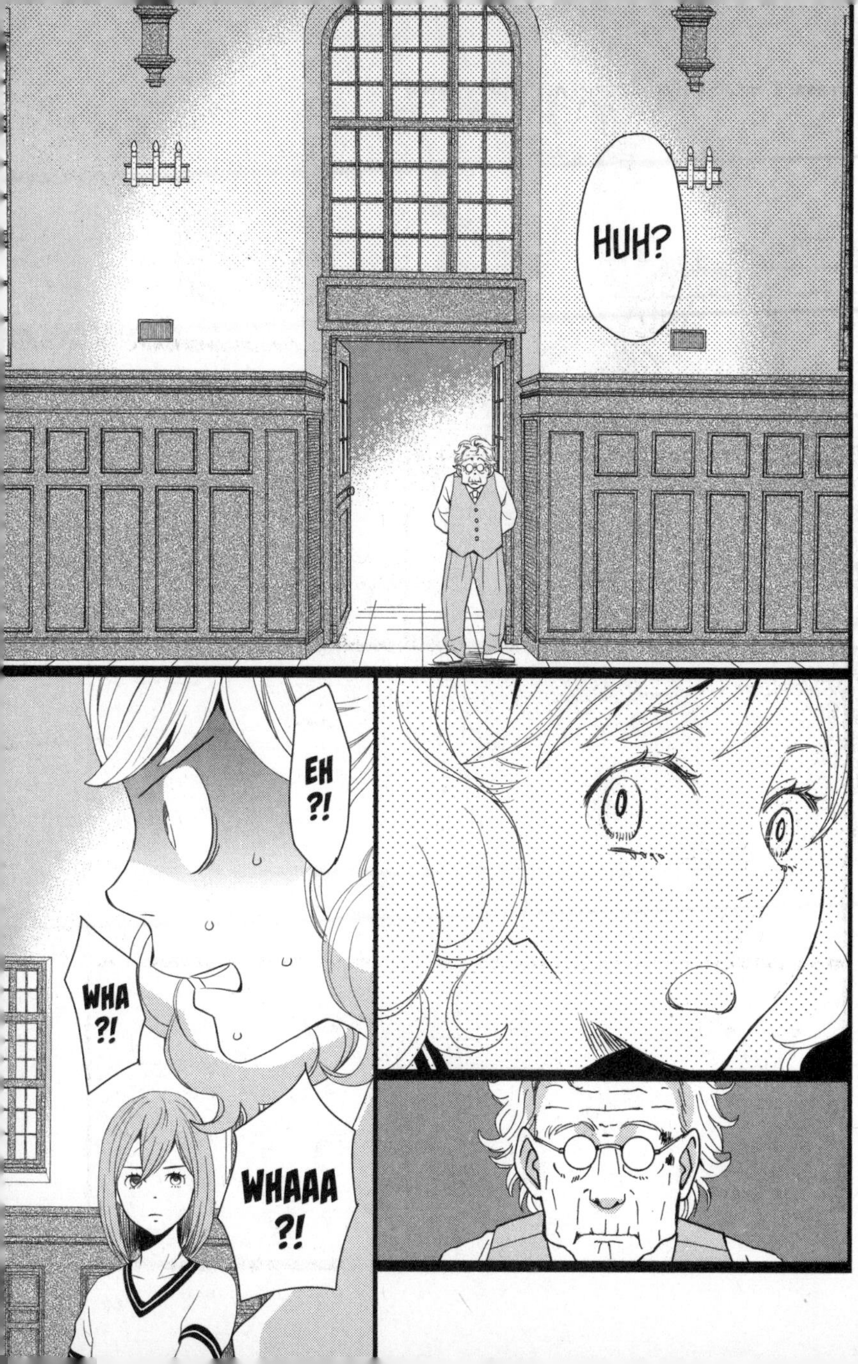
HUH?
EH?!
WHA?!
WHAAA?!

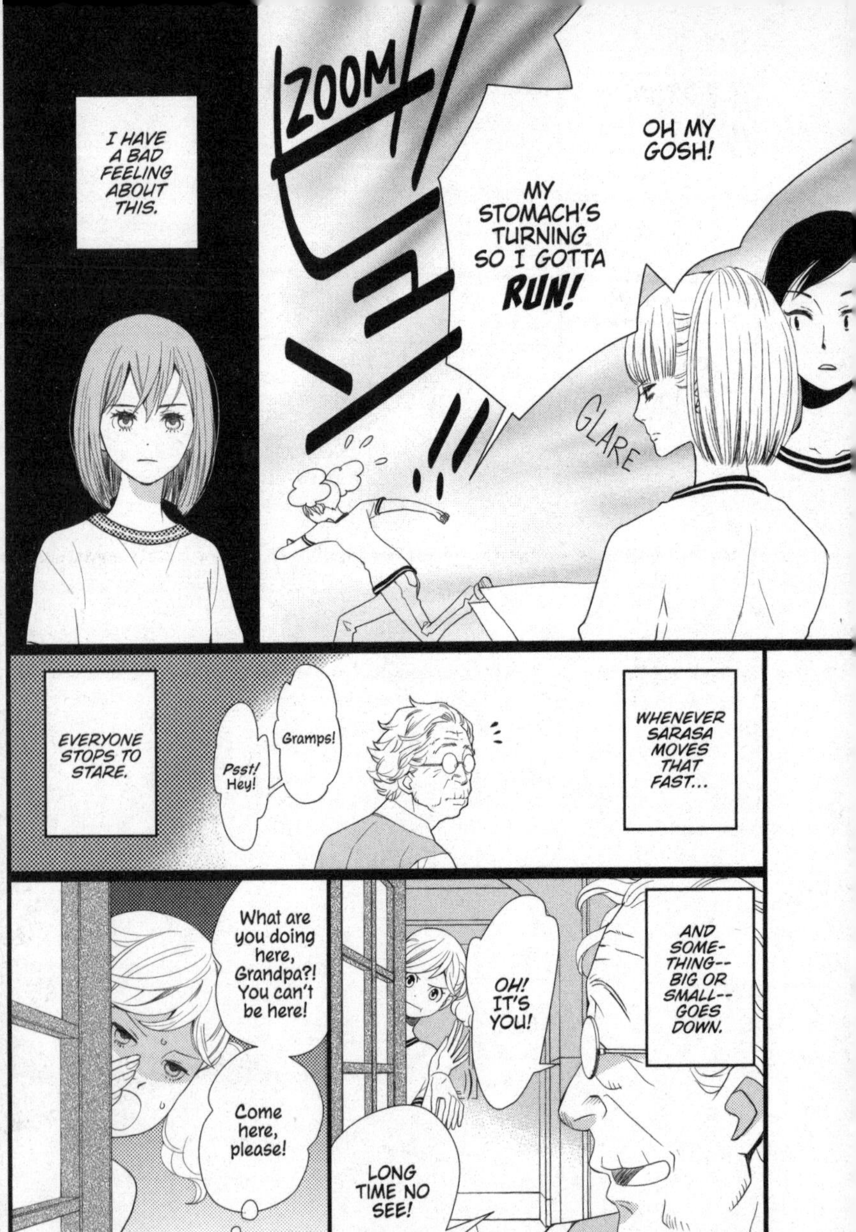
OH MY GOSH!
ZOOM
MY STOMACH'S TURNING SO I GOTTA RUN!
GLARE
I HAVE A BAD FEELING ABOUT THIS.
WHENEVER SARASA MOVES THAT FAST...
Gramps!
Psst! Hey!
EVERYONE STOPS TO STARE.
AND SOME-THING-- BIG OR SMALL-- GOES DOWN.
OH! IT'S YOU!
LONG TIME NO SEE!
What are you doing here, Grandpa?! You can't be here!
Come here, please!

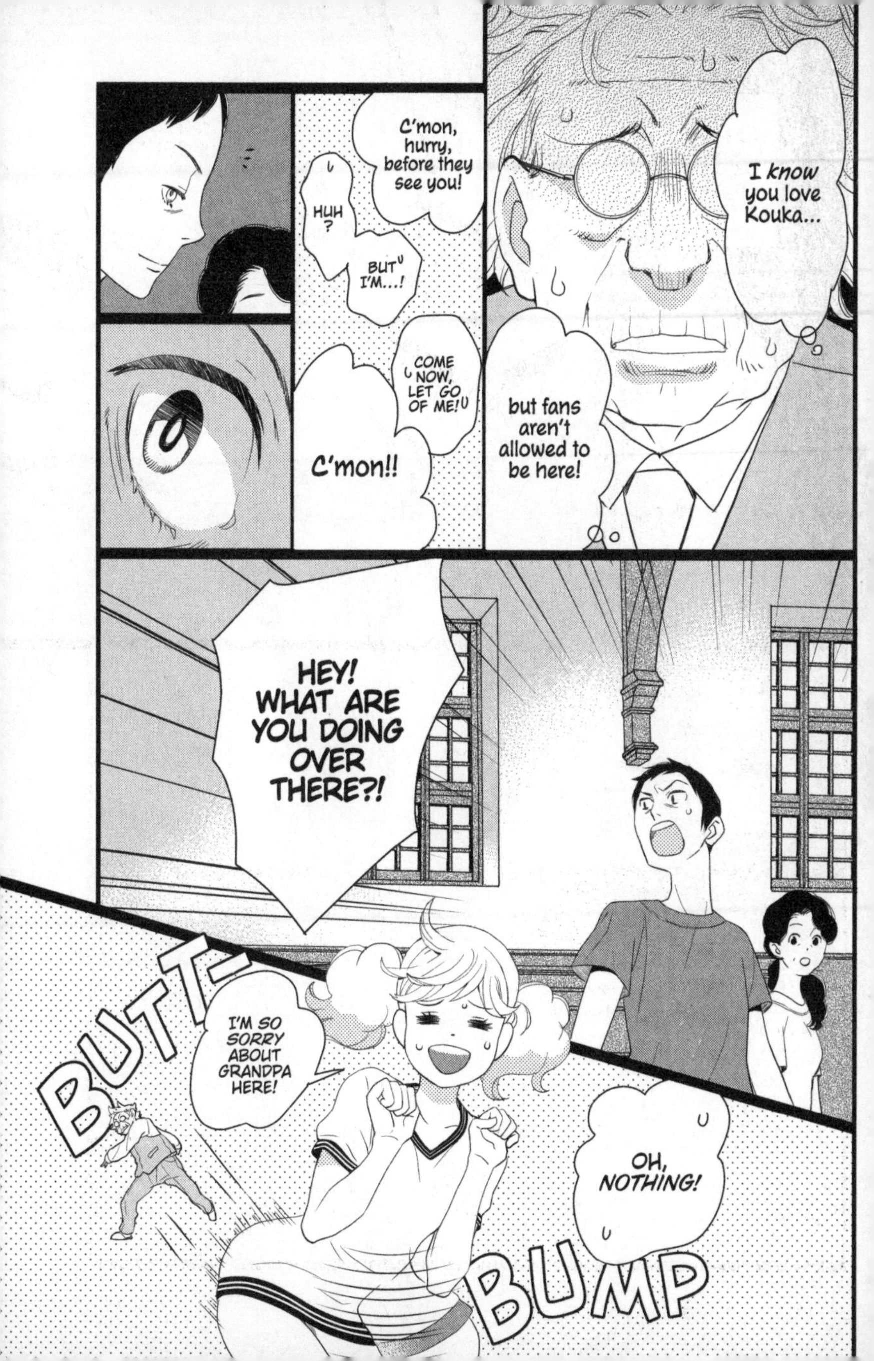
I *know* you love Kouka...
but fans aren't allowed to be here!
C'mon, hurry, before they see you!
HUH?
BUT I'M...!
COME NOW, LET GO OF ME!
C'mon!!
HEY! WHAT ARE YOU DOING OVER THERE?!
OH, *NOTHING!*
I'M SO *SORRY* ABOUT GRANDPA HERE!
BUTT-BUMP

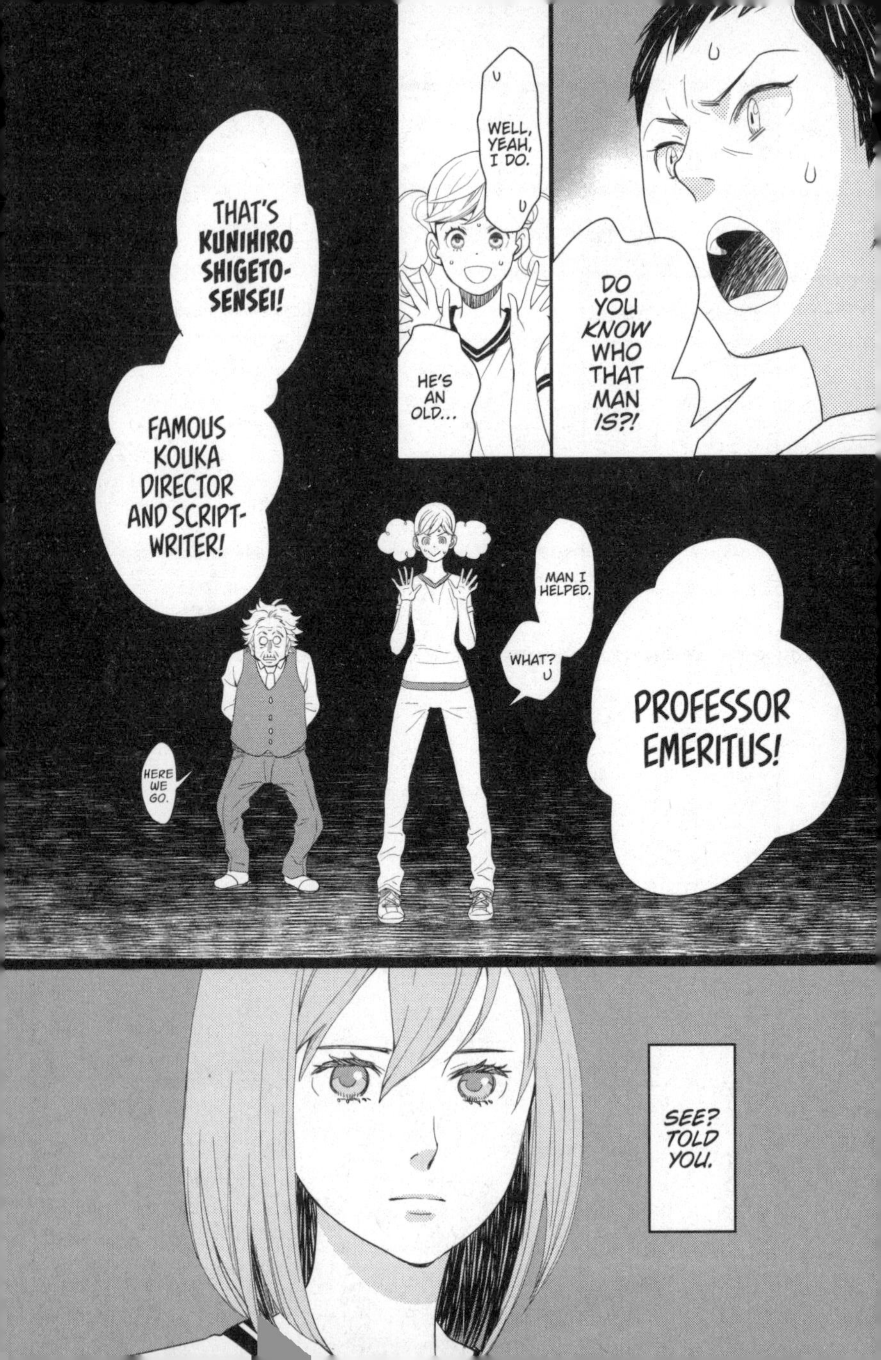
DO YOU KNOW WHO THAT MAN IS?!
WELL, YEAH, I DO.
HE'S AN OLD...
MAN I HELPED.
THAT'S KUNIHIRO SHIGETO-SENSEI!
FAMOUS KOUKA DIRECTOR AND SCRIPT-WRITER!
WHAT?
PROFESSOR EMERITUS!
HERE WE GO.
SEE? TOLD YOU.

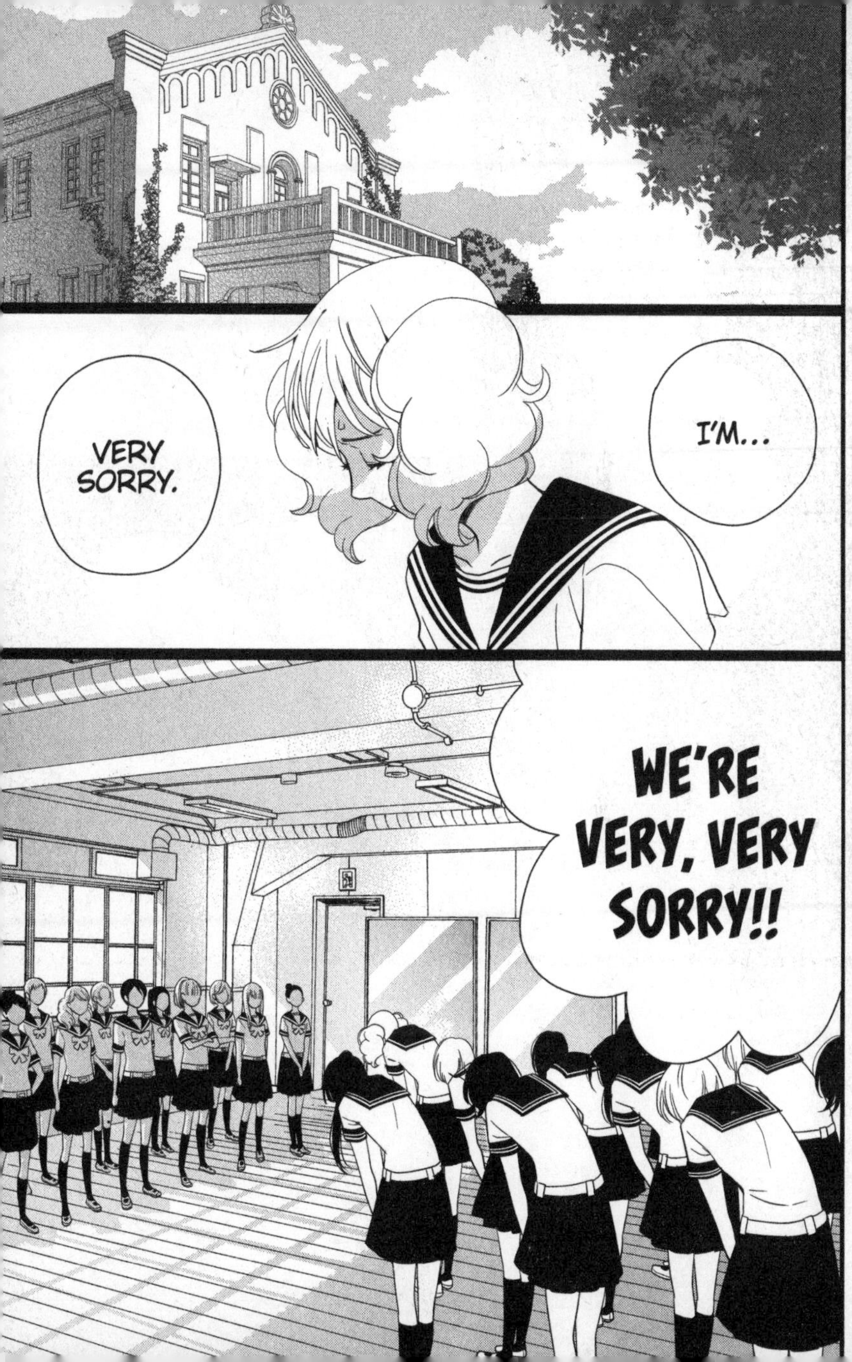
I'M...
VERY SORRY.
WE'RE VERY, VERY SORRY!!

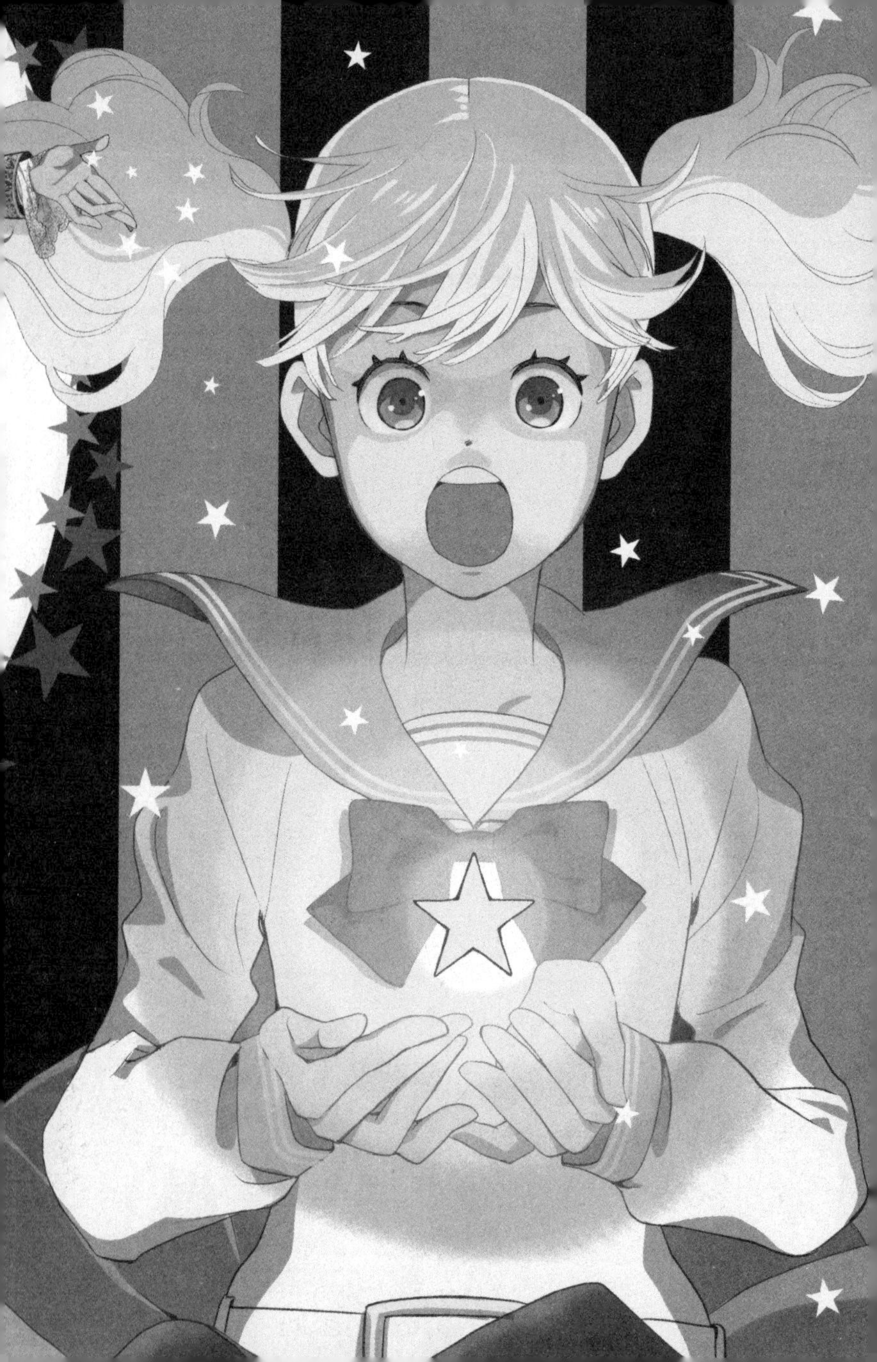

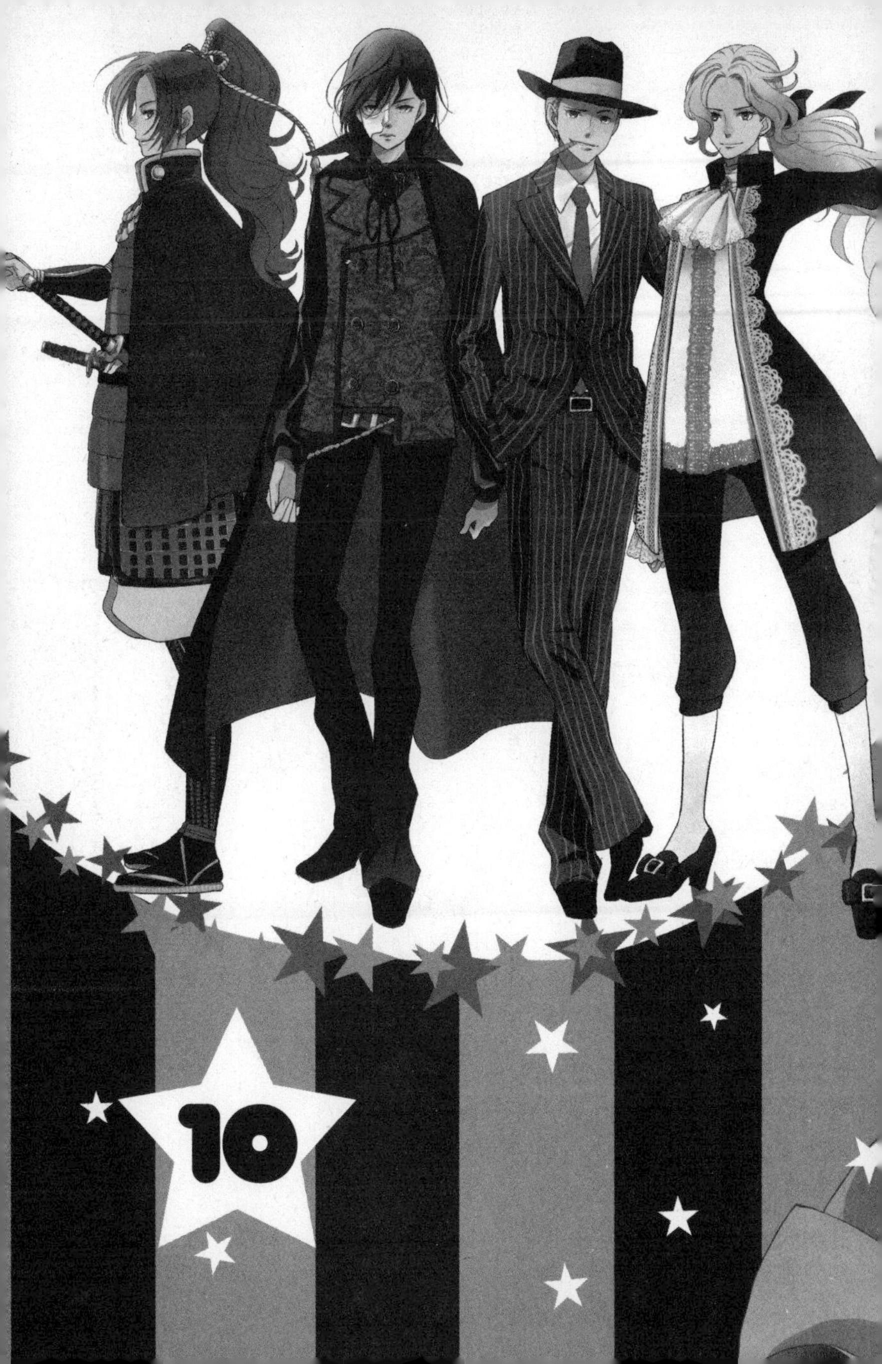
10

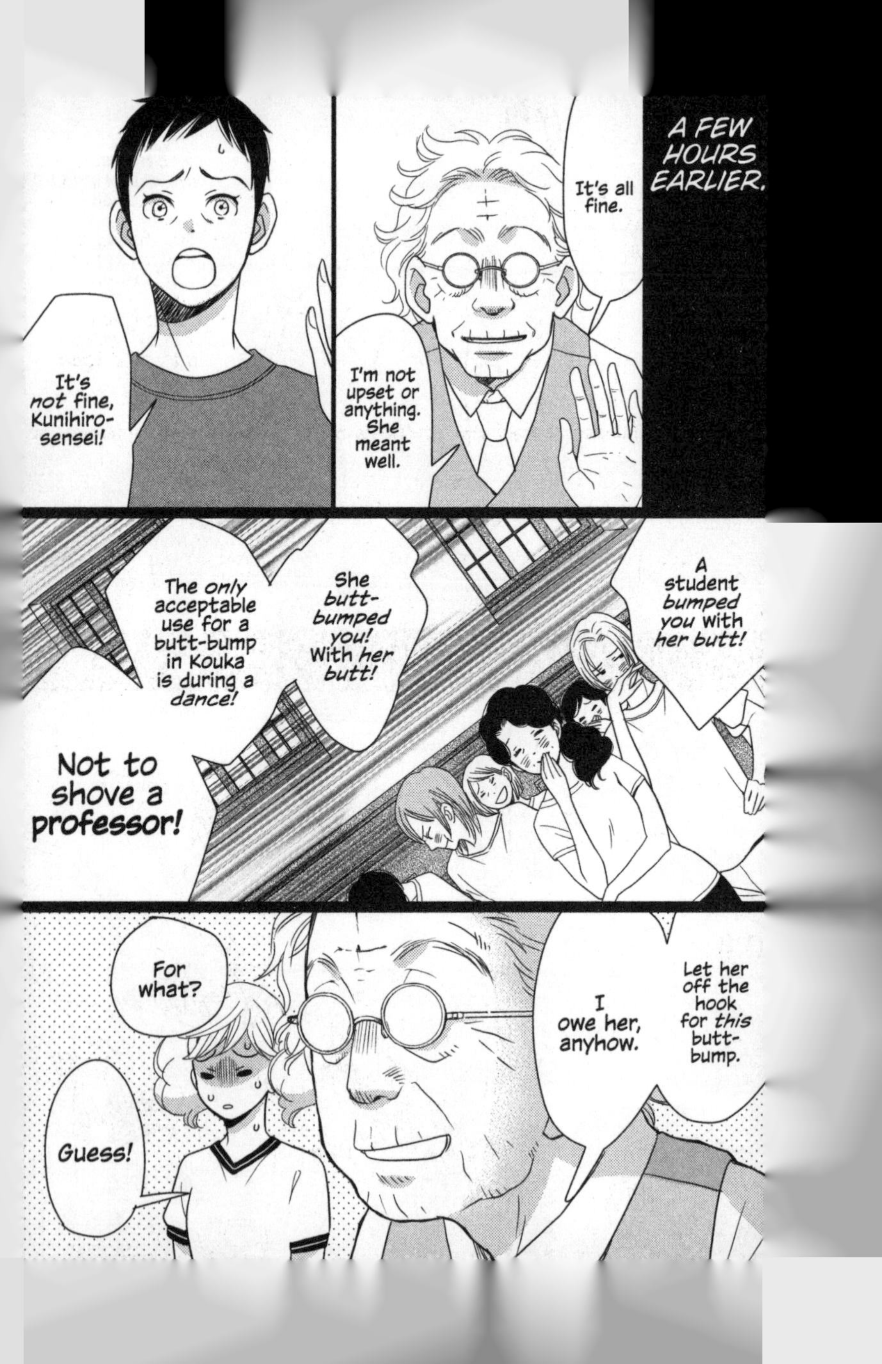
A FEW HOURS EARLIER.
It's all fine.
I'm not upset or anything. She meant well.
It's *not* fine, Kunihiro-sensei!
A student *bumped* you with *her butt!*
She *butt-bumped* you! With *her butt!*
The *only* acceptable use for a butt-bump in Kouka is during a *dance!*
Not to shove a professor!
Let her off the hook for *this* butt-bump.
I owe her, anyhow.
For what?
Guess!

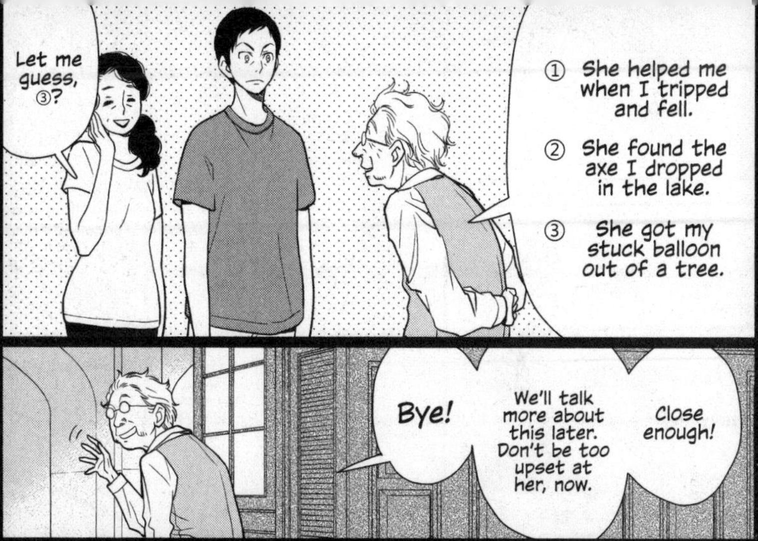
① She helped me when I tripped and fell.
② She found the axe I dropped in the lake.
③ She got my stuck balloon out of a tree.
Let me guess, ③?
Close enough!
We'll talk more about this later. Don't be too upset at her, now.
Bye!

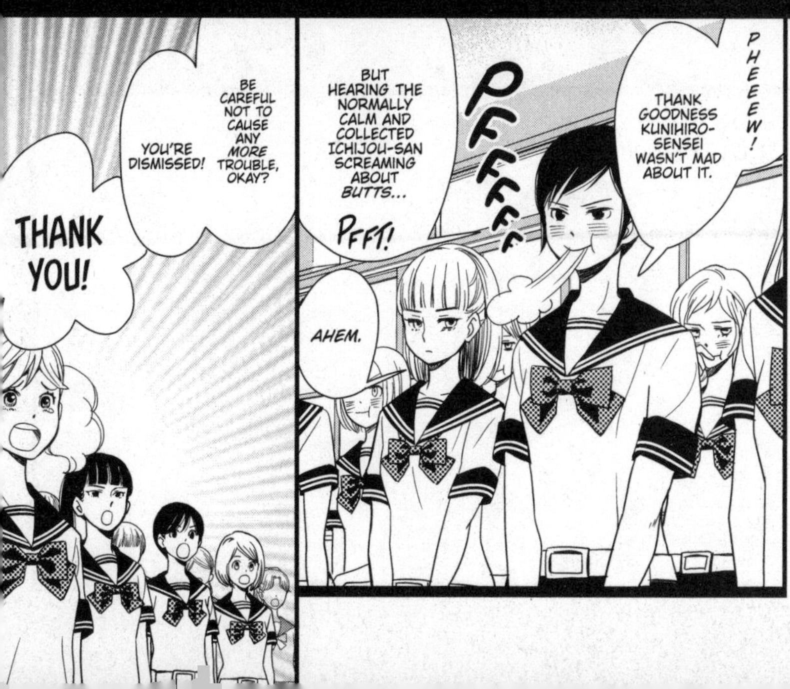
PHEEEW!
THANK GOODNESS KUNIHIRO-SENSEI WASN'T MAD ABOUT IT.
PFFFFF
BUT HEARING THE NORMALLY CALM AND COLLECTED ICHIJOU-SAN SCREAMING ABOUT *BUTTS*...
PFFT!
AHEM.
BE CAREFUL NOT TO CAUSE ANY *MORE* TROUBLE, OKAY?
YOU'RE DISMISSED!
THANK YOU!

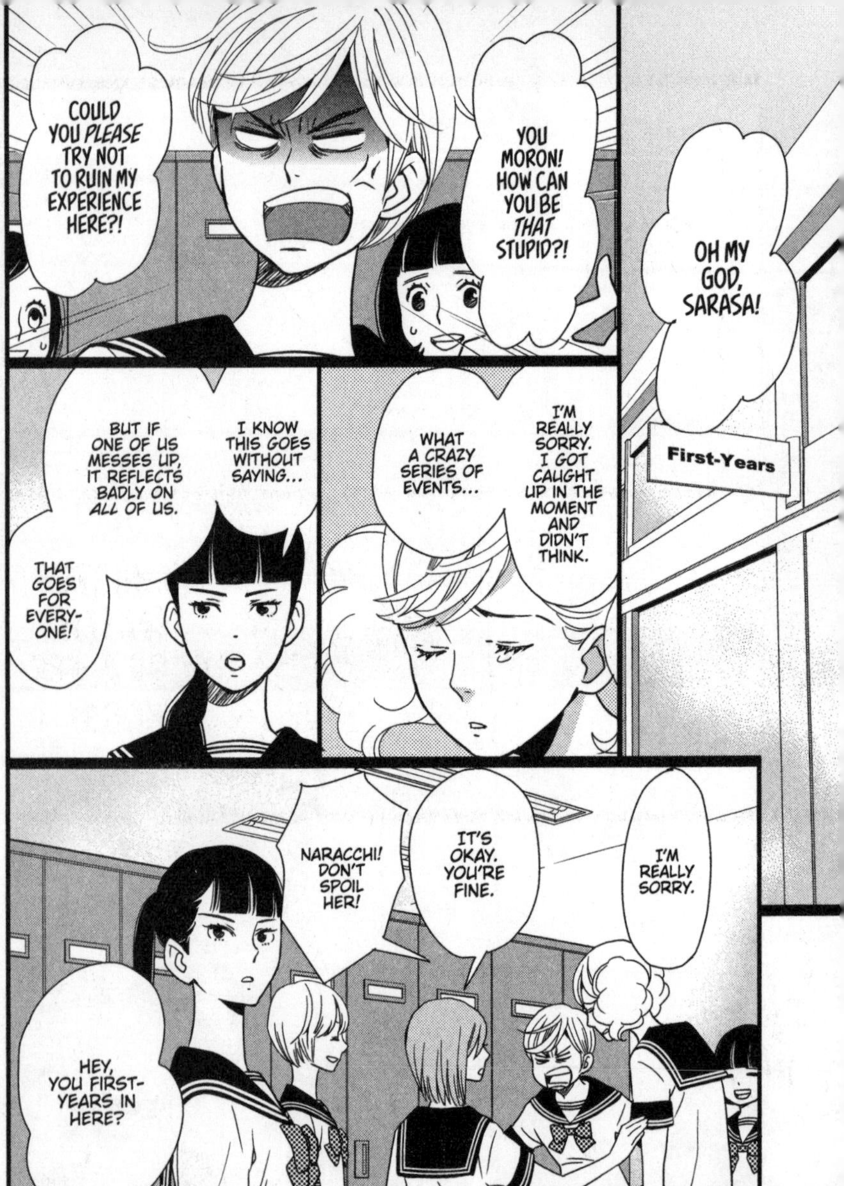
OH MY GOD, SARASA!
First-Years
YOU MORON! HOW CAN YOU BE *THAT* STUPID?!
COULD YOU *PLEASE* TRY NOT TO RUIN MY EXPERIENCE HERE?!
I'M REALLY SORRY. I GOT CAUGHT UP IN THE MOMENT AND DIDN'T THINK.
WHAT A CRAZY SERIES OF EVENTS...
I KNOW THIS GOES WITHOUT SAYING...
BUT IF ONE OF US MESSES UP, IT REFLECTS BADLY ON *ALL* OF US.
THAT GOES FOR EVERY-ONE!
I'M REALLY SORRY.
IT'S OKAY. YOU'RE FINE.
NARACCHI! DON'T SPOIL HER!
HEY, YOU FIRST-YEARS IN HERE?

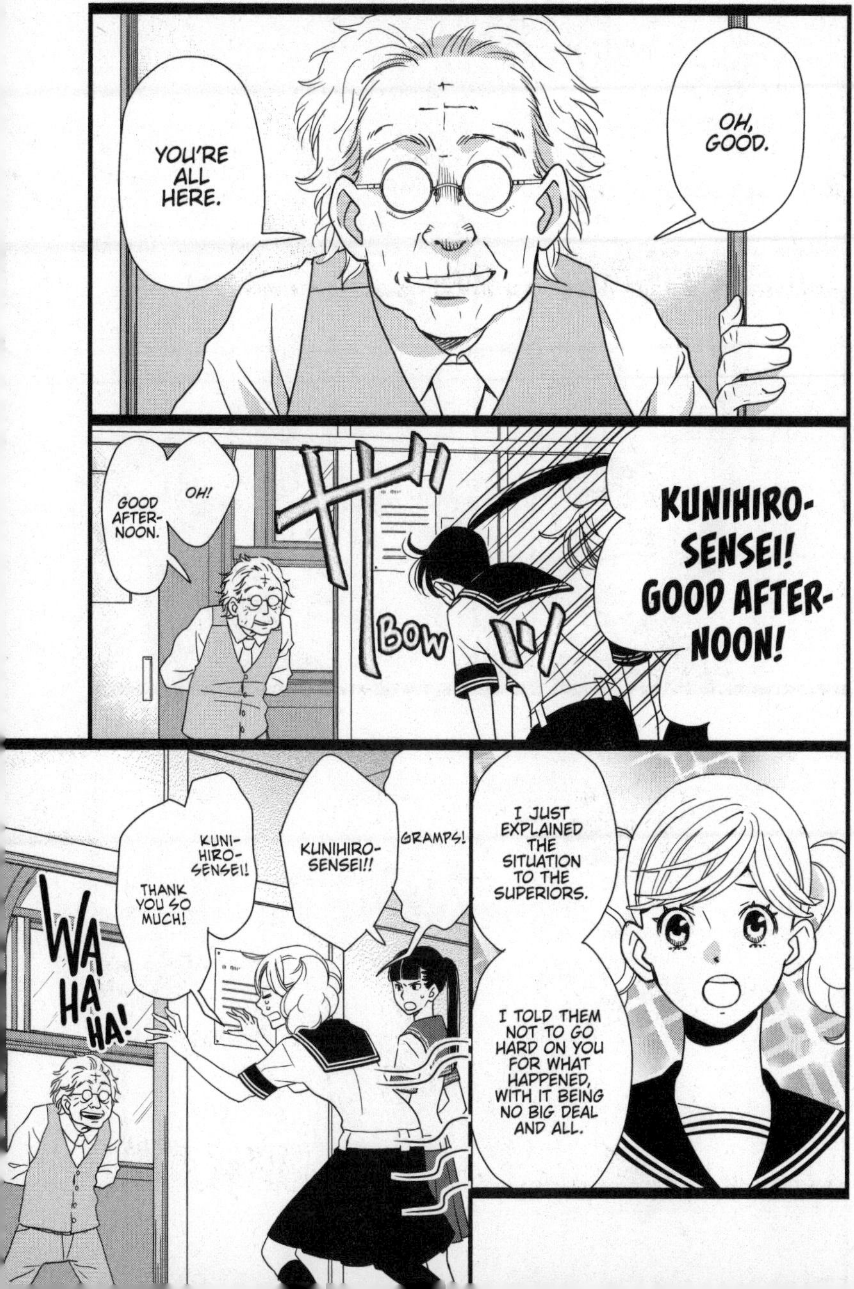
OH, GOOD.
YOU'RE ALL HERE.
KUNIHIRO-SENSEI! GOOD AFTER-NOON!
BOW
OH!
GOOD AFTER-NOON.
I JUST EXPLAINED THE SITUATION TO THE SUPERIORS.
I TOLD THEM NOT TO GO HARD ON YOU FOR WHAT HAPPENED, WITH IT BEING NO BIG DEAL AND ALL.
GRAMPS!
KUNIHIRO-SENSEI!!
KUNI-HIRO-SENSEI!
THANK YOU SO MUCH!
WA HA HA!

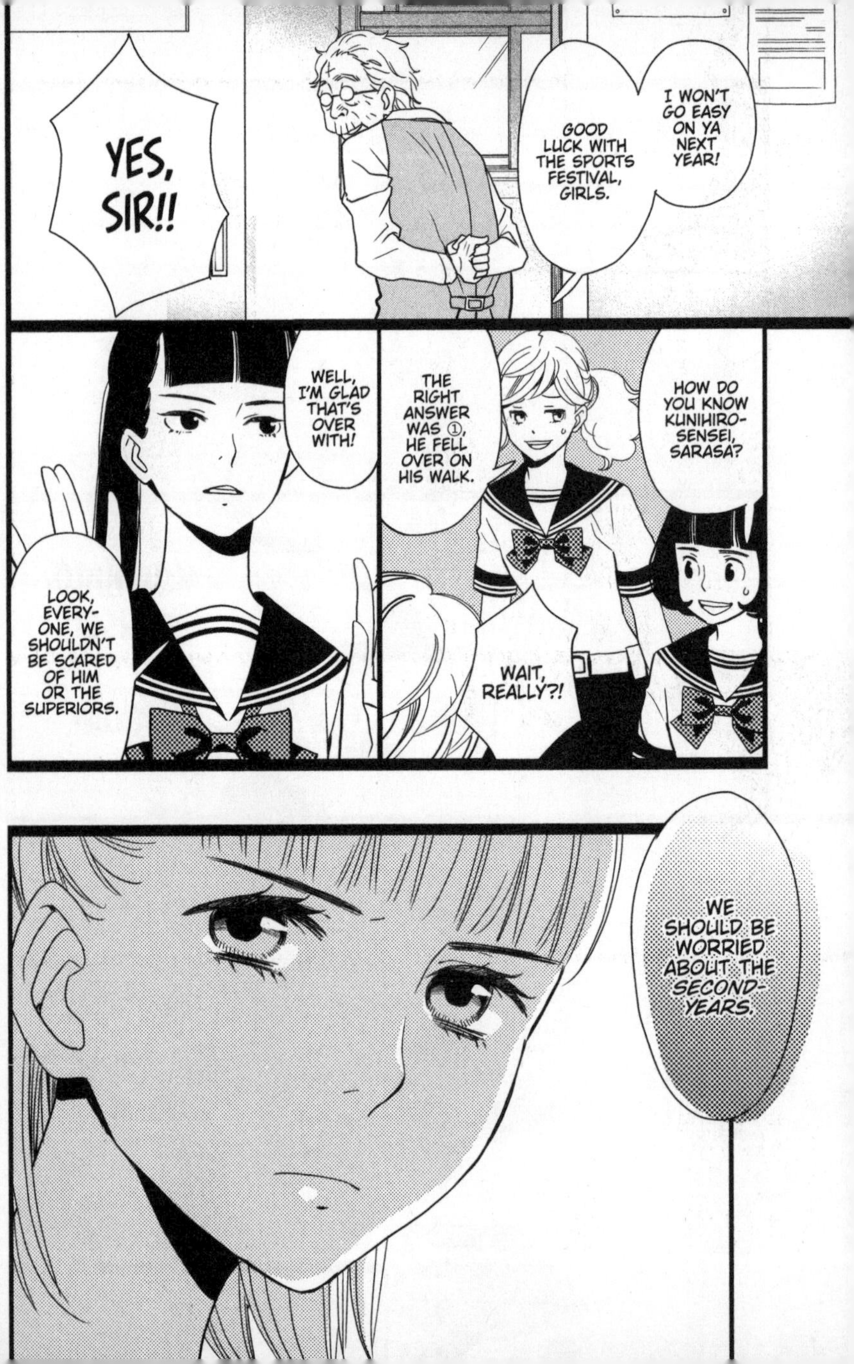
I WON'T GO EASY ON YA NEXT YEAR!
GOOD LUCK WITH THE SPORTS FESTIVAL, GIRLS.
YES, SIR!!
HOW DO YOU KNOW KUNIHIRO-SENSEI, SARASA?
THE RIGHT ANSWER WAS ①, HE FELL OVER ON HIS WALK.
WAIT, REALLY?!
WELL, I'M GLAD THAT'S OVER WITH!
LOOK, EVERY-ONE, WE SHOULDN'T BE SCARED OF HIM OR THE SUPERIORS.
WE SHOULD BE WORRIED ABOUT THE *SECOND-YEARS.*

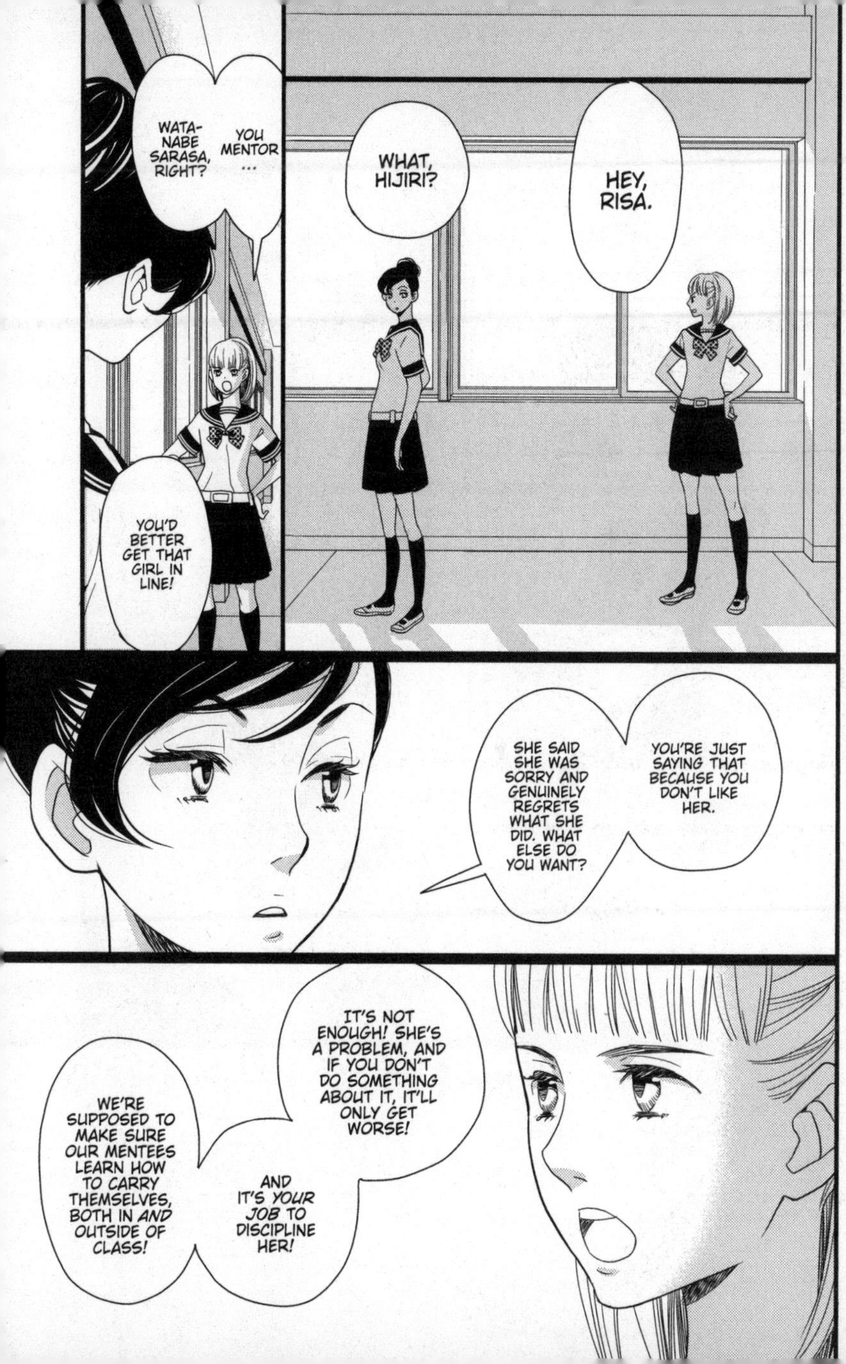
HEY, RISA.
WHAT, HIJIRI?
YOU MENTOR ...
WATA-NABE SARASA, RIGHT?
YOU'D BETTER GET THAT GIRL IN LINE!
YOU'RE JUST SAYING THAT BECAUSE YOU DON'T LIKE HER.
SHE SAID SHE WAS SORRY AND GENUINELY REGRETS WHAT SHE DID. WHAT ELSE DO YOU WANT?
IT'S NOT ENOUGH! SHE'S A PROBLEM, AND IF YOU DON'T DO SOMETHING ABOUT IT, IT'LL ONLY GET WORSE!
AND IT'S *YOUR* JOB TO DISCIPLINE HER!
WE'RE SUPPOSED TO MAKE SURE OUR MENTEES LEARN HOW TO CARRY THEMSELVES, BOTH IN *AND* OUTSIDE OF CLASS!

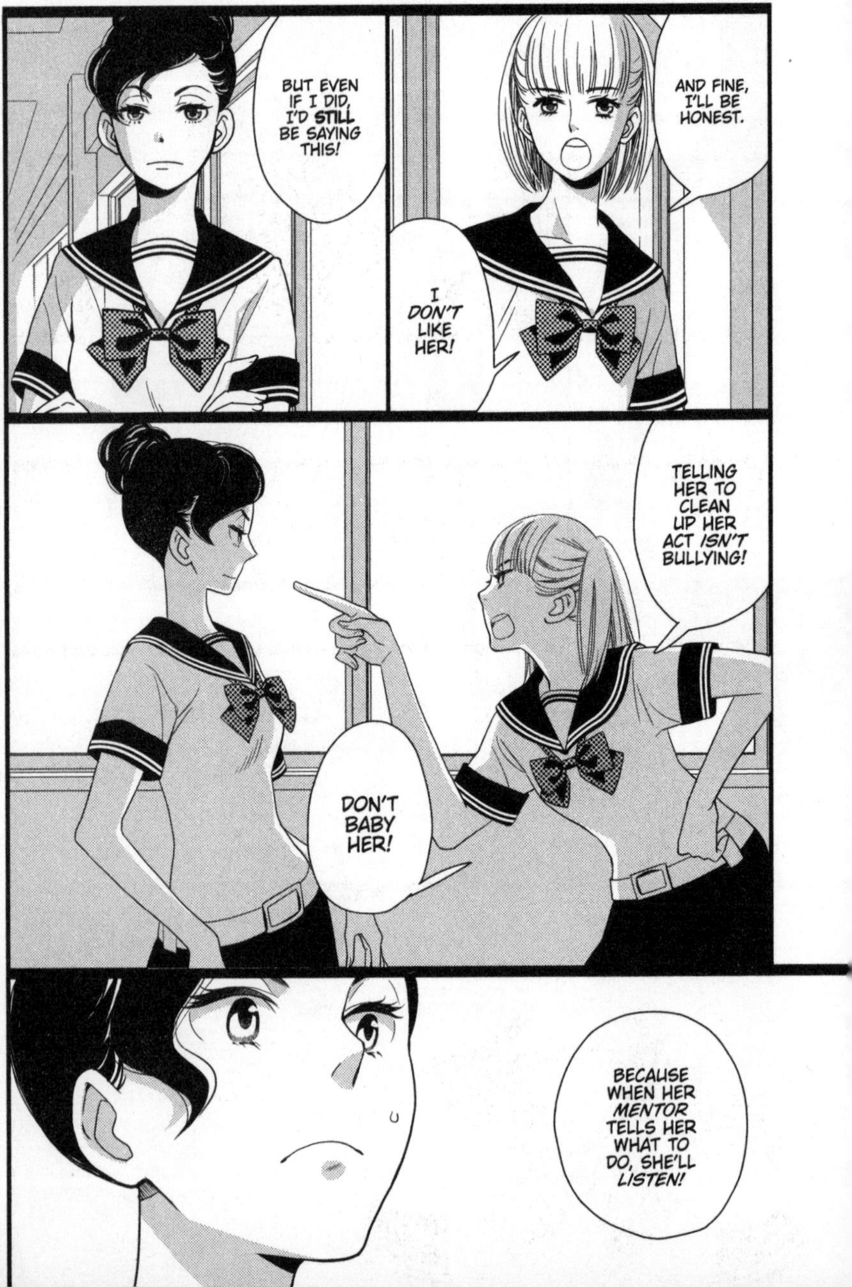
AND FINE, I'LL BE HONEST.
I DON'T LIKE HER!
BUT EVEN IF I DID, I'D STILL BE SAYING THIS!
TELLING HER TO CLEAN UP HER ACT ISN'T BULLYING!
DON'T BABY HER!
BECAUSE WHEN HER MENTOR TELLS HER WHAT TO DO, SHE'LL LISTEN!

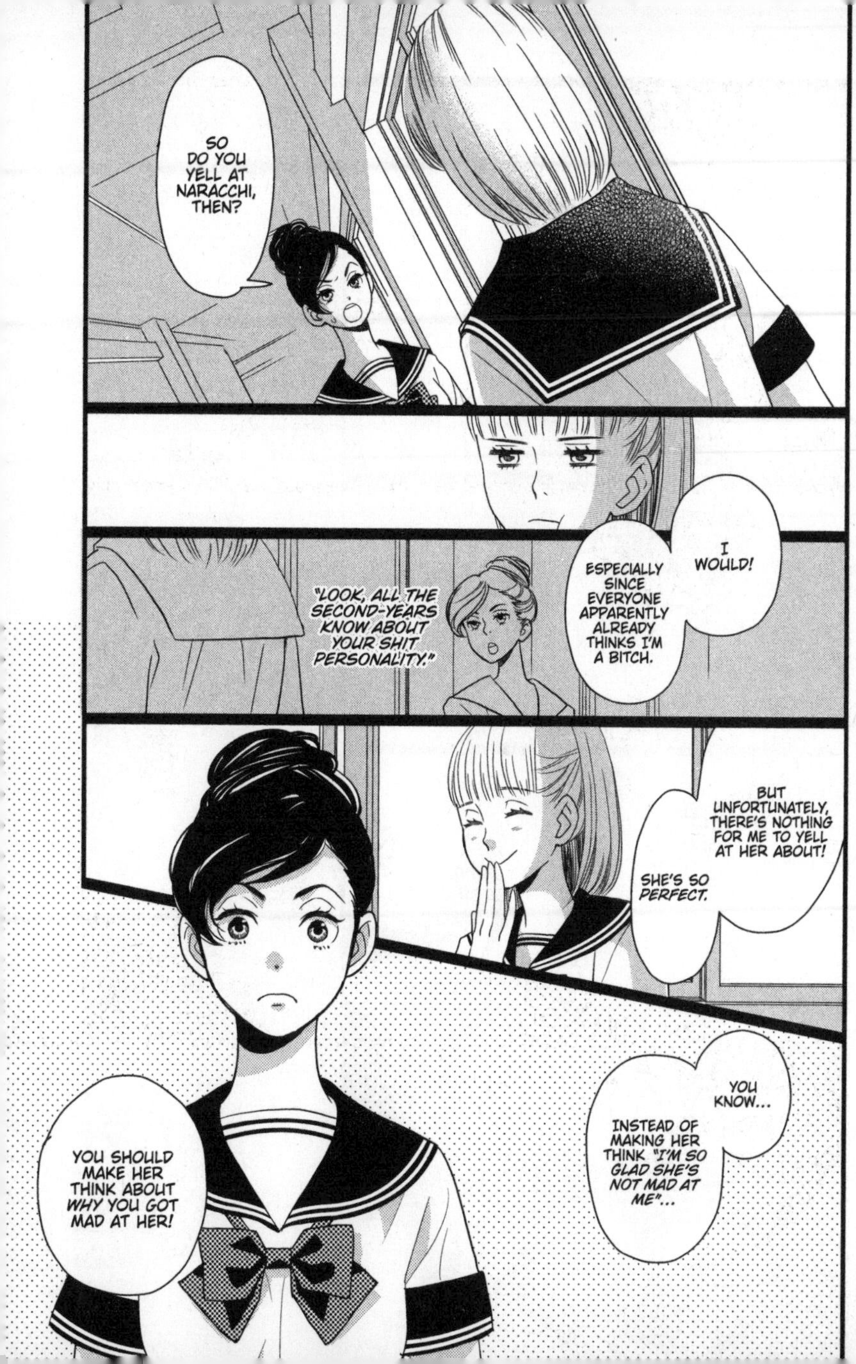
SO DO YOU YELL AT NARACCHI, THEN?
I WOULD!
ESPECIALLY SINCE EVERYONE APPARENTLY ALREADY THINKS I'M A BITCH.
"LOOK, ALL THE SECOND-YEARS KNOW ABOUT YOUR SHIT PERSONALITY."
BUT UNFORTUNATELY, THERE'S NOTHING FOR ME TO YELL AT HER ABOUT!
SHE'S SO *PERFECT.*
YOU KNOW...
INSTEAD OF MAKING HER THINK *"I'M SO GLAD SHE'S NOT MAD AT ME"*...
YOU SHOULD MAKE HER THINK ABOUT *WHY YOU GOT* MAD AT HER!

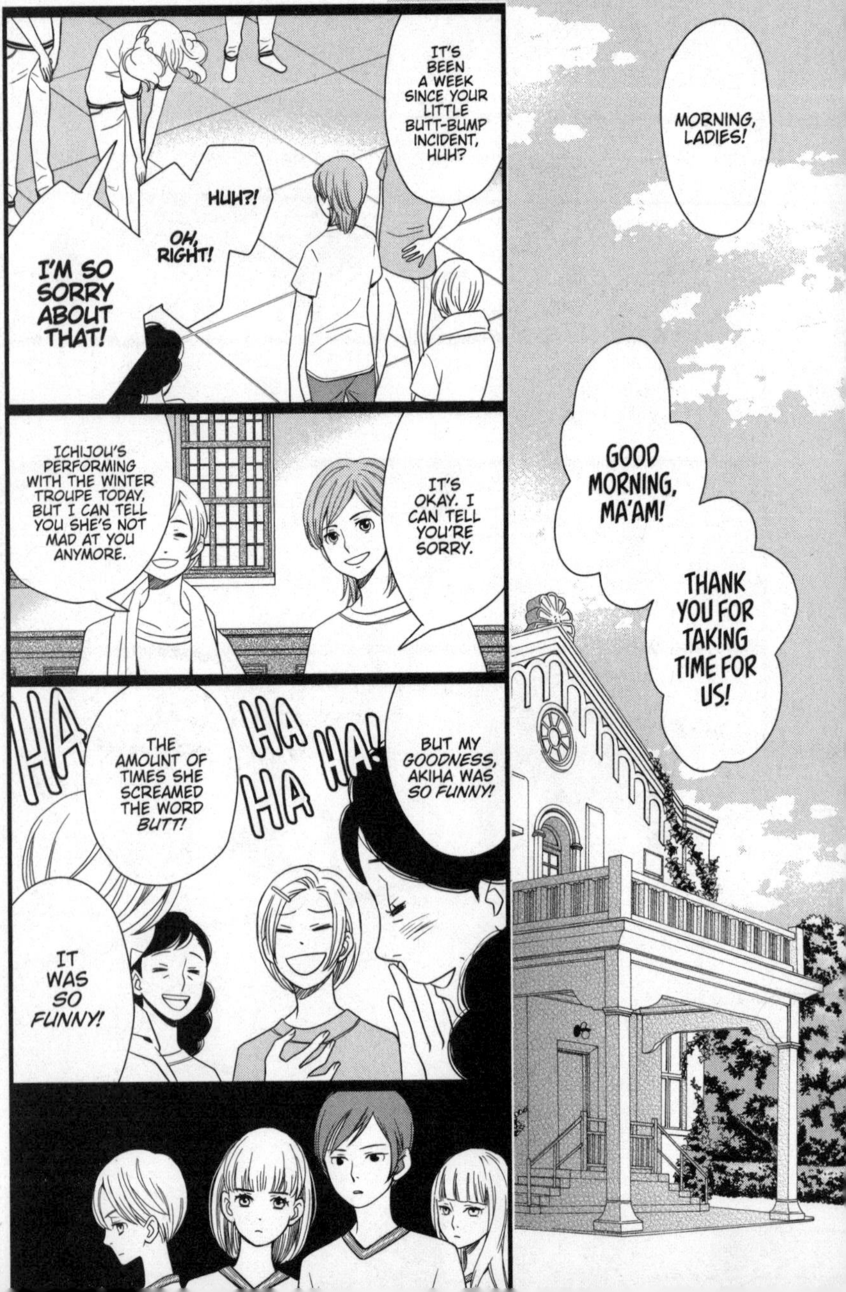
MORNING, LADIES!
GOOD MORNING, MA'AM!
THANK YOU FOR TAKING TIME FOR US!
IT'S BEEN A WEEK SINCE YOUR LITTLE BUTT-BUMP INCIDENT, HUH?
HUH?!
OH, RIGHT!
I'M SO SORRY ABOUT THAT!
IT'S OKAY. I CAN TELL YOU'RE SORRY.
ICHIJOU'S PERFORMING WITH THE WINTER TROUPE TODAY, BUT I CAN TELL YOU SHE'S NOT MAD AT YOU ANYMORE.
BUT MY GOODNESS, AKIHA WAS SO FUNNY!
HA HA HA HA!
THE AMOUNT OF TIMES SHE SCREAMED THE WORD BUTT!
HA
IT WAS SO FUNNY!

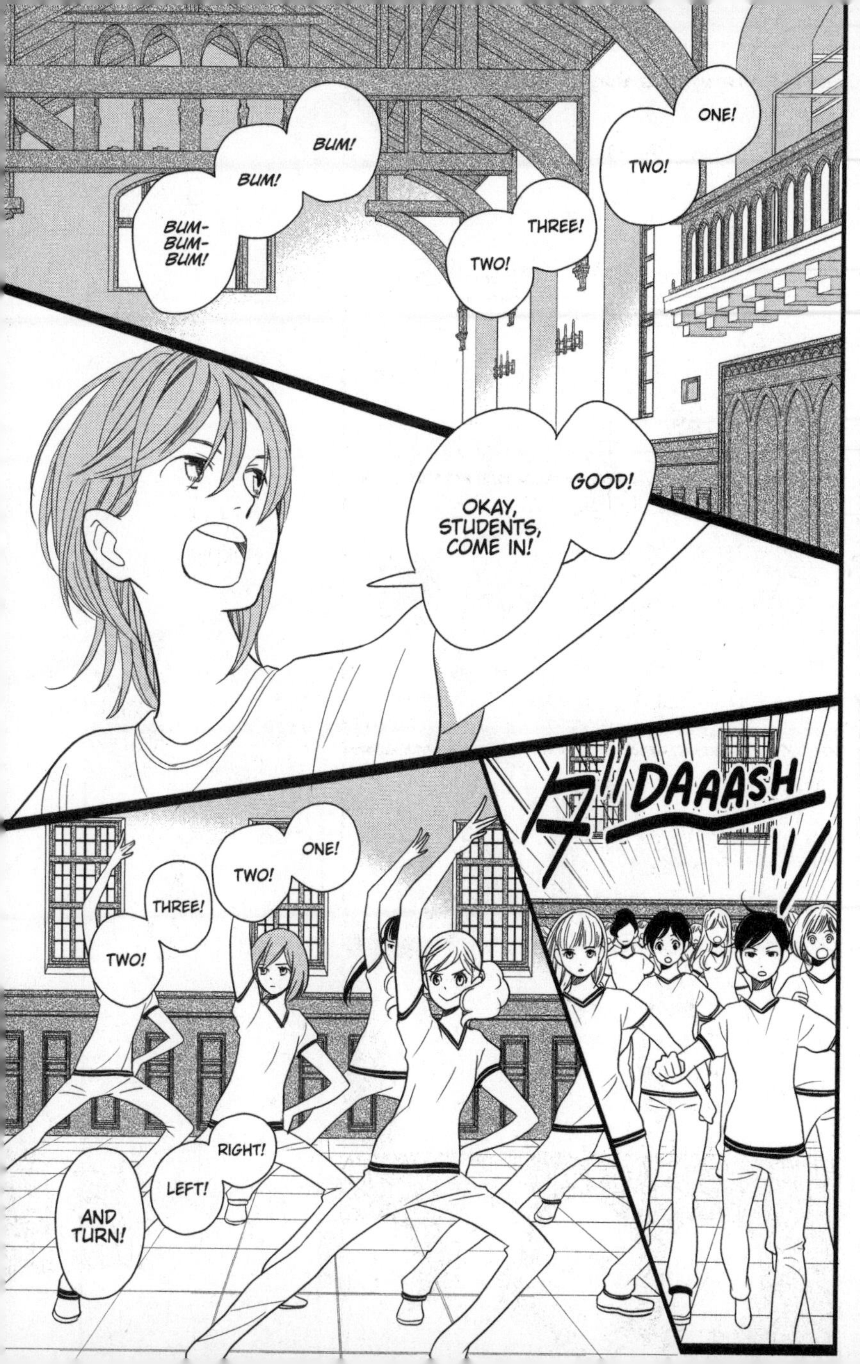

ONE!
TWO!
THREE!
TWO!
BUM!
BUM!
BUM-BUM-BUM!
GOOD!
OKAY, STUDENTS, COME IN!
DAAASH
ONE!
TWO!
THREE!
TWO!
RIGHT!
LEFT!
AND TURN!

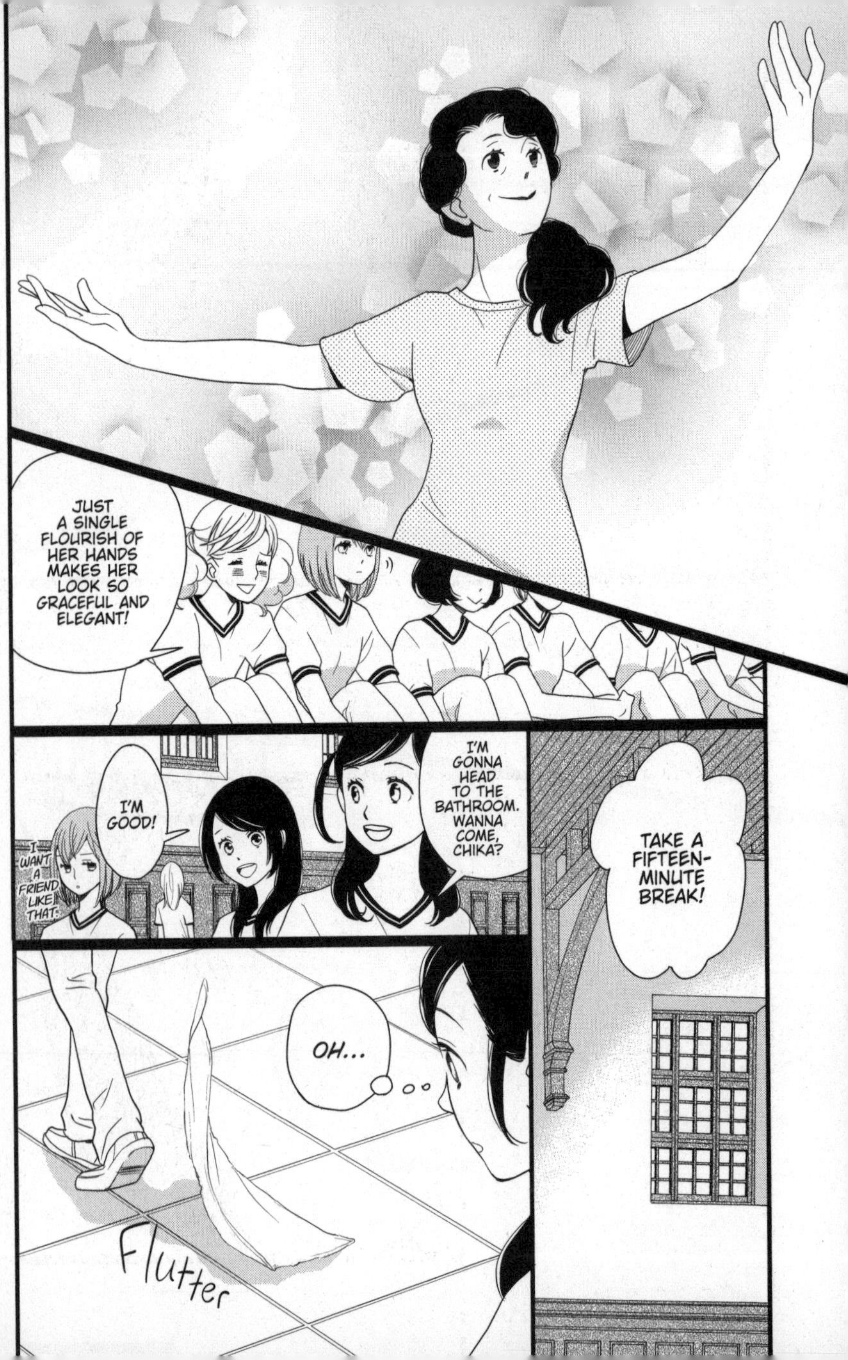
JUST A SINGLE FLOURISH OF HER HANDS MAKES HER LOOK SO GRACEFUL AND ELEGANT!
TAKE A FIFTEEN-MINUTE BREAK!
I'M GONNA HEAD TO THE BATHROOM. WANNA COME, CHIKA?
I'M GOOD!
I WANT A FRIEND LIKE THAT.
OH...
Flutter

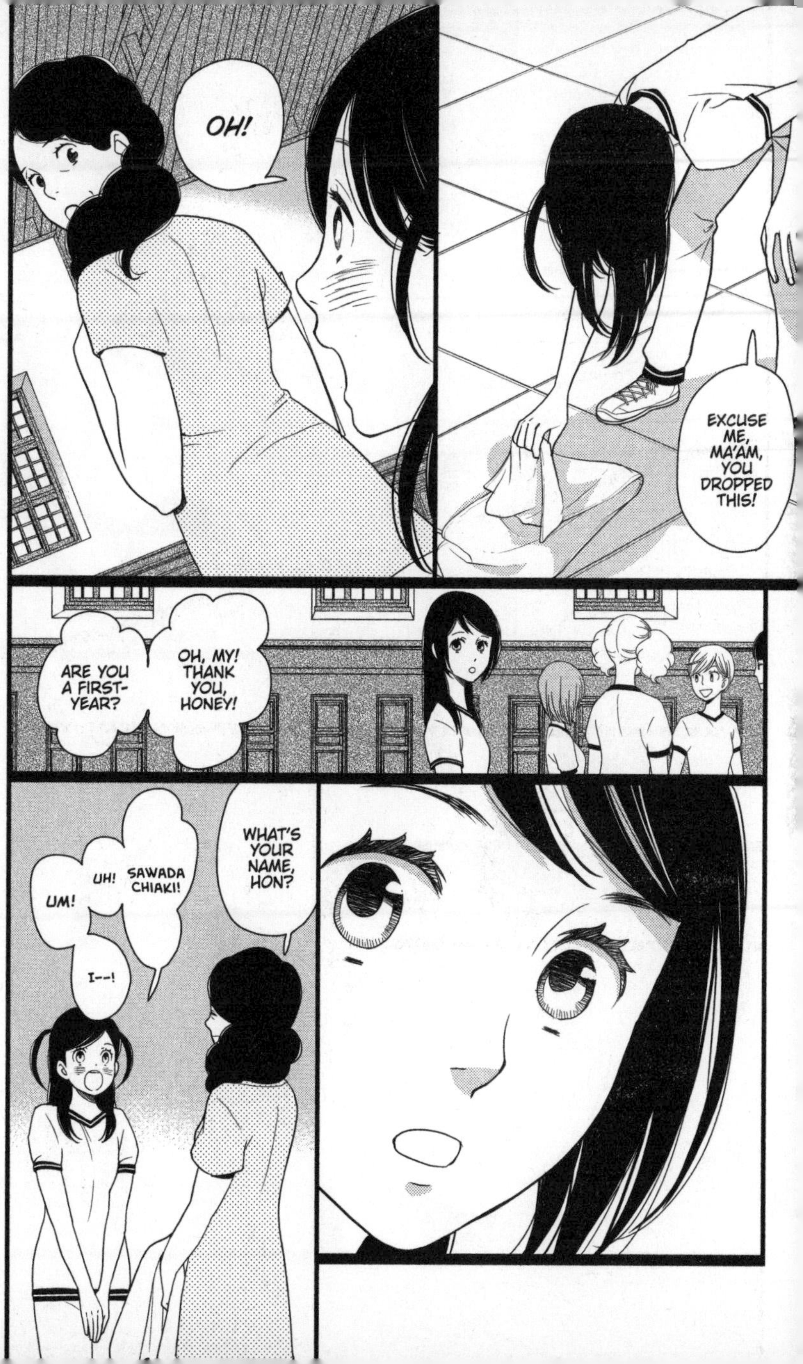
EXCUSE ME, MA'AM, YOU DROPPED THIS!
OH!
OH, MY! THANK YOU, HONEY!
ARE YOU A FIRST-YEAR?
WHAT'S YOUR NAME, HON?
UH! SAWADA CHIAKI!
UM!
I--!

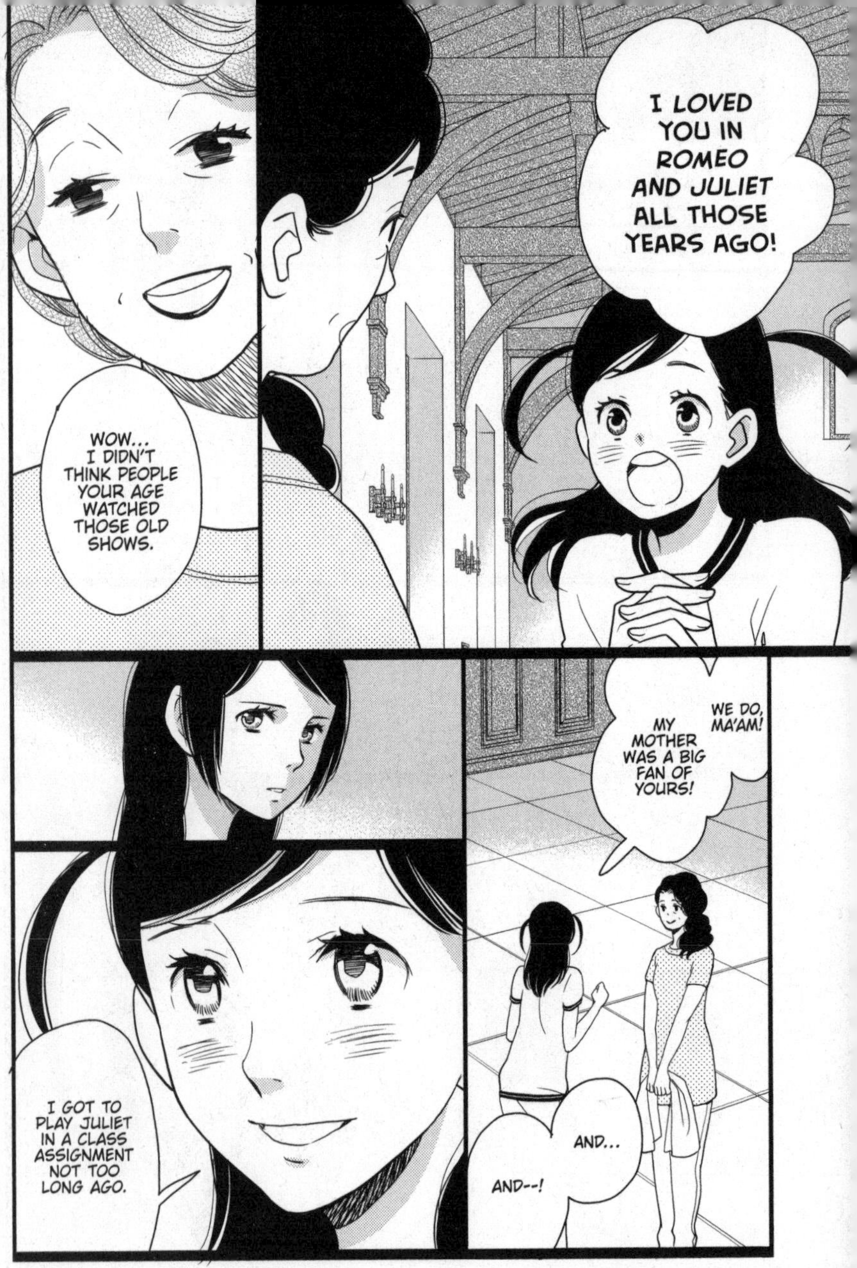
I LOVED YOU IN ROMEO AND JULIET ALL THOSE YEARS AGO!
WOW... I DIDN'T THINK PEOPLE YOUR AGE WATCHED THOSE OLD SHOWS.
WE DO, MA'AM!
MY MOTHER WAS A BIG FAN OF YOURS!
AND...
AND--!
I GOT TO PLAY JULIET IN A CLASS ASSIGNMENT NOT TOO LONG AGO.

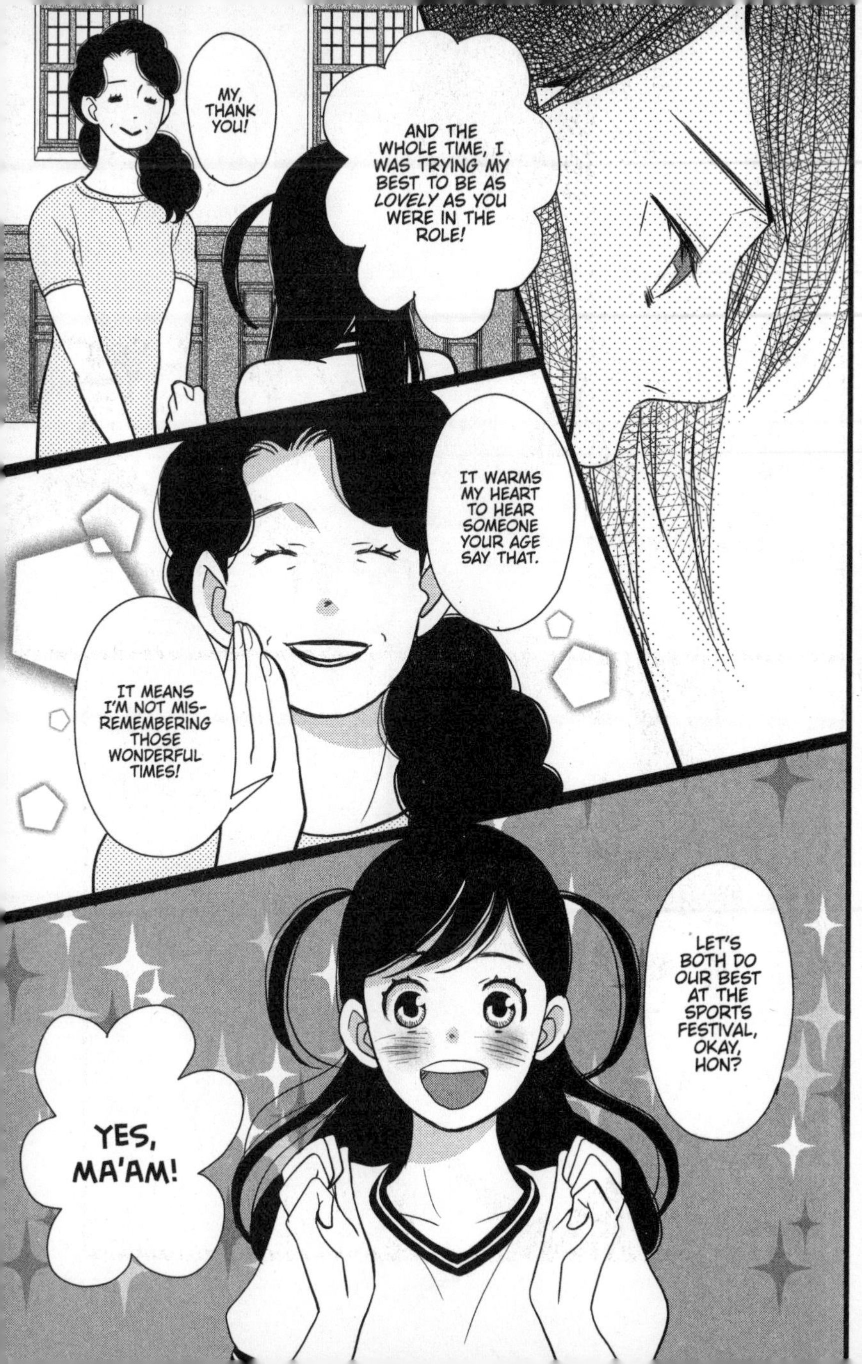
AND THE WHOLE TIME, I WAS TRYING MY BEST TO BE AS *LOVELY* AS YOU WERE IN THE ROLE!
MY, THANK YOU!
IT WARMS MY HEART TO HEAR SOMEONE YOUR AGE SAY THAT.
IT MEANS I'M NOT MIS-REMEMBERING THOSE WONDERFUL TIMES!
LET'S BOTH DO OUR BEST AT THE SPORTS FESTIVAL, OKAY, HON?
YES, MA'AM!

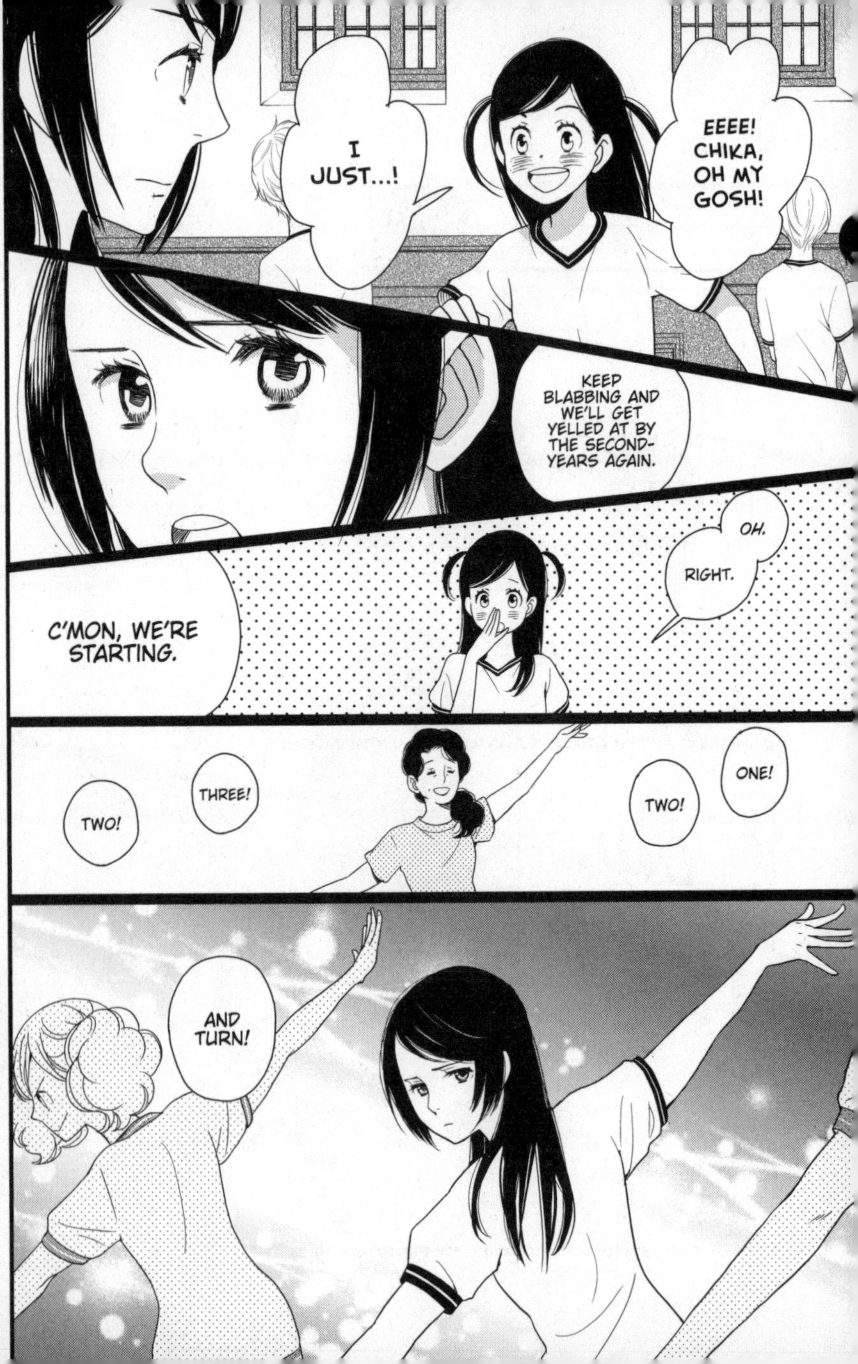
EEEE! CHIKA, OH MY GOSH!
I JUST...!
KEEP BLABBING AND WE'LL GET YELLED AT BY THE SECOND-YEARS AGAIN.
OH. RIGHT.
C'MON, WE'RE STARTING.
ONE!
TWO!
THREE!
TWO!
AND TURN!

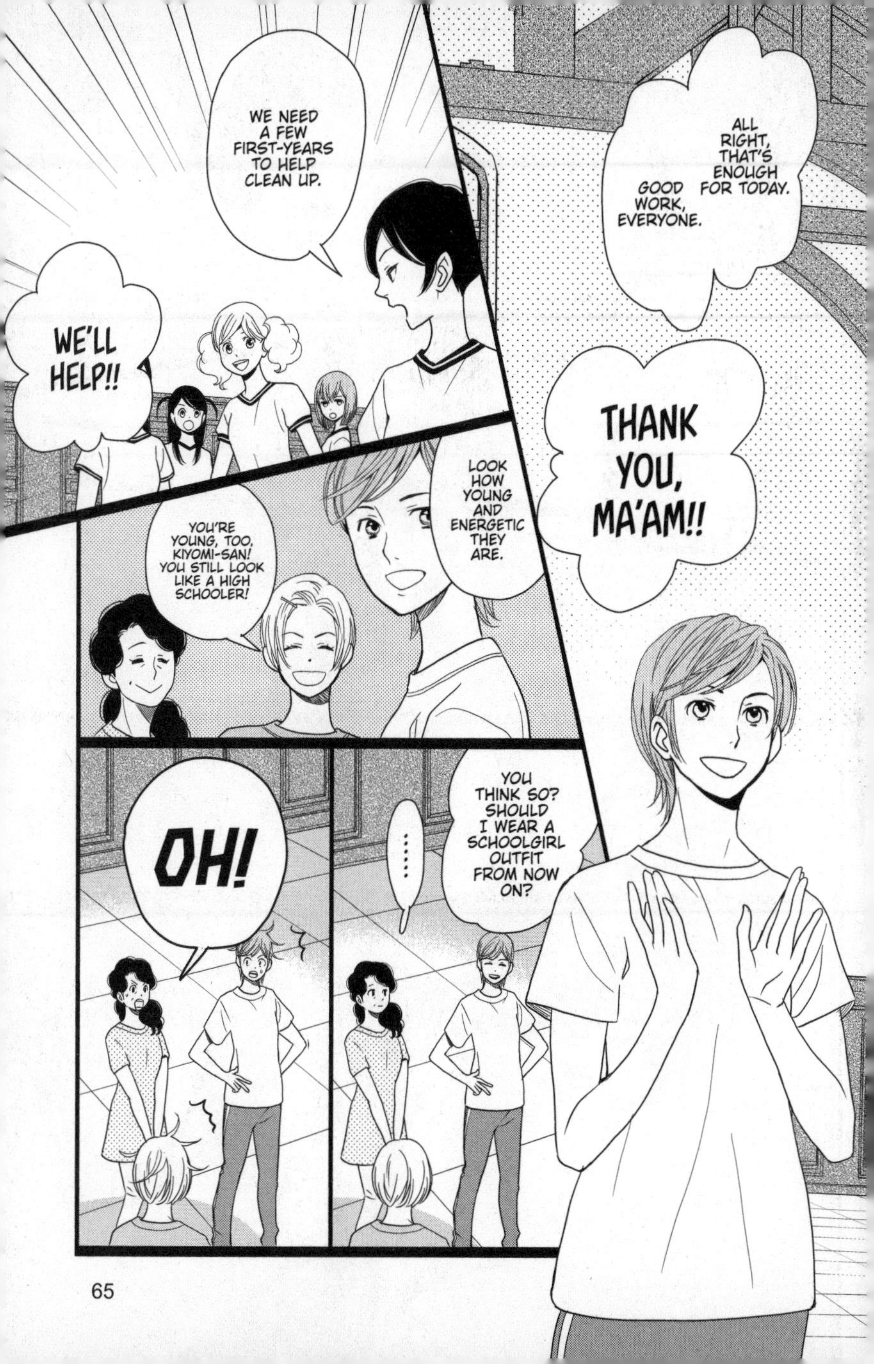
ALL RIGHT, THAT'S ENOUGH FOR TODAY. GOOD WORK, EVERYONE.
THANK YOU, MA'AM!!
WE NEED A FEW FIRST-YEARS TO HELP CLEAN UP.
WE'LL HELP!!
LOOK HOW YOUNG AND ENERGETIC THEY ARE.
YOU'RE YOUNG, TOO, KIYOMI-SAN! YOU STILL LOOK LIKE A HIGH SCHOOLER!
YOU THINK SO? SHOULD I WEAR A SCHOOLGIRL OUTFIT FROM NOW ON?
......
OH!

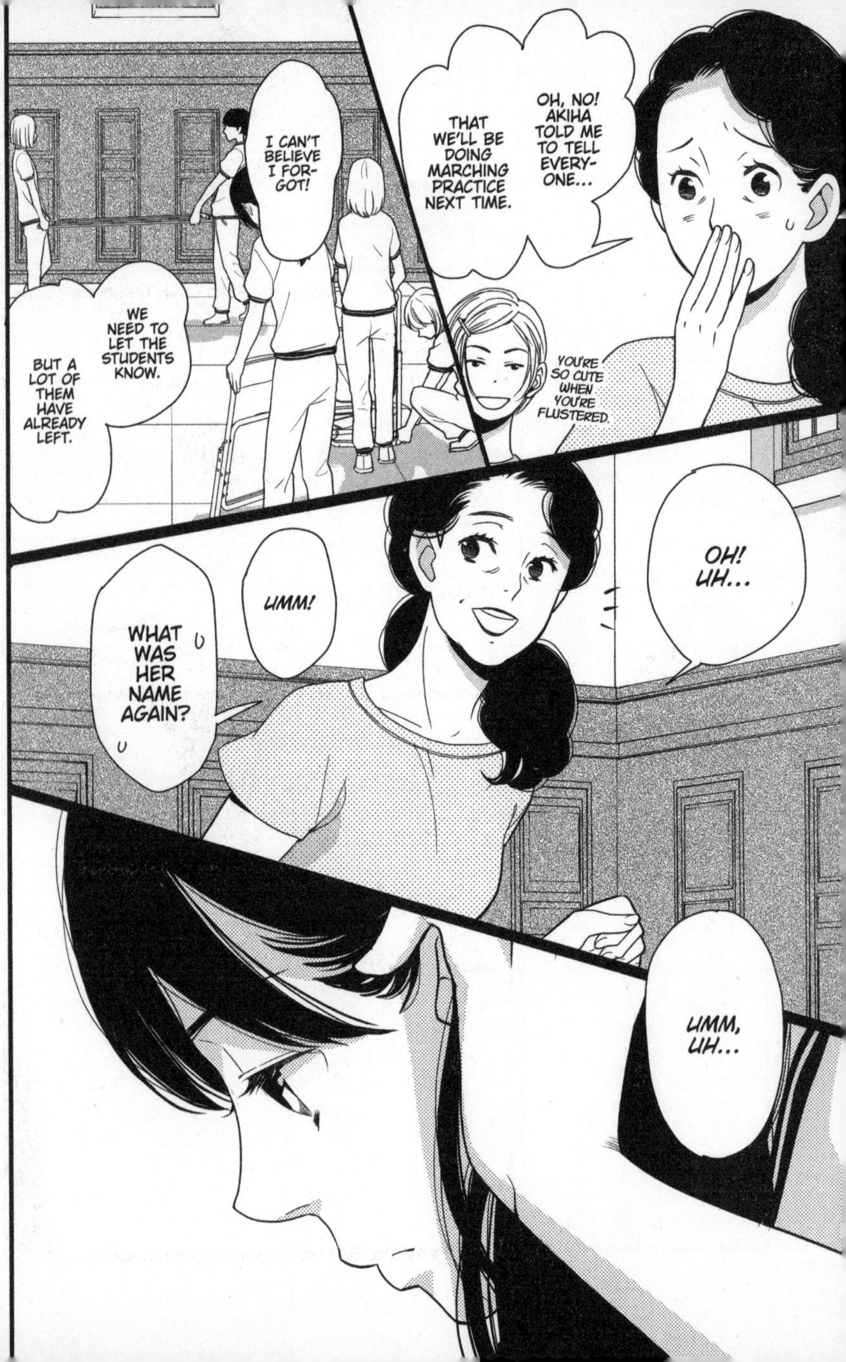
OH, NO! AKIHA TOLD ME TO TELL EVERY-ONE...
THAT WE'LL BE DOING MARCHING PRACTICE NEXT TIME.
YOU'RE SO CUTE WHEN YOU'RE FLUSTERED.
I CAN'T BELIEVE I FOR-GOT!
WE NEED TO LET THE STUDENTS KNOW.
BUT A LOT OF THEM HAVE ALREADY LEFT.
OH! UH...
UMM!
WHAT WAS HER NAME AGAIN?
UMM, UH...

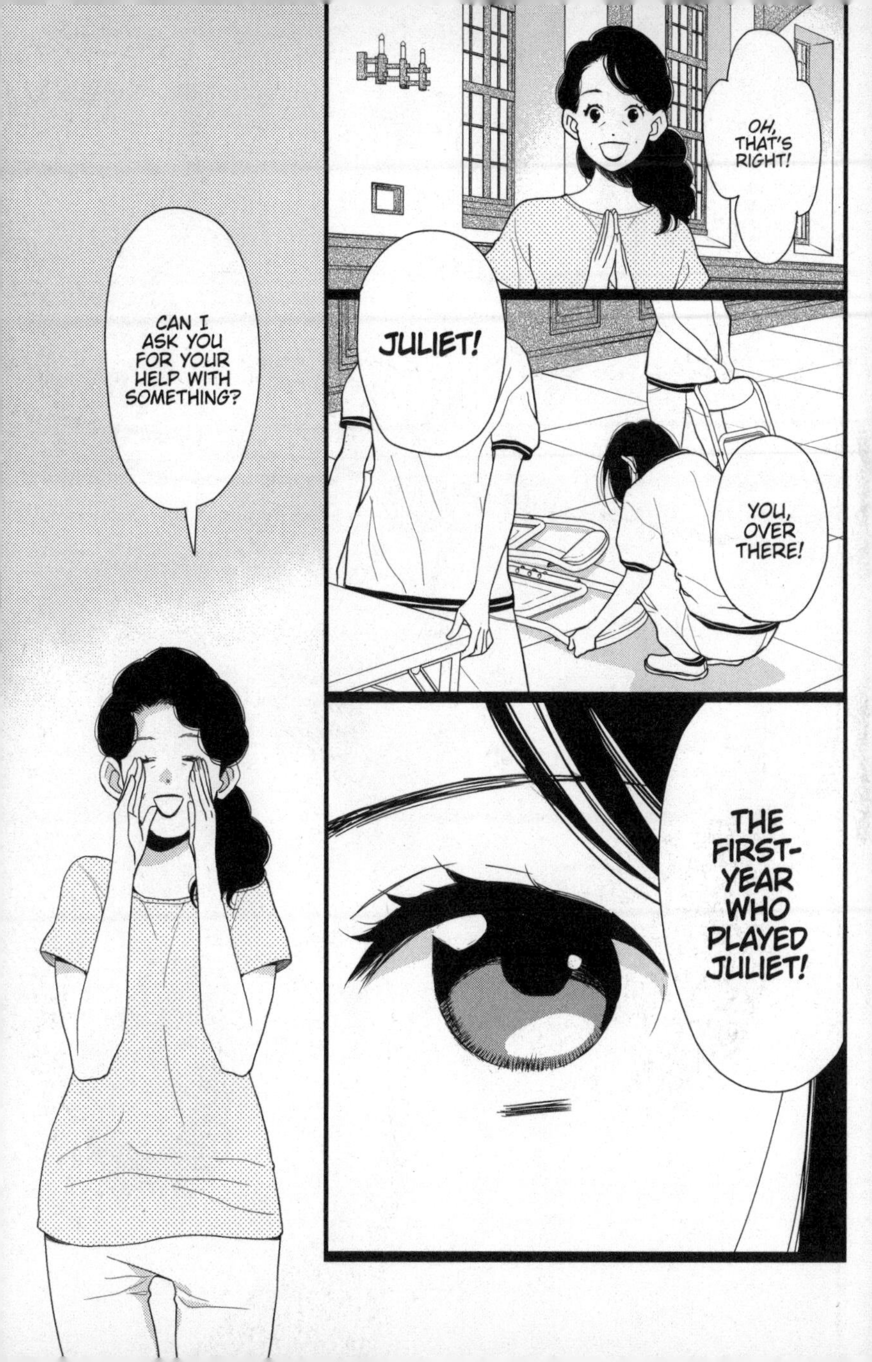
OH, THAT'S RIGHT!
JULIET!
YOU, OVER THERE!
THE FIRST-YEAR WHO PLAYED JULIET!
CAN I ASK YOU FOR YOUR HELP WITH SOMETHING?

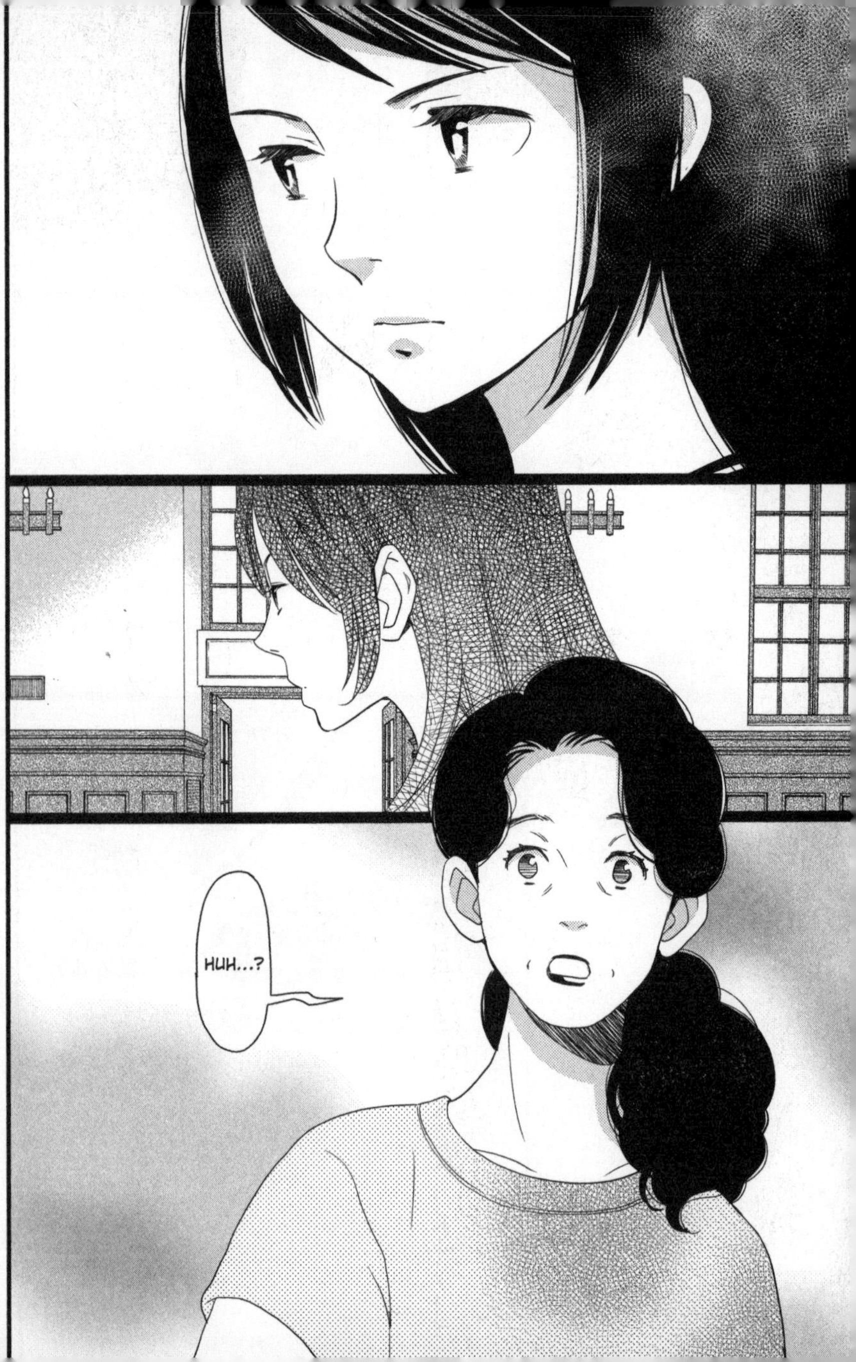
HUH...?

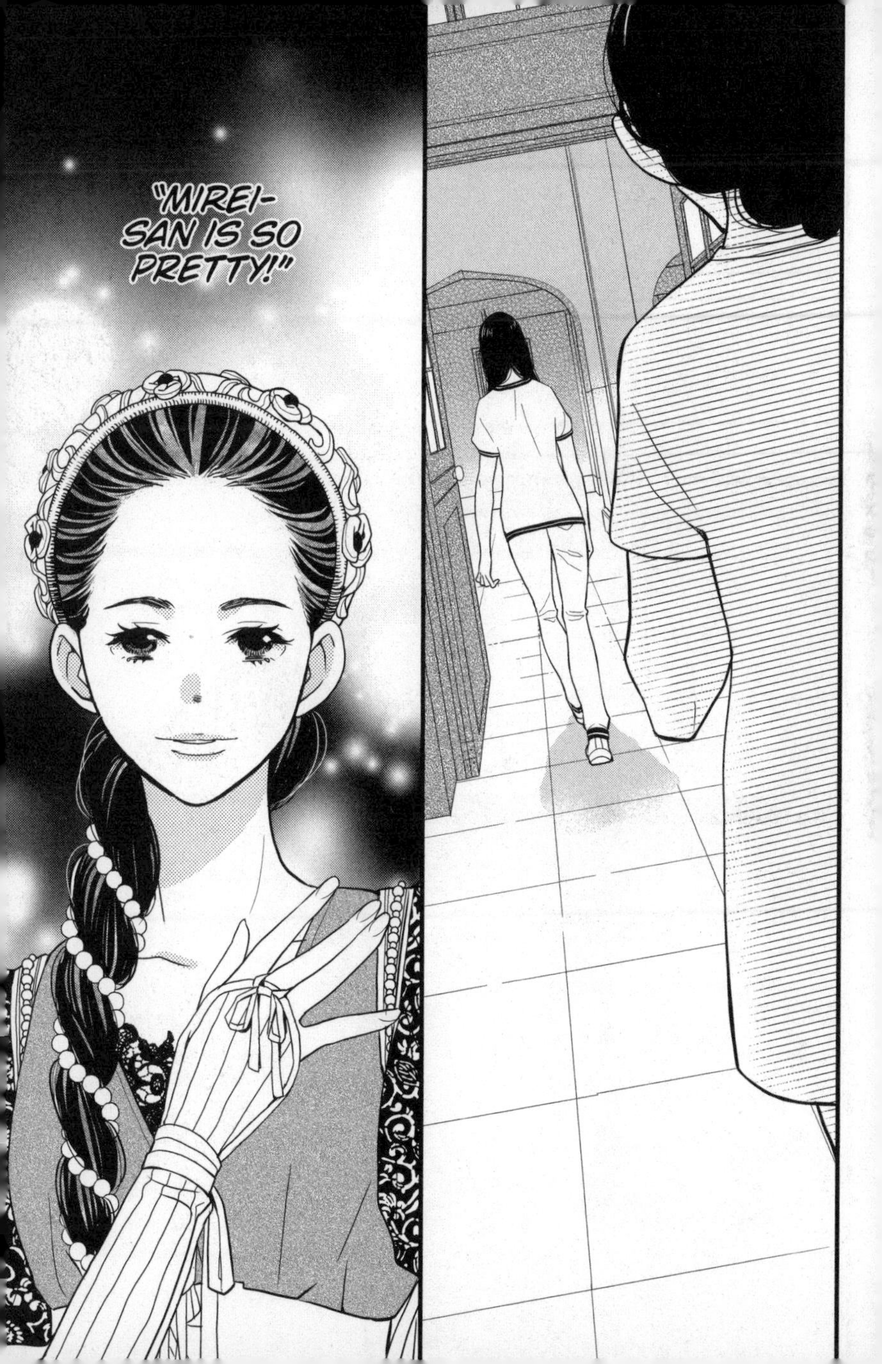
"MIREI-SAN IS SO PRETTY!"

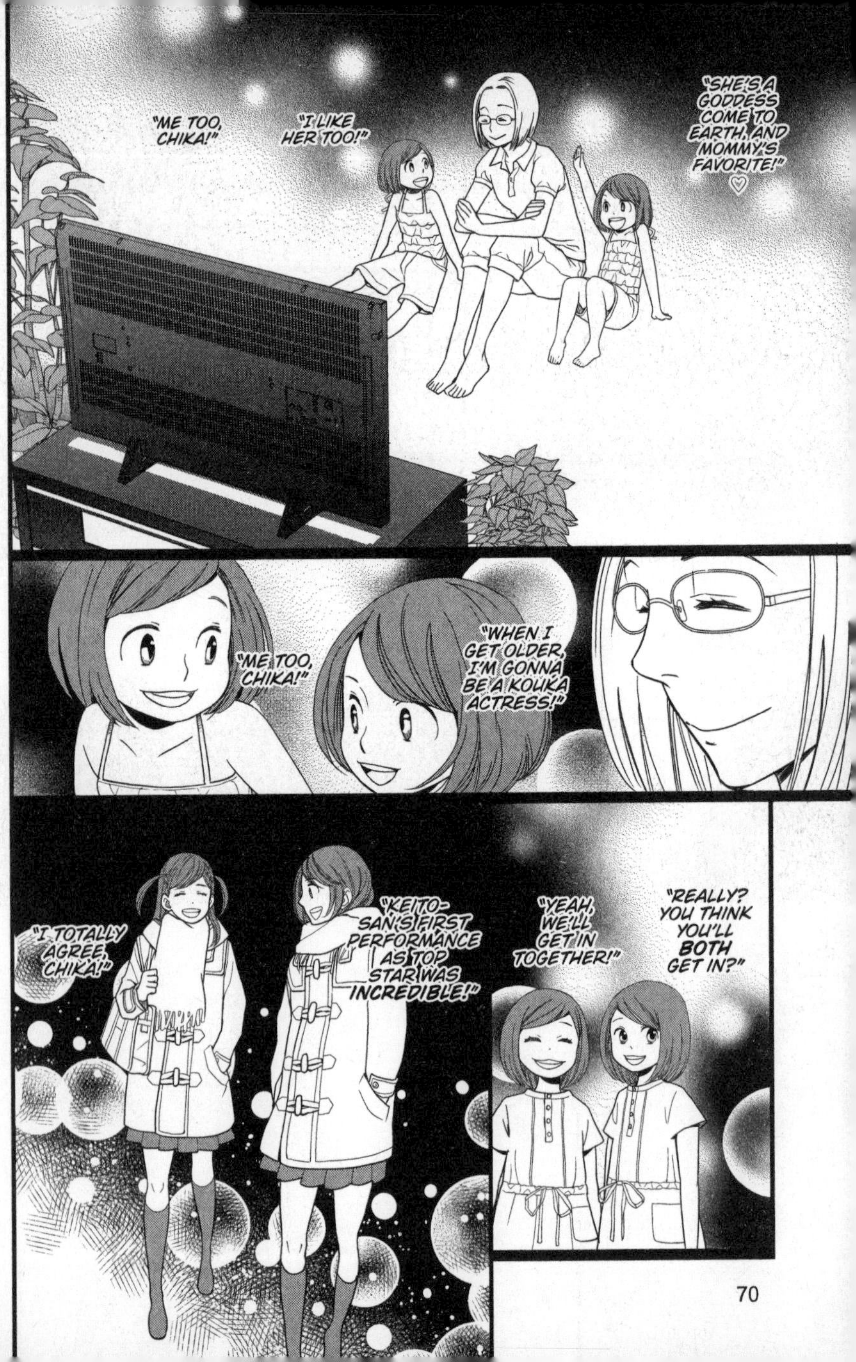
"SHE'S A GODDESS COME TO EARTH, AND MOMMY'S FAVORITE!" ♡
"I LIKE HER TOO!"
"ME TOO, CHIKA!"
"WHEN I GET OLDER, I'M GONNA BE A KOUKA ACTRESS!"
"ME TOO, CHIKA!"
"REALLY? YOU THINK YOU'LL BOTH GET IN?"
"YEAH, WE'LL GET IN TOGETHER!"
"KEITO-SAN'S FIRST PERFORMANCE AS TOP STAR WAS INCREDIBLE!"
"I TOTALLY AGREE, CHIKA!"

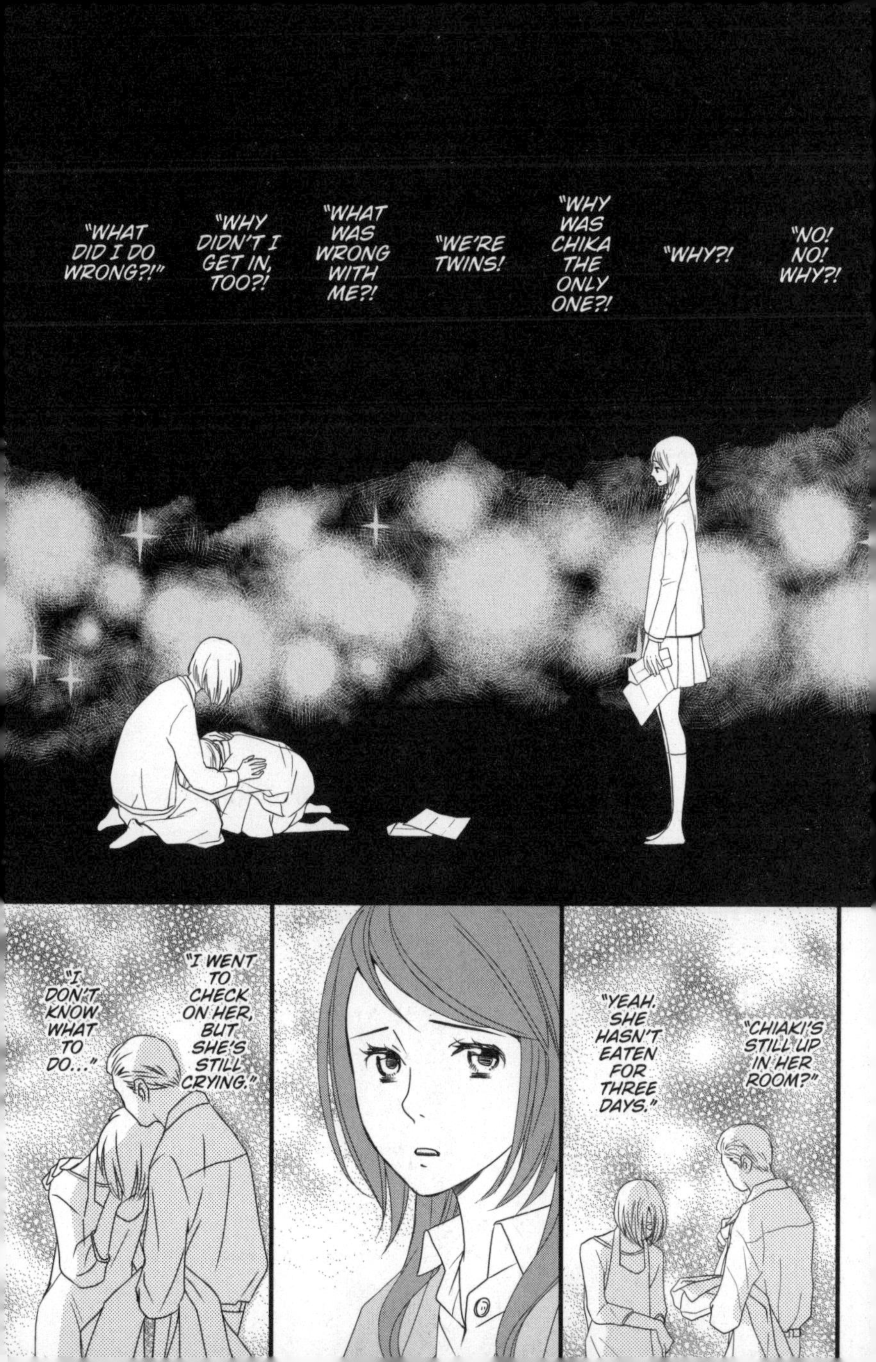
"NO! NO! WHY?!
"WHY?!
"WHY WAS CHIKA THE ONLY ONE?!
"WE'RE TWINS!
"WHAT WAS WRONG WITH ME?!
"WHY DIDN'T I GET IN, TOO?!
"WHAT DID I DO WRONG?!"
"CHIAKI'S STILL UP IN HER ROOM?"
"YEAH. SHE HASN'T EATEN FOR THREE DAYS."
"I WENT TO CHECK ON HER, BUT SHE'S STILL CRYING."
"I DON'T KNOW WHAT TO DO..."

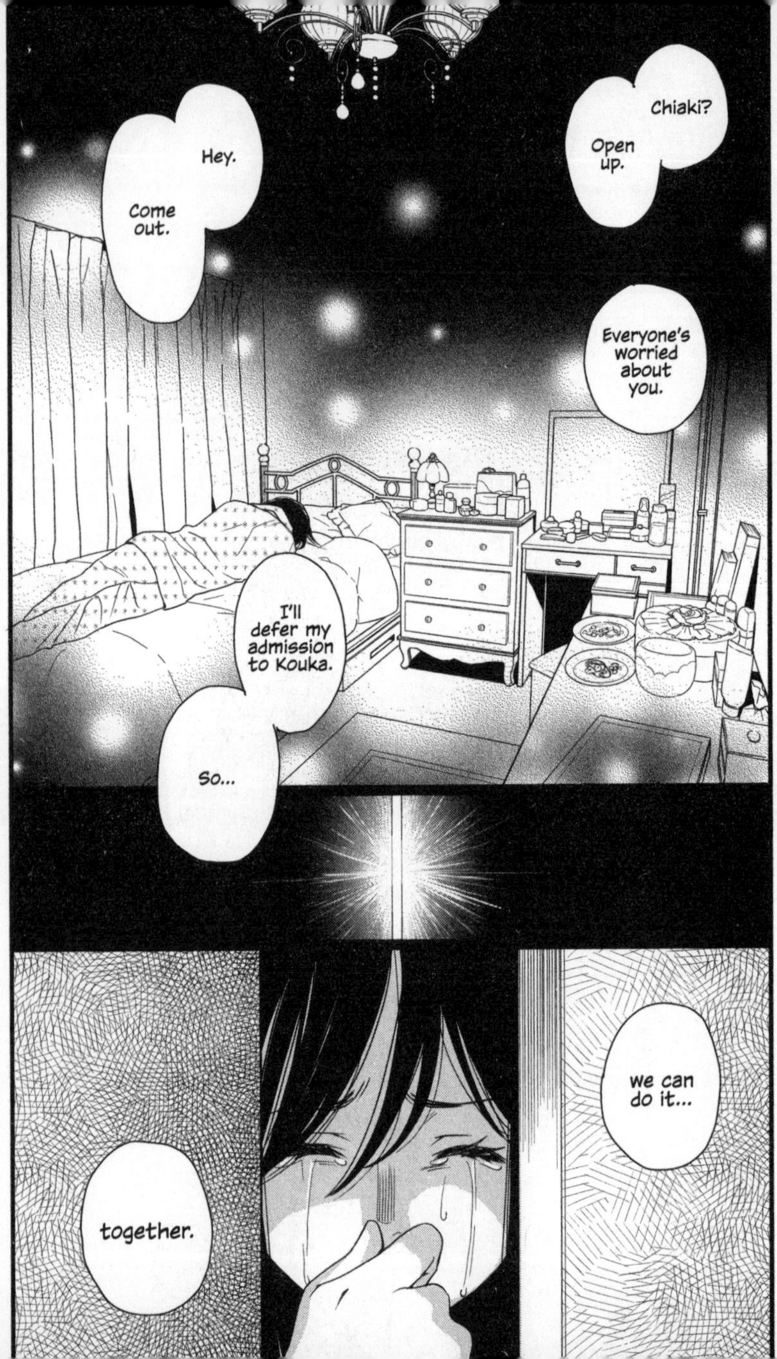
Chiaki?
Open up.
Everyone's worried about you.
Hey.
Come out.
I'll defer my admission to Kouka.
So...
we can do it...
together.

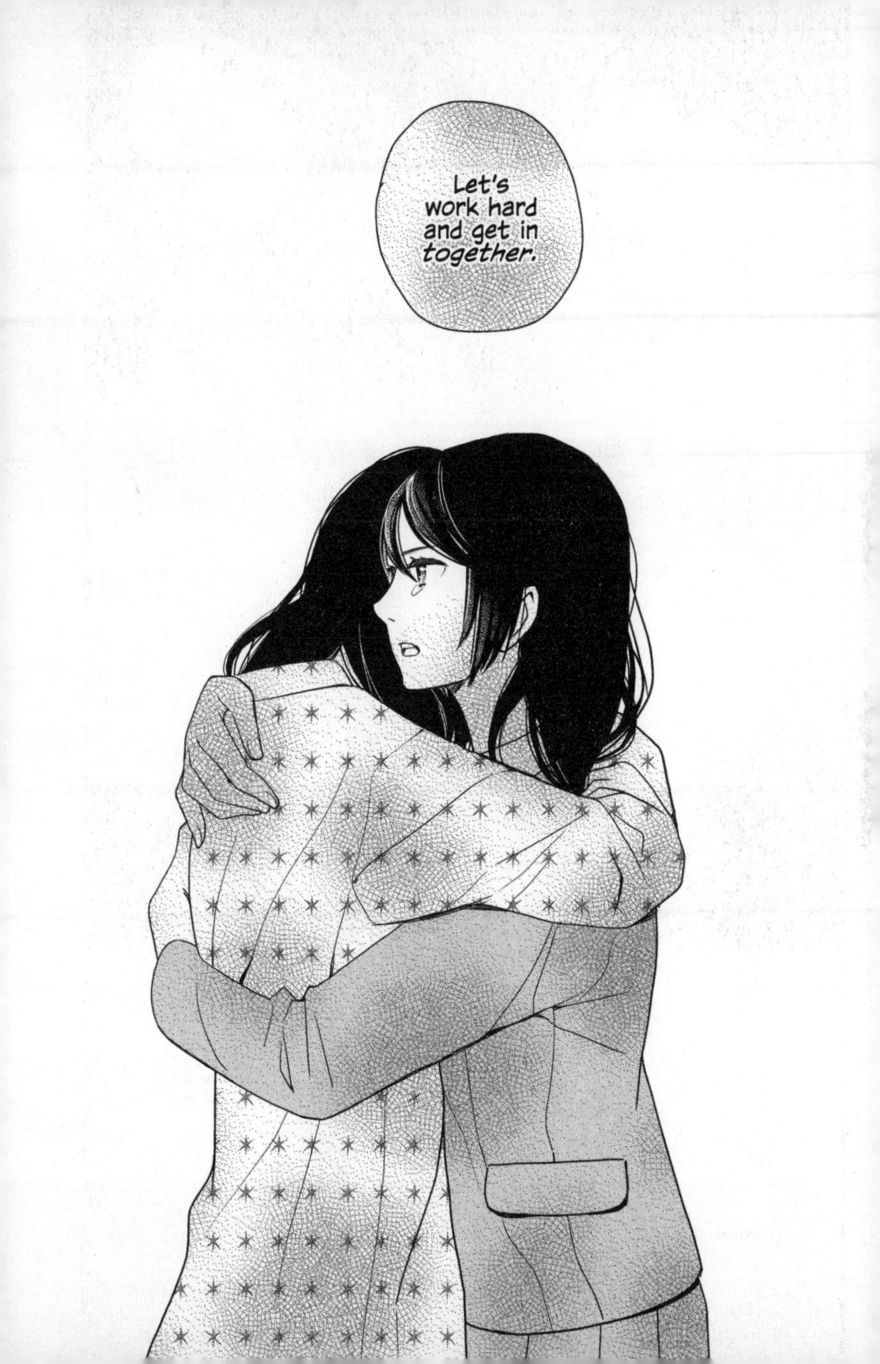
Let's work hard and get in together.

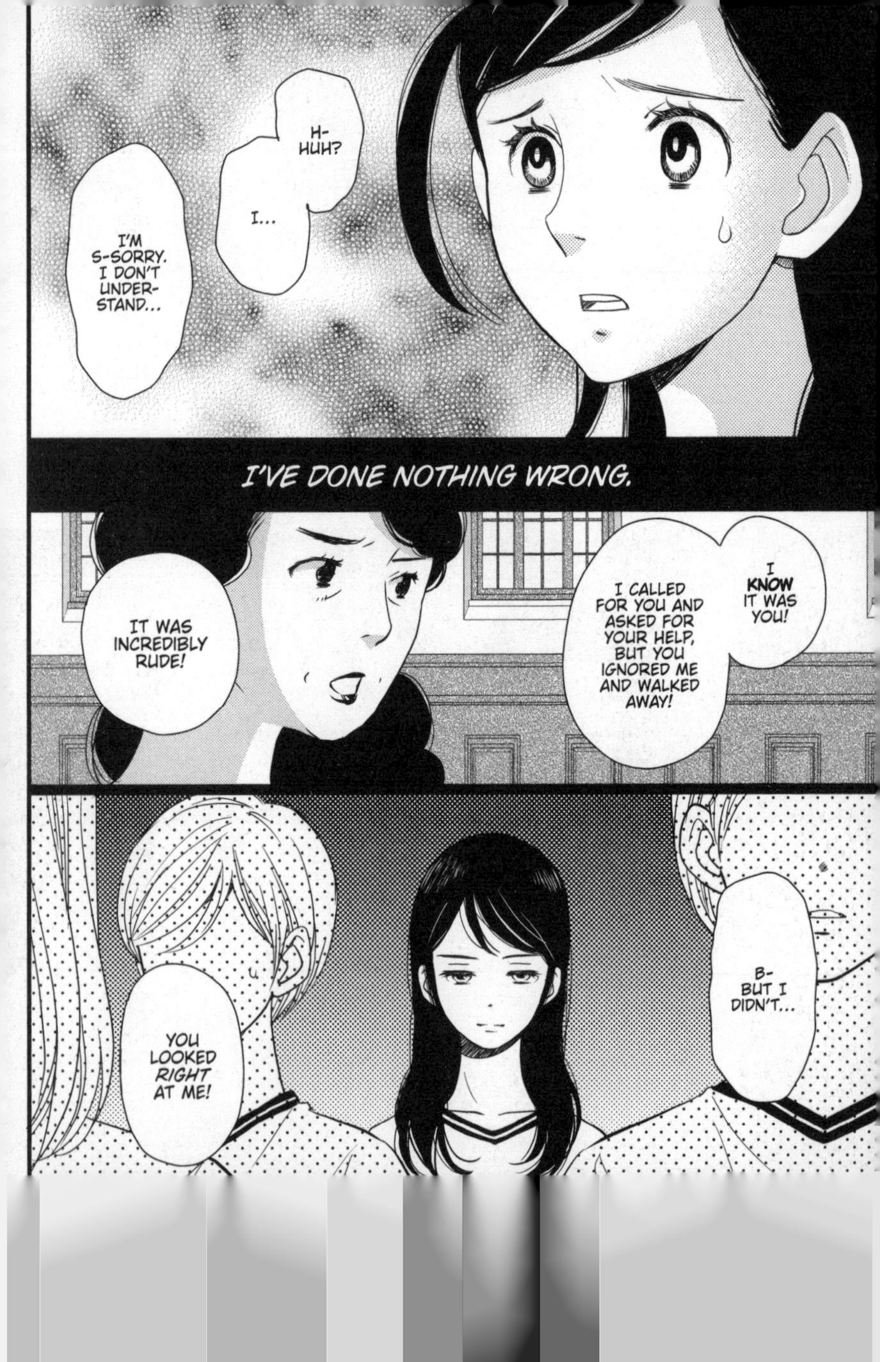

H-HUH?
I...
I'M S-SORRY. I DON'T UNDER-STAND...
I'VE DONE NOTHING WRONG.
I **KNOW** IT WAS YOU!
I CALLED FOR YOU AND ASKED FOR YOUR HELP, BUT YOU IGNORED ME AND WALKED AWAY!
IT WAS INCREDIBLY RUDE!
B-BUT I DIDN'T...
YOU LOOKED *RIGHT* AT ME!

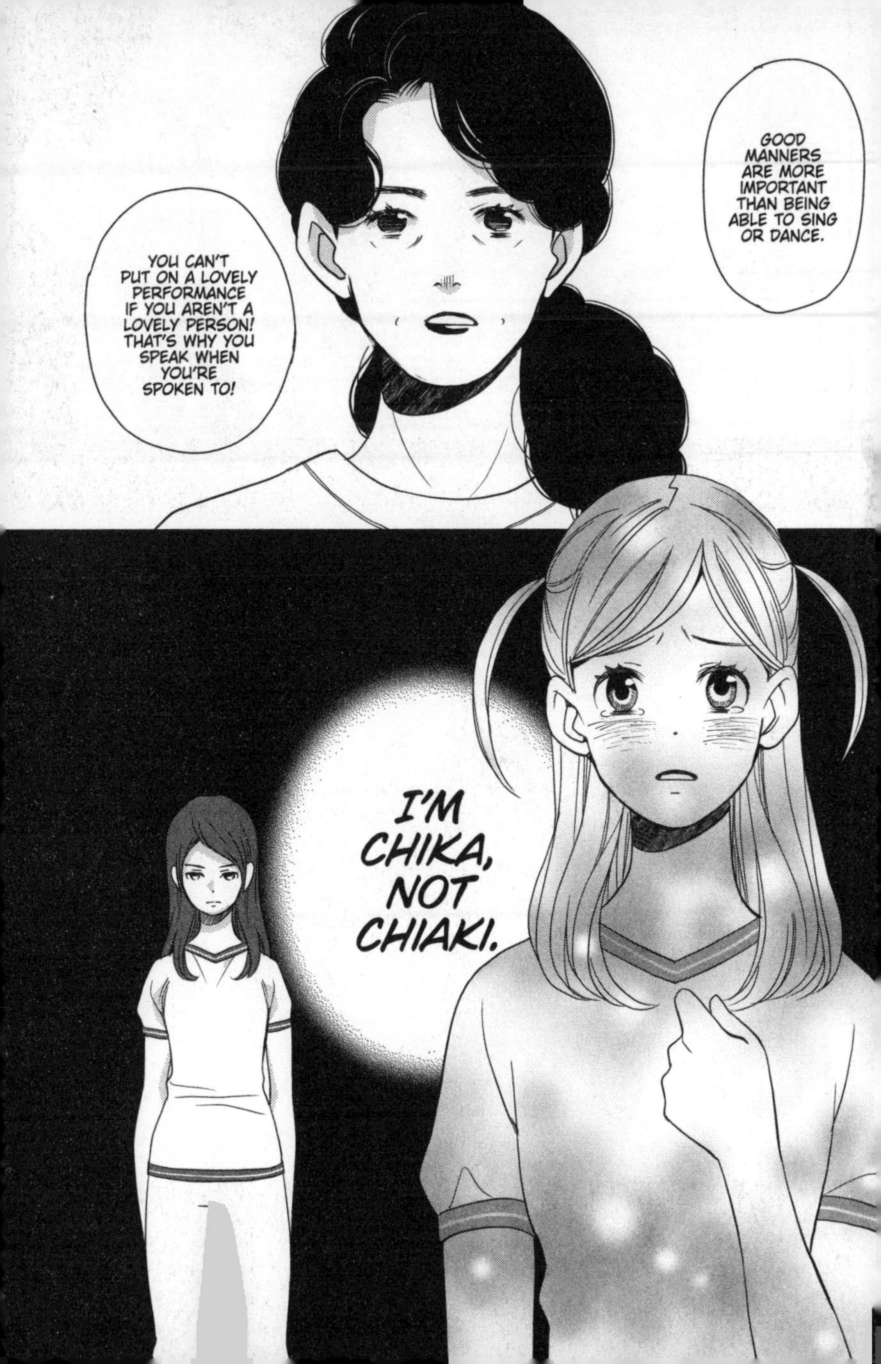
GOOD MANNERS ARE MORE IMPORTANT THAN BEING ABLE TO SING OR DANCE.
YOU CAN'T PUT ON A LOVELY PERFORMANCE IF YOU AREN'T A LOVELY PERSON! THAT'S WHY YOU SPEAK WHEN YOU'RE SPOKEN TO!
I'M CHIKA, NOT CHIAKI.

Special Thanks

Tara-chan
Asai-san
Kazami-san
Takato-san
Yoshida-san
Ishigaki-san
Kuroki-san
Takahashi-san
Nono & Jill
&
all my readers

Love From
斉木久美子
Kumiko Saiki

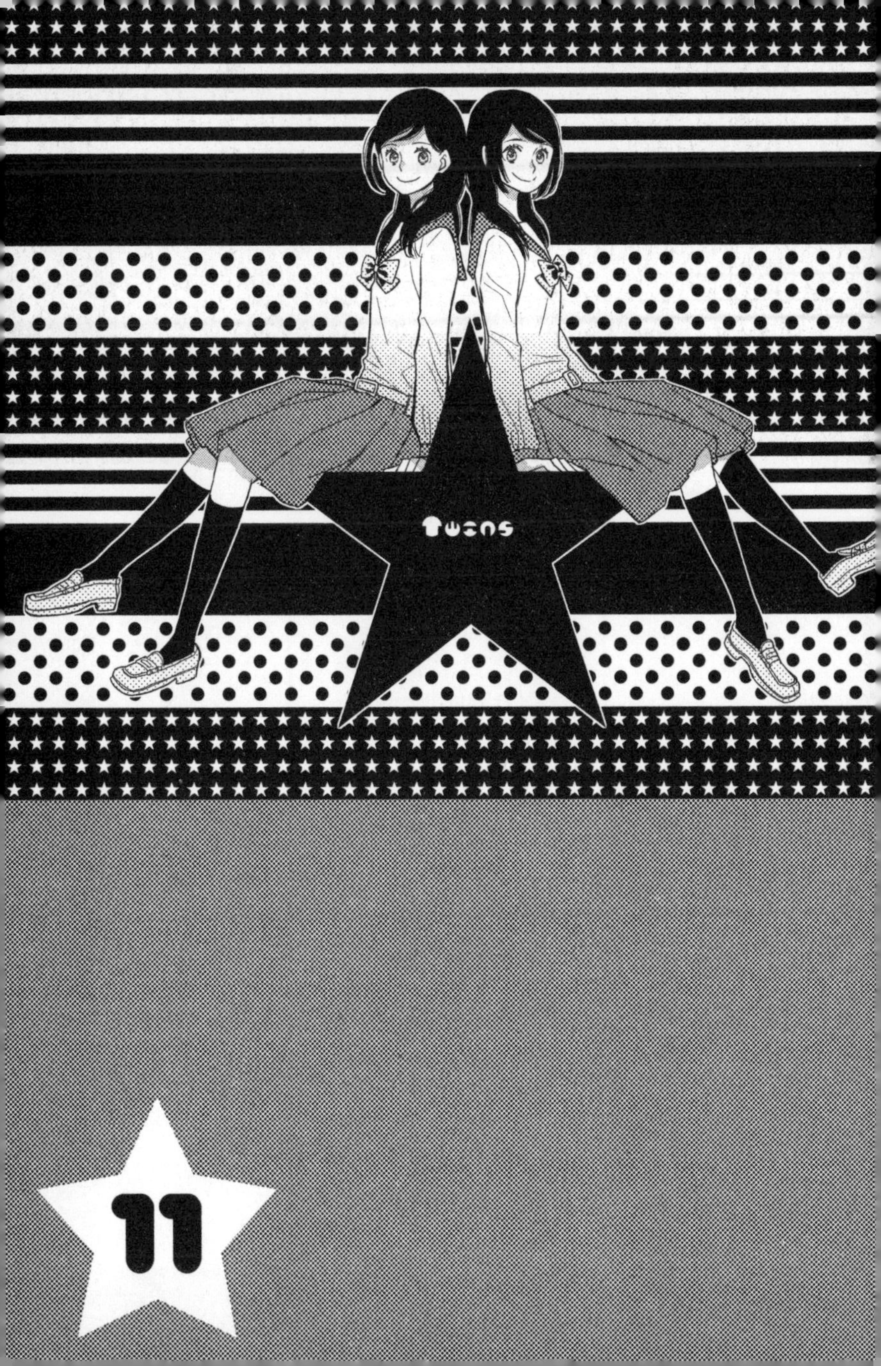
twins
11

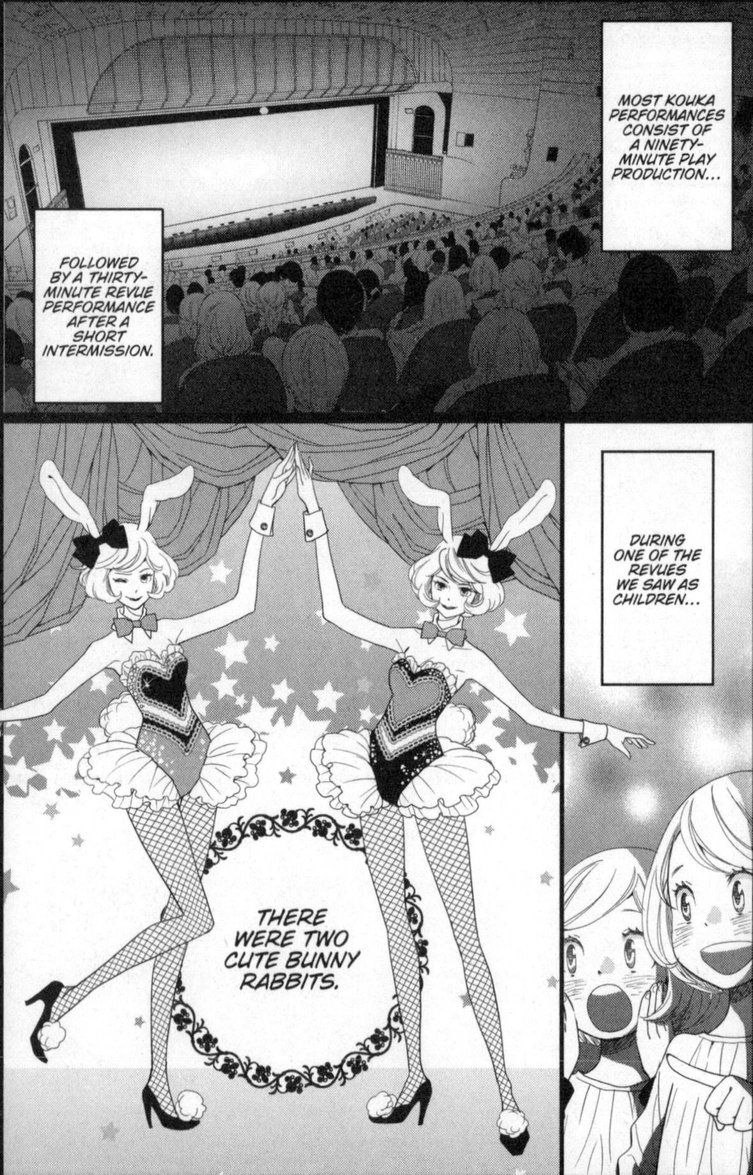
MOST KOUKA PERFORMANCES CONSIST OF A NINETY-MINUTE PLAY PRODUCTION...
FOLLOWED BY A THIRTY-MINUTE REVUE PERFORMANCE AFTER A SHORT INTERMISSION.
DURING ONE OF THE REVUES WE SAW AS CHILDREN...
THERE WERE TWO CUTE BUNNY RABBITS.

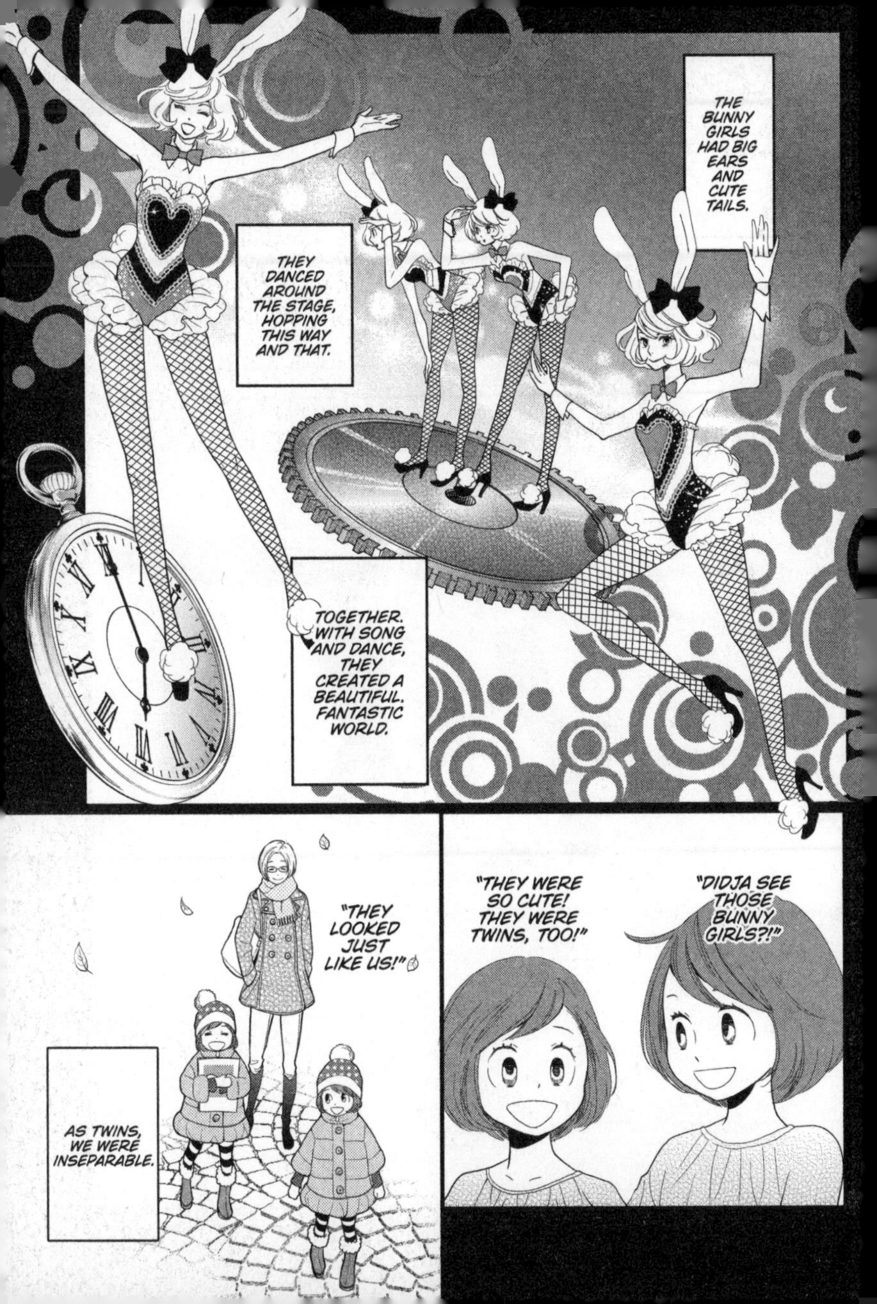
THE BUNNY GIRLS HAD BIG EARS AND CUTE TAILS.
THEY DANCED AROUND THE STAGE, HOPPING THIS WAY AND THAT.
TOGETHER. WITH SONG AND DANCE, THEY CREATED A BEAUTIFUL. FANTASTIC WORLD.
"DIDJA SEE THOSE BUNNY GIRLS?!"
"THEY WERE SO CUTE! THEY WERE TWINS, TOO!"
"THEY LOOKED JUST LIKE US!"
AS TWINS, WE WERE INSEPARABLE.

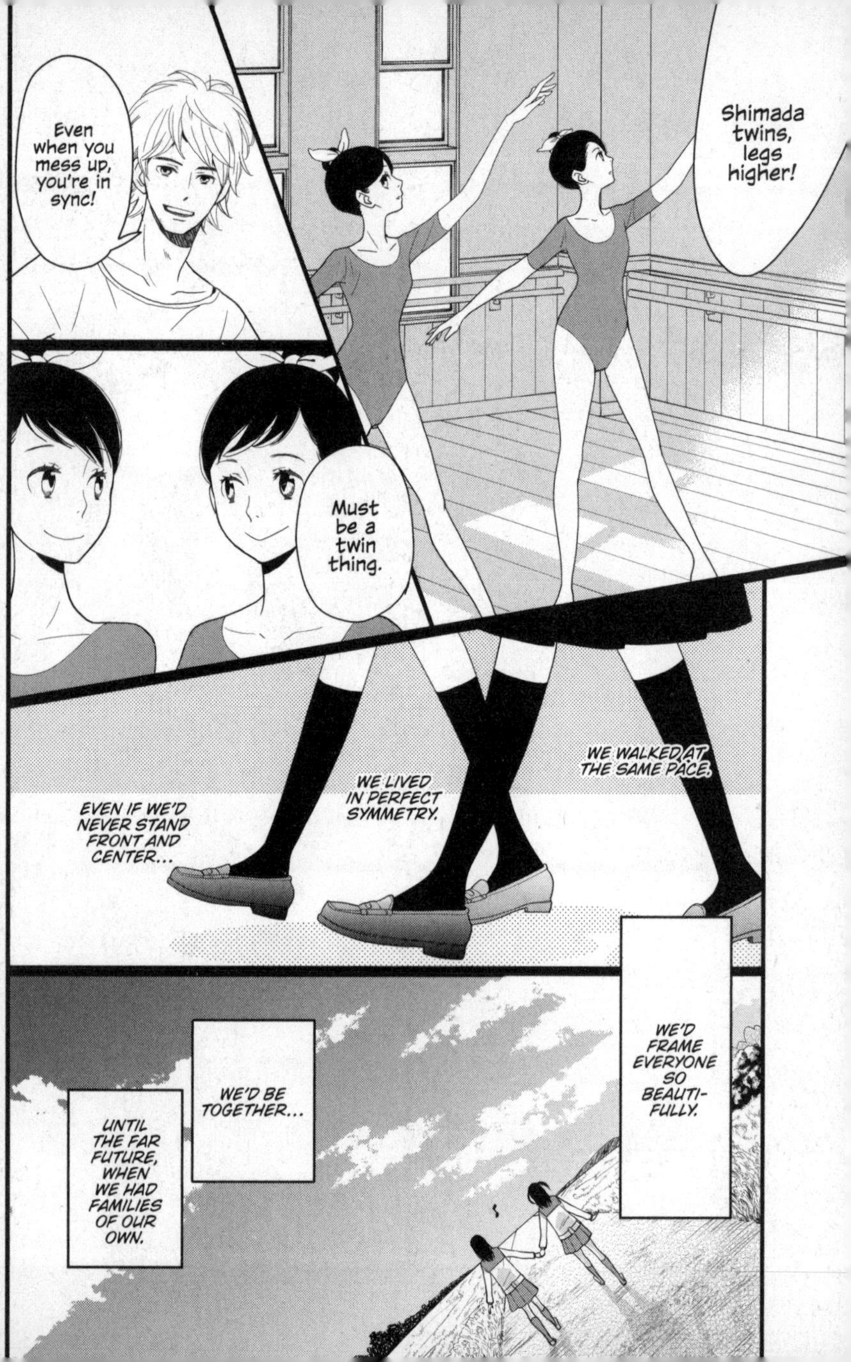
Shimada twins, legs higher!
Even when you mess up, you're in sync!
Must be a twin thing.
WE WALKED AT THE SAME PACE.
WE LIVED IN PERFECT SYMMETRY.
EVEN IF WE'D NEVER STAND FRONT AND CENTER...
WE'D FRAME EVERYONE SO BEAUTIFULLY.
WE'D BE TOGETHER...
UNTIL THE FAR FUTURE, WHEN WE HAD FAMILIES OF OUR OWN.

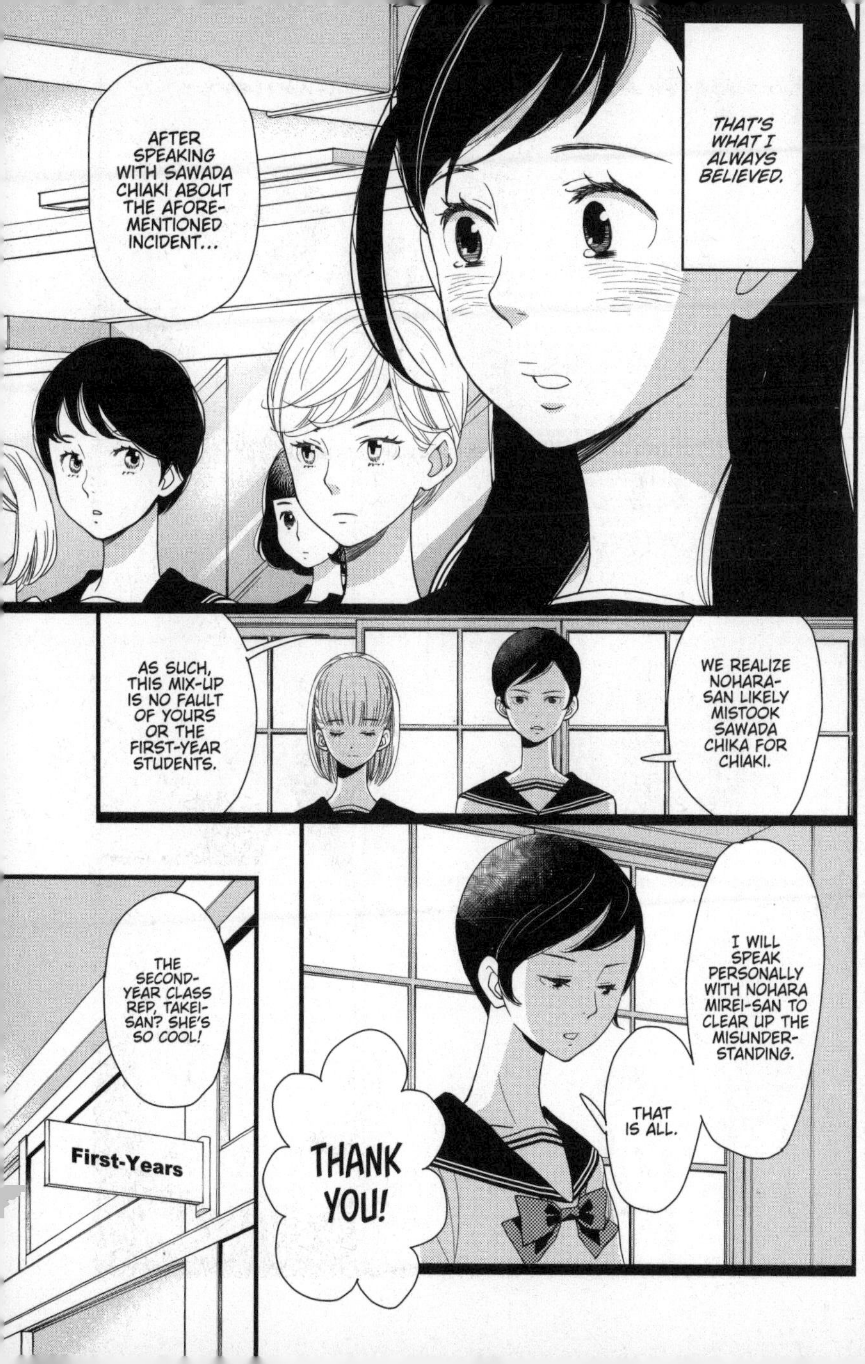
THAT'S WHAT I ALWAYS BELIEVED.
AFTER SPEAKING WITH SAWADA CHIAKI ABOUT THE AFORE-MENTIONED INCIDENT...
WE REALIZE NOHARA-SAN LIKELY MISTOOK SAWADA CHIKA FOR CHIAKI.
AS SUCH, THIS MIX-UP IS NO FAULT OF YOURS OR THE FIRST-YEAR STUDENTS.
I WILL SPEAK PERSONALLY WITH NOHARA MIREI-SAN TO CLEAR UP THE MISUNDER-STANDING.
THAT IS ALL.
THANK YOU!
THE SECOND-YEAR CLASS REP, TAKEI-SAN? SHE'S SO COOL!
First-Years

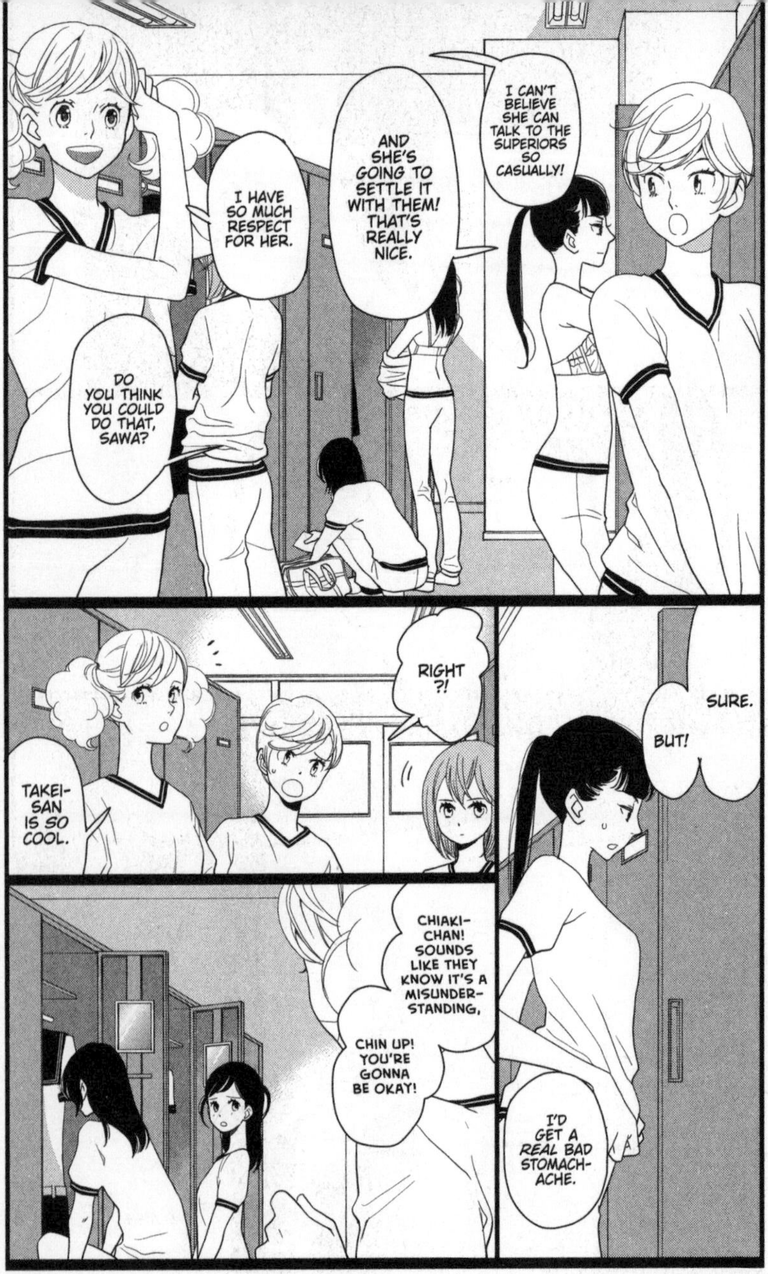
I CAN'T BELIEVE SHE CAN TALK TO THE SUPERIORS SO CASUALLY!
AND SHE'S GOING TO SETTLE IT WITH THEM! THAT'S REALLY NICE.
I HAVE SO MUCH RESPECT FOR HER.
DO YOU THINK YOU COULD DO THAT, SAWA?
SURE.
BUT!
I'D GET A *REAL* BAD STOMACH-ACHE.
RIGHT?!
TAKEI-SAN IS SO COOL.
CHIAKI-CHAN! SOUNDS LIKE THEY KNOW IT'S A MISUNDER-STANDING,
CHIN UP! YOU'RE GONNA BE OKAY!

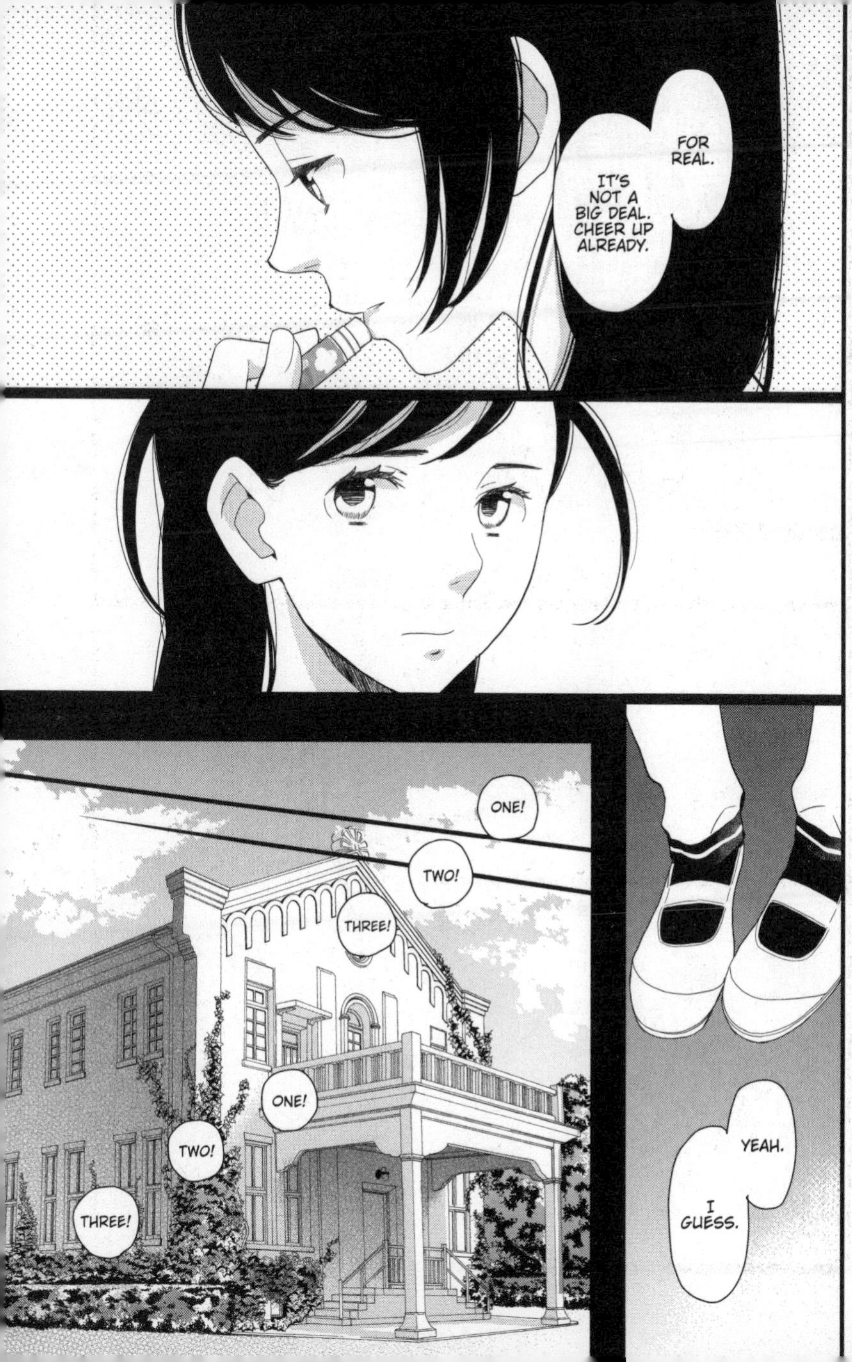
FOR REAL.
IT'S NOT A BIG DEAL. CHEER UP ALREADY.
YEAH.
I GUESS.
ONE!
TWO!
THREE!
ONE!
TWO!
THREE!

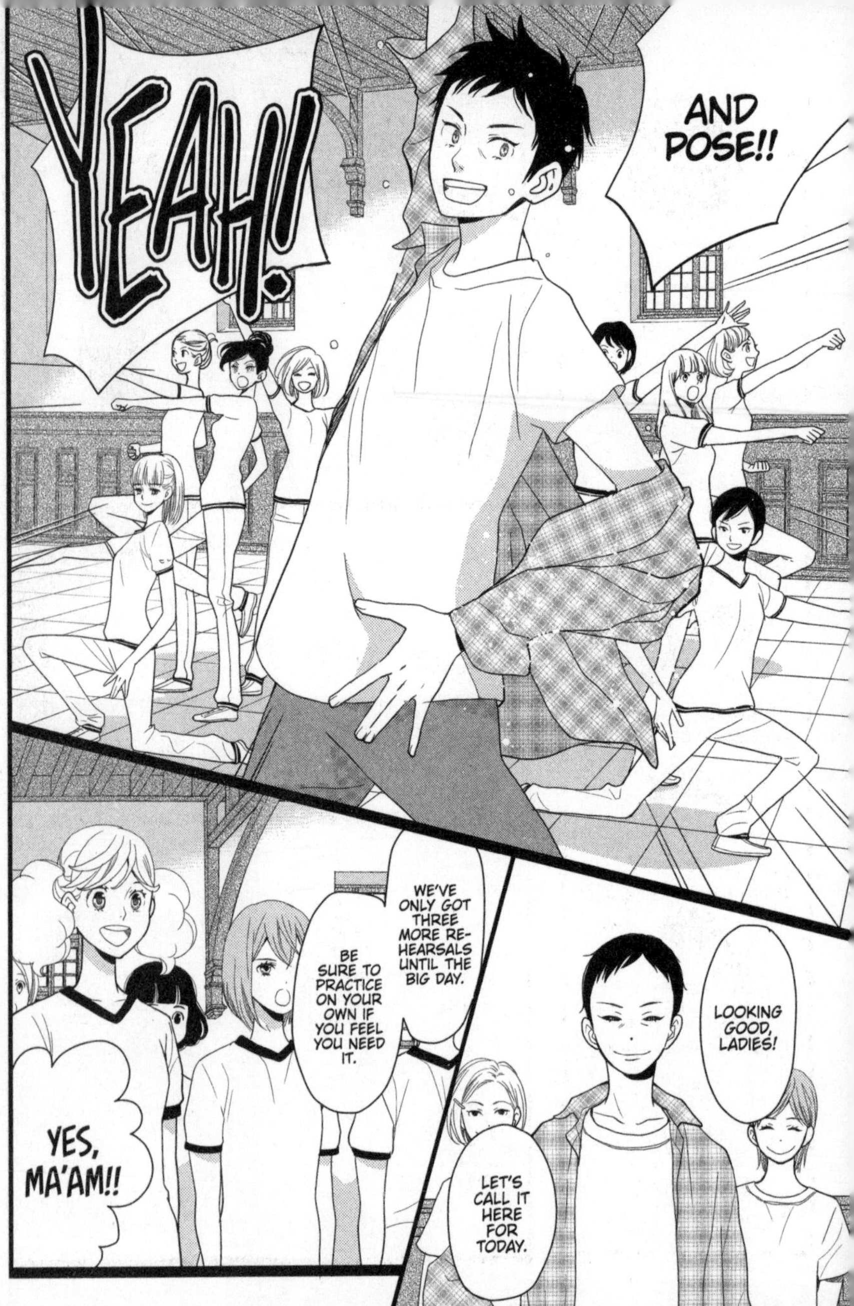
AND POSE!!
YEAH!
LOOKING GOOD, LADIES!
LET'S CALL IT HERE FOR TODAY.
WE'VE ONLY GOT THREE MORE RE-HEARSALS UNTIL THE BIG DAY.
BE SURE TO PRACTICE ON YOUR OWN IF YOU FEEL YOU NEED IT.
YES, MA'AM!!

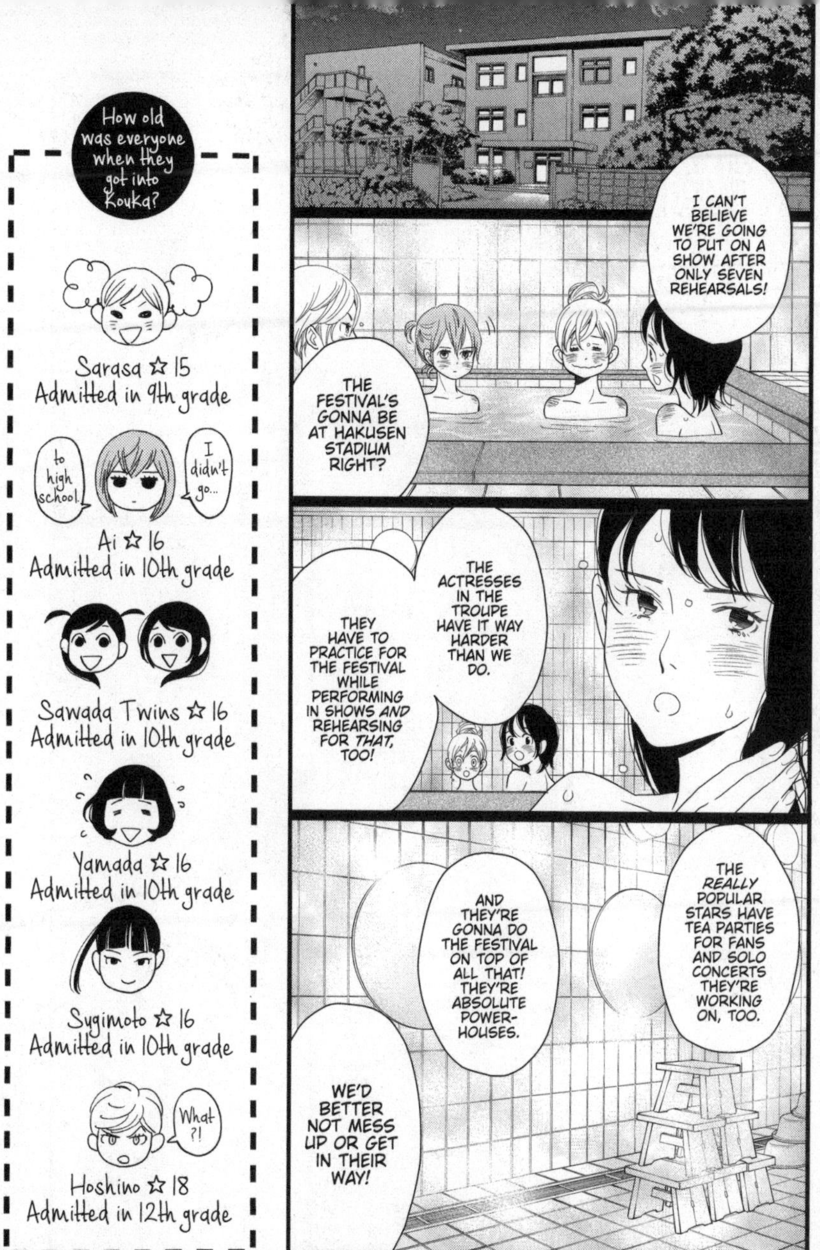
I CAN'T BELIEVE WE'RE GOING TO PUT ON A SHOW AFTER ONLY SEVEN REHEARSALS!
THE FESTIVAL'S GONNA BE AT HAKUSEN STADIUM RIGHT?
THE ACTRESSES IN THE TROUPE HAVE IT WAY HARDER THAN WE DO.
THEY HAVE TO PRACTICE FOR THE FESTIVAL WHILE PERFORMING IN SHOWS *AND* REHEARSING FOR *THAT*, TOO!
THE *REALLY* POPULAR STARS HAVE TEA PARTIES FOR FANS AND SOLO CONCERTS THEY'RE WORKING ON, TOO.
AND THEY'RE GONNA DO THE FESTIVAL ON TOP OF ALL THAT! THEY'RE ABSOLUTE POWER-HOUSES.
WE'D BETTER NOT MESS UP OR GET IN THEIR WAY!

How old was everyone when they got into Kouka?

Sarasa ☆ 15
Admitted in 9th grade

I didn't go...
to high school.

Ai ☆ 16
Admitted in 10th grade

Sawada Twins ☆ 16
Admitted in 10th grade

Yamada ☆ 16
Admitted in 10th grade

Sugimoto ☆ 16
Admitted in 10th grade

What?!

Hoshino ☆ 18
Admitted in 12th grade

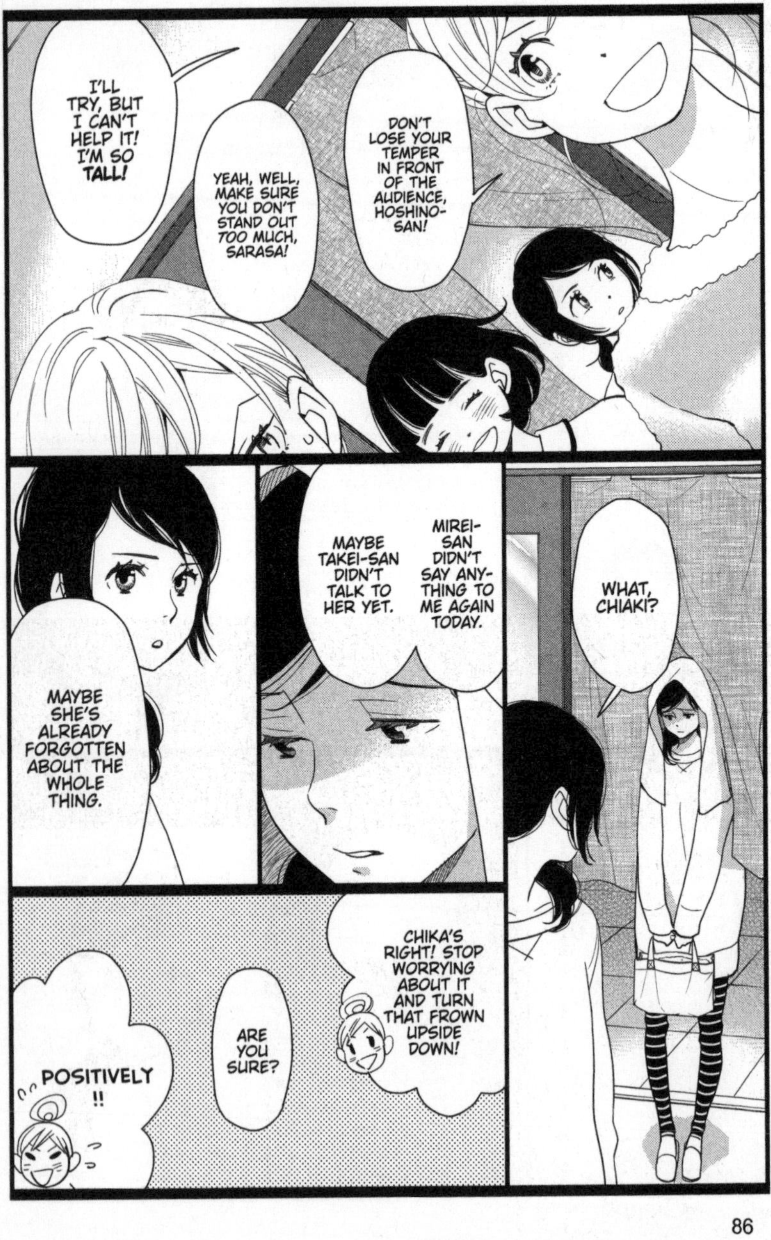
DON'T LOSE YOUR TEMPER IN FRONT OF THE AUDIENCE, HOSHINO-SAN!
YEAH, WELL, MAKE SURE YOU DON'T STAND OUT *TOO* MUCH, SARASA!
I'LL TRY, BUT I CAN'T HELP IT! I'M SO **TALL!**
WHAT, CHIAKI?
MIREI-SAN DIDN'T SAY ANYTHING TO ME AGAIN TODAY.
MAYBE TAKEI-SAN DIDN'T TALK TO HER YET.
MAYBE SHE'S ALREADY FORGOTTEN ABOUT THE WHOLE THING.
CHIKA'S RIGHT! STOP WORRYING ABOUT IT AND TURN THAT FROWN UPSIDE DOWN!
ARE YOU SURE?
POSITIVELY!!

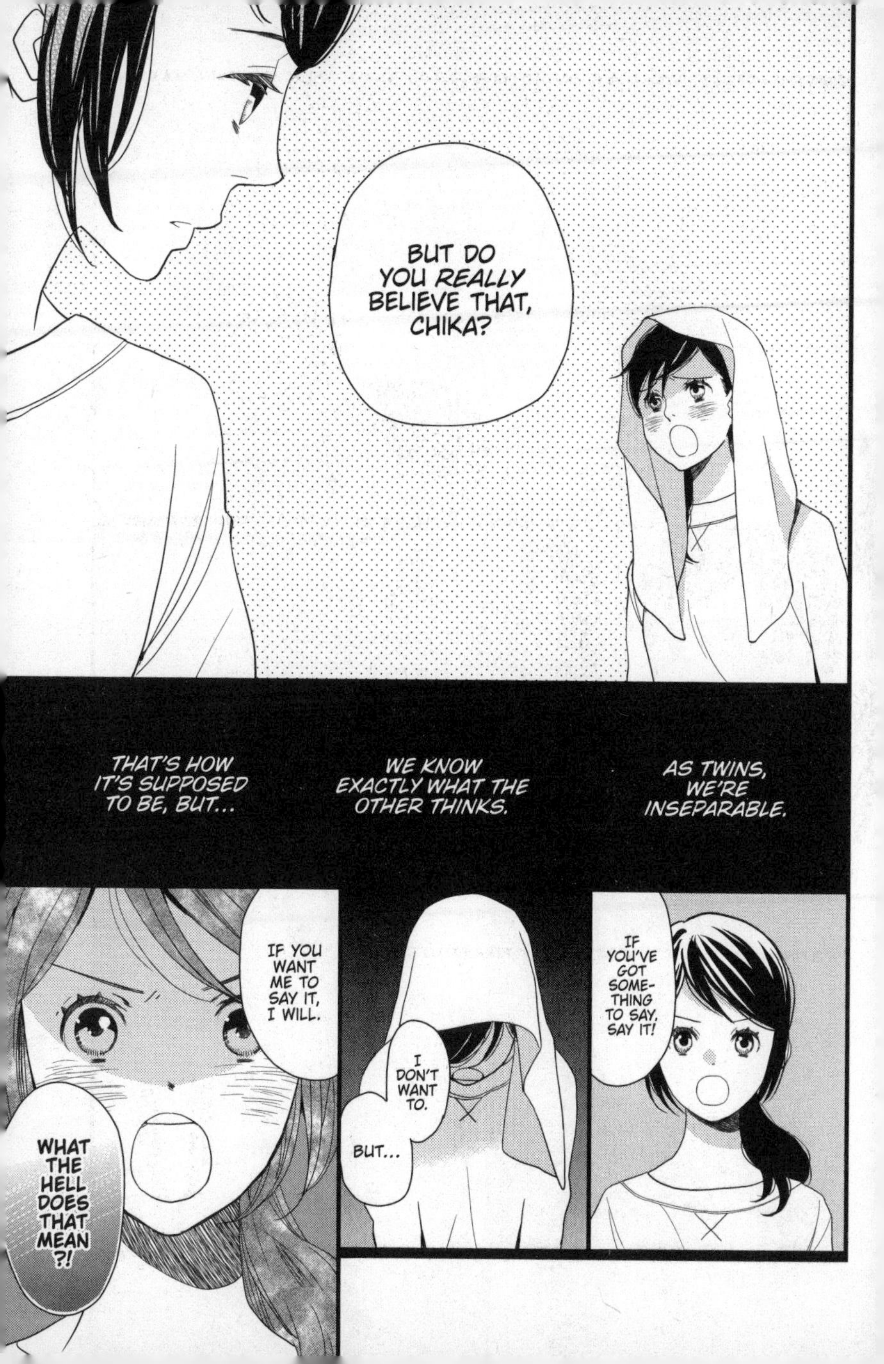
BUT DO YOU *REALLY* BELIEVE THAT, CHIKA?
AS TWINS, WE'RE INSEPARABLE.
WE KNOW EXACTLY WHAT THE OTHER THINKS.
THAT'S HOW IT'S SUPPOSED TO BE, BUT...
IF YOU'VE GOT SOME-THING TO SAY, SAY IT!
I DON'T WANT TO.
BUT...
IF YOU WANT ME TO SAY IT, I WILL.
WHAT THE HELL DOES THAT MEAN?!

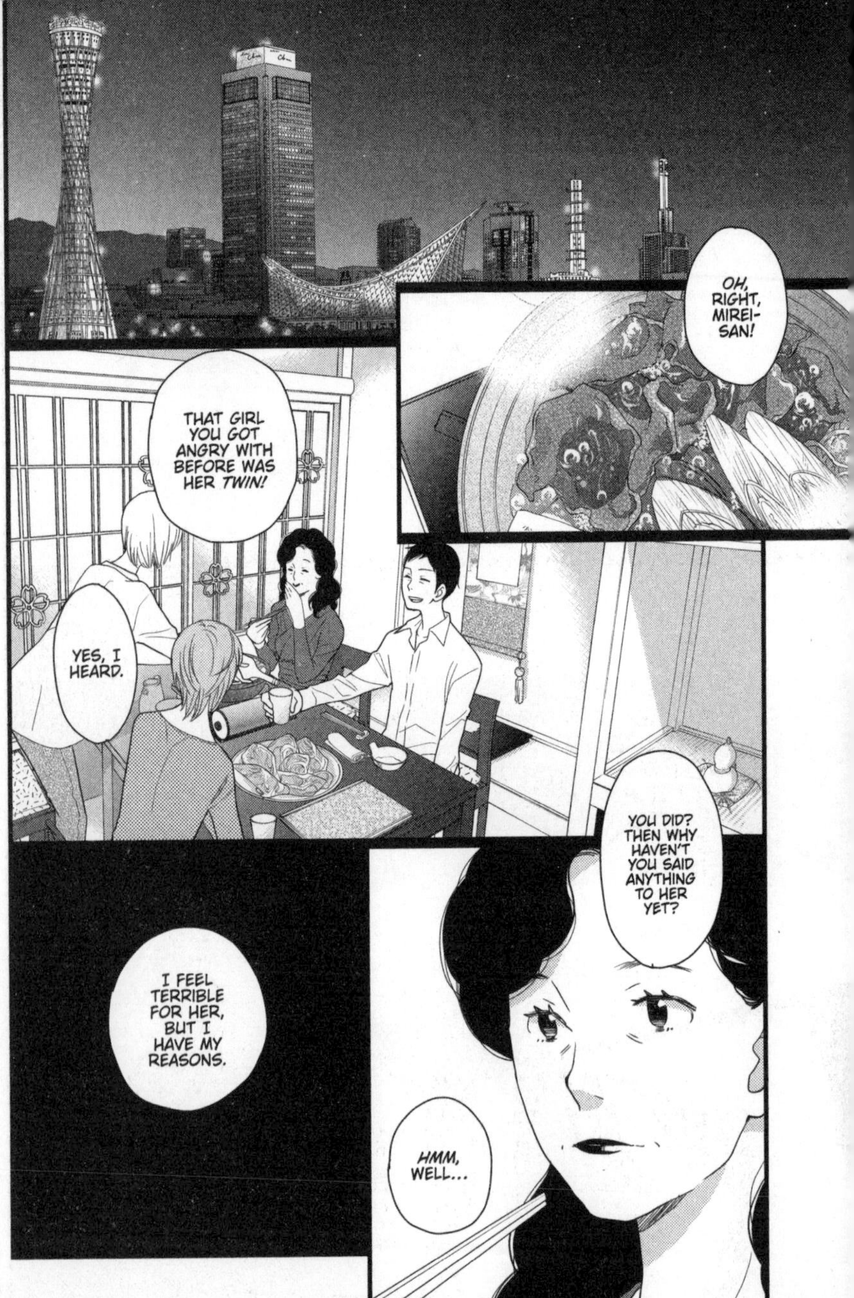
OH, RIGHT, MIREI-SAN!
THAT GIRL YOU GOT ANGRY WITH BEFORE WAS HER *TWIN!*
YES, I HEARD.
YOU DID? THEN WHY HAVEN'T YOU SAID ANYTHING TO HER YET?
HMM, WELL...
I FEEL TERRIBLE FOR HER, BUT I HAVE MY REASONS.

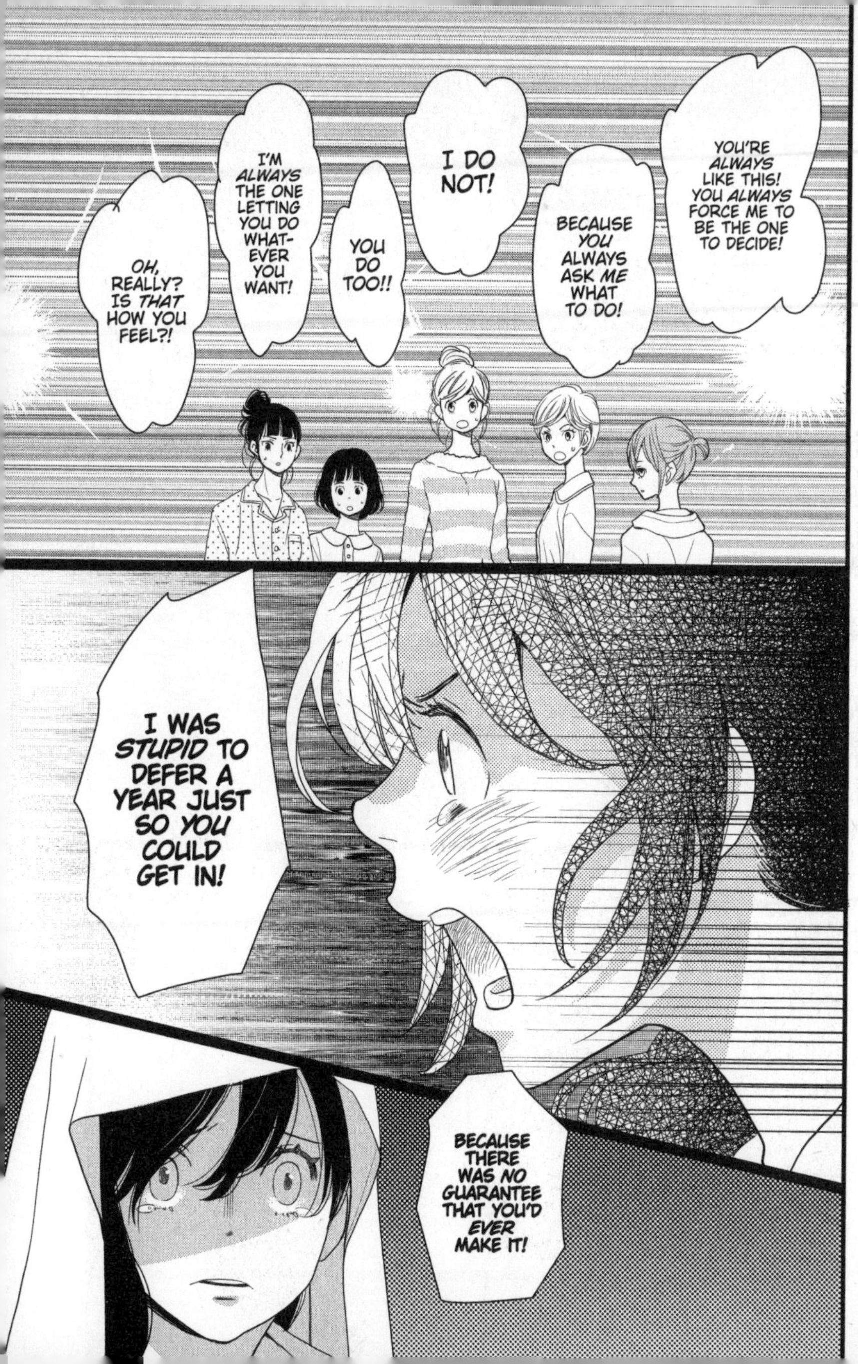
YOU'RE *ALWAYS* LIKE THIS! YOU *ALWAYS* FORCE ME TO BE THE ONE TO DECIDE!
BECAUSE *YOU* ALWAYS ASK *ME* WHAT TO DO!
I DO NOT!
YOU DO TOO!!
I'M *ALWAYS* THE ONE LETTING YOU DO WHAT-EVER YOU WANT!
OH, REALLY? IS *THAT* HOW YOU FEEL?!
I WAS *STUPID* TO DEFER A YEAR JUST SO *YOU* COULD GET IN!
BECAUSE THERE WAS *NO* GUARANTEE THAT YOU'D *EVER* MAKE IT!

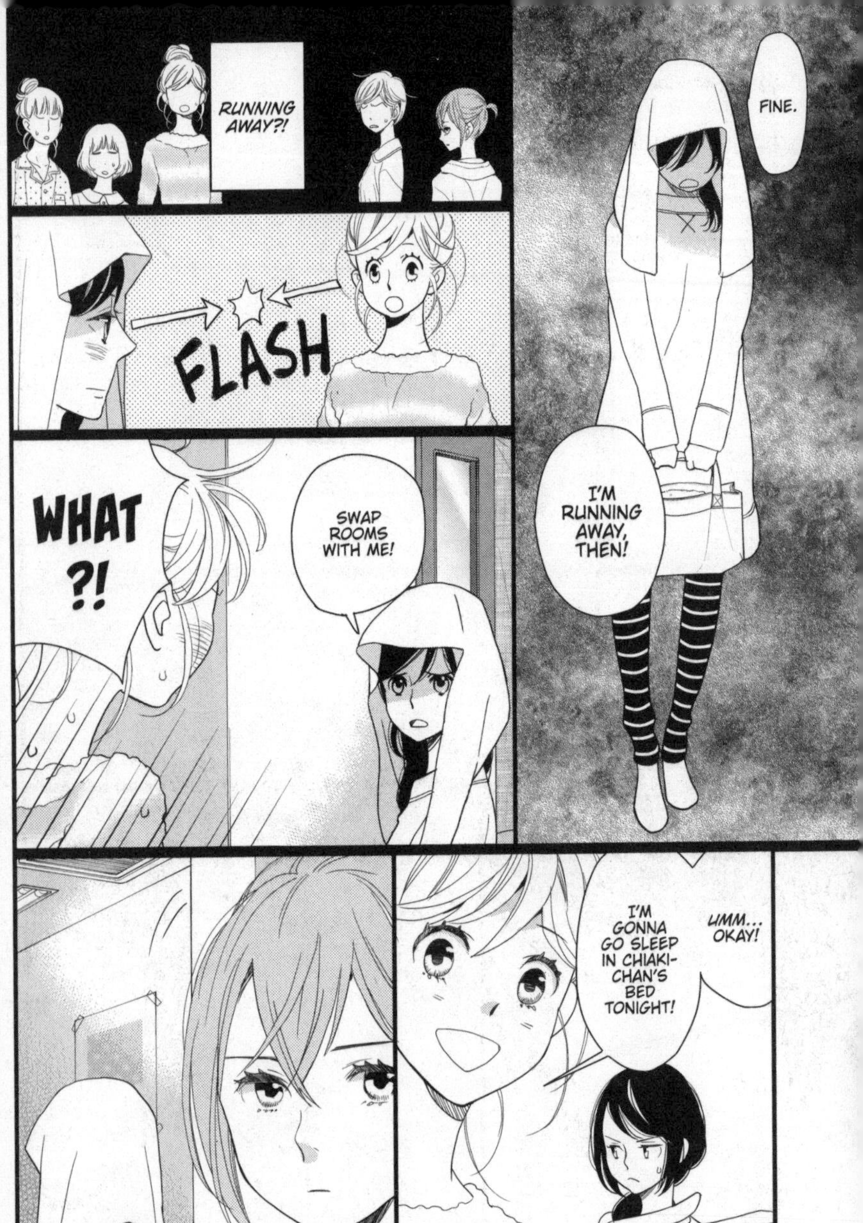
FINE.
I'M RUNNING AWAY, THEN!
RUNNING AWAY?!
FLASH
SWAP ROOMS WITH ME!
WHAT ?!
UMM... OKAY!
I'M GONNA GO SLEEP IN CHIAKI-CHAN'S BED TONIGHT!

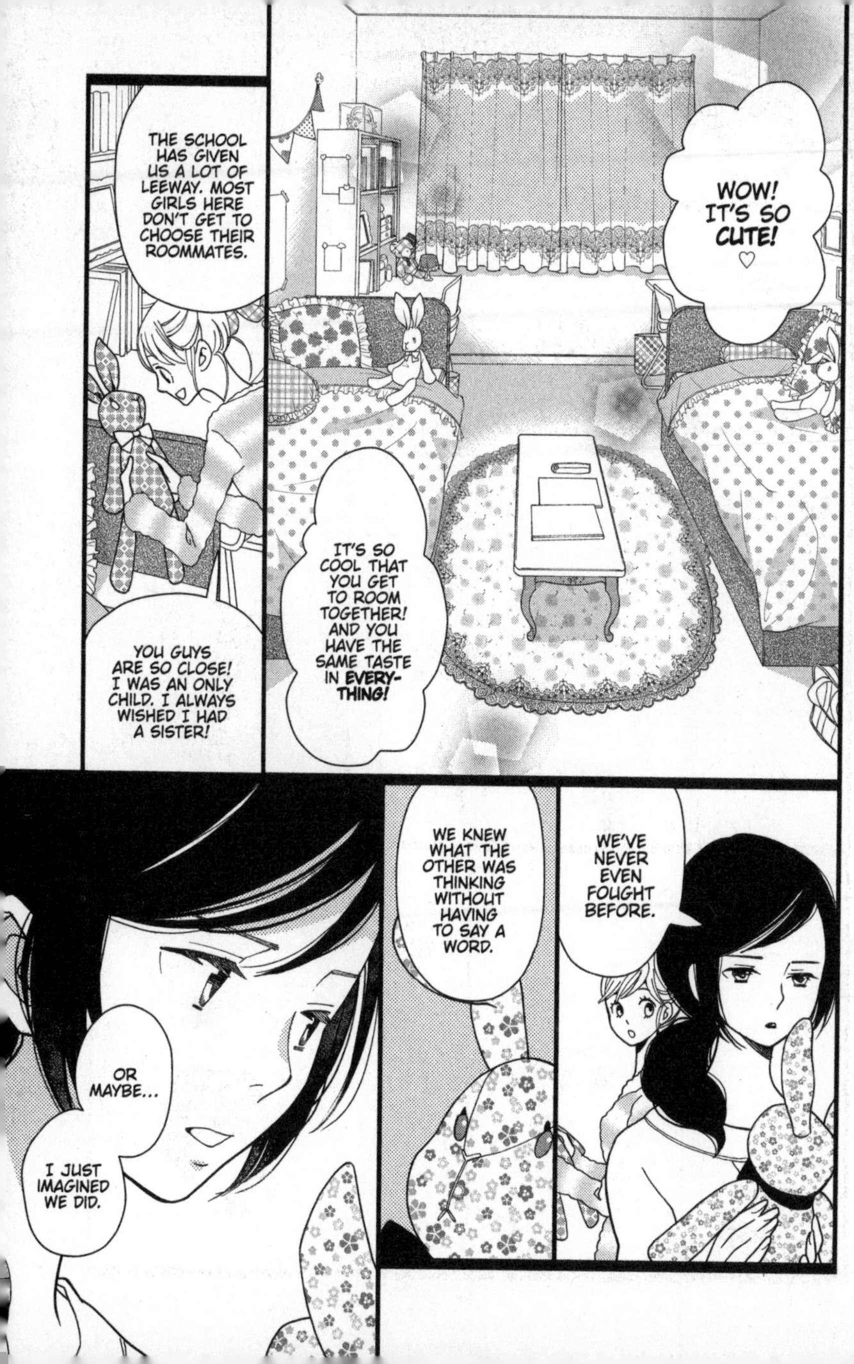
WOW! IT'S SO CUTE! ♡
IT'S SO COOL THAT YOU GET TO ROOM TOGETHER! AND YOU HAVE THE SAME TASTE IN EVERYTHING!
THE SCHOOL HAS GIVEN US A LOT OF LEEWAY. MOST GIRLS HERE DON'T GET TO CHOOSE THEIR ROOMMATES.
YOU GUYS ARE SO CLOSE! I WAS AN ONLY CHILD. I ALWAYS WISHED I HAD A SISTER!
WE'VE NEVER EVEN FOUGHT BEFORE.
WE KNEW WHAT THE OTHER WAS THINKING WITHOUT HAVING TO SAY A WORD.
OR MAYBE...
I JUST IMAGINED WE DID.

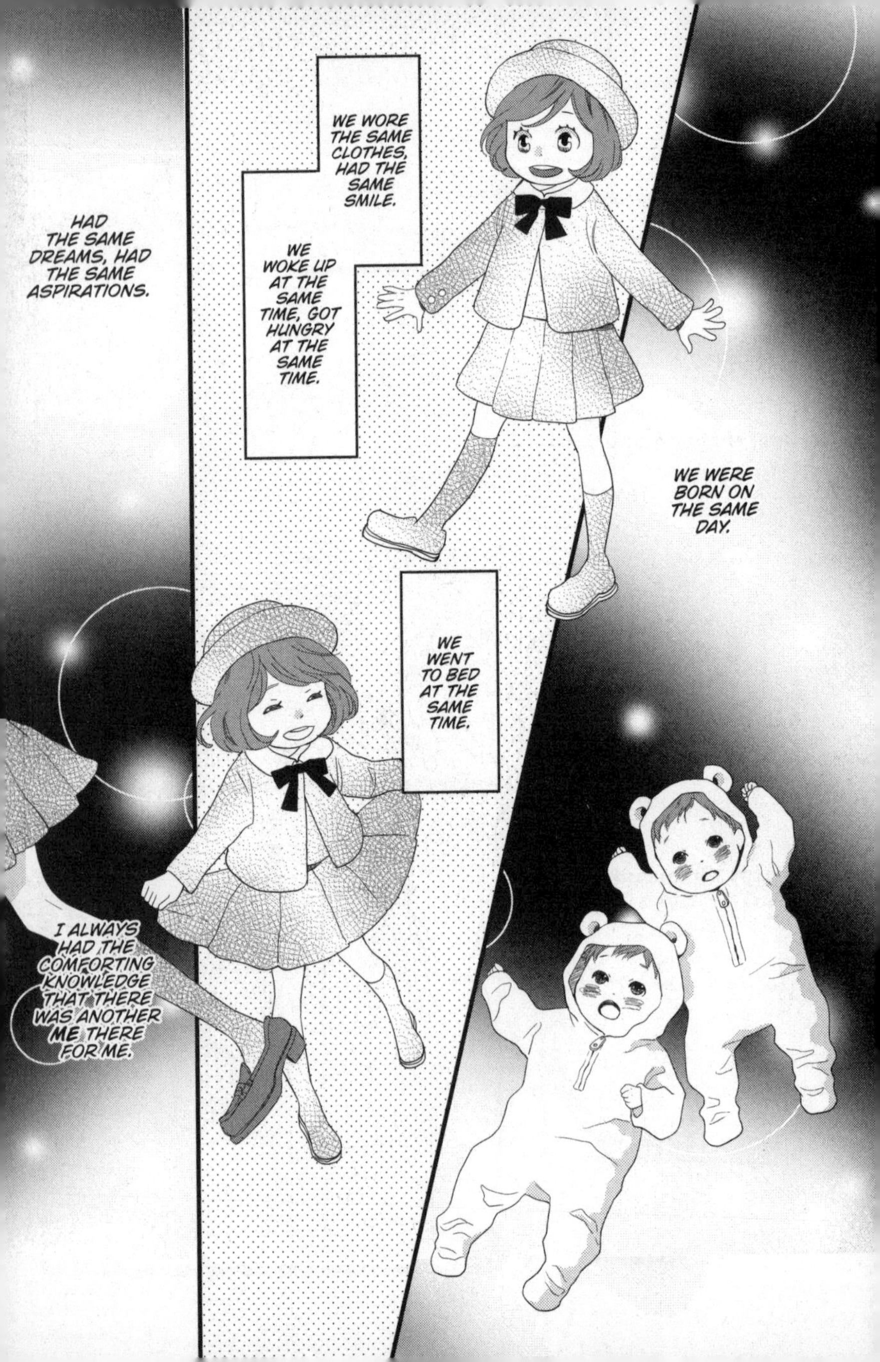
WE WERE BORN ON THE SAME DAY.
WE WORE THE SAME CLOTHES, HAD THE SAME SMILE.
WE WOKE UP AT THE SAME TIME, GOT HUNGRY AT THE SAME TIME.
WE WENT TO BED AT THE SAME TIME.
HAD THE SAME DREAMS, HAD THE SAME ASPIRATIONS.
I ALWAYS HAD THE COMFORTING KNOWLEDGE THAT THERE WAS ANOTHER ME THERE FOR ME.

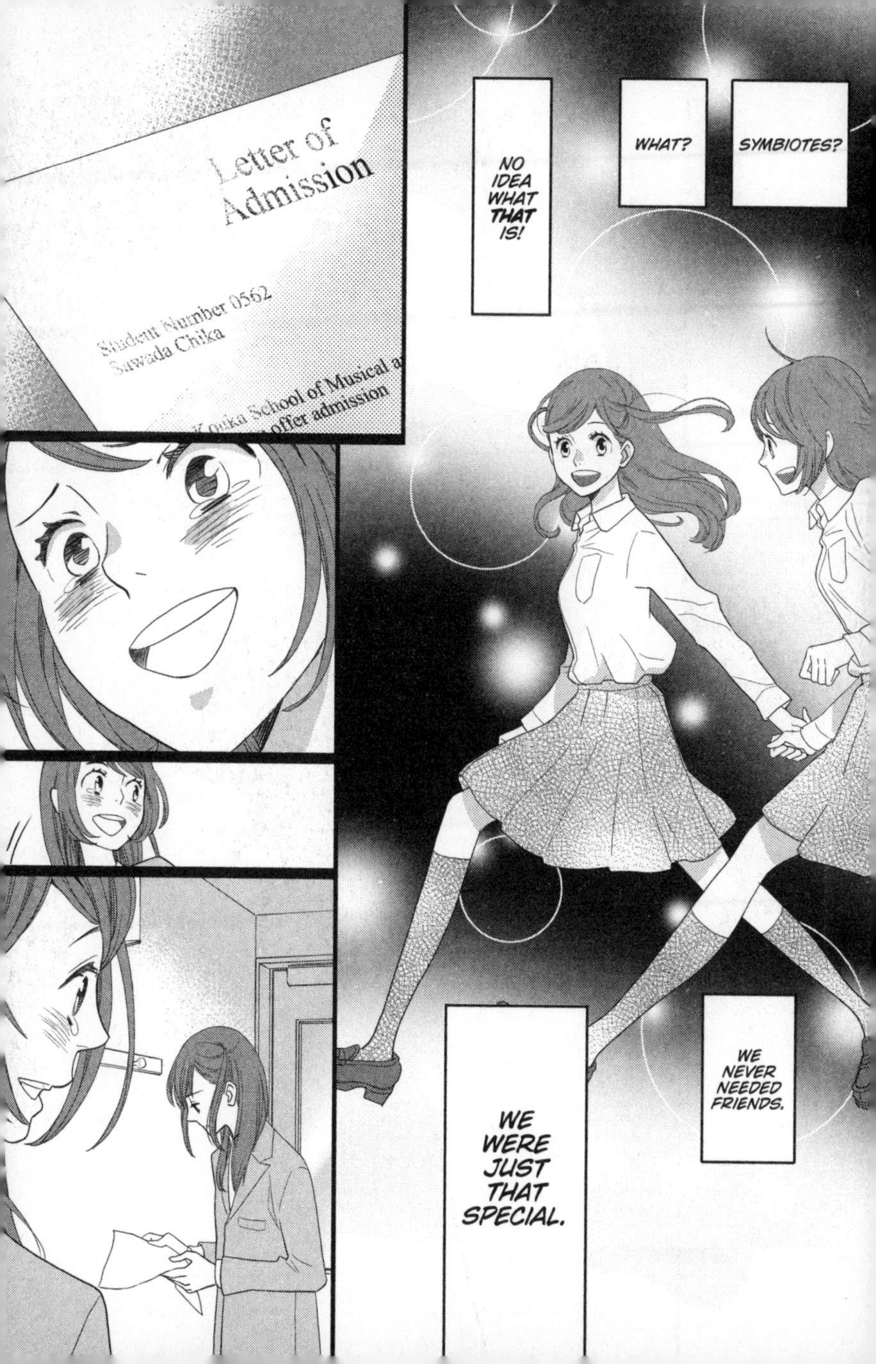
SYMBIOTES?
WHAT?
NO IDEA WHAT THAT IS!
WE NEVER NEEDED FRIENDS.
WE WERE JUST THAT SPECIAL.
Letter of Admission
Student Number 0562
Sawada Chika
School of Musical
offer admission

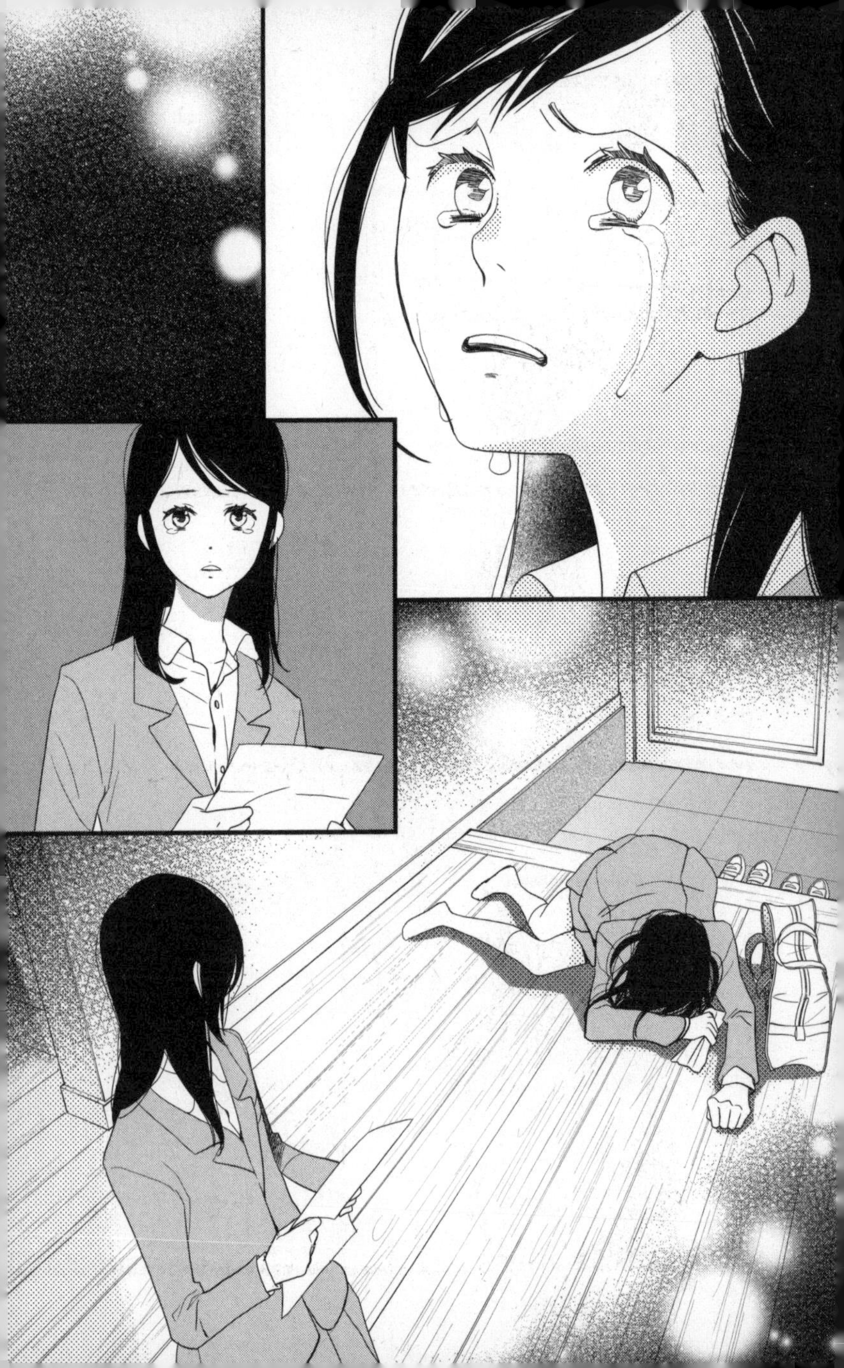

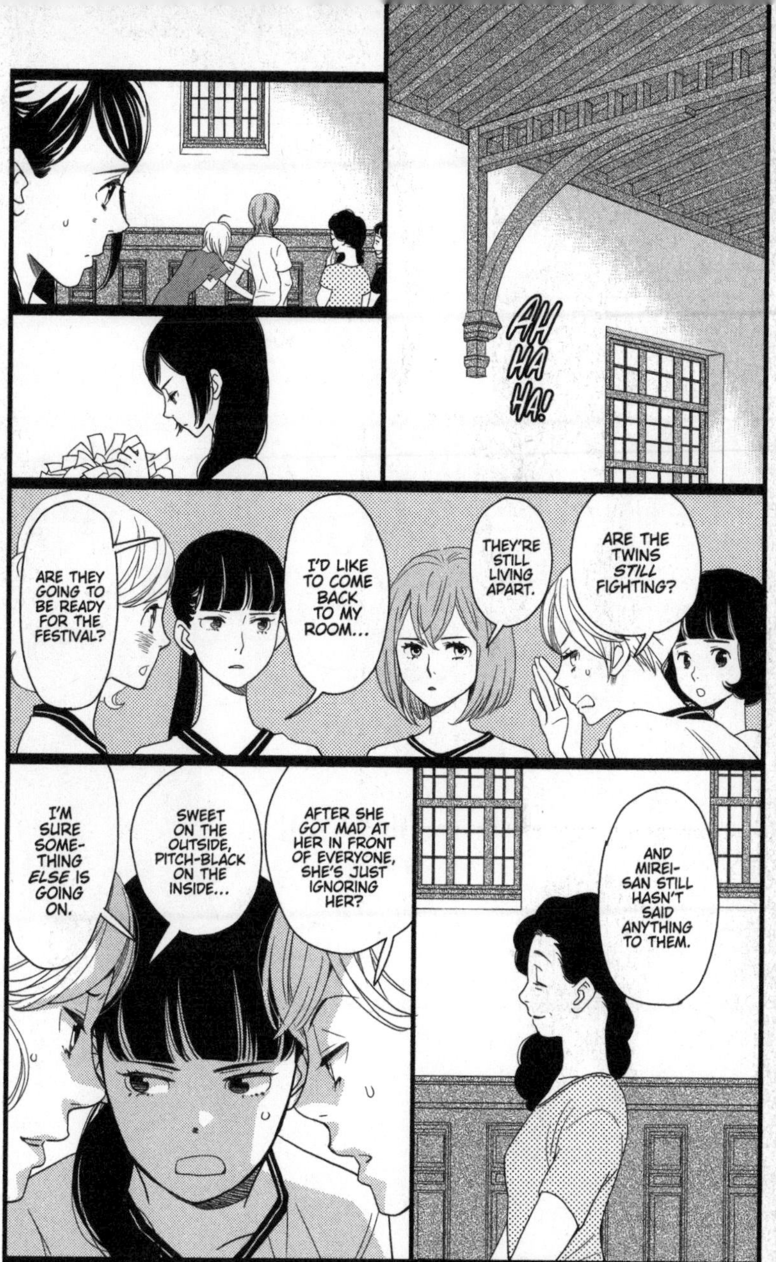
AH HA HA!
ARE THE TWINS *STILL* FIGHTING?
THEY'RE STILL LIVING APART.
I'D LIKE TO COME BACK TO MY ROOM...
ARE THEY GOING TO BE READY FOR THE FESTIVAL?
AND MIREI-SAN STILL HASN'T SAID ANYTHING TO THEM.
AFTER SHE GOT MAD AT HER IN FRONT OF EVERYONE, SHE'S JUST IGNORING HER?
SWEET ON THE OUTSIDE, PITCH-BLACK ON THE INSIDE...
I'M SURE SOMETHING *ELSE* IS GOING ON.

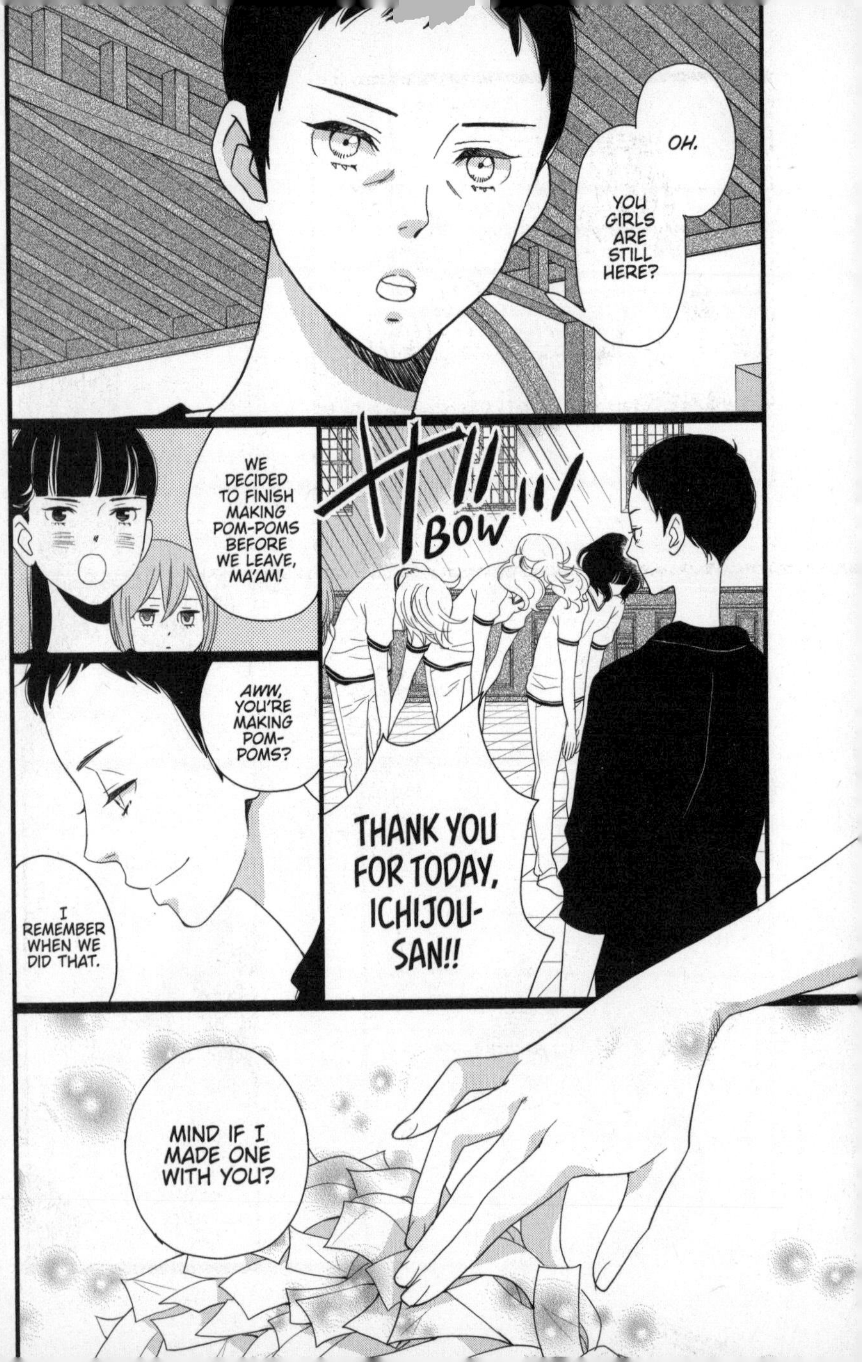
OH.
YOU GIRLS ARE STILL HERE?
BOW
THANK YOU FOR TODAY, ICHIJOU-SAN!!
WE DECIDED TO FINISH MAKING POM-POMS BEFORE WE LEAVE, MA'AM!
AWW, YOU'RE MAKING POM-POMS?
I REMEMBER WHEN WE DID THAT.
MIND IF I MADE ONE WITH YOU?

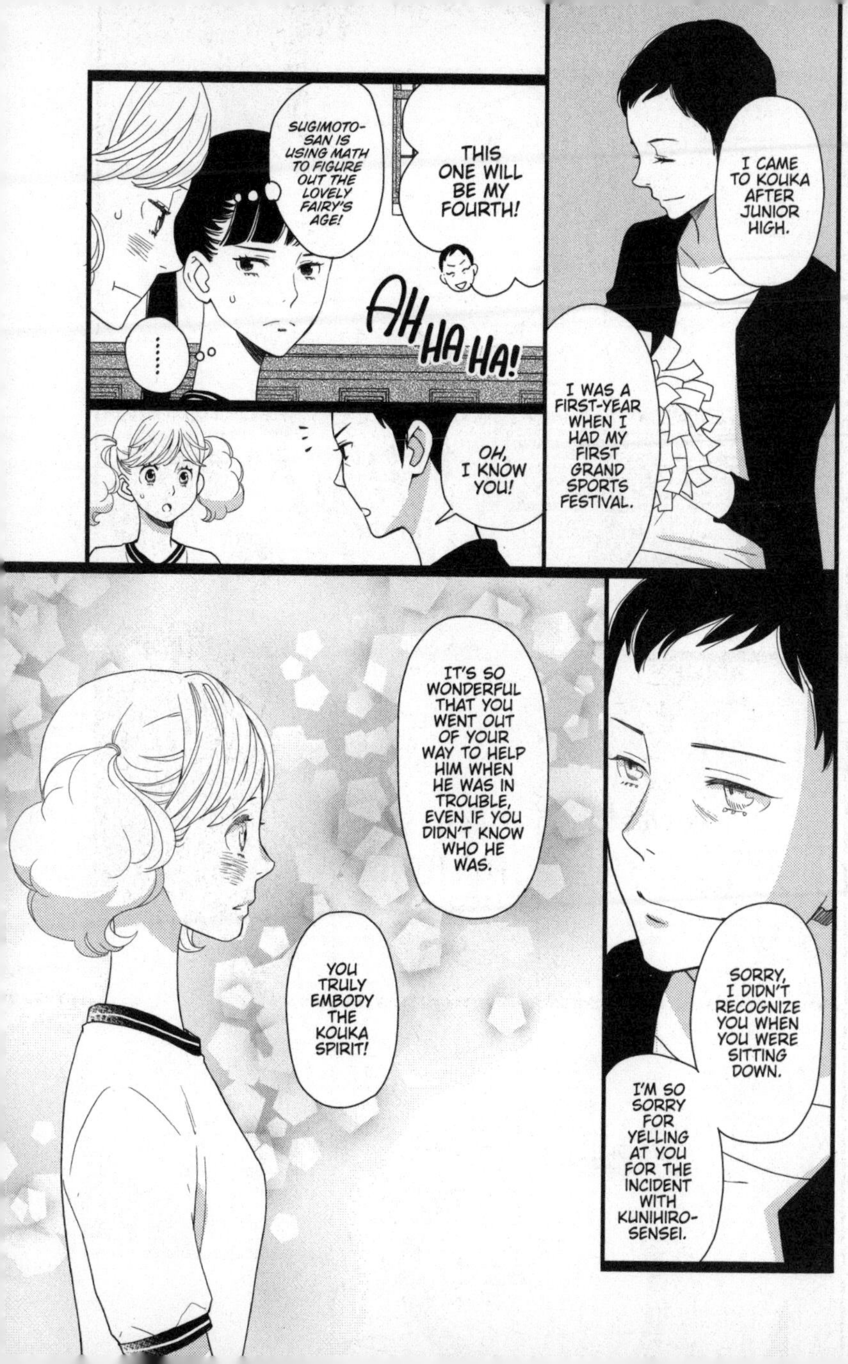
I CAME TO KOUKA AFTER JUNIOR HIGH.
I WAS A FIRST-YEAR WHEN I HAD MY FIRST GRAND SPORTS FESTIVAL.
THIS ONE WILL BE MY FOURTH!
SUGIMOTO-SAN IS USING MATH TO FIGURE OUT THE LOVELY FAIRY'S AGE!
AH HA HA!
......
OH, I KNOW YOU!
SORRY, I DIDN'T RECOGNIZE YOU WHEN YOU WERE SITTING DOWN.
I'M SO SORRY FOR YELLING AT YOU FOR THE INCIDENT WITH KUNIHIRO-SENSEI.
IT'S SO WONDERFUL THAT YOU WENT OUT OF YOUR WAY TO HELP HIM WHEN HE WAS IN TROUBLE, EVEN IF YOU DIDN'T KNOW WHO HE WAS.
YOU TRULY EMBODY THE KOUKA SPIRIT!

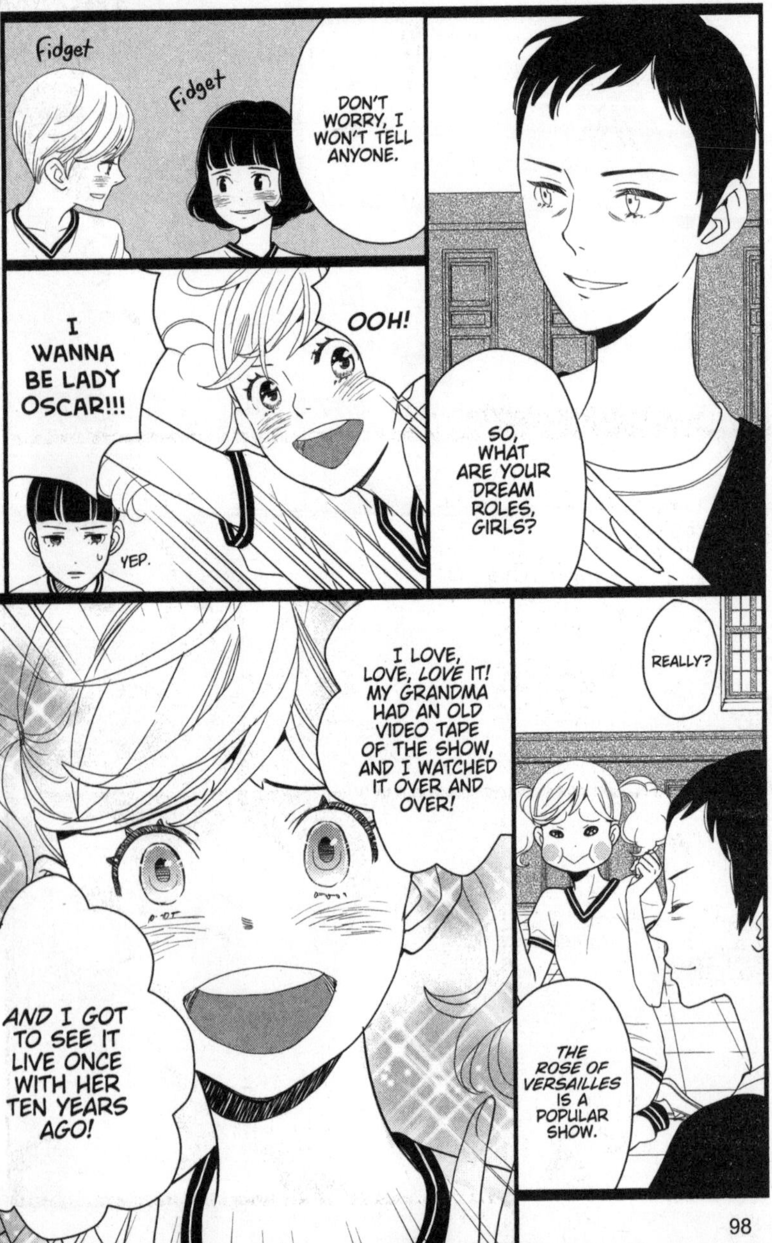
SO, WHAT ARE YOUR DREAM ROLES, GIRLS?
Fidget
Fidget
DON'T WORRY, I WON'T TELL ANYONE.
OOH!
I WANNA BE LADY OSCAR!!!
YEP.
REALLY?
THE ROSE OF VERSAILLES IS A POPULAR SHOW.
I LOVE, LOVE, LOVE IT! MY GRANDMA HAD AN OLD VIDEO TAPE OF THE SHOW, AND I WATCHED IT OVER AND OVER!
AND I GOT TO SEE IT LIVE ONCE WITH HER TEN YEARS AGO!

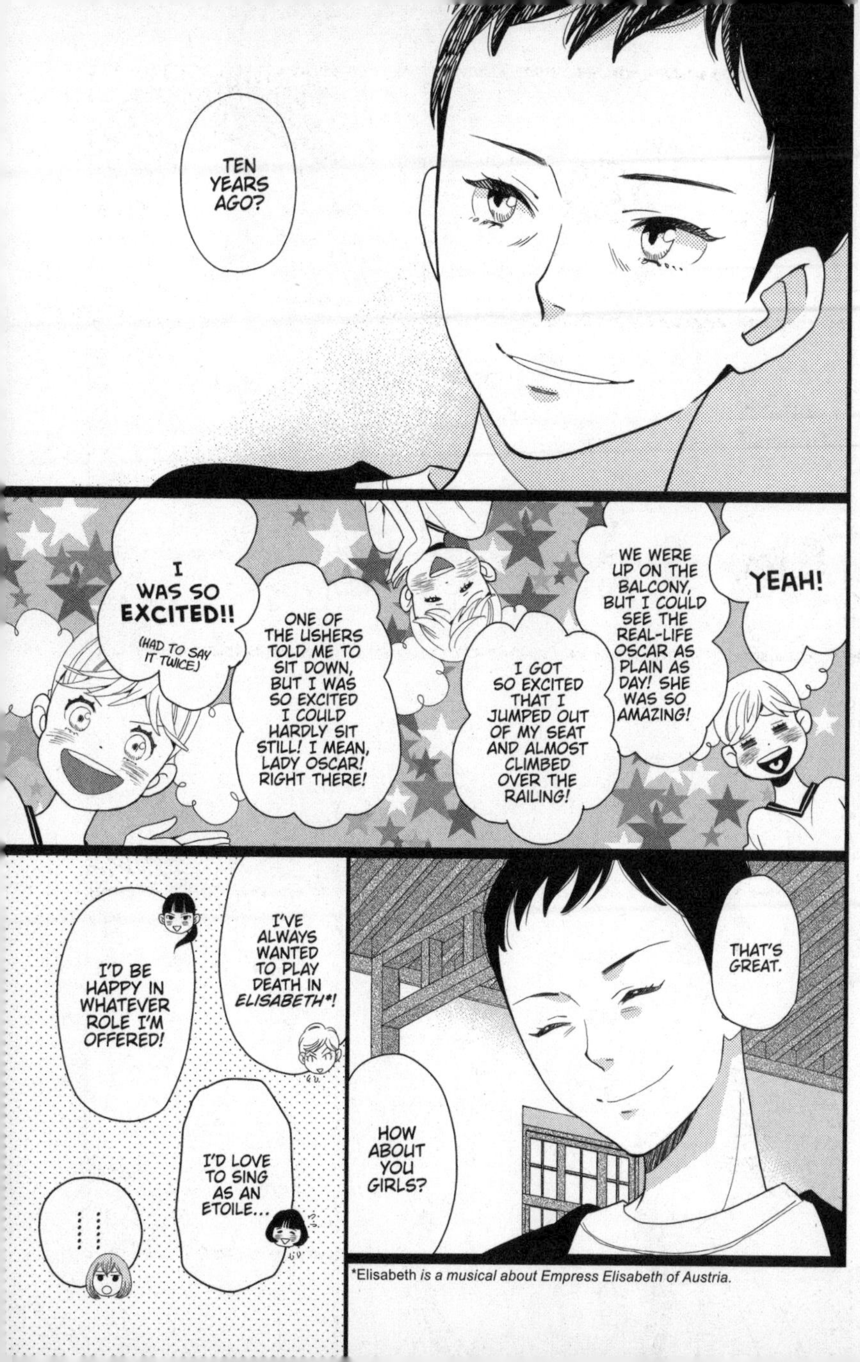
TEN YEARS AGO?
YEAH!
WE WERE UP ON THE BALCONY, BUT I COULD SEE THE REAL-LIFE OSCAR AS PLAIN AS DAY! SHE WAS SO AMAZING!
I GOT SO EXCITED THAT I JUMPED OUT OF MY SEAT AND ALMOST CLIMBED OVER THE RAILING!
ONE OF THE USHERS TOLD ME TO SIT DOWN, BUT I WAS SO EXCITED I COULD HARDLY SIT STILL! I MEAN, LADY OSCAR! RIGHT THERE!
I WAS SO EXCITED!!
(HAD TO SAY IT TWICE)
THAT'S GREAT.
HOW ABOUT YOU GIRLS?
I'VE ALWAYS WANTED TO PLAY DEATH IN *ELISABETH**!
I'D BE HAPPY IN WHATEVER ROLE I'M OFFERED!
I'D LOVE TO SING AS AN ETOILE...
……

*Elisabeth *is a musical about Empress Elisabeth of Austria.*

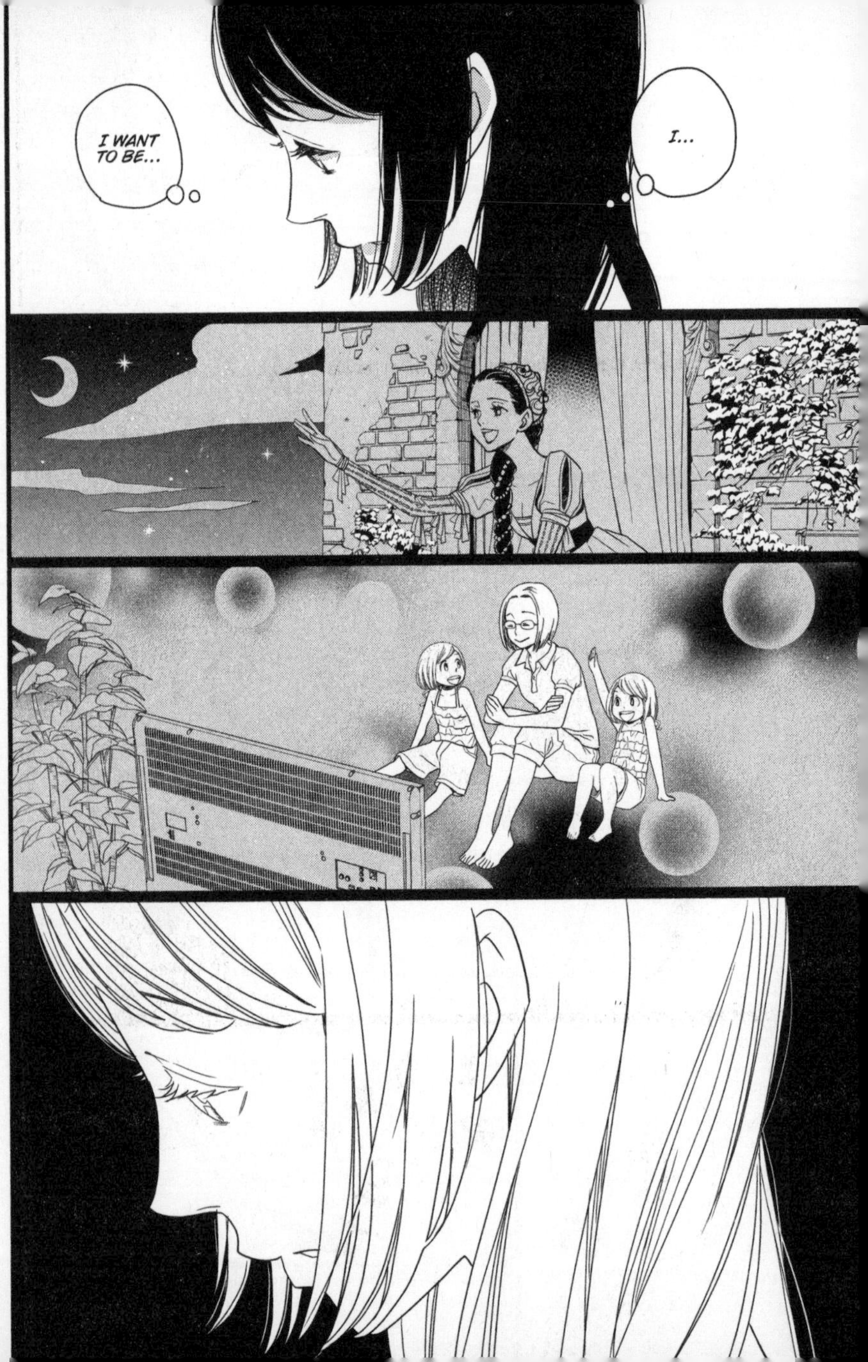
I...
I WANT TO BE...

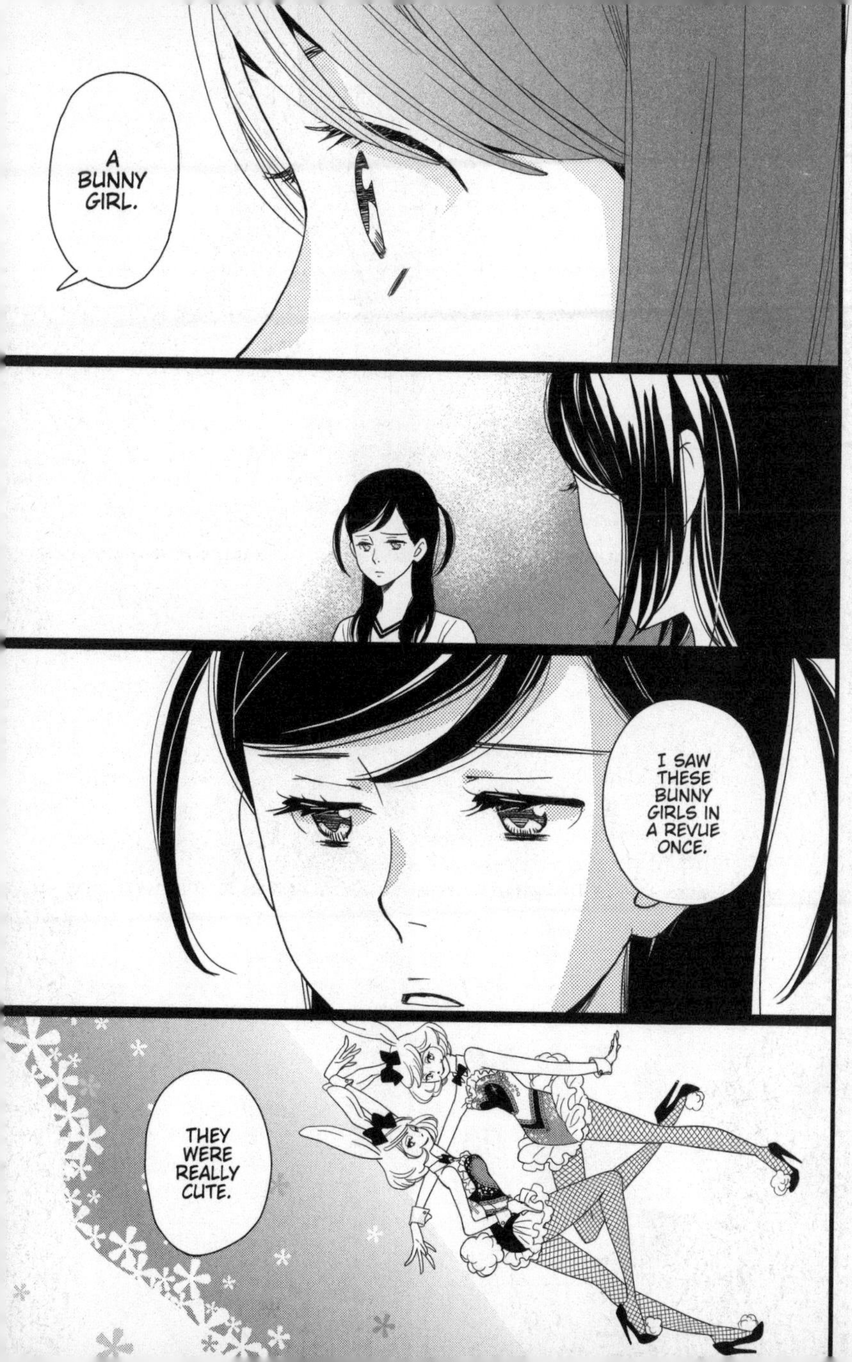
A BUNNY GIRL.
I SAW THESE BUNNY GIRLS IN A REVUE ONCE.
THEY WERE REALLY CUTE.

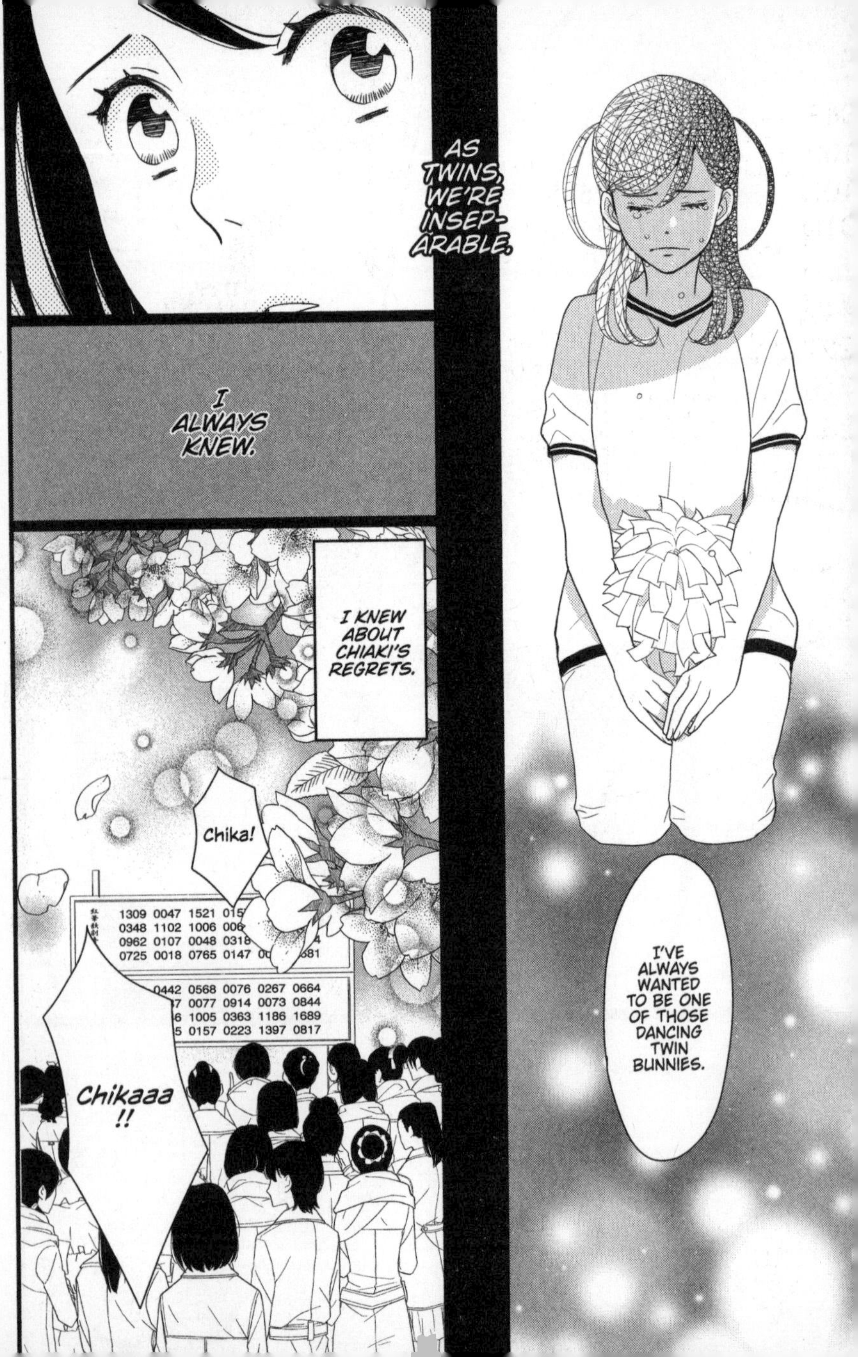
AS TWINS, WE'RE INSEP-ARABLE.
I'VE ALWAYS WANTED TO BE ONE OF THOSE DANCING TWIN BUNNIES.
I ALWAYS KNEW.
I KNEW ABOUT CHIAKI'S REGRETS.
Chika!
Chikaaa !!

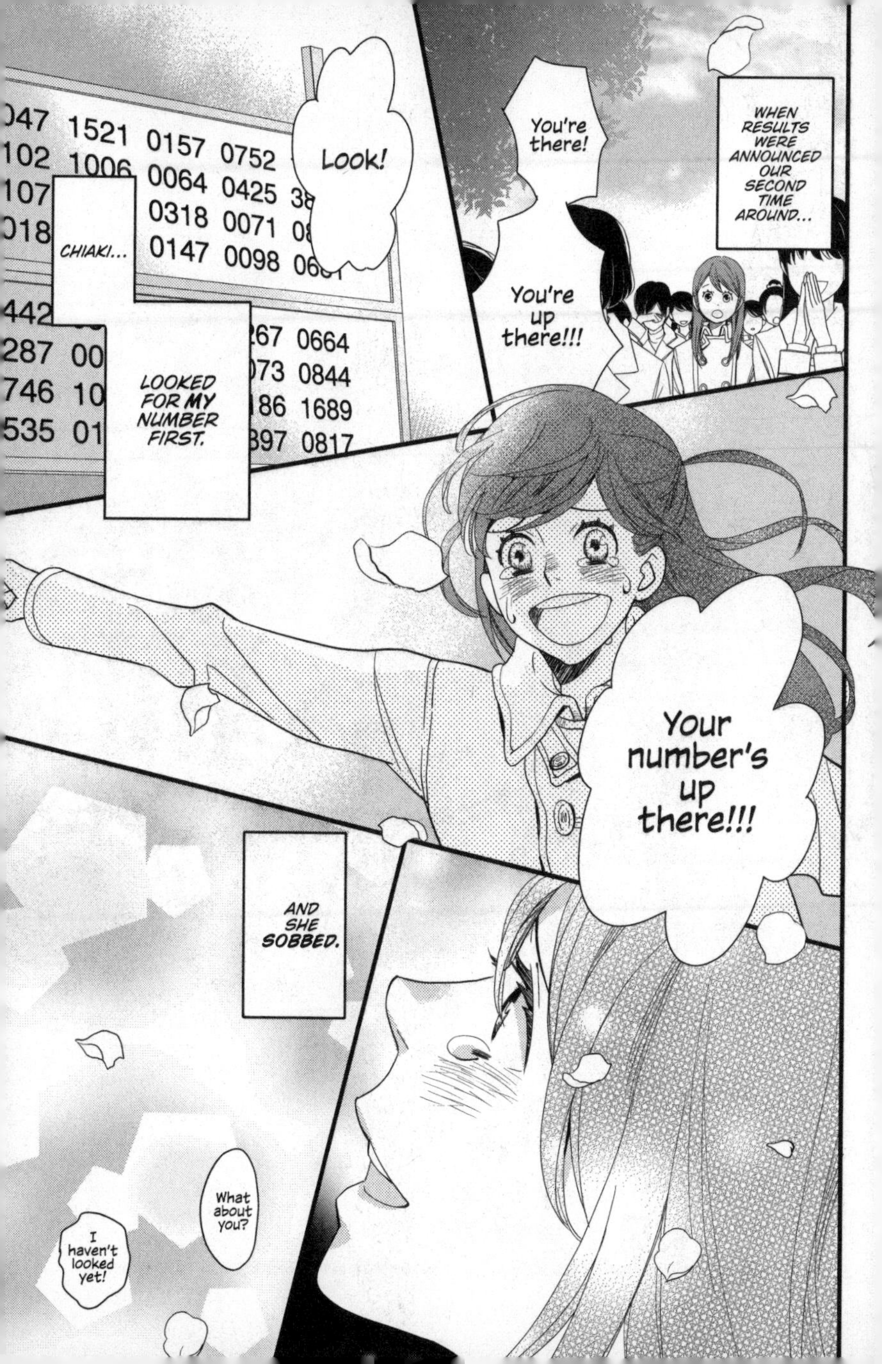
WHEN RESULTS WERE ANNOUNCED OUR SECOND TIME AROUND...
You're there!
You're up there!!!
Look!
CHIAKI...
LOOKED FOR MY NUMBER FIRST.
Your number's up there!!!
AND SHE SOBBED.
What about you?
I haven't looked yet!

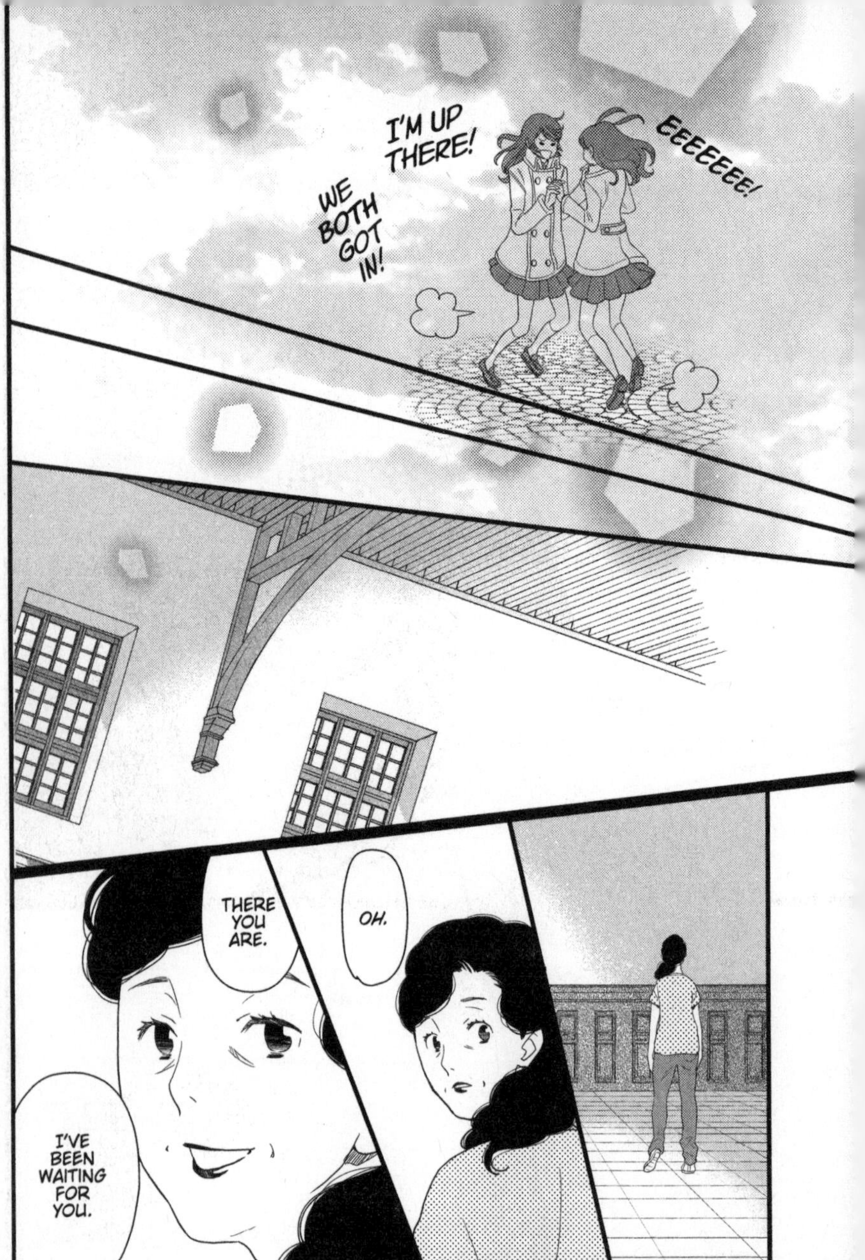
EEEEEEE!
I'M UP THERE!
WE BOTH GOT IN!
OH.
THERE YOU ARE.
I'VE BEEN WAITING FOR YOU.

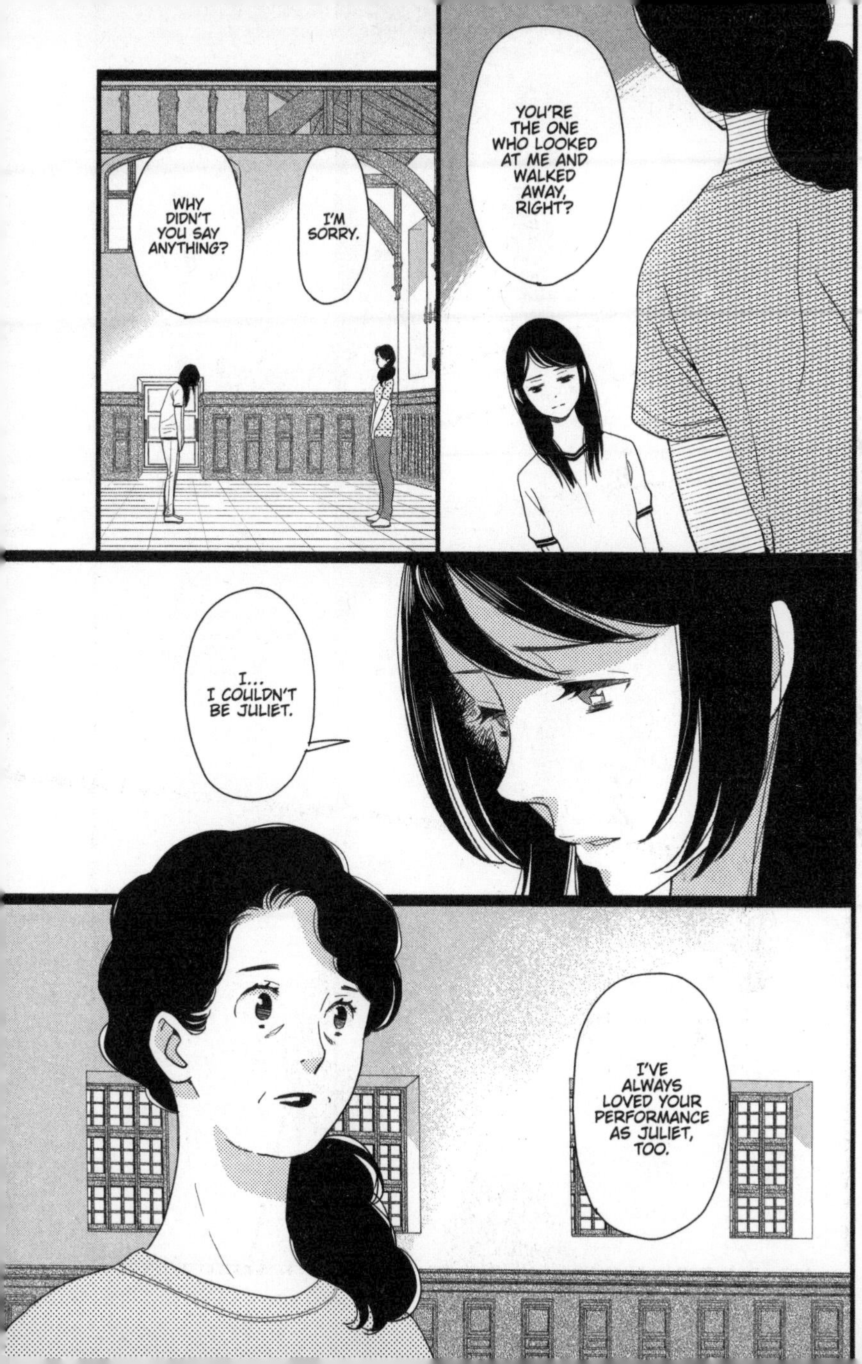
YOU'RE THE ONE WHO LOOKED AT ME AND WALKED AWAY, RIGHT?
I'M SORRY.
WHY DIDN'T YOU SAY ANYTHING?
I... I COULDN'T BE JULIET.
I'VE ALWAYS LOVED YOUR PERFORMANCE AS JULIET, TOO.

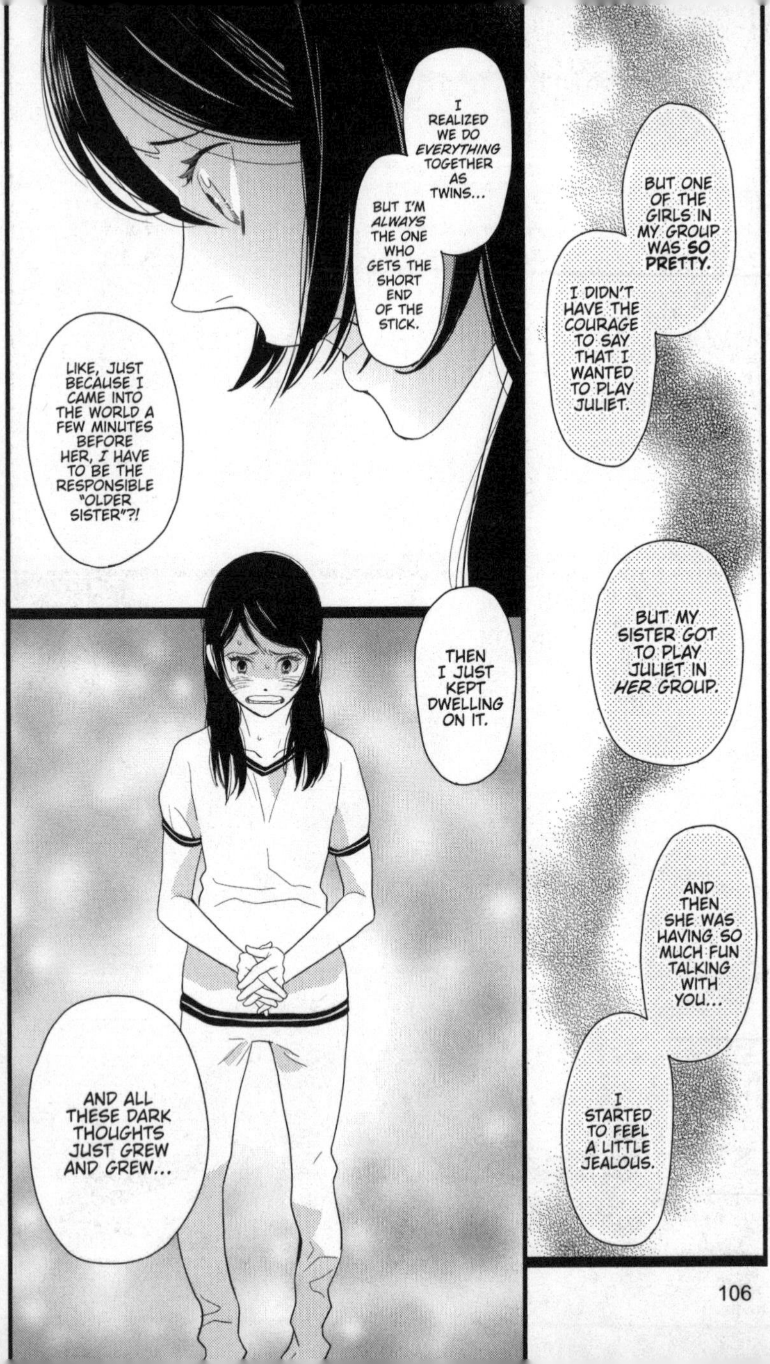
BUT ONE OF THE GIRLS IN MY GROUP WAS **SO PRETTY.**
I DIDN'T HAVE THE COURAGE TO SAY THAT I WANTED TO PLAY JULIET.
BUT MY SISTER GOT TO PLAY JULIET IN *HER* GROUP.
AND THEN SHE WAS HAVING SO MUCH FUN TALKING WITH YOU...
I STARTED TO FEEL A LITTLE JEALOUS.
I REALIZED WE DO *EVERYTHING* TOGETHER AS TWINS...
BUT I'M *ALWAYS* THE ONE WHO GETS THE SHORT END OF THE STICK.
LIKE, JUST BECAUSE I CAME INTO THE WORLD A FEW MINUTES BEFORE HER, *I* HAVE TO BE THE RESPONSIBLE "OLDER SISTER"?!
THEN I JUST KEPT DWELLING ON IT.
AND ALL THESE DARK THOUGHTS JUST GREW AND GREW...

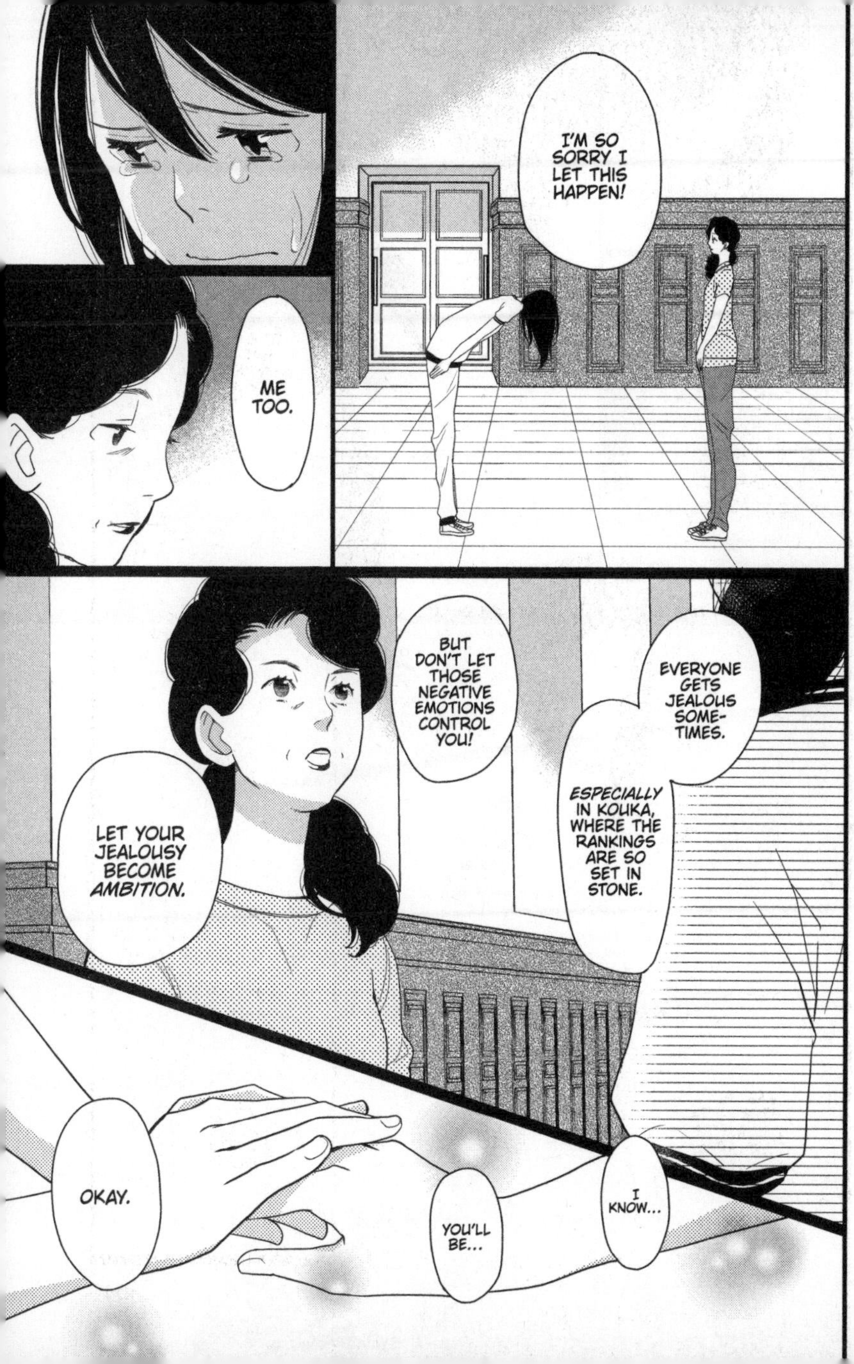
I'M SO SORRY I LET THIS HAPPEN!
ME TOO.
EVERYONE GETS JEALOUS SOME-TIMES.
ESPECIALLY IN KOUKA, WHERE THE RANKINGS ARE SO SET IN STONE.
BUT DON'T LET THOSE NEGATIVE EMOTIONS CONTROL YOU!
LET YOUR JEALOUSY BECOME *AMBITION*.
I KNOW...
YOU'LL BE...
OKAY.

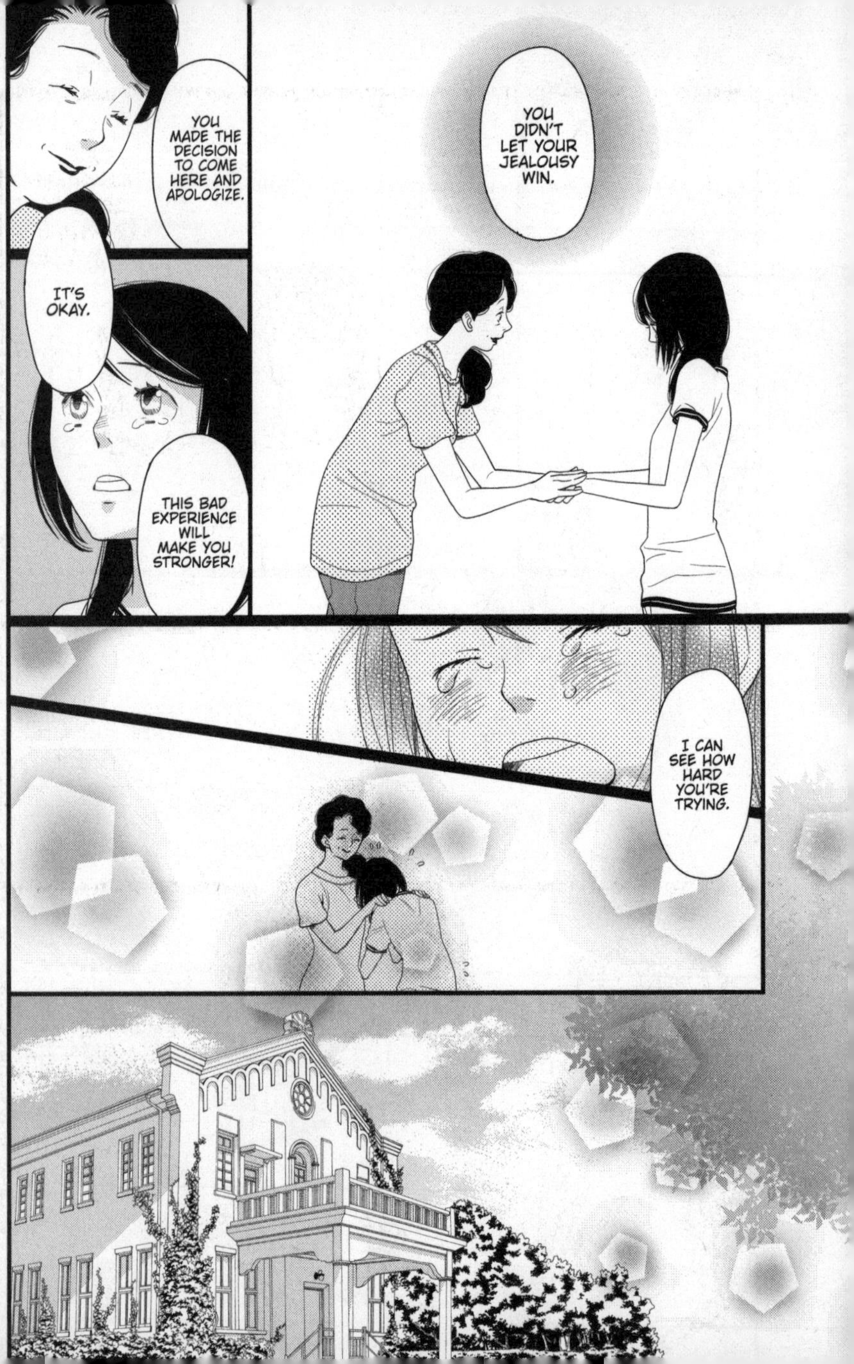
YOU DIDN'T LET YOUR JEALOUSY WIN.
YOU MADE THE DECISION TO COME HERE AND APOLOGIZE.
IT'S OKAY.
THIS BAD EXPERIENCE WILL MAKE YOU STRONGER!
I CAN SEE HOW HARD YOU'RE TRYING.

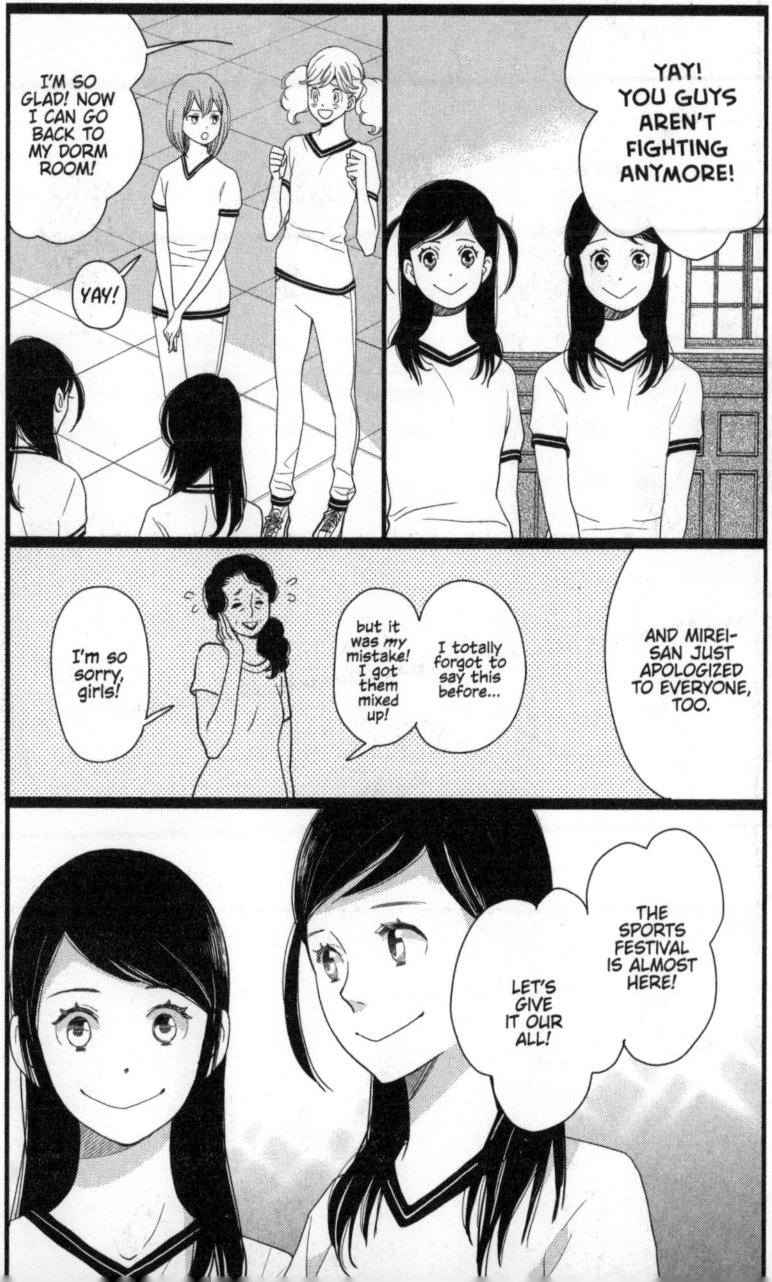
YAY! YOU GUYS AREN'T FIGHTING ANYMORE!
I'M SO GLAD! NOW I CAN GO BACK TO MY DORM ROOM!
YAY!
AND MIREI-SAN JUST APOLOGIZED TO EVERYONE, TOO.
I totally forgot to say this before...
but it was *my* mistake! I got them mixed up!
I'm so sorry, girls!
THE SPORTS FESTIVAL IS ALMOST HERE!
LET'S GIVE IT OUR ALL!

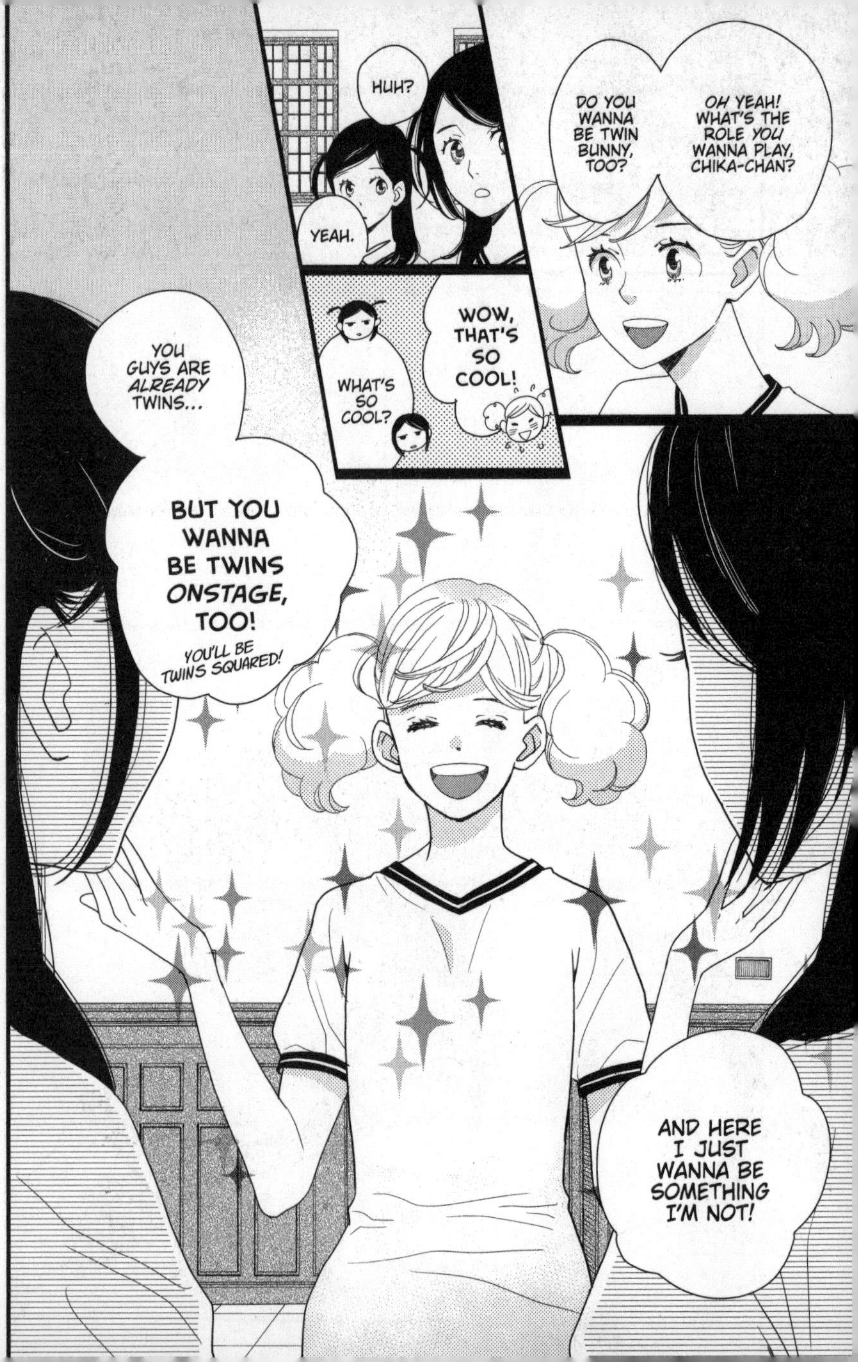

OH YEAH! WHAT'S THE ROLE YOU WANNA PLAY, CHIKA-CHAN?
DO YOU WANNA BE TWIN BUNNY, TOO?
HUH?
YEAH.
WOW, THAT'S SO COOL!
WHAT'S SO COOL?
YOU GUYS ARE ALREADY TWINS...
BUT YOU WANNA BE TWINS ONSTAGE, TOO!
YOU'LL BE TWINS SQUARED!
AND HERE I JUST WANNA BE SOMETHING I'M NOT!

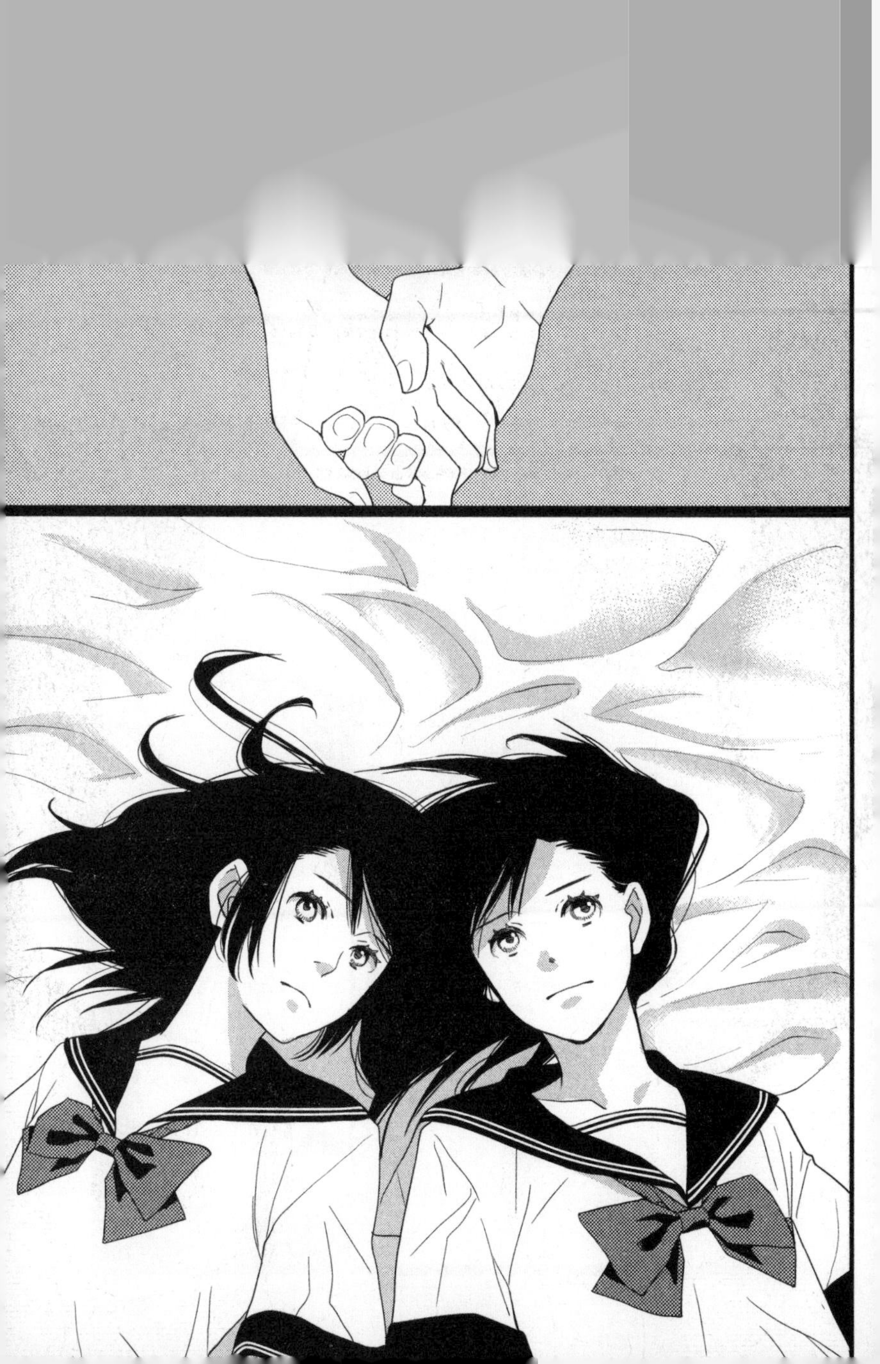

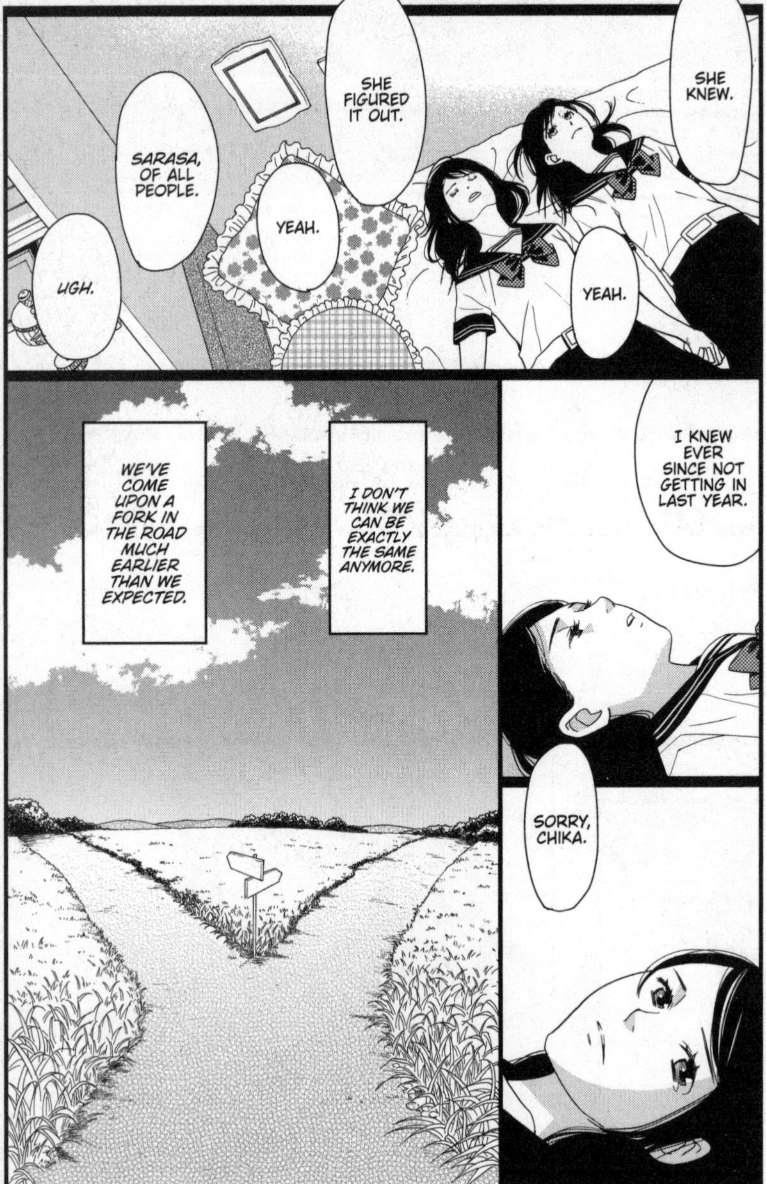
SHE KNEW.
YEAH.
SHE FIGURED IT OUT.
YEAH.
SARASA, OF ALL PEOPLE.
UGH.
I KNEW EVER SINCE NOT GETTING IN LAST YEAR.
SORRY, CHIKA.
I DON'T THINK WE CAN BE EXACTLY THE SAME ANYMORE.
WE'VE COME UPON A FORK IN THE ROAD MUCH EARLIER THAN WE EXPECTED.

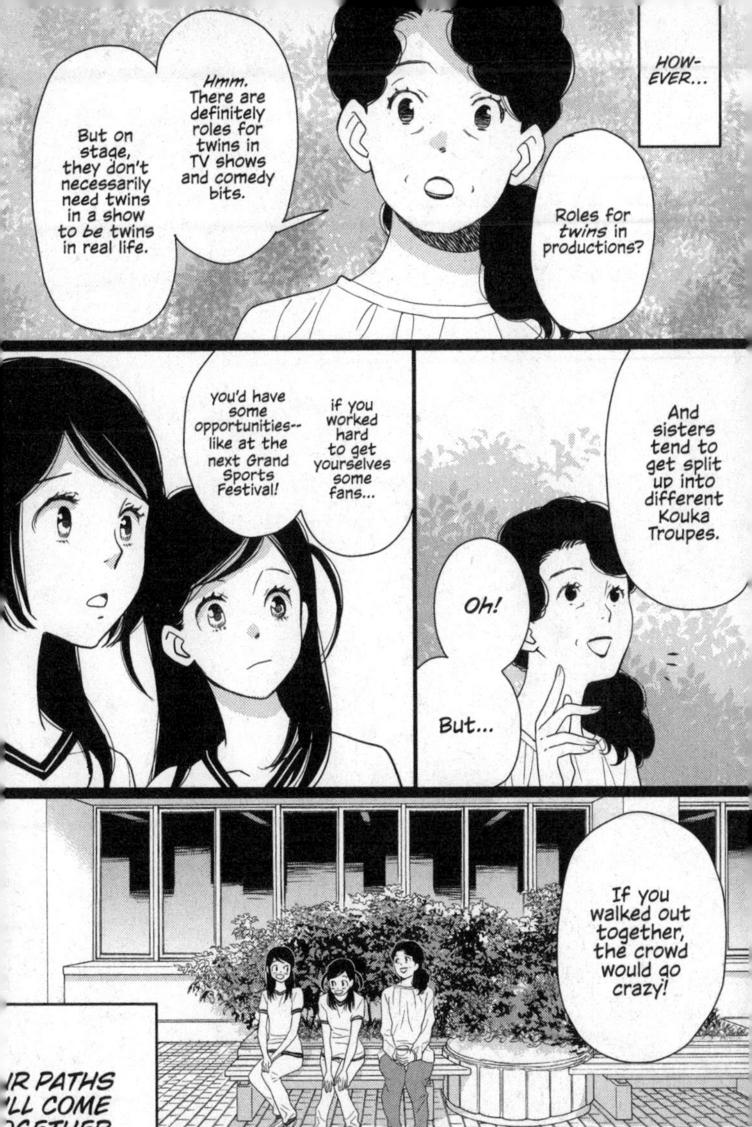
HOW-EVER...
Roles for twins in productions?
Hmm. There are definitely roles for twins in TV shows and comedy bits.
But on stage, they don't necessarily need twins in a show to be twins in real life.
And sisters tend to get split up into different Kouka Troupes.
Oh!
But...
if you worked hard to get yourselves some fans...
you'd have some opportunities--like at the next Grand Sports Festival!
If you walked out together, the crowd would go crazy!
IR PATHS
LL COME
OGETHER
GAIN ONE

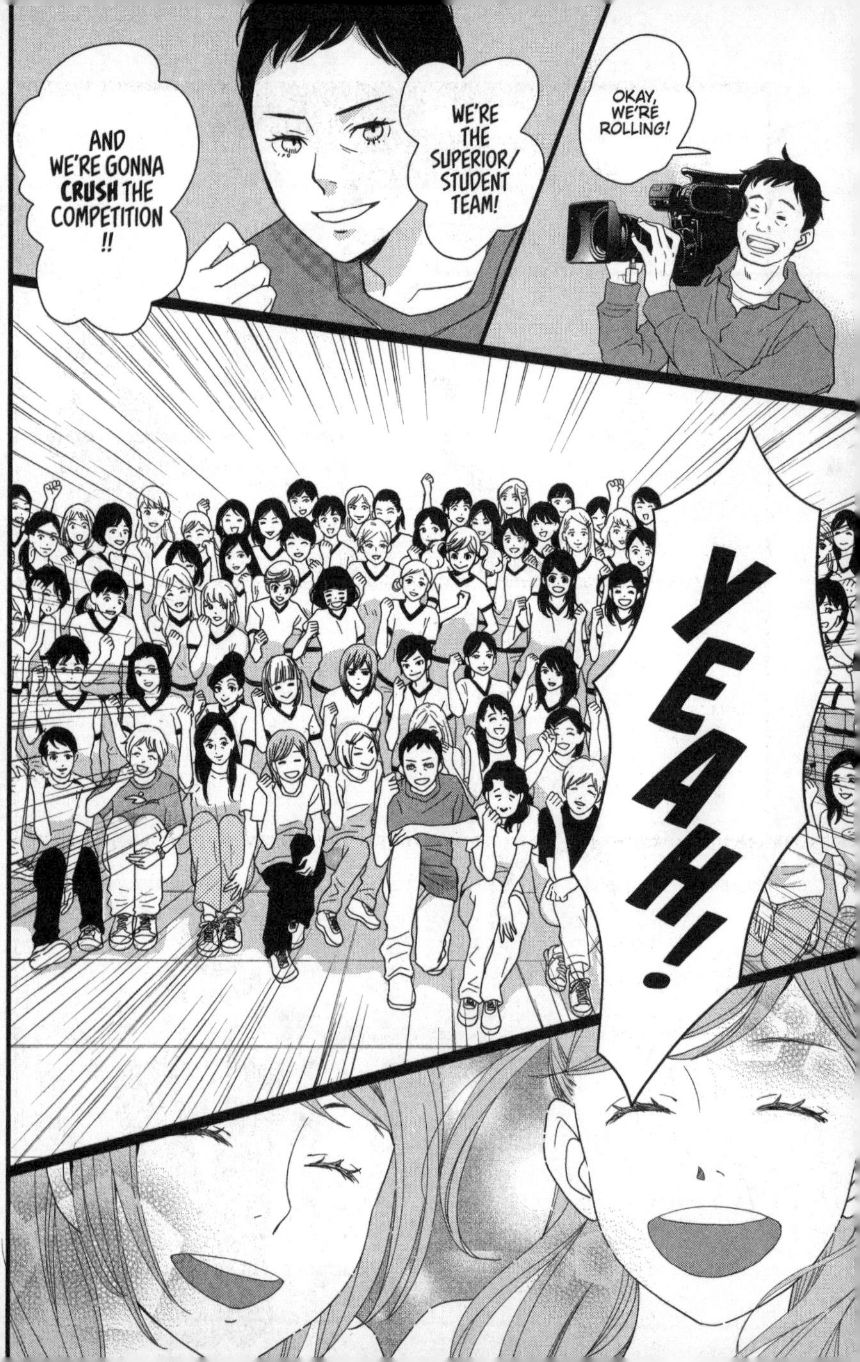
OKAY, WE'RE ROLLING!
WE'RE THE SUPERIOR/STUDENT TEAM!
AND WE'RE GONNA CRUSH THE COMPETITION !!
YEAH!

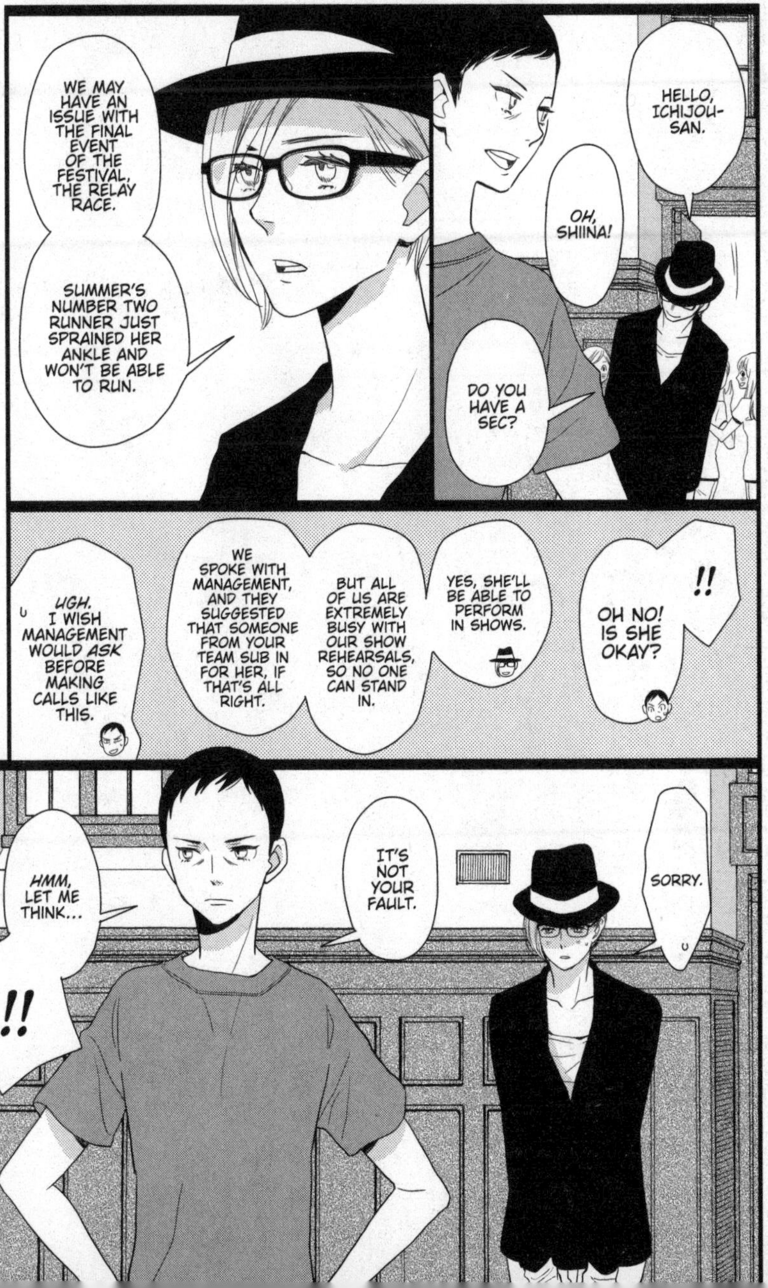
HELLO, ICHIJOU-SAN.
OH, SHIINA!
DO YOU HAVE A SEC?
WE MAY HAVE AN ISSUE WITH THE FINAL EVENT OF THE FESTIVAL, THE RELAY RACE.
SUMMER'S NUMBER TWO RUNNER JUST SPRAINED HER ANKLE AND WON'T BE ABLE TO RUN.
!!
OH NO! IS SHE OKAY?
YES, SHE'LL BE ABLE TO PERFORM IN SHOWS.
BUT ALL OF US ARE EXTREMELY BUSY WITH OUR SHOW REHEARSALS, SO NO ONE CAN STAND IN.
WE SPOKE WITH MANAGEMENT, AND THEY SUGGESTED THAT SOMEONE FROM YOUR TEAM SUB IN FOR HER, IF THAT'S ALL RIGHT.
UGH. I WISH MANAGEMENT WOULD *ASK* BEFORE MAKING CALLS LIKE THIS.
SORRY.
IT'S NOT YOUR FAULT.
HMM, LET ME THINK...
!!

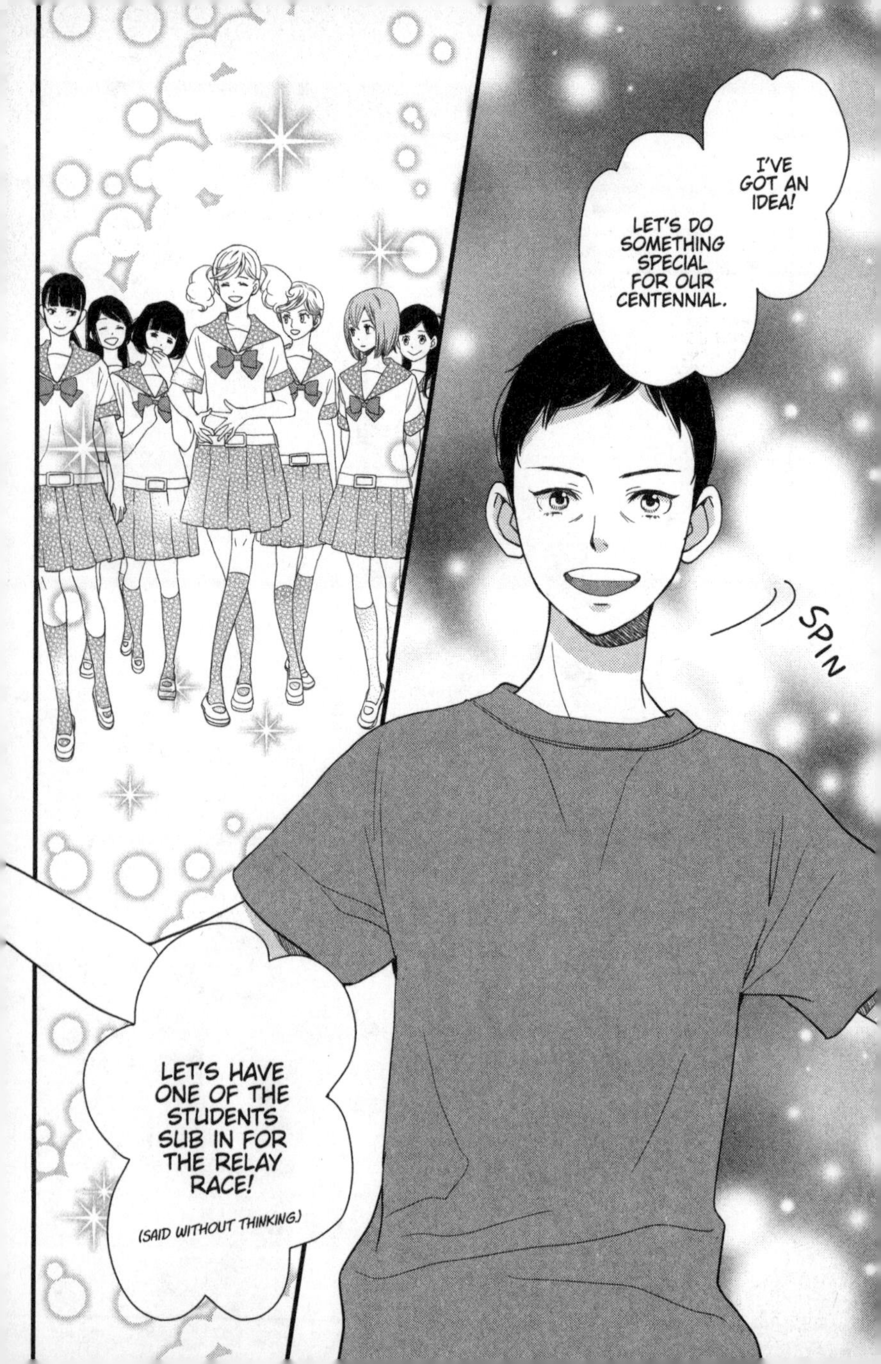
I'VE GOT AN IDEA!
LET'S DO SOMETHING SPECIAL FOR OUR CENTENNIAL.
SPIN
LET'S HAVE ONE OF THE STUDENTS SUB IN FOR THE RELAY RACE!
(SAID WITHOUT THINKING.)

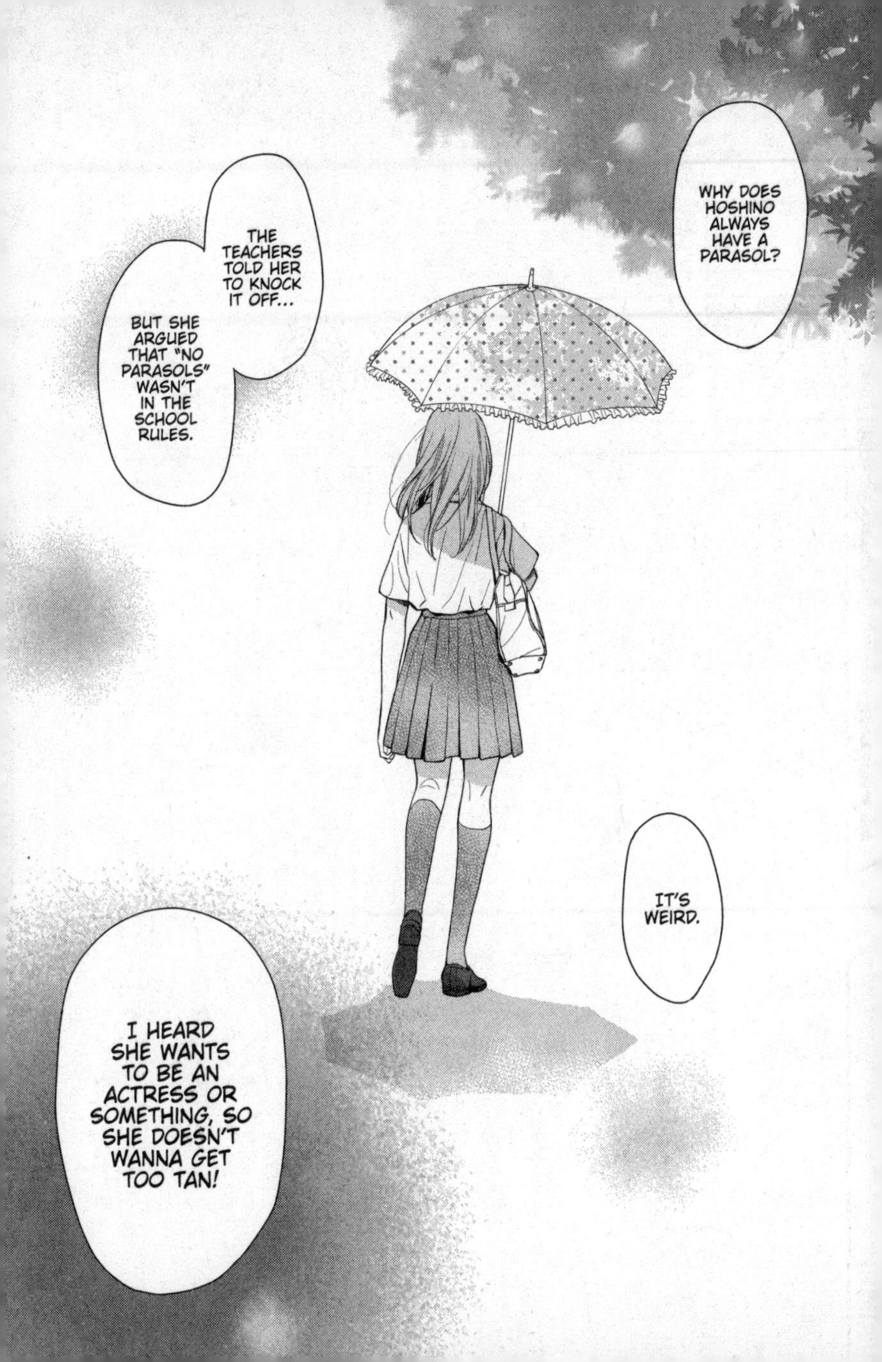
WHY DOES HOSHINO ALWAYS HAVE A PARASOL?
THE TEACHERS TOLD HER TO KNOCK IT OFF...
BUT SHE ARGUED THAT "NO PARASOLS" WASN'T IN THE SCHOOL RULES.
IT'S WEIRD.
I HEARD SHE WANTS TO BE AN ACTRESS OR SOMETHING, SO SHE DOESN'T WANNA GET TOO TAN!

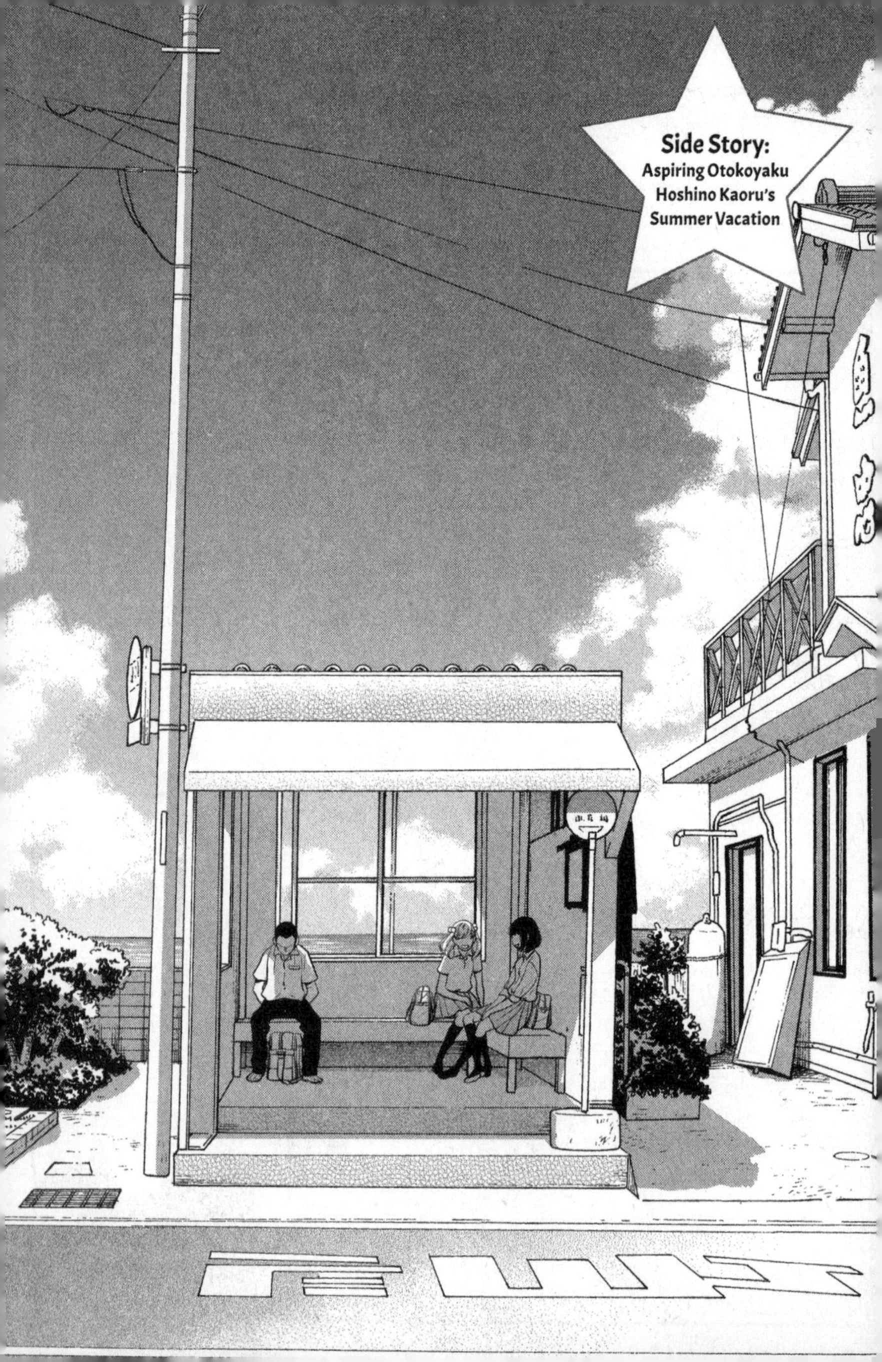
Side Story:
Aspiring Otokoyaku
Hoshino Kaoru's
Summer Vacation

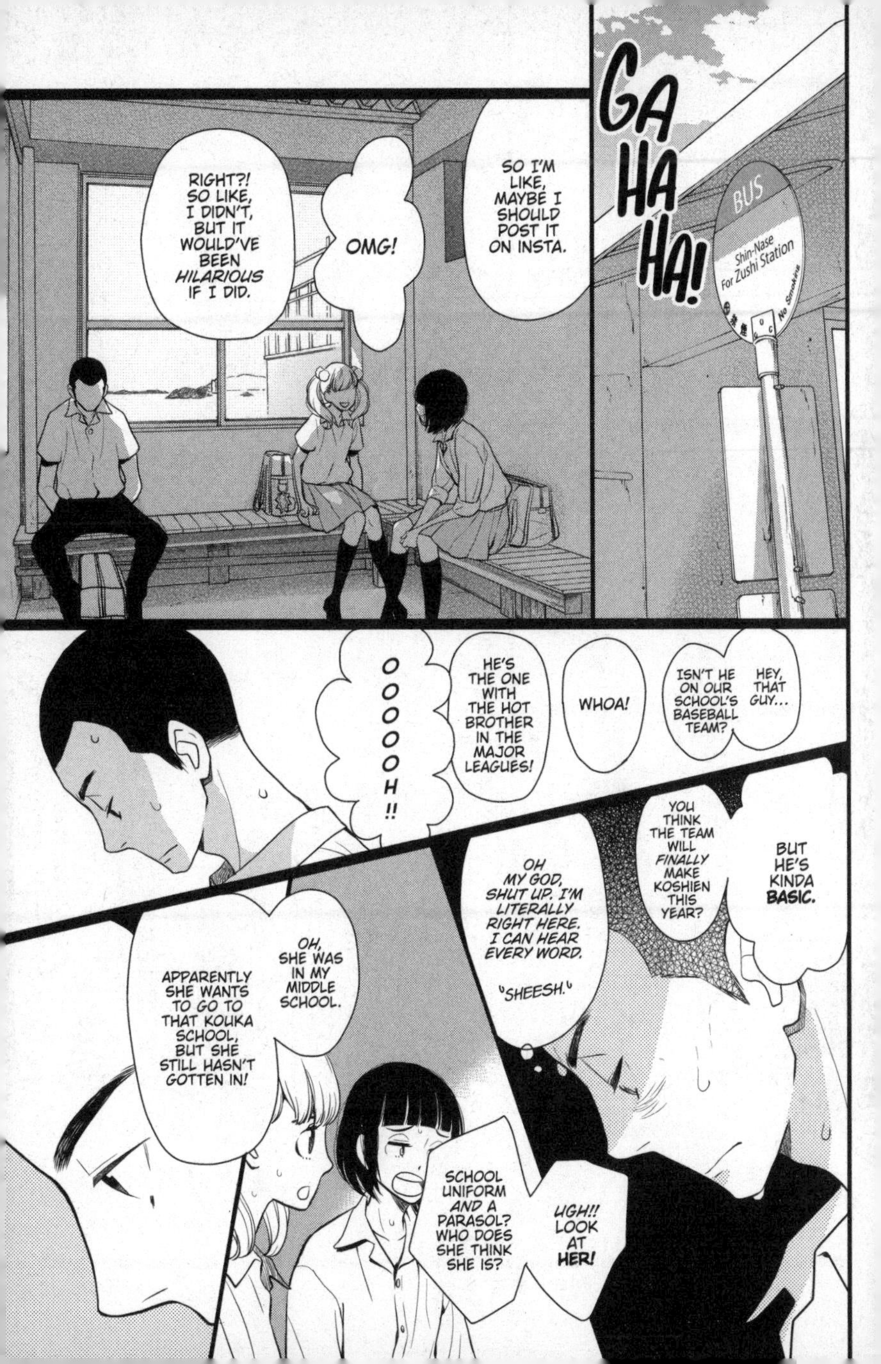
GA HA HA!
BUS
Shin-Nase
For Zushi Station
No Smoking
SO I'M LIKE, MAYBE I SHOULD POST IT ON INSTA.
OMG!
RIGHT?! SO LIKE, I DIDN'T, BUT IT WOULD'VE BEEN *HILARIOUS* IF I DID.
HEY, THAT GUY...
ISN'T HE ON OUR SCHOOL'S BASEBALL TEAM?
WHOA!
HE'S THE ONE WITH THE HOT BROTHER IN THE MAJOR LEAGUES!
OOOOOOH!!
BUT HE'S KINDA **BASIC.**
YOU THINK THE TEAM WILL *FINALLY* MAKE KOSHIEN THIS YEAR?
OH MY GOD, SHUT UP. I'M LITERALLY RIGHT HERE. I CAN HEAR EVERY WORD.
"SHEESH."
OH, SHE WAS IN MY MIDDLE SCHOOL.
APPARENTLY SHE WANTS TO GO TO THAT KOUKA SCHOOL, BUT SHE STILL HASN'T GOTTEN IN!
UGH!! LOOK AT **HER!**
SCHOOL UNIFORM *AND* A PARASOL? WHO DOES SHE THINK SHE IS?

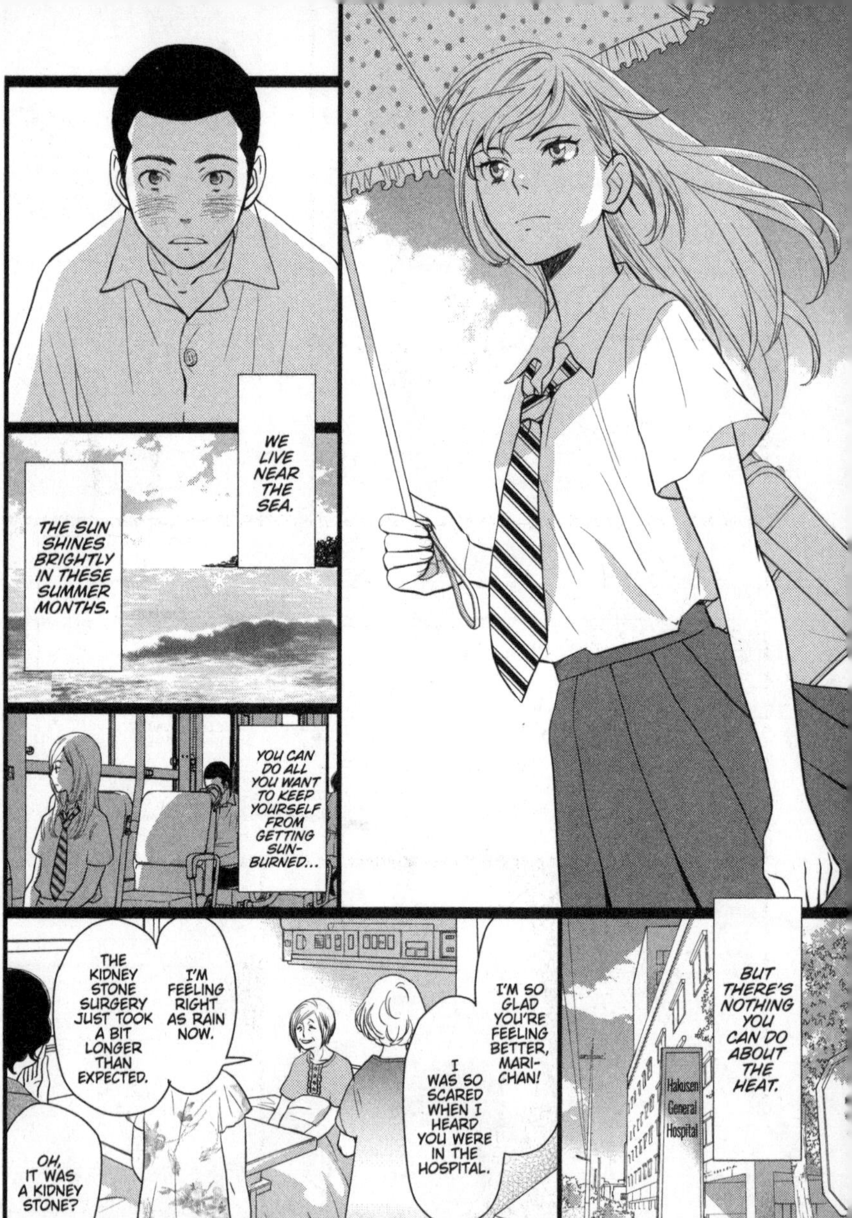
WE LIVE NEAR THE SEA.
THE SUN SHINES BRIGHTLY IN THESE SUMMER MONTHS.
YOU CAN DO ALL YOU WANT TO KEEP YOURSELF FROM GETTING SUN-BURNED...
BUT THERE'S NOTHING YOU CAN DO ABOUT THE HEAT.
Hakusen General Hospital
I'M SO GLAD YOU'RE FEELING BETTER, MARI-CHAN!
I WAS SO SCARED WHEN I HEARD YOU WERE IN THE HOSPITAL.
I'M FEELING RIGHT AS RAIN NOW.
THE KIDNEY STONE SURGERY JUST TOOK A BIT LONGER THAN EXPECTED.
OH, IT WAS A KIDNEY STONE?

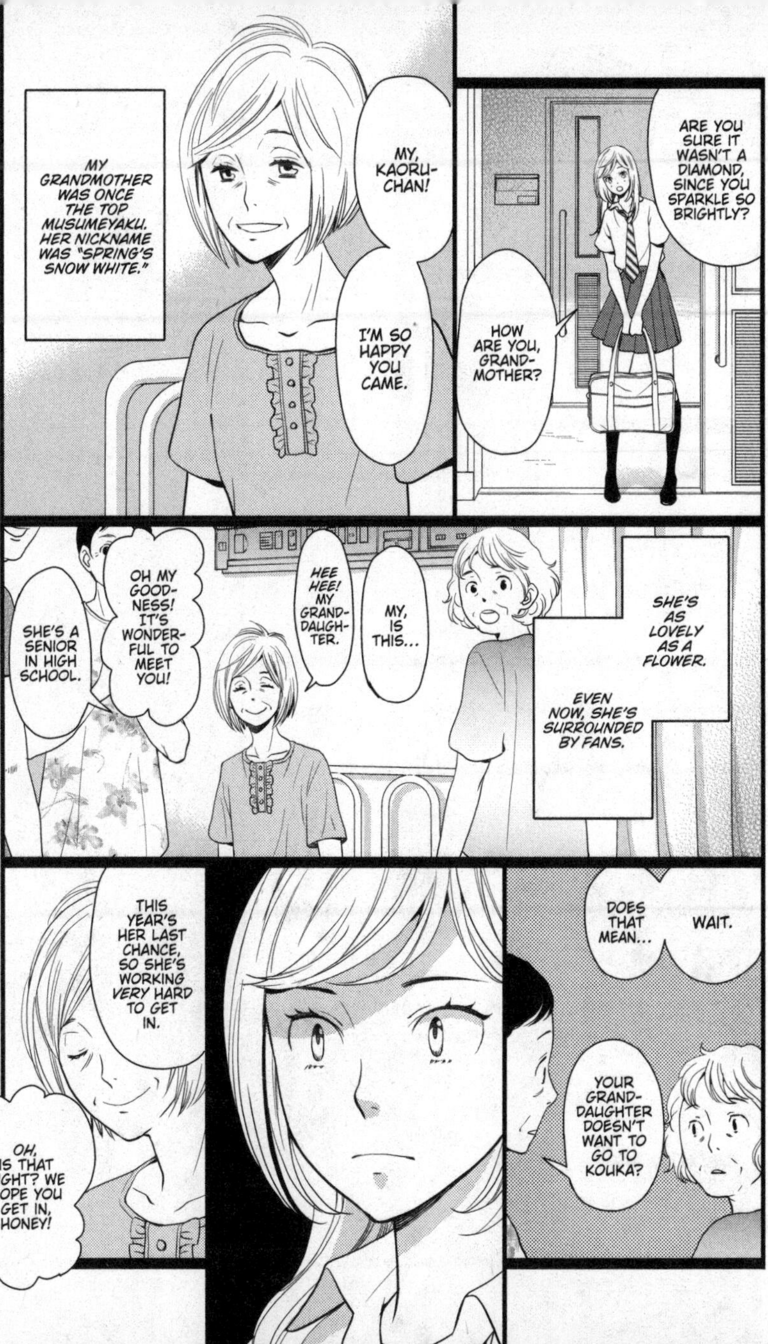
ARE YOU SURE IT WASN'T A DIAMOND, SINCE YOU SPARKLE SO BRIGHTLY?
HOW ARE YOU, GRANDMOTHER?
MY, KAORU-CHAN!
I'M SO HAPPY YOU CAME.
MY GRANDMOTHER WAS ONCE THE TOP MUSUMEYAKU. HER NICKNAME WAS "SPRING'S SNOW WHITE."
SHE'S AS LOVELY AS A FLOWER.
EVEN NOW, SHE'S SURROUNDED BY FANS.
MY, IS THIS...
HEE HEE! MY GRANDDAUGHTER.
OH MY GOODNESS! IT'S WONDERFUL TO MEET YOU!
SHE'S A SENIOR IN HIGH SCHOOL.
WAIT.
DOES THAT MEAN...
YOUR GRANDDAUGHTER DOESN'T WANT TO GO TO KOUKA?
THIS YEAR'S HER LAST CHANCE, SO SHE'S WORKING VERY HARD TO GET IN.
OH, IS THAT RIGHT? WE HOPE YOU GET IN, HONEY!

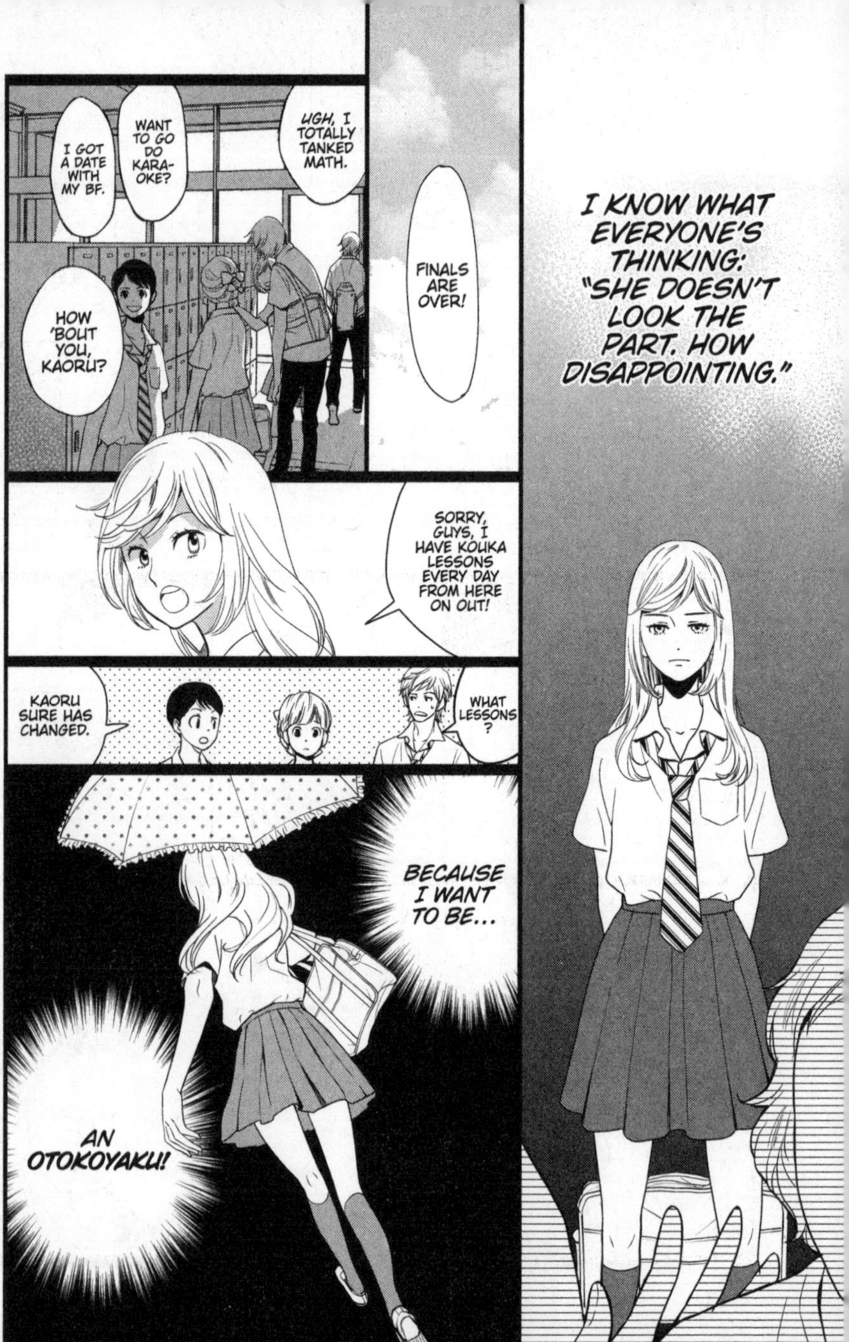
I KNOW WHAT EVERYONE'S THINKING: "SHE DOESN'T LOOK THE PART. HOW DISAPPOINTING."
FINALS ARE OVER!
UGH, I TOTALLY TANKED MATH.
WANT TO GO DO KARA-OKE?
I GOT A DATE WITH MY BF.
HOW 'BOUT YOU, KAORU?
SORRY, GUYS, I HAVE KOUKA LESSONS EVERY DAY FROM HERE ON OUT!
WHAT LESSONS?
KAORU SURE HAS CHANGED.
BECAUSE I WANT TO BE...
AN OTOKOYAKU!

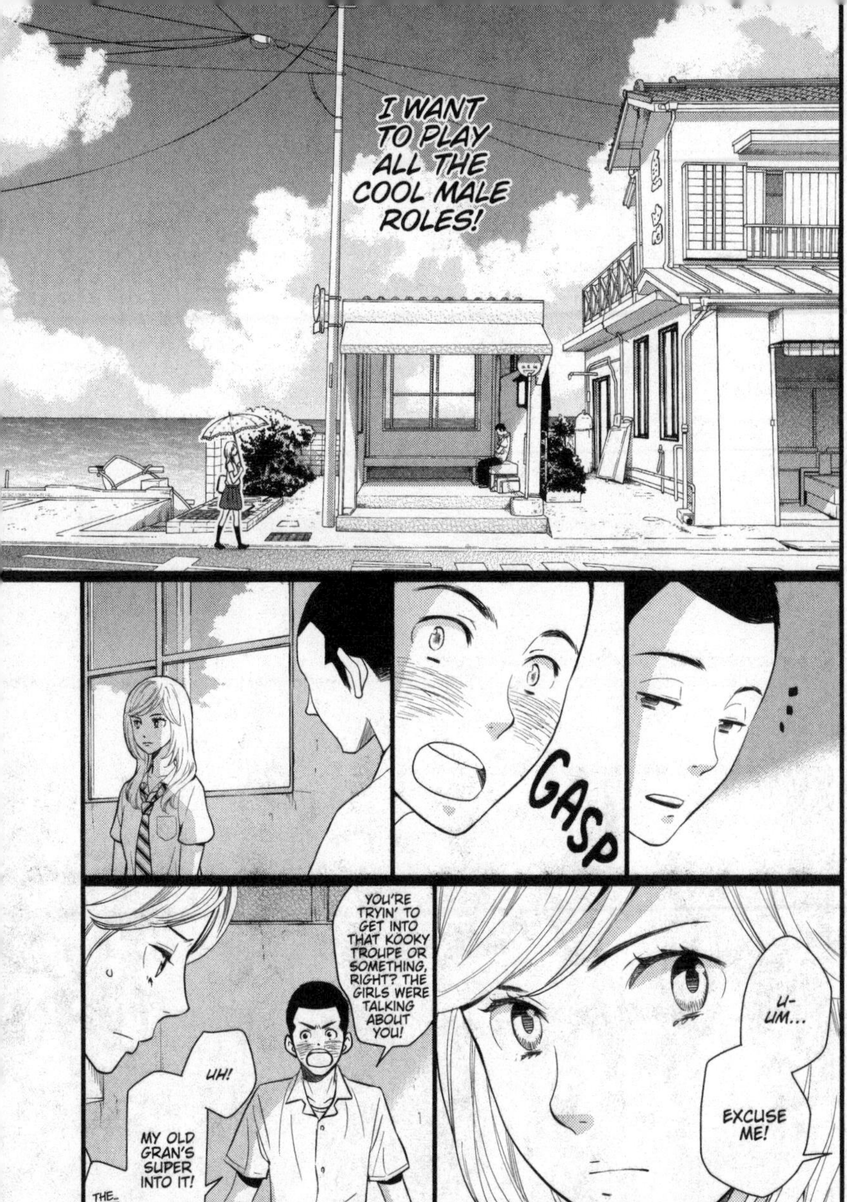
I WANT TO PLAY ALL THE COOL MALE ROLES!
GASP
U-UM...
EXCUSE ME!
YOU'RE TRYIN' TO GET INTO THAT KOOKY TROUPE OR SOMETHING, RIGHT? THE GIRLS WERE TALKING ABOUT YOU!
UH!
MY OLD GRAN'S SUPER INTO IT!
THE... WHATEVER TROUPE!

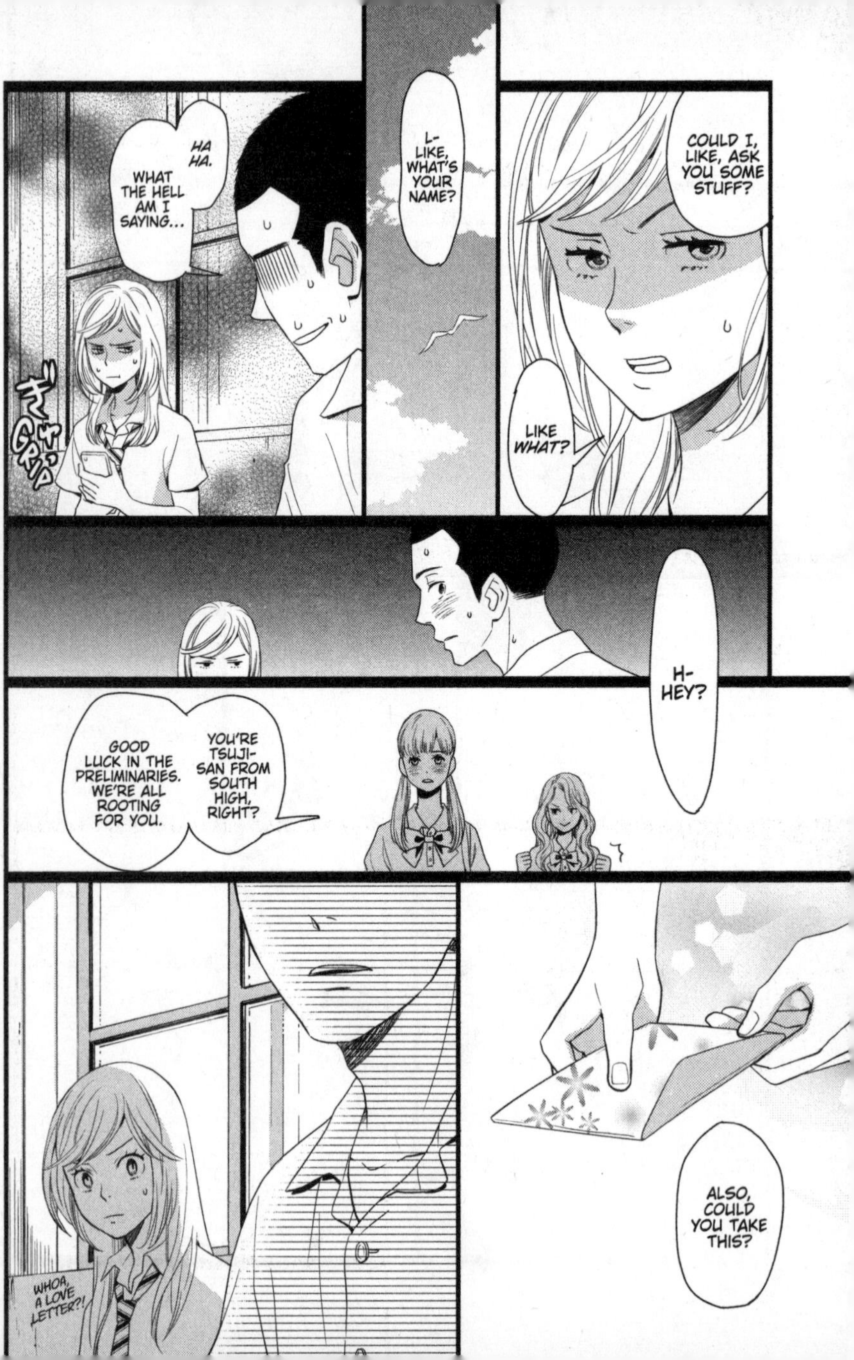
COULD I, LIKE, ASK YOU SOME STUFF?
LIKE WHAT?
L-LIKE, WHAT'S YOUR NAME?
HA HA. WHAT THE HELL AM I SAYING...
ぎゅっ GRIP
H-HEY?
YOU'RE TSUJI-SAN FROM SOUTH HIGH, RIGHT?
GOOD LUCK IN THE PRELIMINARIES. WE'RE ALL ROOTING FOR YOU.
ALSO, COULD YOU TAKE THIS?
WHOA, A LOVE LETTER?!

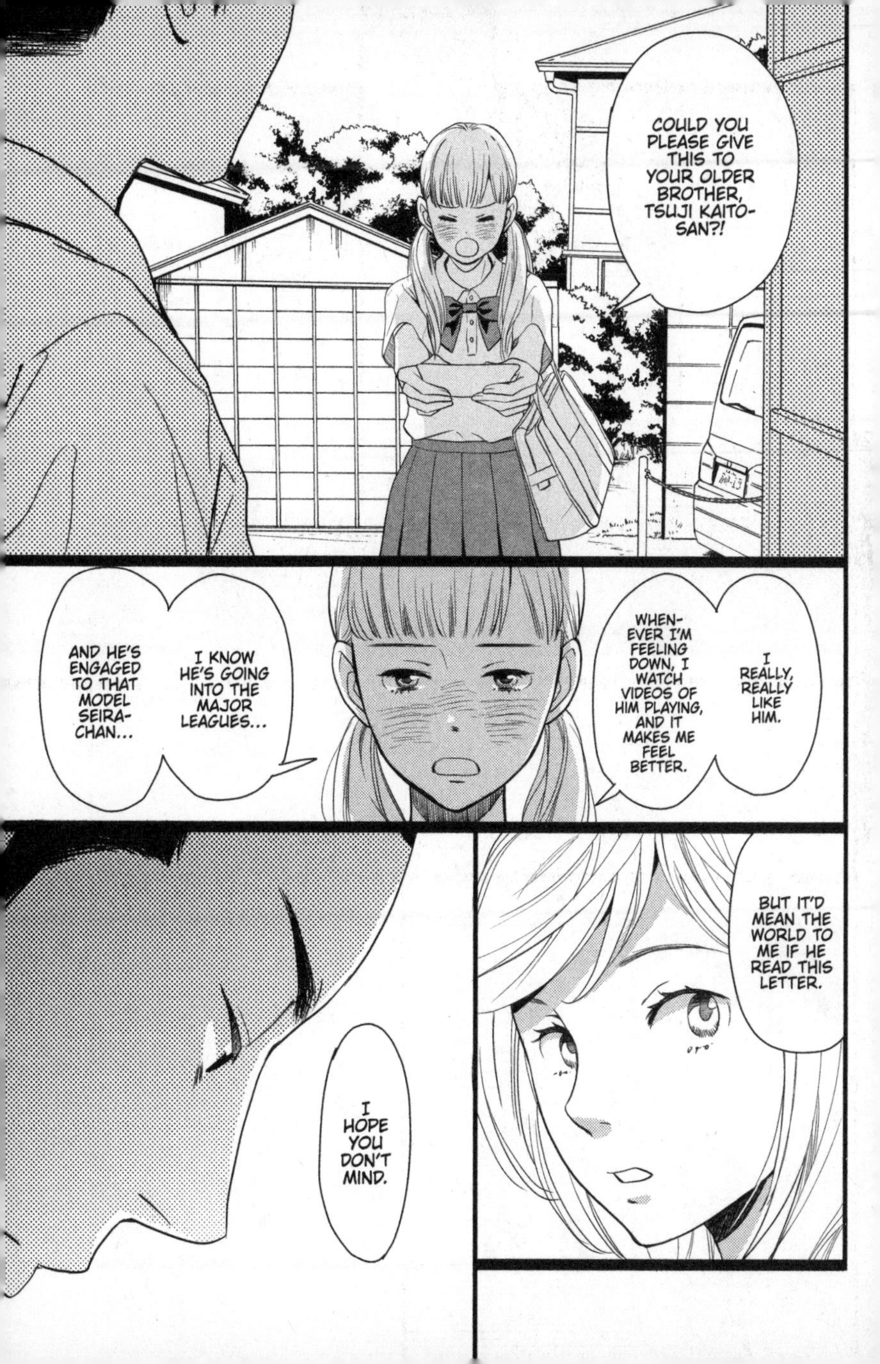
COULD YOU PLEASE GIVE THIS TO YOUR OLDER BROTHER, TSUJI KAITO-SAN?!
I REALLY, REALLY LIKE HIM.
WHEN-EVER I'M FEELING DOWN, I WATCH VIDEOS OF HIM PLAYING, AND IT MAKES ME FEEL BETTER.
I KNOW HE'S GOING INTO THE MAJOR LEAGUES...
AND HE'S ENGAGED TO THAT MODEL SEIRA-CHAN...
BUT IT'D MEAN THE WORLD TO ME IF HE READ THIS LETTER.
I HOPE YOU DON'T MIND.

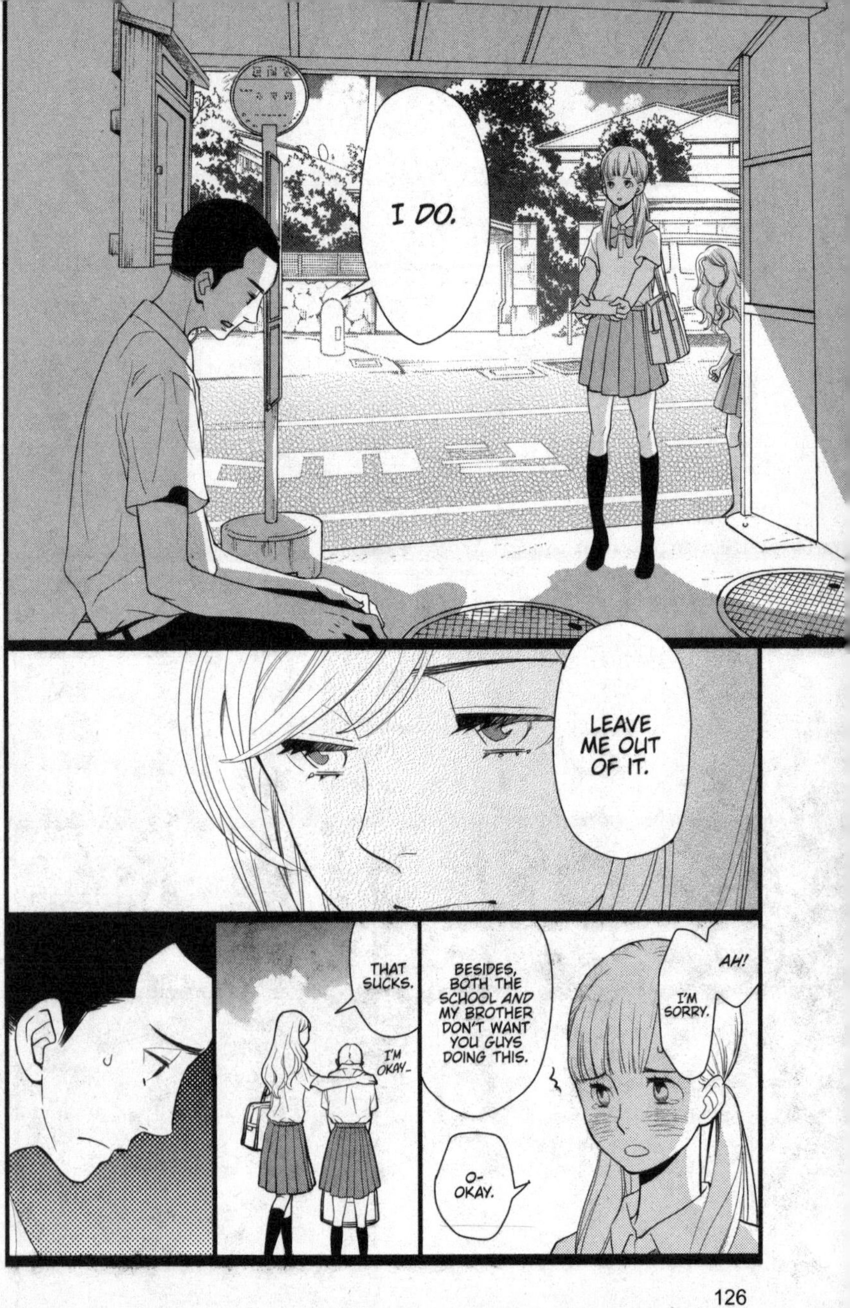
I DO.
LEAVE ME OUT OF IT.
AH!
I'M SORRY.
BESIDES, BOTH THE SCHOOL AND MY BROTHER DON'T WANT YOU GUYS DOING THIS.
O-OKAY.
THAT SUCKS.
I'M OKAY..

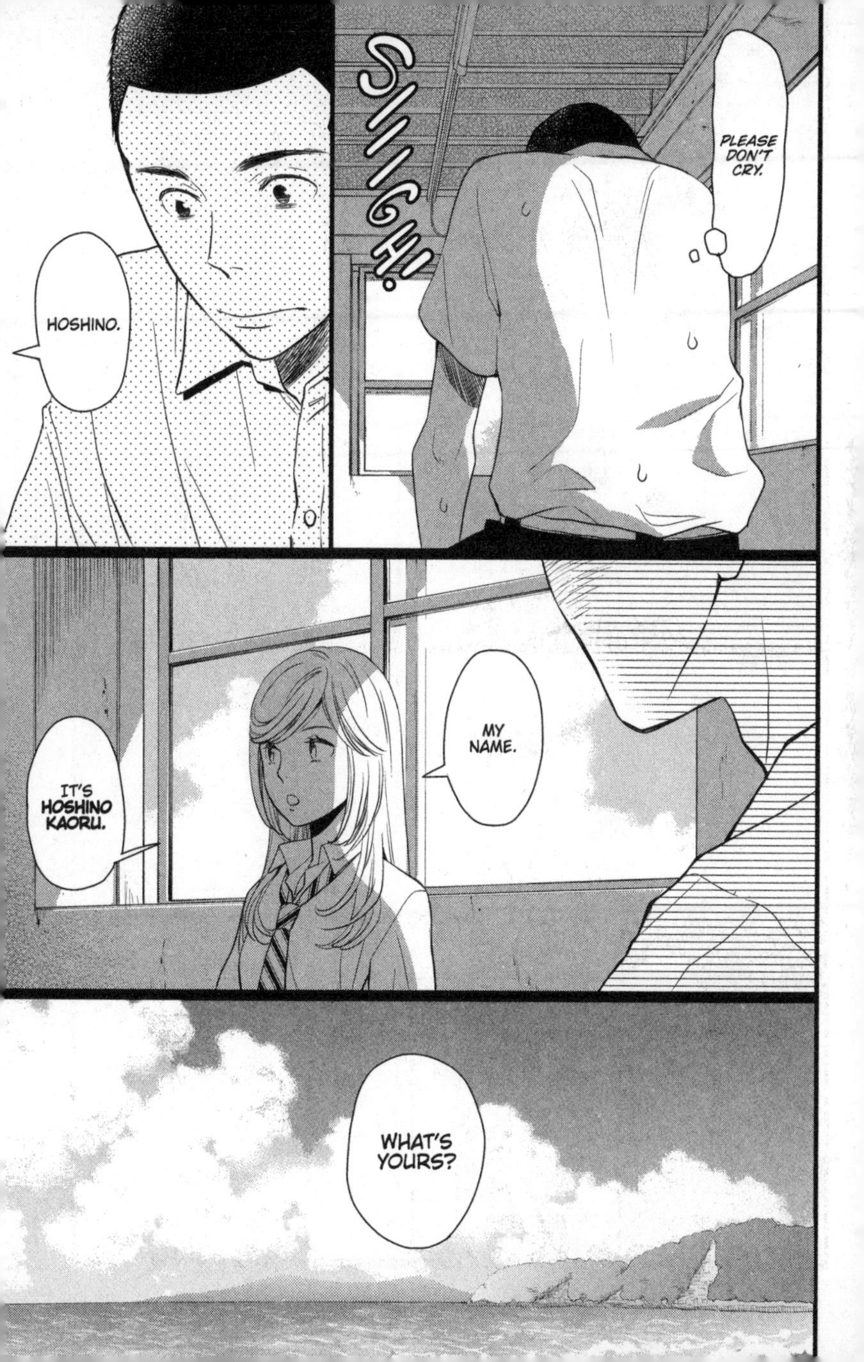
PLEASE DON'T CRY.
SIIIGH!
HOSHINO.
MY NAME.
IT'S HOSHINO KAORU.
WHAT'S YOURS?

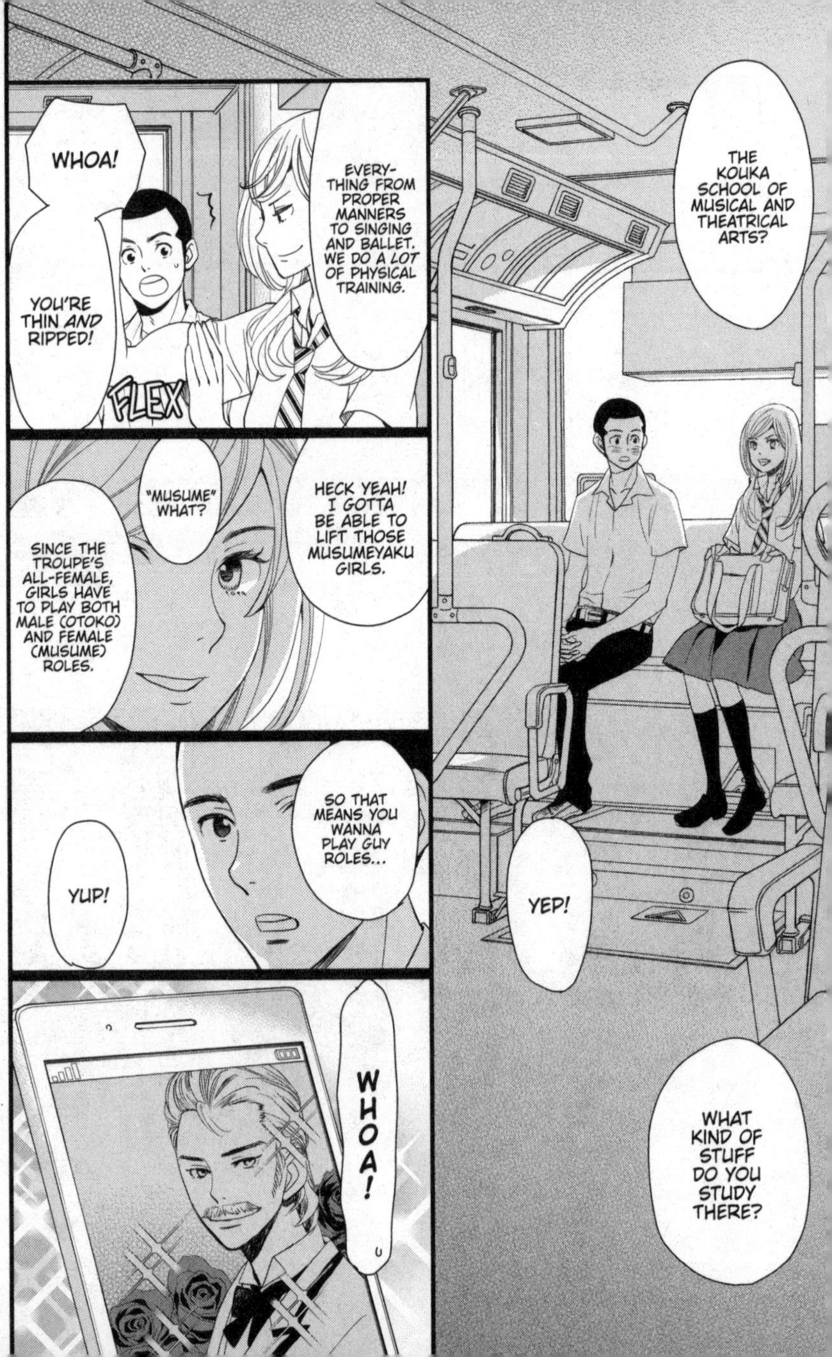
THE KOUKA SCHOOL OF MUSICAL AND THEATRICAL ARTS?
YEP!
WHAT KIND OF STUFF DO YOU STUDY THERE?
EVERY-THING FROM PROPER MANNERS TO SINGING AND BALLET. WE DO A LOT OF PHYSICAL TRAINING.
WHOA!
YOU'RE THIN *AND* RIPPED!
FLEX
HECK YEAH! I GOTTA BE ABLE TO LIFT THOSE MUSUMEYAKU GIRLS.
"MUSUME" WHAT?
SINCE THE TROUPE'S ALL-FEMALE, GIRLS HAVE TO PLAY BOTH MALE (OTOKO) AND FEMALE (MUSUME) ROLES.
SO THAT MEANS YOU WANNA PLAY GUY ROLES...
YUP!
WHOA!

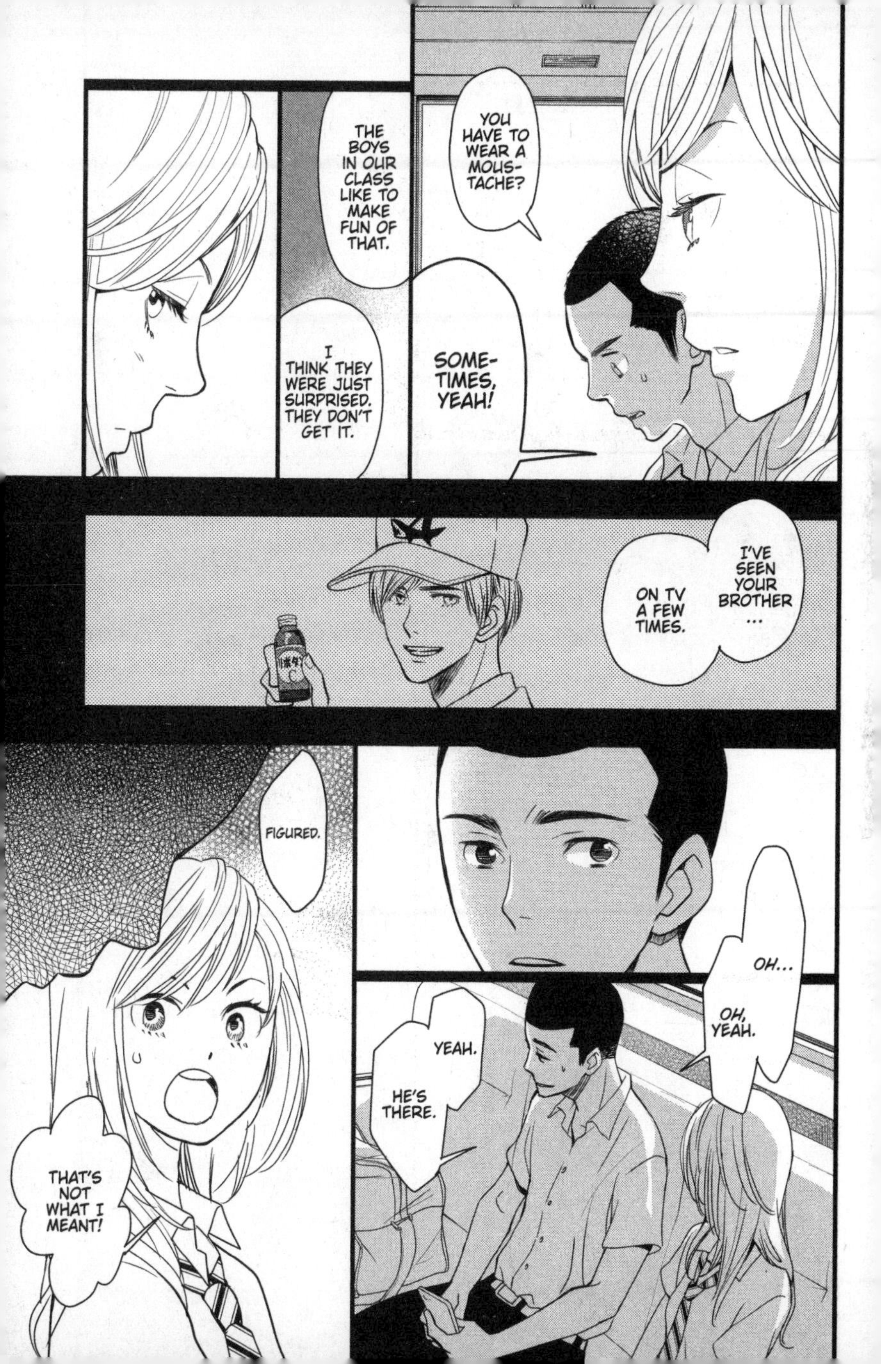
YOU HAVE TO WEAR A MOUS-TACHE?
SOME-TIMES, YEAH!
THE BOYS IN OUR CLASS LIKE TO MAKE FUN OF THAT.
I THINK THEY WERE JUST SURPRISED. THEY DON'T GET IT.
I'VE SEEN YOUR BROTHER ... ON TV A FEW TIMES.
OH... OH, YEAH.
YEAH. HE'S THERE.
FIGURED.
THAT'S NOT WHAT I MEANT!

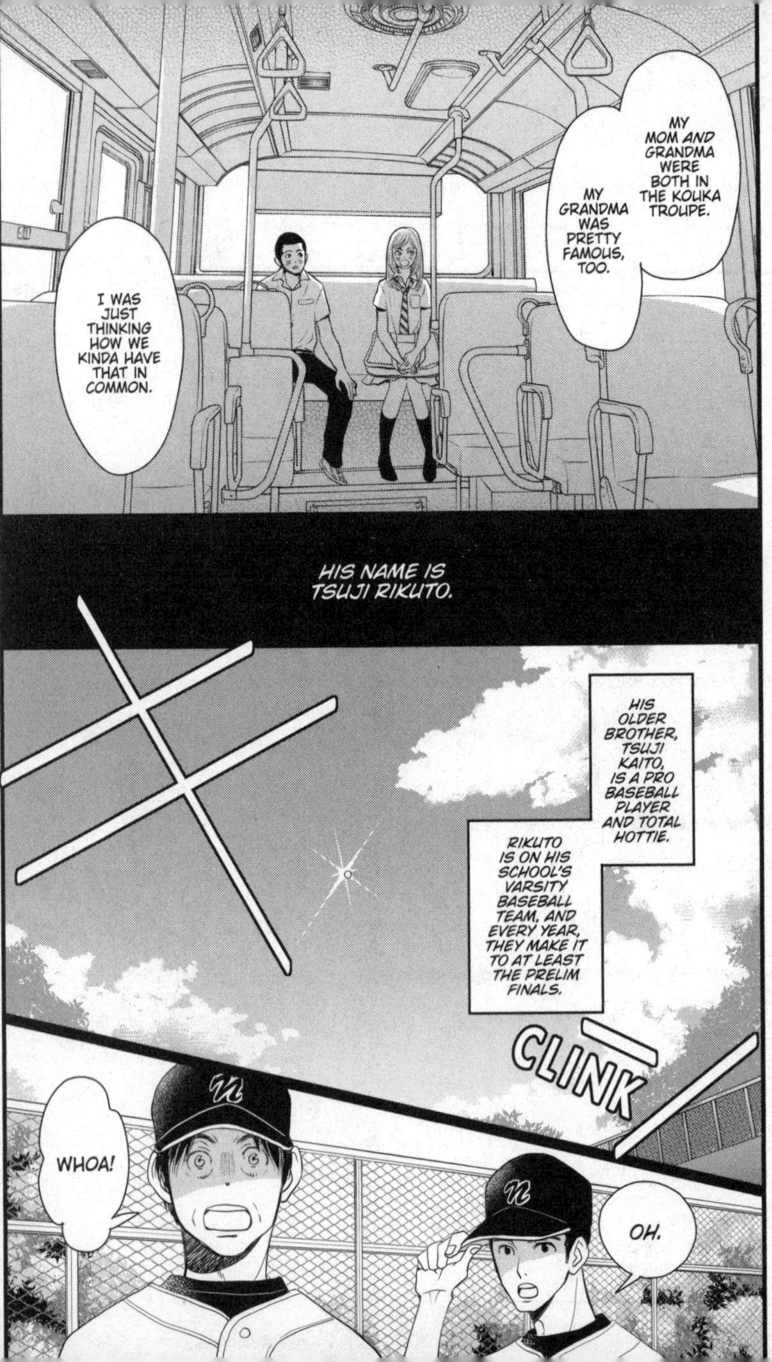
MY MOM AND GRANDMA WERE BOTH IN THE KOUKA TROUPE.
MY GRANDMA WAS PRETTY FAMOUS, TOO.
I WAS JUST THINKING HOW WE KINDA HAVE THAT IN COMMON.
HIS NAME IS TSUJI RIKUTO.
HIS OLDER BROTHER, TSUJI KAITO, IS A PRO BASEBALL PLAYER AND TOTAL HOTTIE.
RIKUTO IS ON HIS SCHOOL'S VARSITY BASEBALL TEAM, AND EVERY YEAR, THEY MAKE IT TO AT LEAST THE PRELIM FINALS.
CLINK
OH.
WHOA!

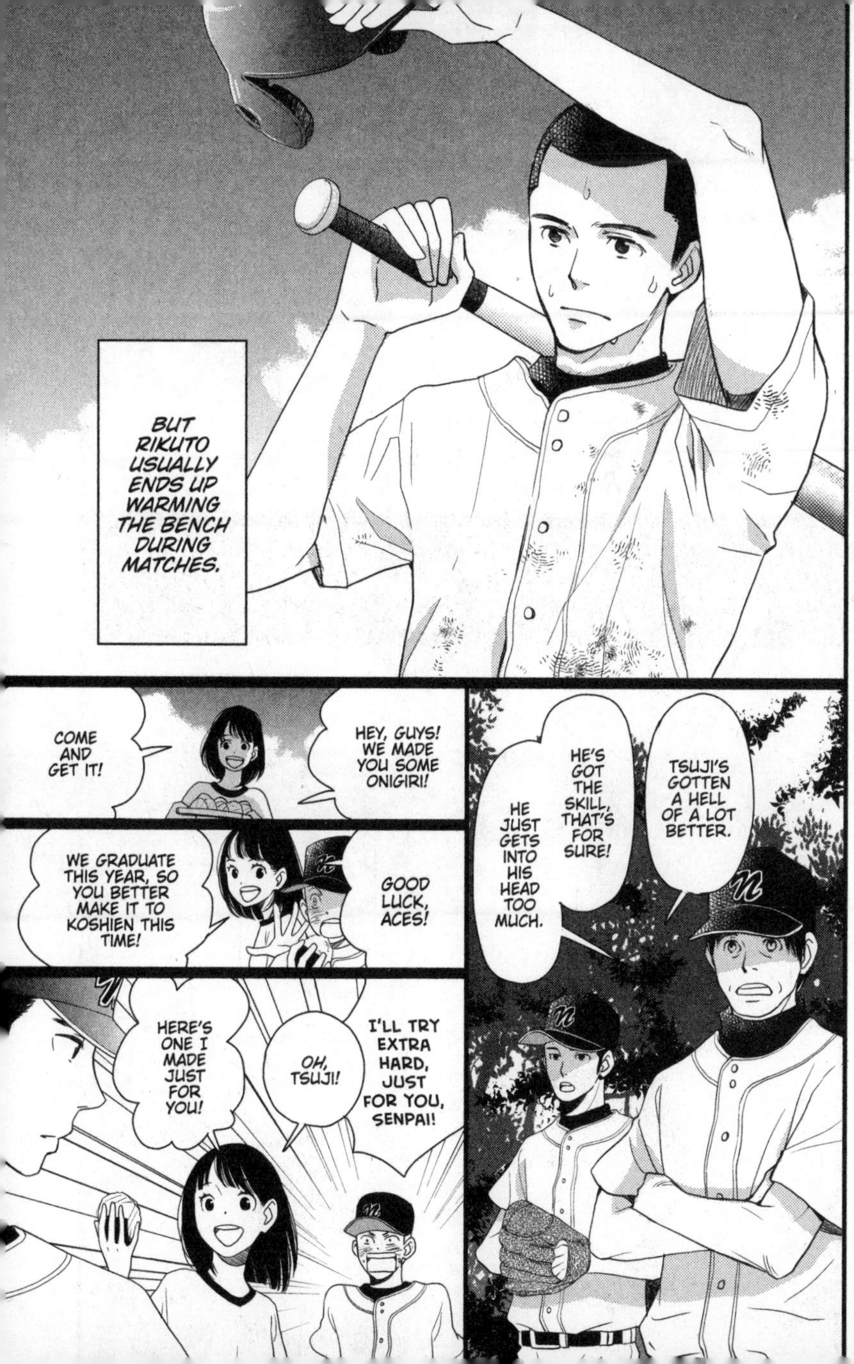
BUT RIKUTO USUALLY ENDS UP WARMING THE BENCH DURING MATCHES.
TSUJI'S GOTTEN A HELL OF A LOT BETTER.
HE'S GOT THE SKILL, THAT'S FOR SURE!
HE JUST GETS INTO HIS HEAD TOO MUCH.
HEY, GUYS! WE MADE YOU SOME ONIGIRI!
COME AND GET IT!
GOOD LUCK, ACES!
WE GRADUATE THIS YEAR, SO YOU BETTER MAKE IT TO KOSHIEN THIS TIME!
I'LL TRY EXTRA HARD, JUST FOR YOU, SENPAI!
OH, TSUJI!
HERE'S ONE I MADE JUST FOR YOU!

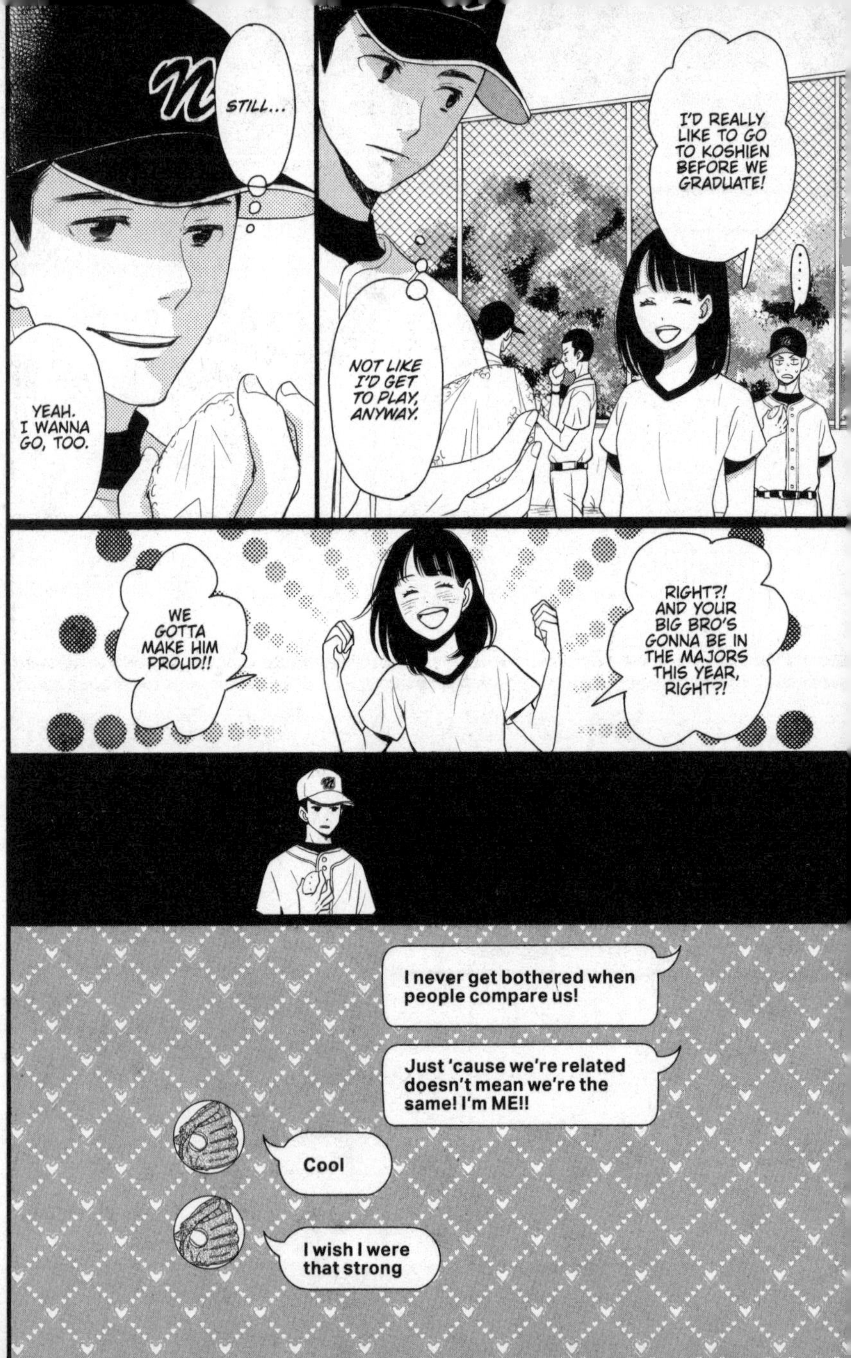
I'D REALLY LIKE TO GO TO KOSHIEN BEFORE WE GRADUATE!
...
NOT LIKE I'D GET TO PLAY, ANYWAY.
STILL...
YEAH. I WANNA GO, TOO.
RIGHT?! AND YOUR BIG BRO'S GONNA BE IN THE MAJORS THIS YEAR, RIGHT?!
WE GOTTA MAKE HIM PROUD!!
I never get bothered when people compare us!
Just 'cause we're related doesn't mean we're the same! I'm ME!!
Cool
I wish I were that strong

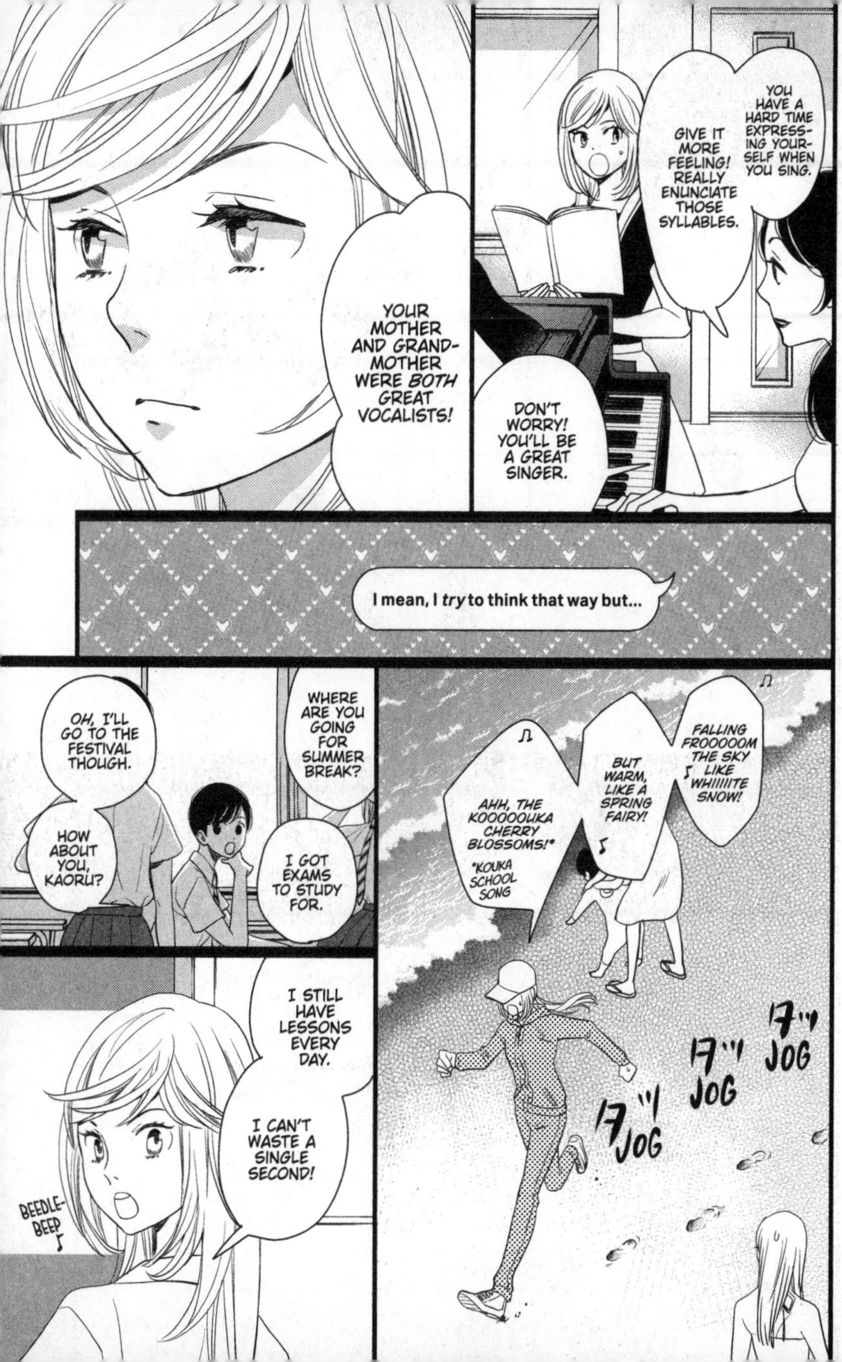
YOU HAVE A HARD TIME EXPRESSING YOURSELF WHEN YOU SING.
GIVE IT MORE FEELING! REALLY ENUNCIATE THOSE SYLLABLES.
DON'T WORRY! YOU'LL BE A GREAT SINGER.
YOUR MOTHER AND GRANDMOTHER WERE *BOTH* GREAT VOCALISTS!
I mean, I *try* to think that way but...
FALLING FROOOOOM THE SKY LIKE WHIIIIITE SNOW!
BUT WARM, LIKE A SPRING FAIRY!
AHH, THE KOOOOOUKA CHERRY BLOSSOMS!*
*KOUKA SCHOOL SONG
JOG
JOG
JOG
WHERE ARE YOU GOING FOR SUMMER BREAK?
OH, I'LL GO TO THE FESTIVAL THOUGH.
I GOT EXAMS TO STUDY FOR.
HOW ABOUT YOU, KAORU?
I STILL HAVE LESSONS EVERY DAY.
I CAN'T WASTE A SINGLE SECOND!
BEEDLE-BEEP

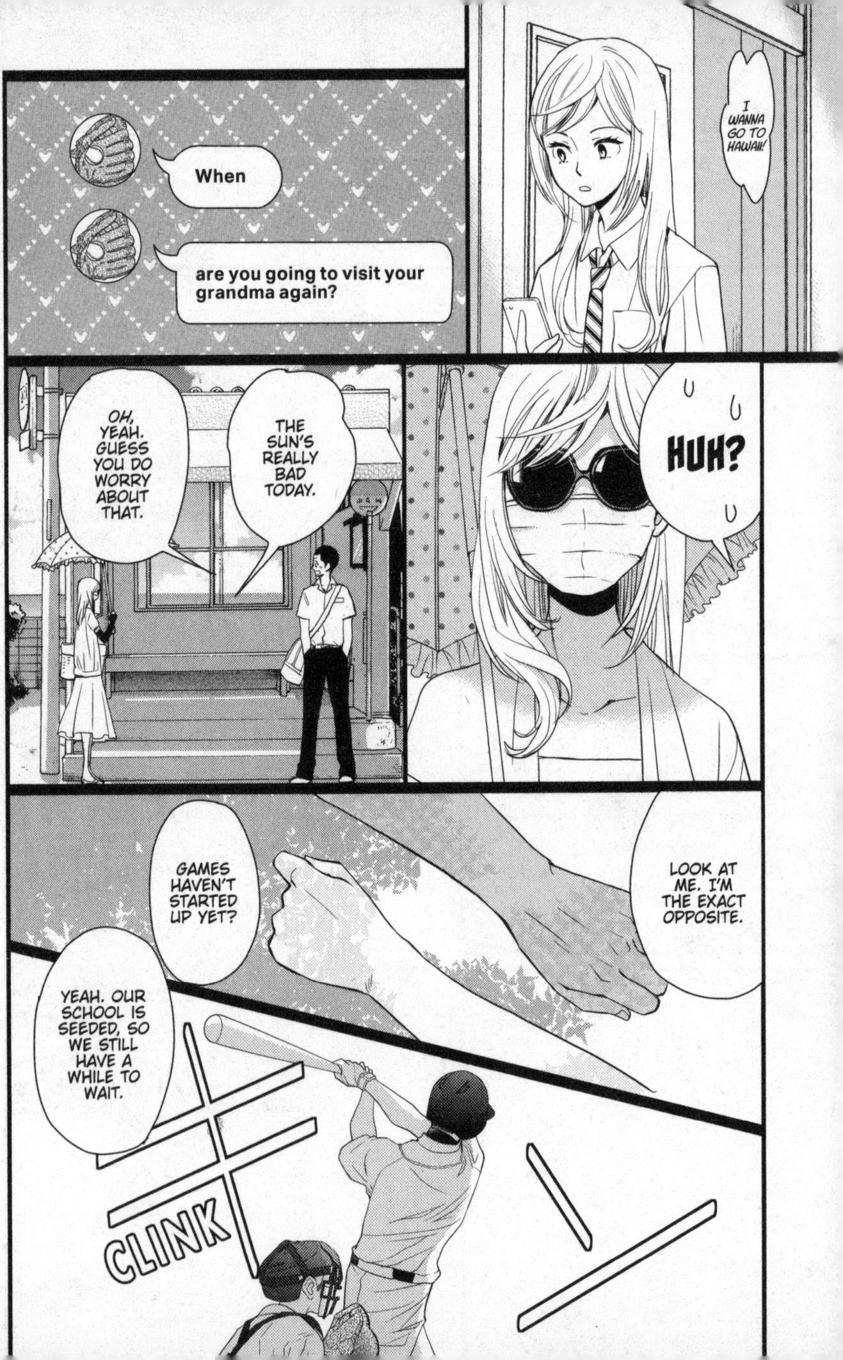
I WANNA GO TO HAWAII!
When
are you going to visit your grandma again?
HUH?
THE SUN'S REALLY BAD TODAY.
OH, YEAH. GUESS YOU DO WORRY ABOUT THAT.
LOOK AT ME. I'M THE EXACT OPPOSITE.
GAMES HAVEN'T STARTED UP YET?
YEAH. OUR SCHOOL IS SEEDED, SO WE STILL HAVE A WHILE TO WAIT.
CLINK

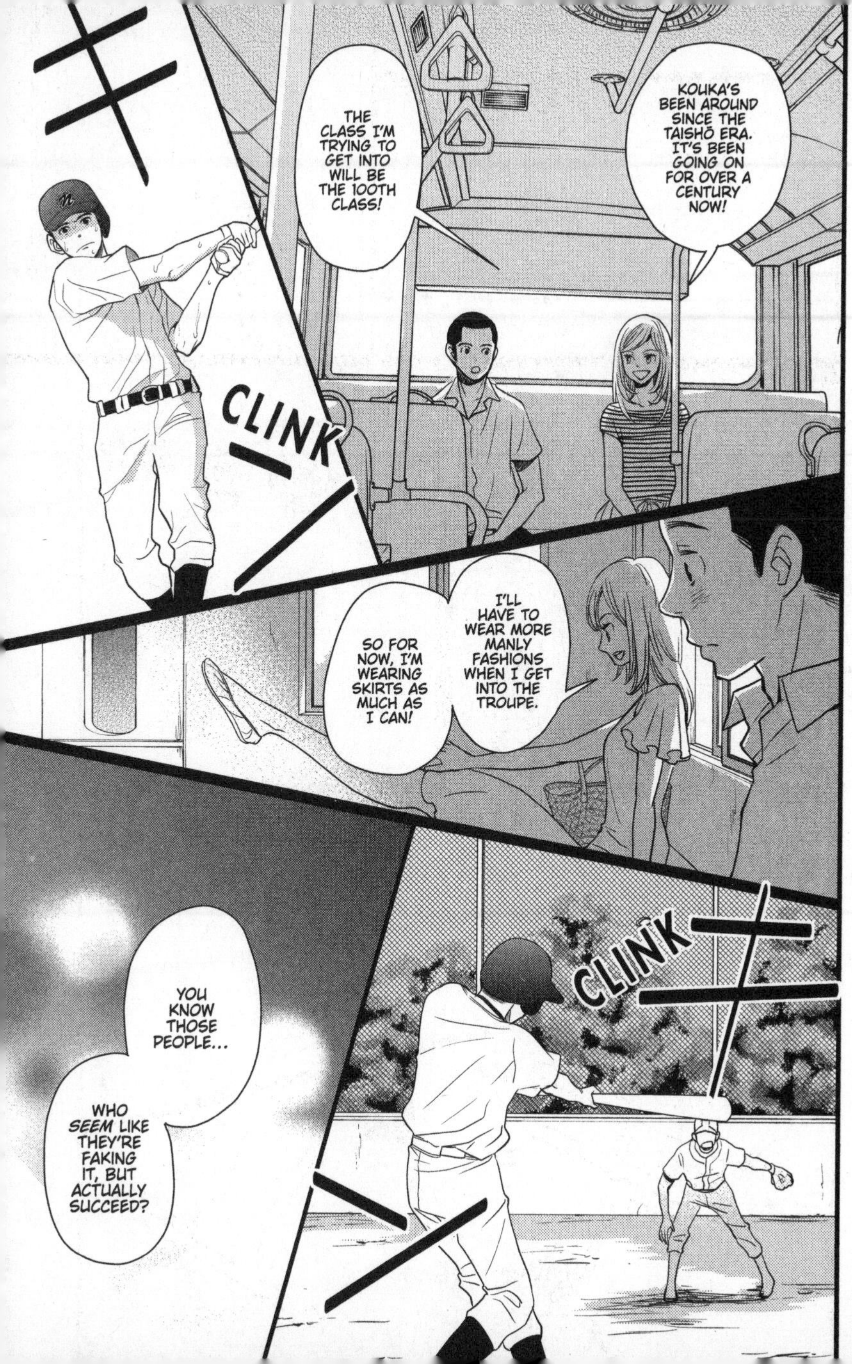
KOUKA'S BEEN AROUND SINCE THE TAISHŌ ERA. IT'S BEEN GOING ON FOR OVER A CENTURY NOW!
THE CLASS I'M TRYING TO GET INTO WILL BE THE 100TH CLASS!
CLINK
I'LL HAVE TO WEAR MORE MANLY FASHIONS WHEN I GET INTO THE TROUPE.
SO FOR NOW, I'M WEARING SKIRTS AS MUCH AS I CAN!
CLINK
YOU KNOW THOSE PEOPLE...
WHO SEEM LIKE THEY'RE FAKING IT, BUT ACTUALLY SUCCEED?

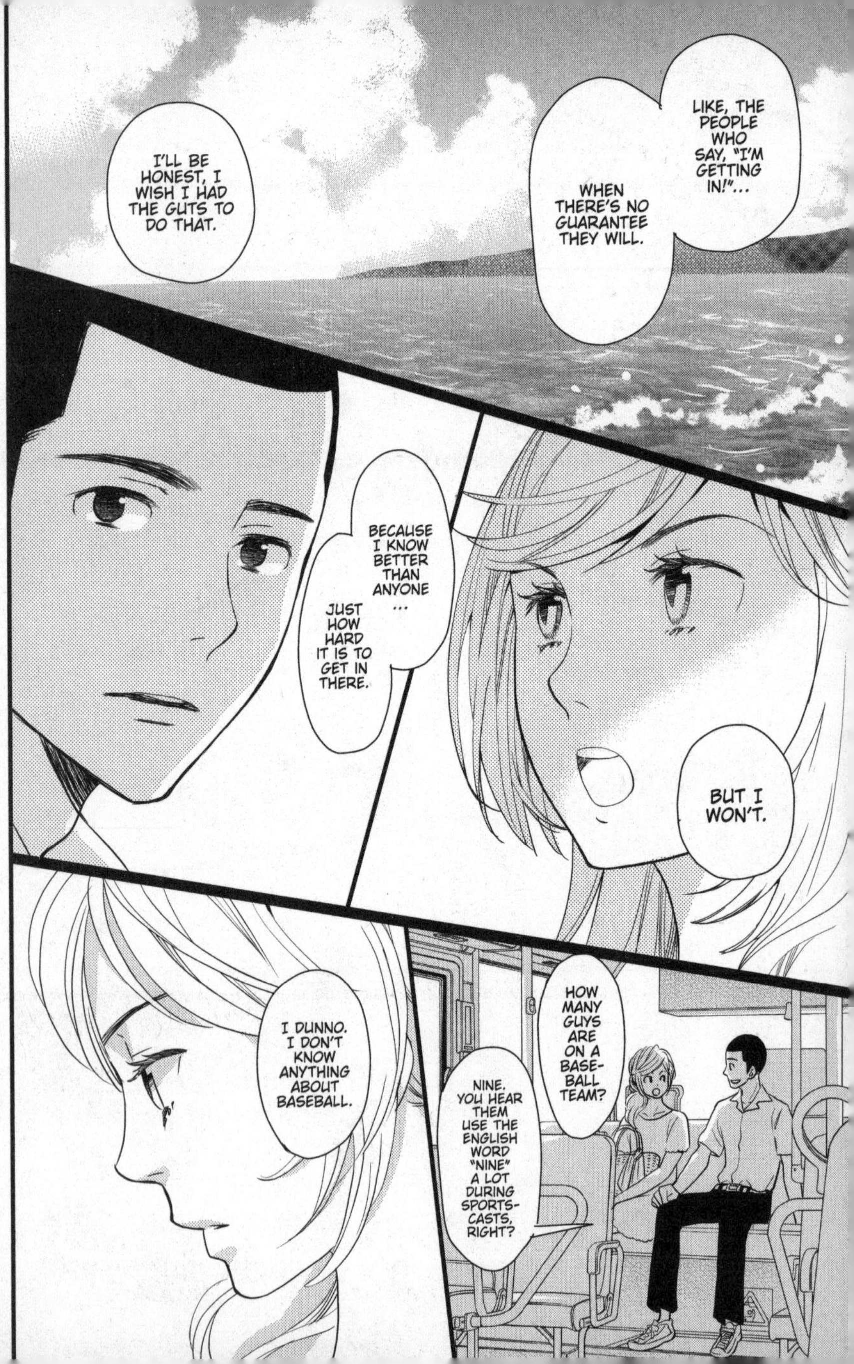
LIKE, THE PEOPLE WHO SAY, "I'M GETTING IN!"...
WHEN THERE'S NO GUARANTEE THEY WILL.
I'LL BE HONEST, I WISH I HAD THE GUTS TO DO THAT.
BUT I WON'T.
BECAUSE I KNOW BETTER THAN ANYONE...
JUST HOW HARD IT IS TO GET IN THERE.
HOW MANY GUYS ARE ON A BASEBALL TEAM?
NINE. YOU HEAR THEM USE THE ENGLISH WORD "NINE" A LOT DURING SPORTSCASTS, RIGHT?
I DUNNO. I DON'T KNOW ANYTHING ABOUT BASEBALL.

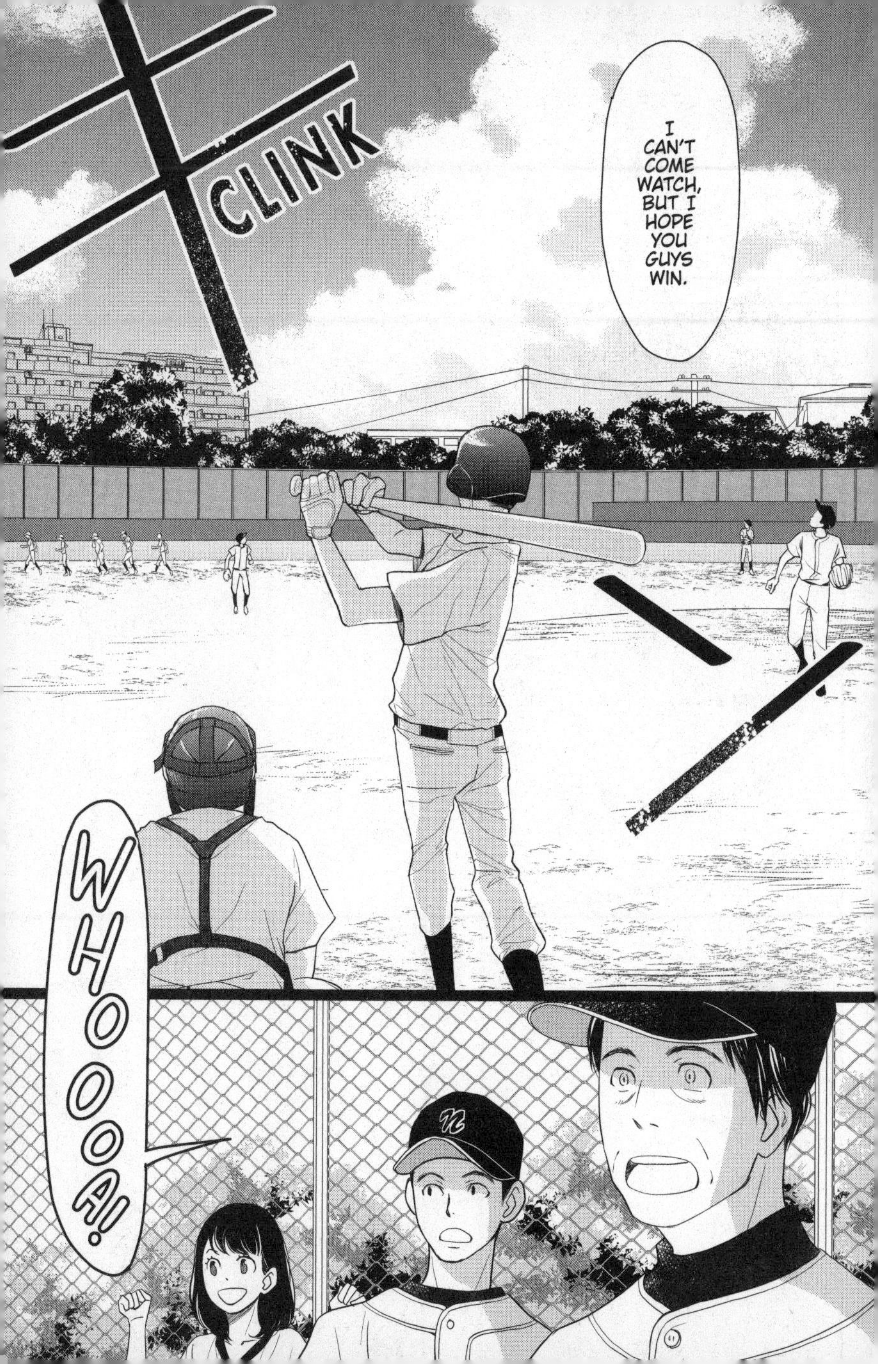
I CAN'T COME WATCH, BUT I HOPE YOU GUYS WIN.
CLINK
WHOOOOA!

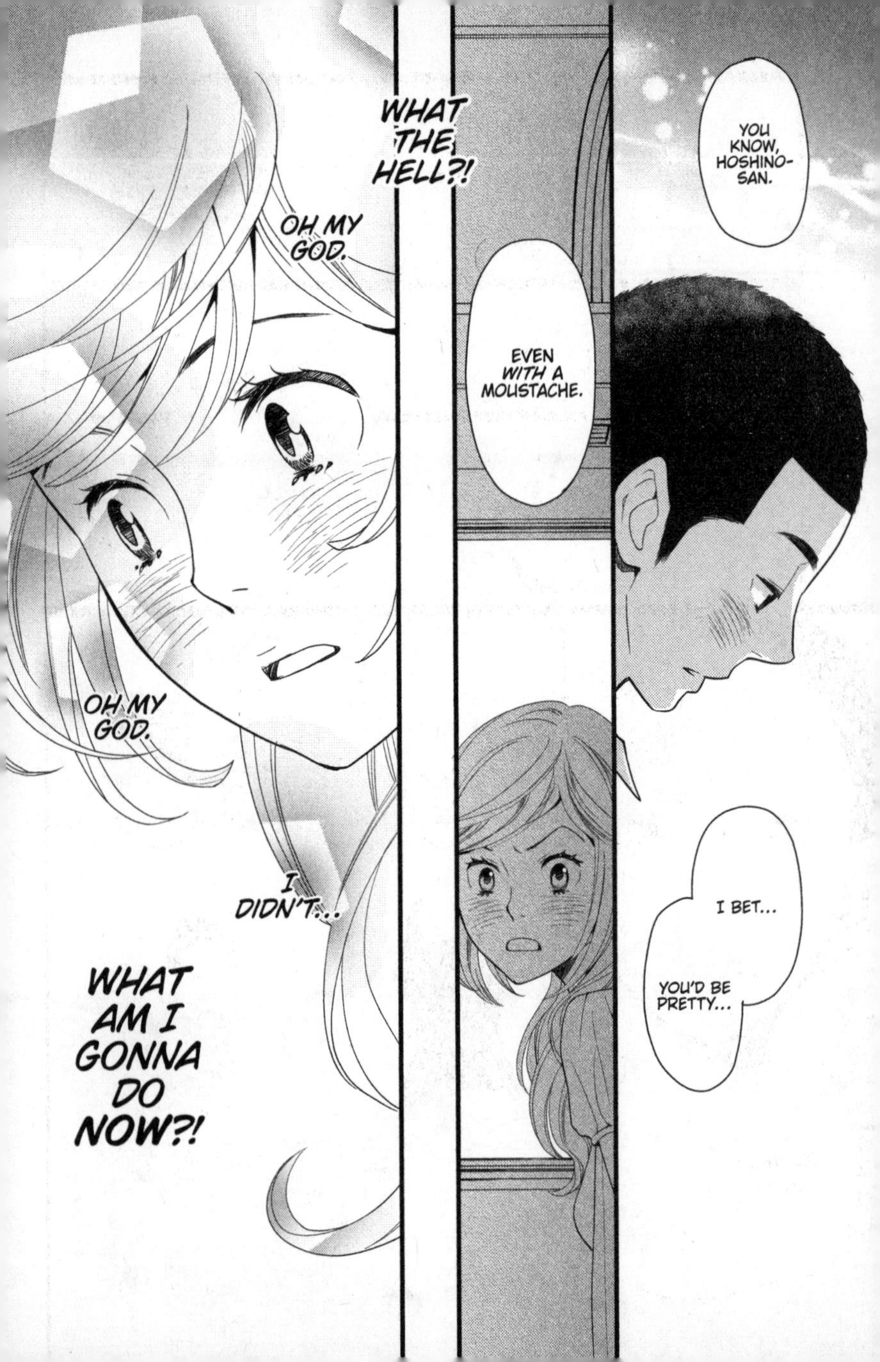
YOU KNOW, HOSHINO-SAN.
I BET...
YOU'D BE PRETTY...
EVEN WITH A MOUSTACHE.
WHAT THE HELL?!
OH MY GOD.
OH MY GOD.
I DIDN'T...
WHAT AM I GONNA DO NOW?!

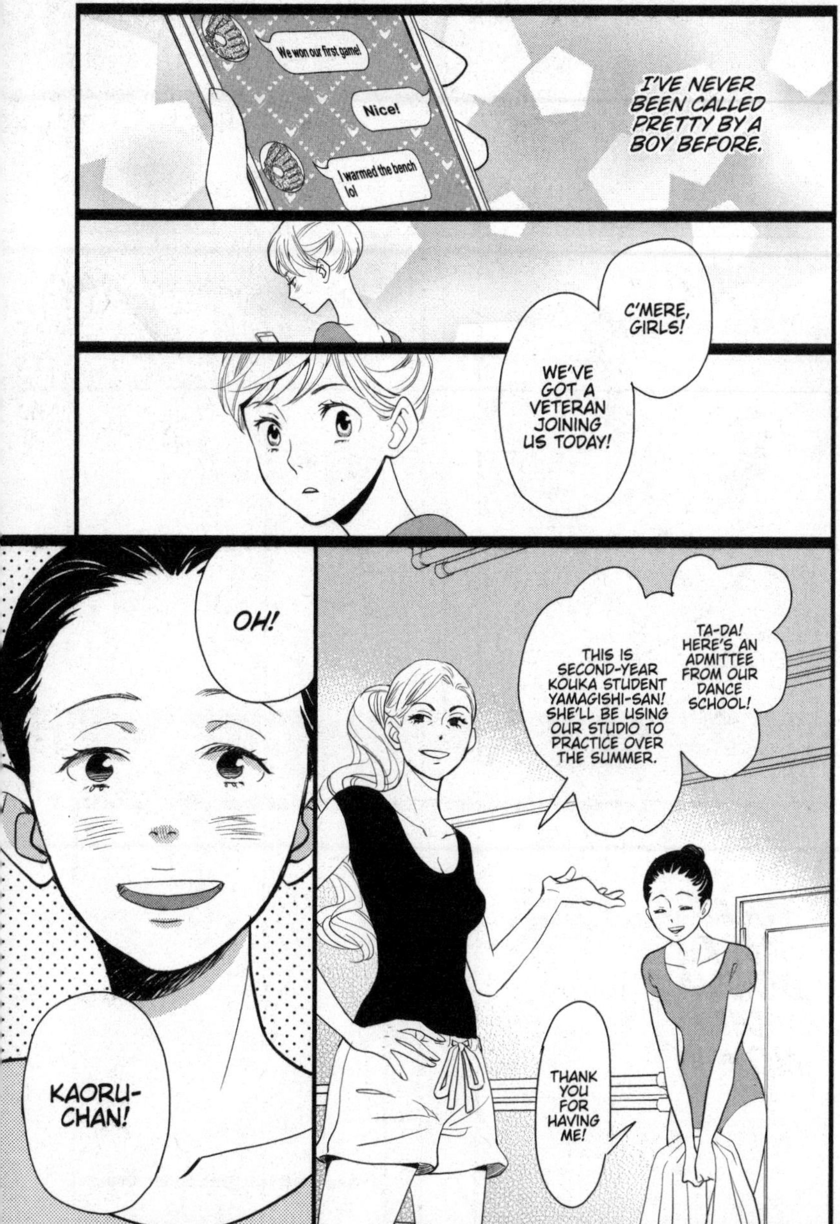
I'VE NEVER BEEN CALLED PRETTY BY A BOY BEFORE.
We won our first game!
Nice!
I warmed the bench lol
C'MERE, GIRLS!
WE'VE GOT A VETERAN JOINING US TODAY!
TA-DA! HERE'S AN ADMITTEE FROM OUR DANCE SCHOOL!
THIS IS SECOND-YEAR KOUKA STUDENT YAMAGISHI-SAN! SHE'LL BE USING OUR STUDIO TO PRACTICE OVER THE SUMMER.
THANK YOU FOR HAVING ME!
OH!
KAORU-CHAN!

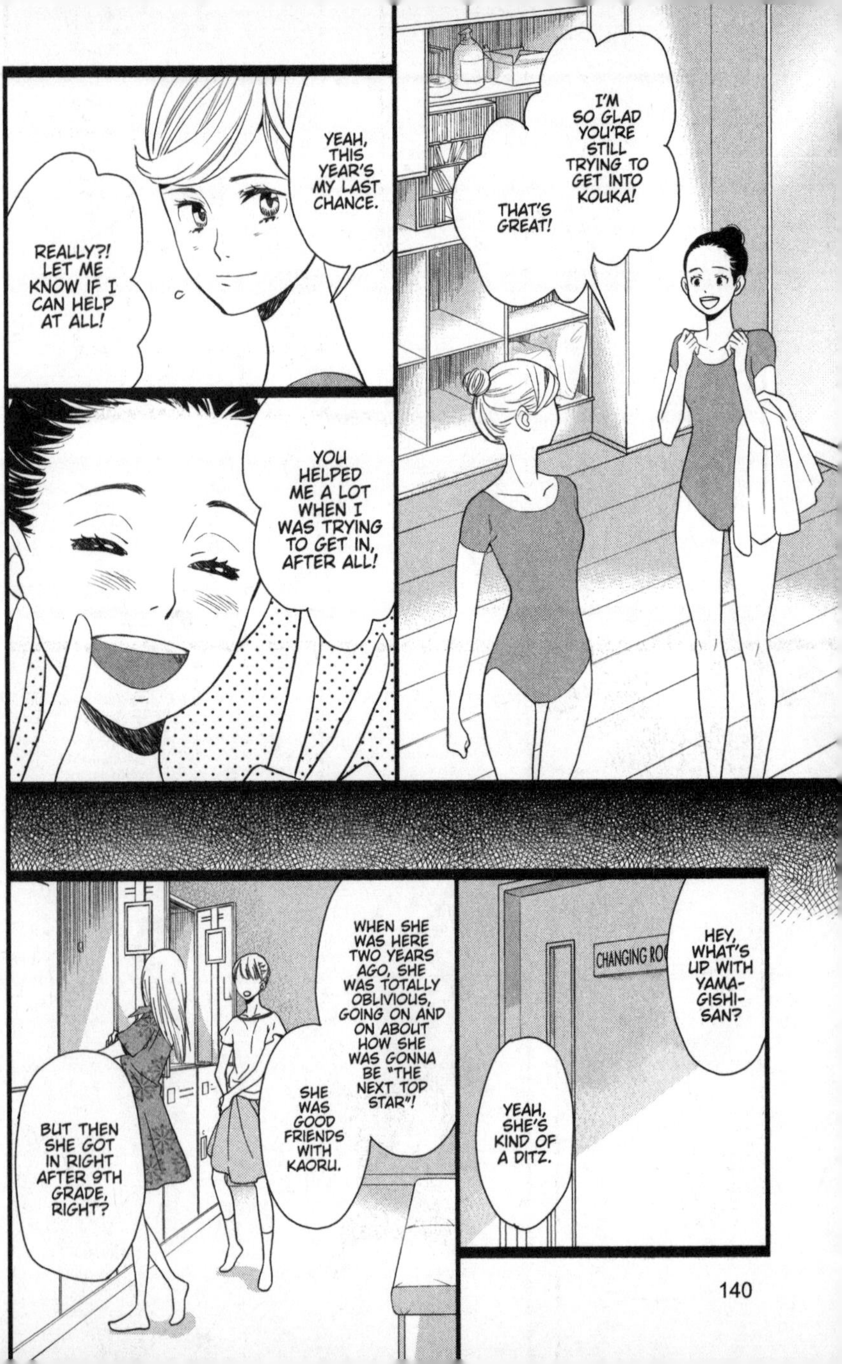
I'M SO GLAD YOU'RE STILL TRYING TO GET INTO KOUKA!
THAT'S GREAT!
YEAH, THIS YEAR'S MY LAST CHANCE.
REALLY?! LET ME KNOW IF I CAN HELP AT ALL!
YOU HELPED ME A LOT WHEN I WAS TRYING TO GET IN, AFTER ALL!
HEY, WHAT'S UP WITH YAMA-GISHI-SAN?
CHANGING RO
YEAH, SHE'S KIND OF A DITZ.
WHEN SHE WAS HERE TWO YEARS AGO, SHE WAS TOTALLY OBLIVIOUS, GOING ON AND ON ABOUT HOW SHE WAS GONNA BE "THE NEXT TOP STAR"!
SHE WAS GOOD FRIENDS WITH KAORU.
BUT THEN SHE GOT IN RIGHT AFTER 9TH GRADE, RIGHT?

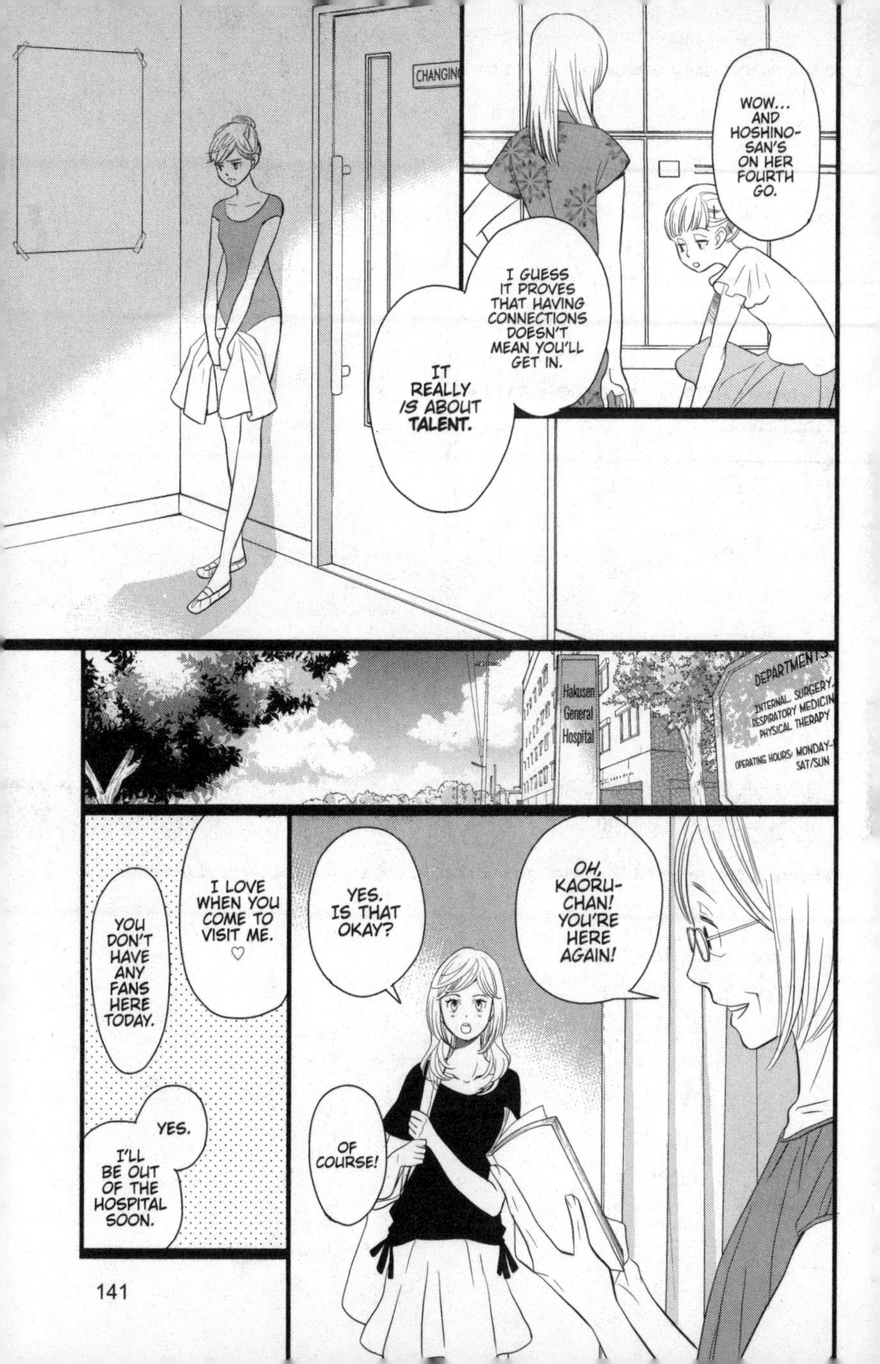
CHANGIN
WOW... AND HOSHINO-SAN'S ON HER FOURTH GO.
I GUESS IT PROVES THAT HAVING CONNECTIONS DOESN'T MEAN YOU'LL GET IN.
IT REALLY IS ABOUT TALENT.
Hakusen General Hospital
DEPARTMENTS
INTERNAL, SURGERY,
RESPIRATORY MEDICIN
PHYSICAL THERAPY
OPERATING HOURS: MONDAY-
SAT/SUN
OH, KAORU-CHAN! YOU'RE HERE AGAIN!
YES. IS THAT OKAY?
OF COURSE!
I LOVE WHEN YOU COME TO VISIT ME. ♡
YOU DON'T HAVE ANY FANS HERE TODAY.
YES. I'LL BE OUT OF THE HOSPITAL SOON.

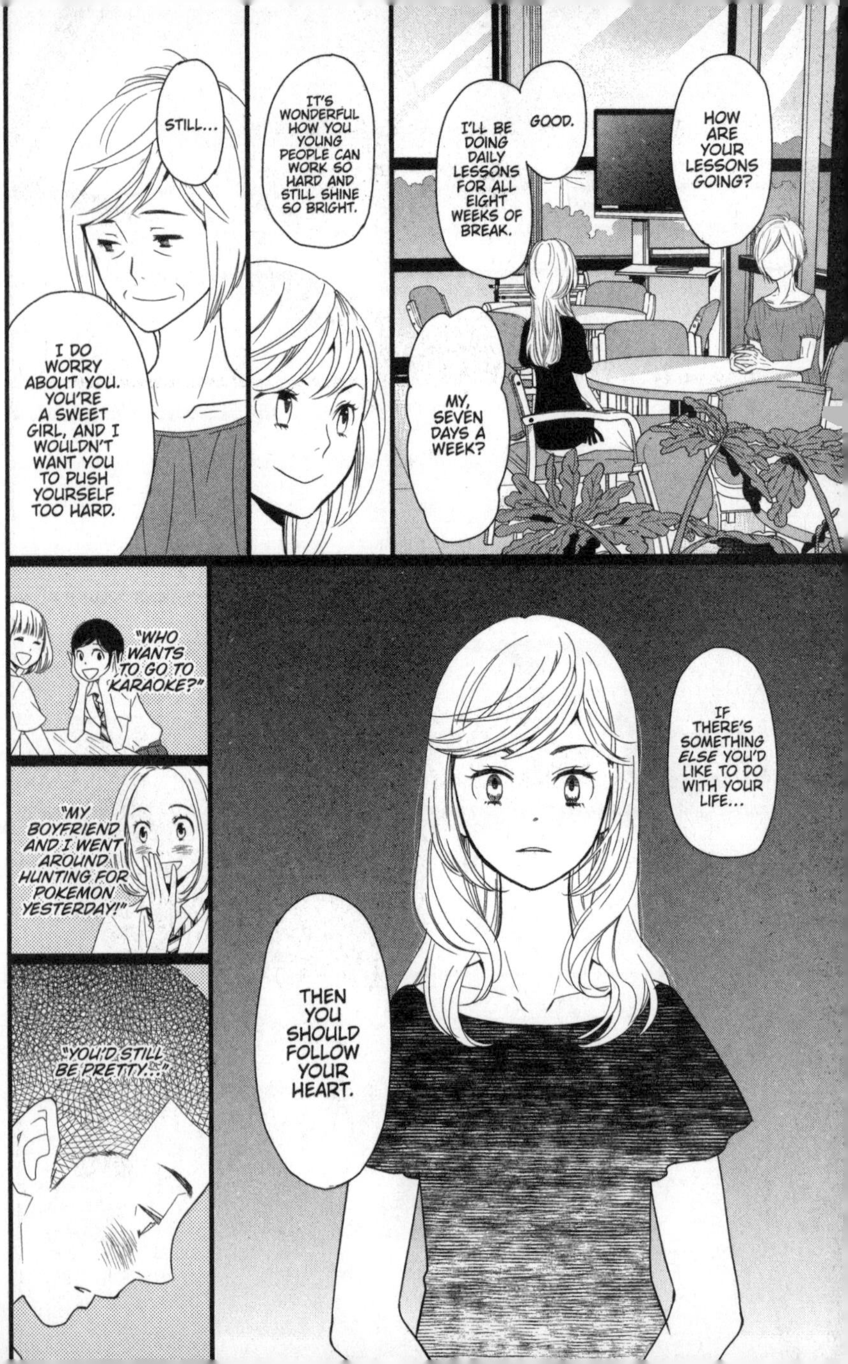
HOW ARE YOUR LESSONS GOING?
GOOD.
I'LL BE DOING DAILY LESSONS FOR ALL EIGHT WEEKS OF BREAK.
MY, SEVEN DAYS A WEEK?
IT'S WONDERFUL HOW YOU YOUNG PEOPLE CAN WORK SO HARD AND STILL SHINE SO BRIGHT.
STILL...
I DO WORRY ABOUT YOU. YOU'RE A SWEET GIRL, AND I WOULDN'T WANT YOU TO PUSH YOURSELF TOO HARD.
IF THERE'S SOMETHING ELSE YOU'D LIKE TO DO WITH YOUR LIFE...
THEN YOU SHOULD FOLLOW YOUR HEART.
"WHO WANTS TO GO TO KARAOKE?"
"MY BOYFRIEND AND I WENT AROUND HUNTING FOR POKEMON YESTERDAY!"
"YOU'D STILL BE PRETTY..."

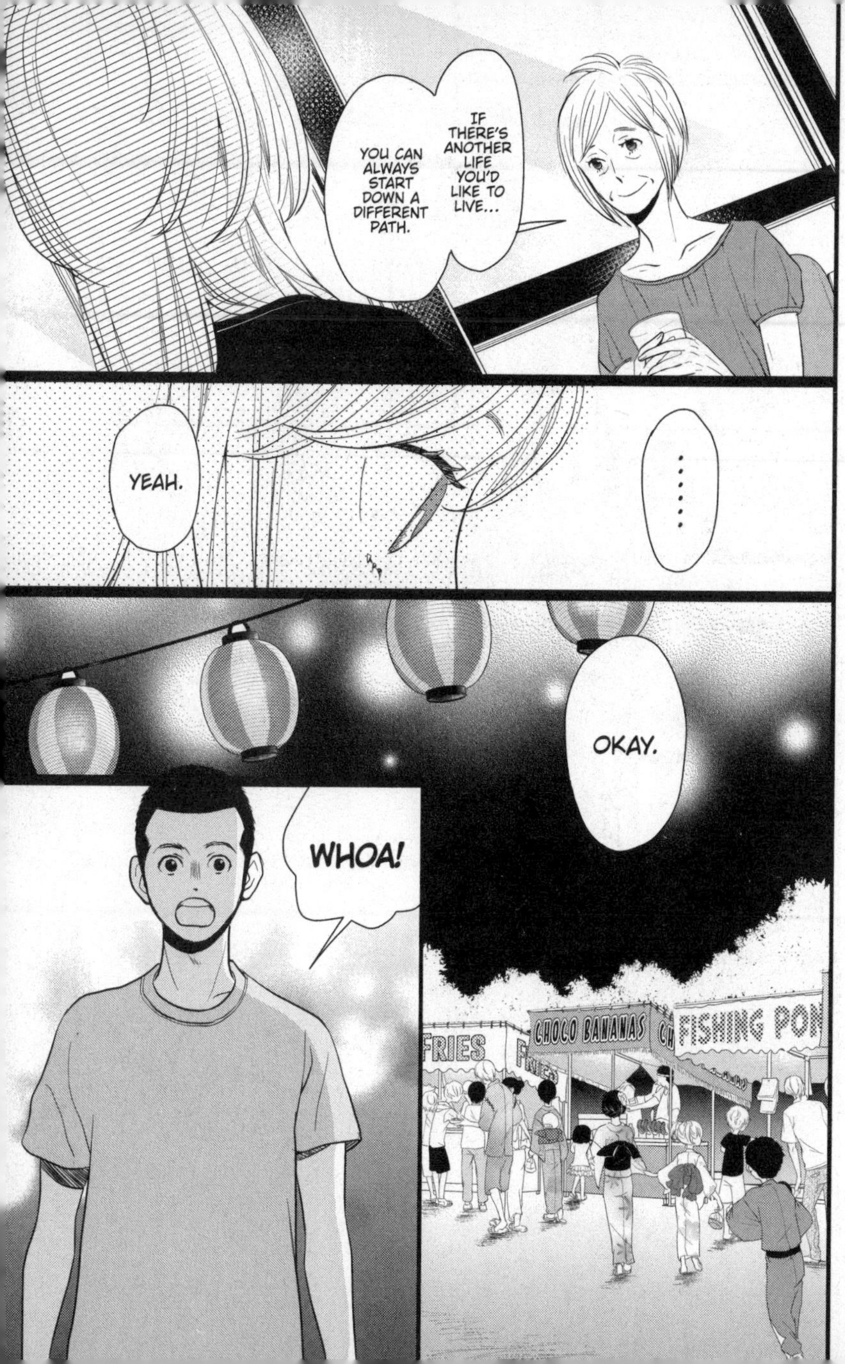
IF THERE'S ANOTHER LIFE YOU'D LIKE TO LIVE...
YOU CAN ALWAYS START DOWN A DIFFERENT PATH.
......
YEAH.
OKAY.
FISHING PON
CHOCO BANANAS
FRIES
WHOA!

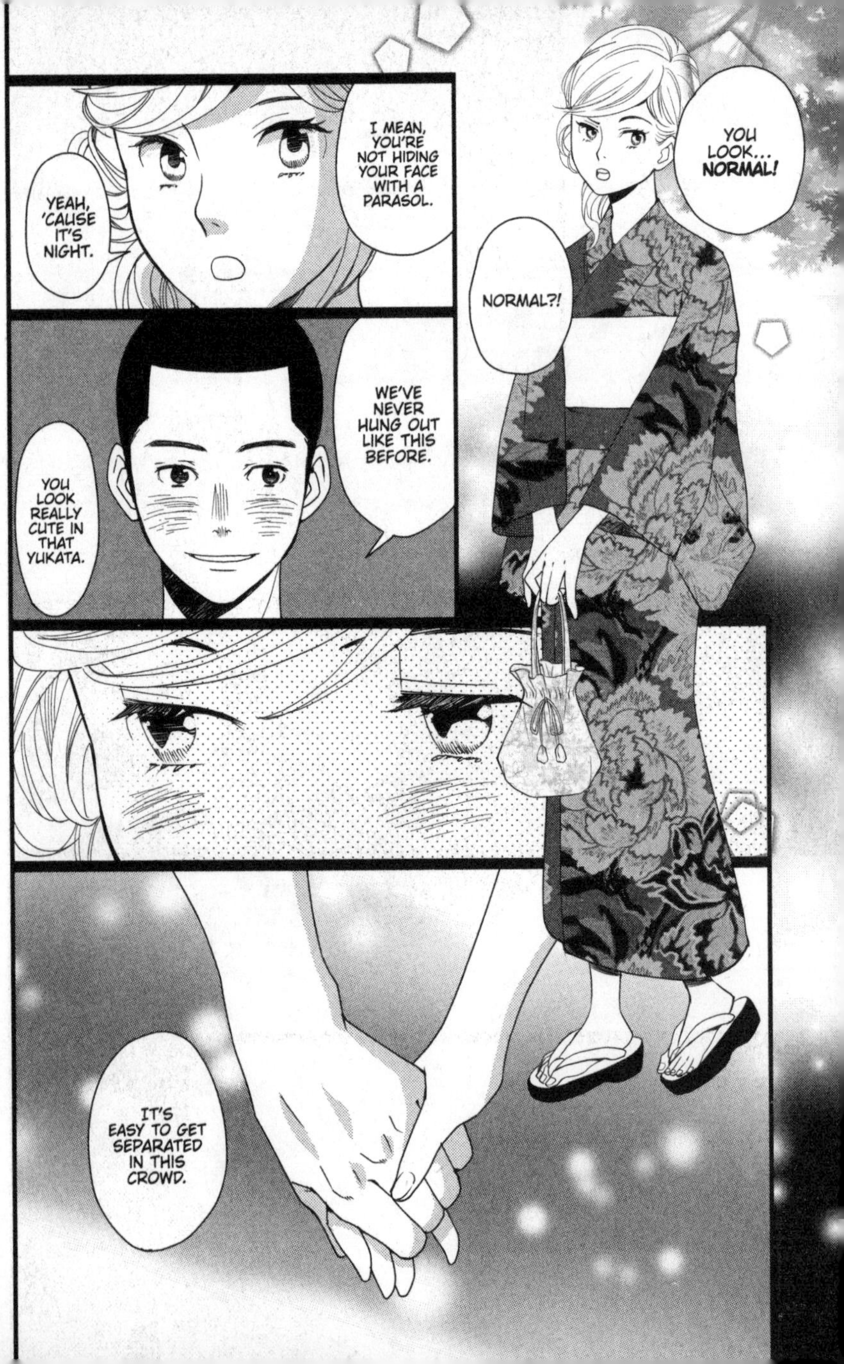
YOU LOOK... NORMAL!
NORMAL?!
I MEAN, YOU'RE NOT HIDING YOUR FACE WITH A PARASOL.
YEAH, 'CAUSE IT'S NIGHT.
WE'VE NEVER HUNG OUT LIKE THIS BEFORE.
YOU LOOK REALLY CUTE IN THAT YUKATA.
IT'S EASY TO GET SEPARATED IN THIS CROWD.

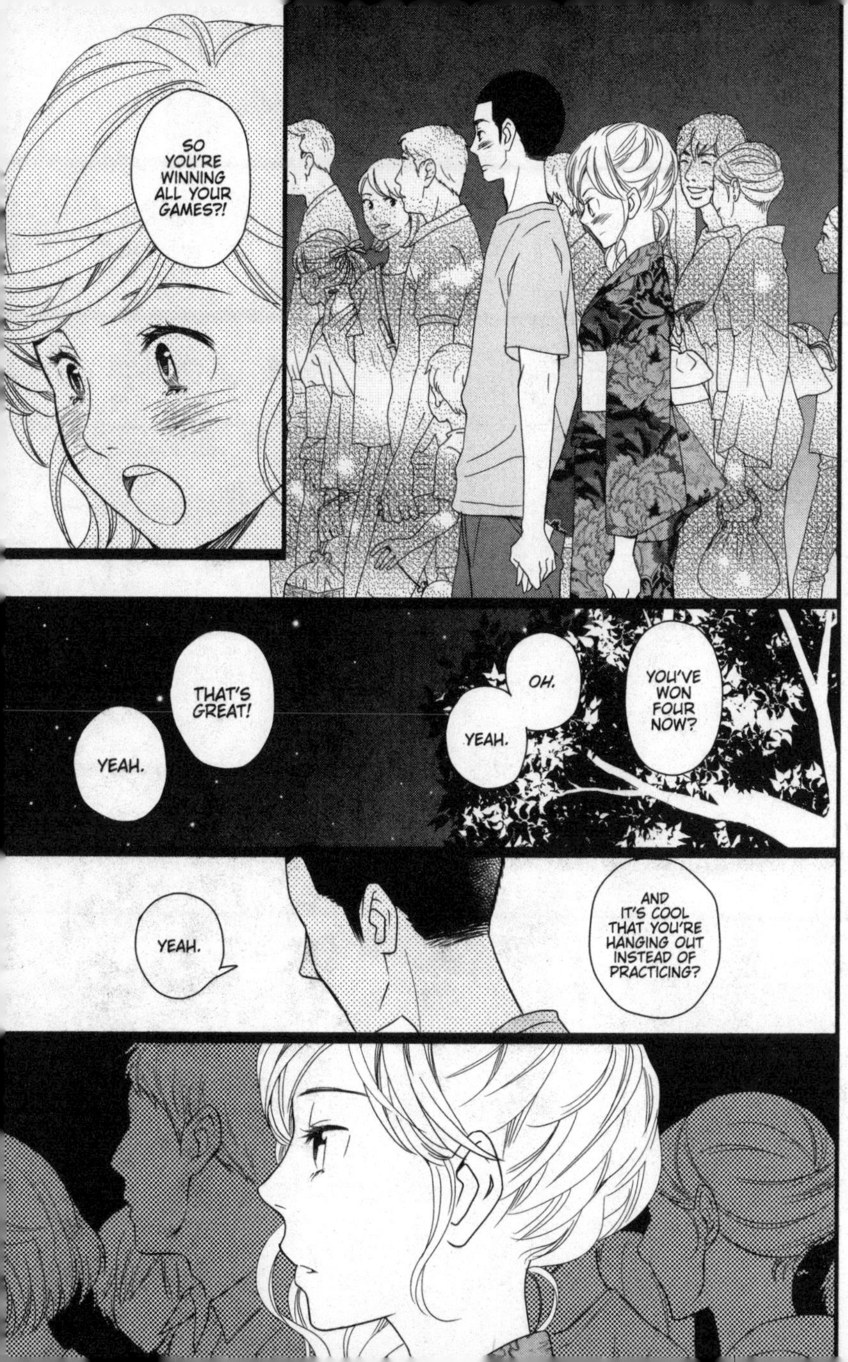
SO YOU'RE WINNING ALL YOUR GAMES?!
YOU'VE WON FOUR NOW?
OH.
YEAH.
THAT'S GREAT!
YEAH.
AND IT'S COOL THAT YOU'RE HANGING OUT INSTEAD OF PRACTICING?
YEAH.

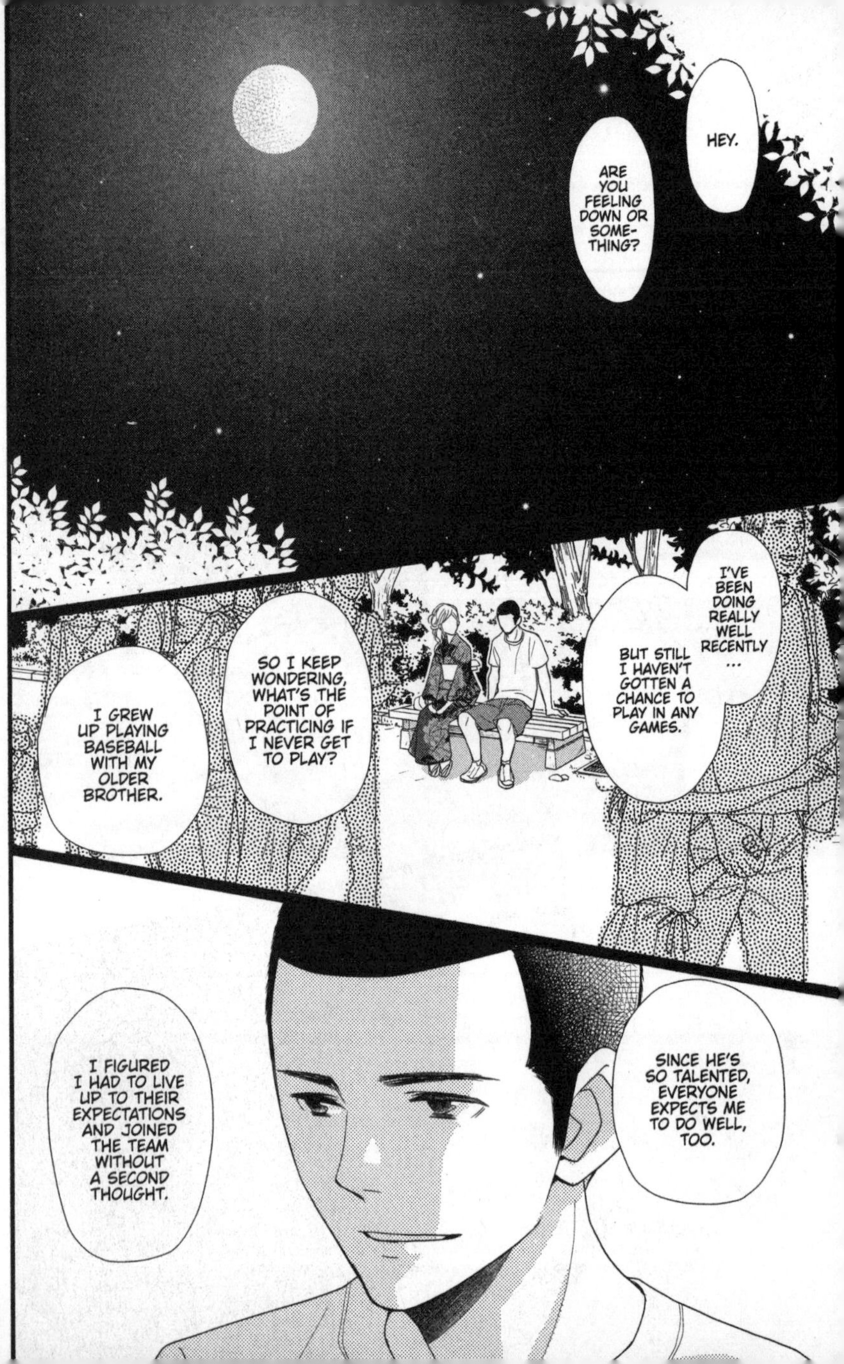
HEY.
ARE YOU FEELING DOWN OR SOME-THING?
I'VE BEEN DOING REALLY WELL RECENTLY ...
BUT STILL I HAVEN'T GOTTEN A CHANCE TO PLAY IN ANY GAMES.
SO I KEEP WONDERING, WHAT'S THE POINT OF PRACTICING IF I NEVER GET TO PLAY?
I GREW UP PLAYING BASEBALL WITH MY OLDER BROTHER.
SINCE HE'S SO TALENTED, EVERYONE EXPECTS ME TO DO WELL, TOO.
I FIGURED I HAD TO LIVE UP TO THEIR EXPECTATIONS AND JOINED THE TEAM WITHOUT A SECOND THOUGHT.

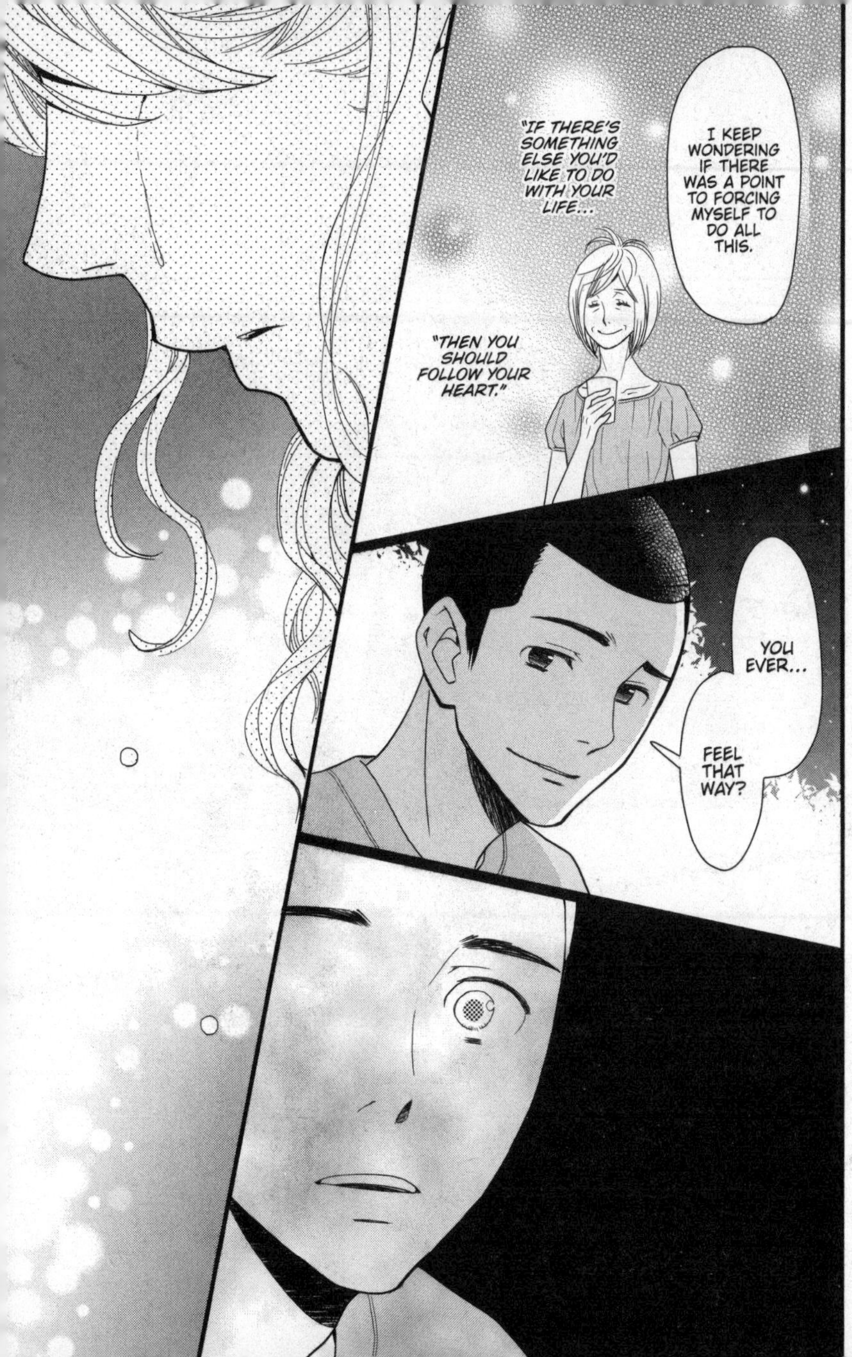
I KEEP WONDERING IF THERE WAS A POINT TO FORCING MYSELF TO DO ALL THIS.
"IF THERE'S SOMETHING ELSE YOU'D LIKE TO DO WITH YOUR LIFE...
"THEN YOU SHOULD FOLLOW YOUR HEART."
YOU EVER...
FEEL THAT WAY?

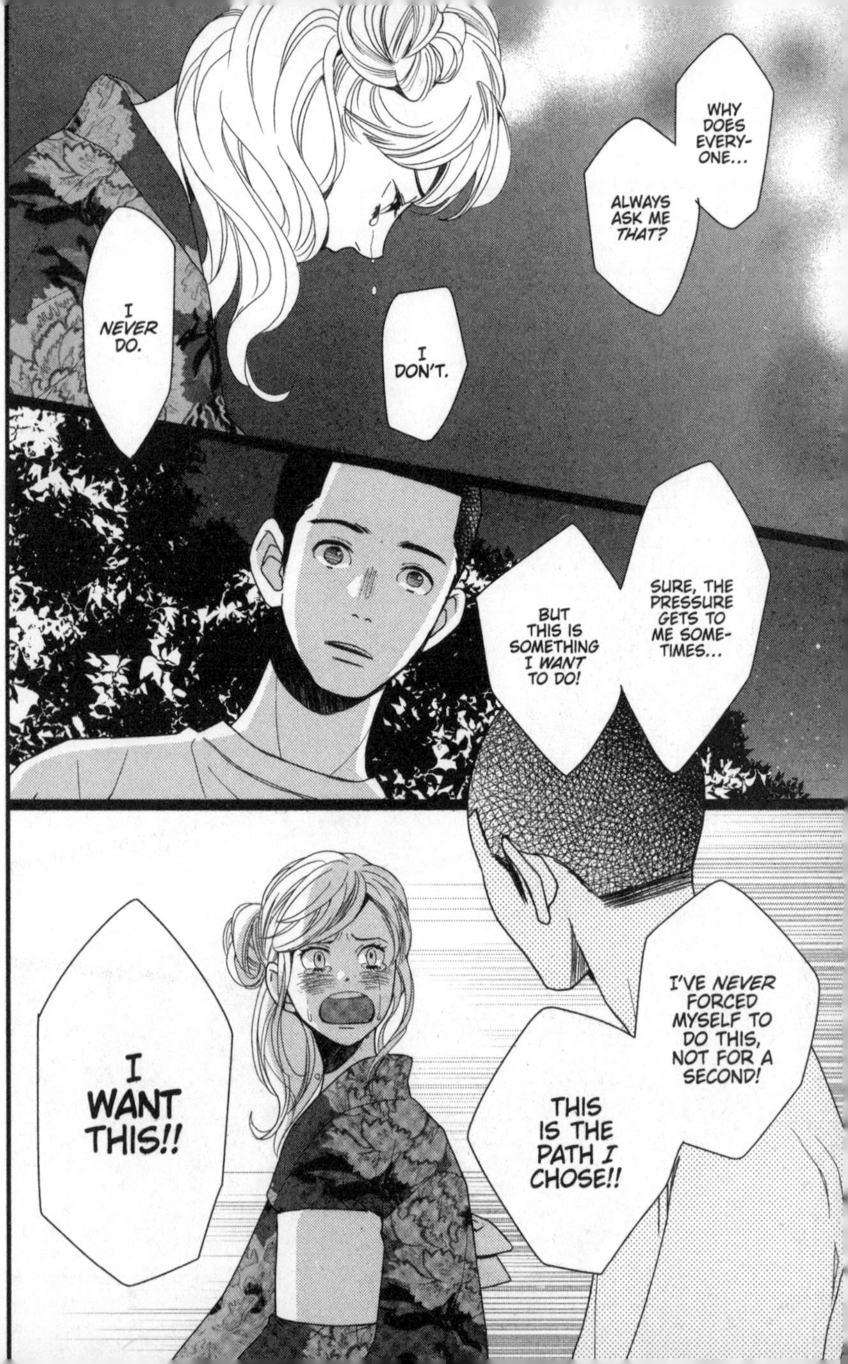
WHY DOES EVERY-ONE...
ALWAYS ASK ME THAT?
I DON'T.
I NEVER DO.
SURE, THE PRESSURE GETS TO ME SOME-TIMES...
BUT THIS IS SOMETHING I WANT TO DO!
I'VE NEVER FORCED MYSELF TO DO THIS, NOT FOR A SECOND!
THIS IS THE PATH I CHOSE!!
I WANT THIS!!

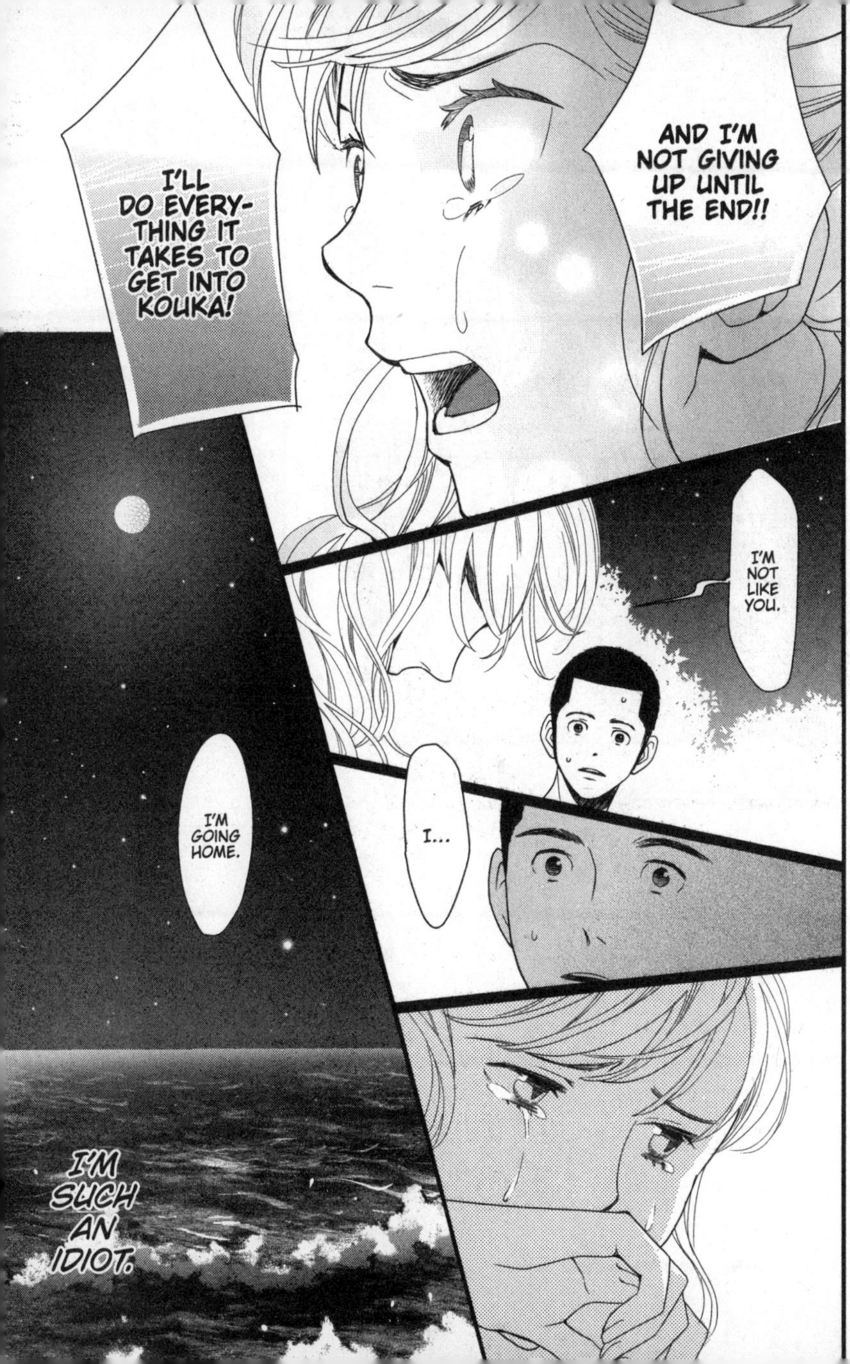
I'LL DO EVERY-THING IT TAKES TO GET INTO KOUKA!
AND I'M NOT GIVING UP UNTIL THE END!!
I'M NOT LIKE YOU.
I...
I'M GOING HOME.
I'M SUCH AN IDIOT.

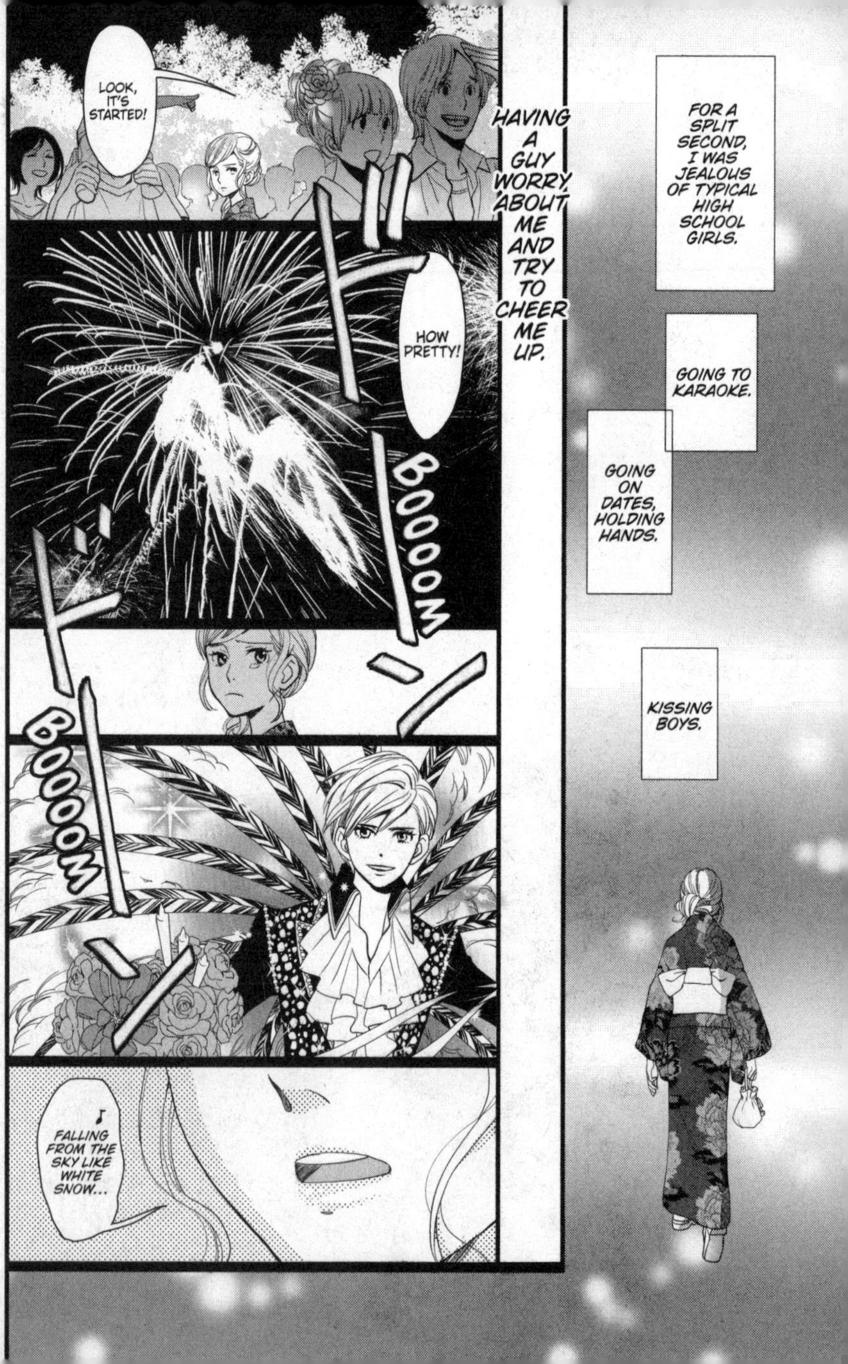
FOR A SPLIT SECOND, I WAS JEALOUS OF TYPICAL HIGH SCHOOL GIRLS.
GOING TO KARAOKE.
GOING ON DATES, HOLDING HANDS.
KISSING BOYS.
HAVING A GUY WORRY ABOUT ME AND TRY TO CHEER ME UP.
LOOK, IT'S STARTED!
HOW PRETTY!
BOOOOOM
BOOOOM
♪ FALLING FROM THE SKY LIKE WHITE SNOW...

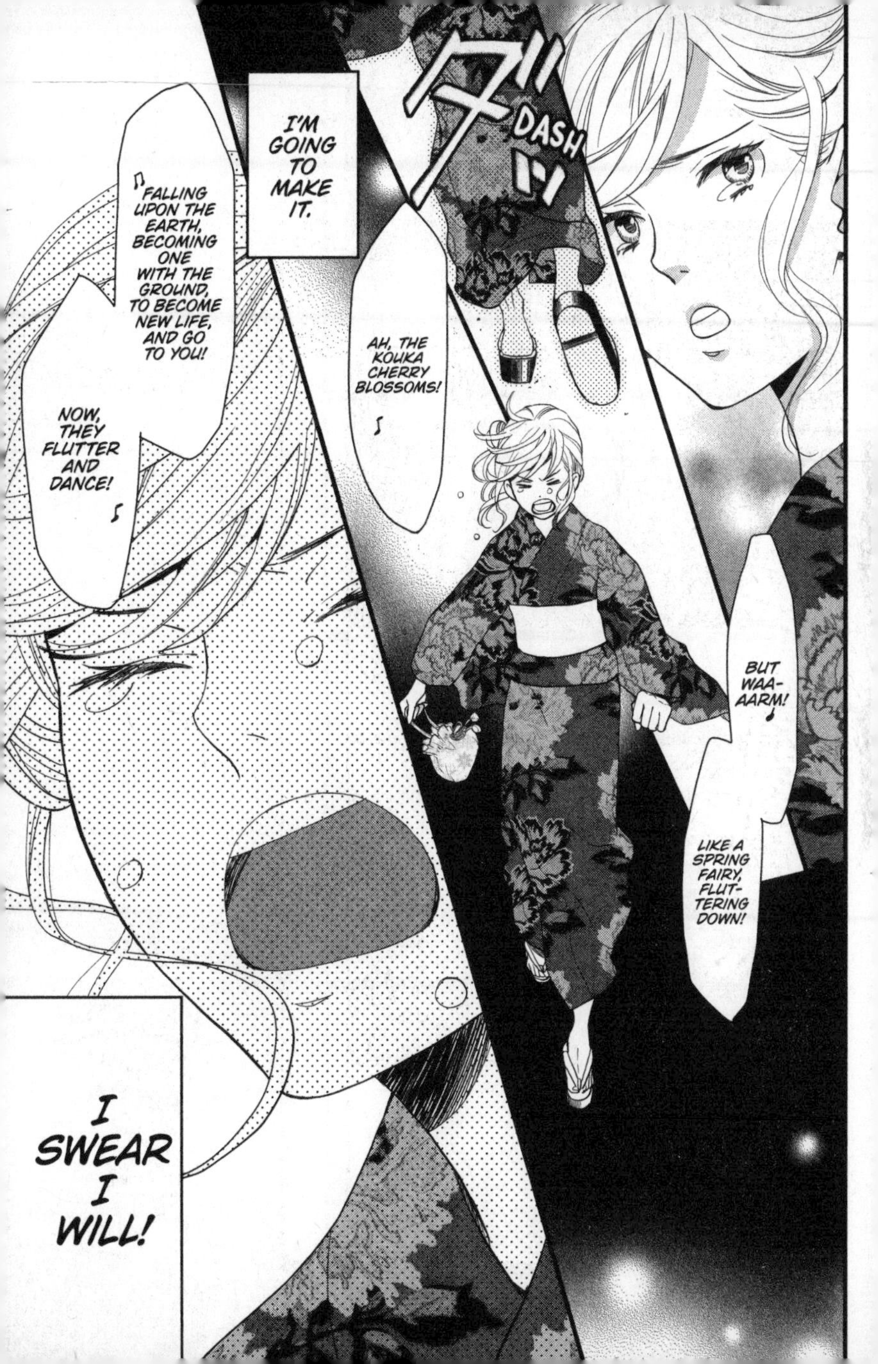
BUT WAA-AARM!
LIKE A SPRING FAIRY, FLUT-TERING DOWN!
ダッ DASH
I'M GOING TO MAKE IT.
AH, THE KOUKA CHERRY BLOSSOMS!
FALLING UPON THE EARTH, BECOMING ONE WITH THE GROUND, TO BECOME NEW LIFE, AND GO TO YOU!
NOW, THEY FLUTTER AND DANCE!
I SWEAR I WILL!

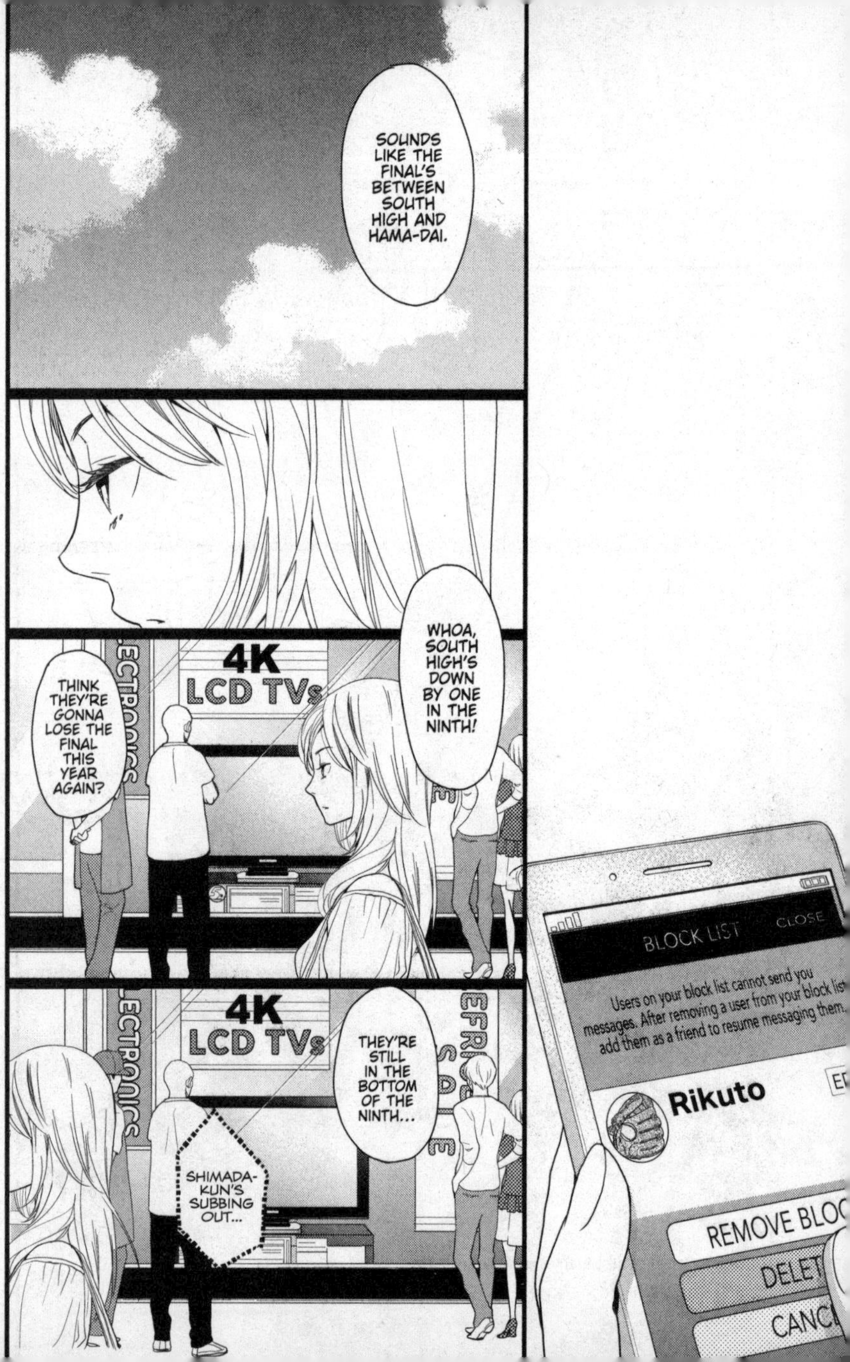
BLOCK LIST
CLOSE
Users on your block list cannot send you messages. After removing a user from your block lis
add them as a friend to resume messaging them.
Rikuto
REMOVE BLOC
DELET
CANC
SOUNDS LIKE THE FINAL'S BETWEEN SOUTH HIGH AND HAMA-DAI.
4K LCD TVs
WHOA, SOUTH HIGH'S DOWN BY ONE IN THE NINTH!
THINK THEY'RE GONNA LOSE THE FINAL THIS YEAR AGAIN?
4K LCD TVs
THEY'RE STILL IN THE BOTTOM OF THE NINTH...
SHIMADA-KUN'S SUBBING OUT...

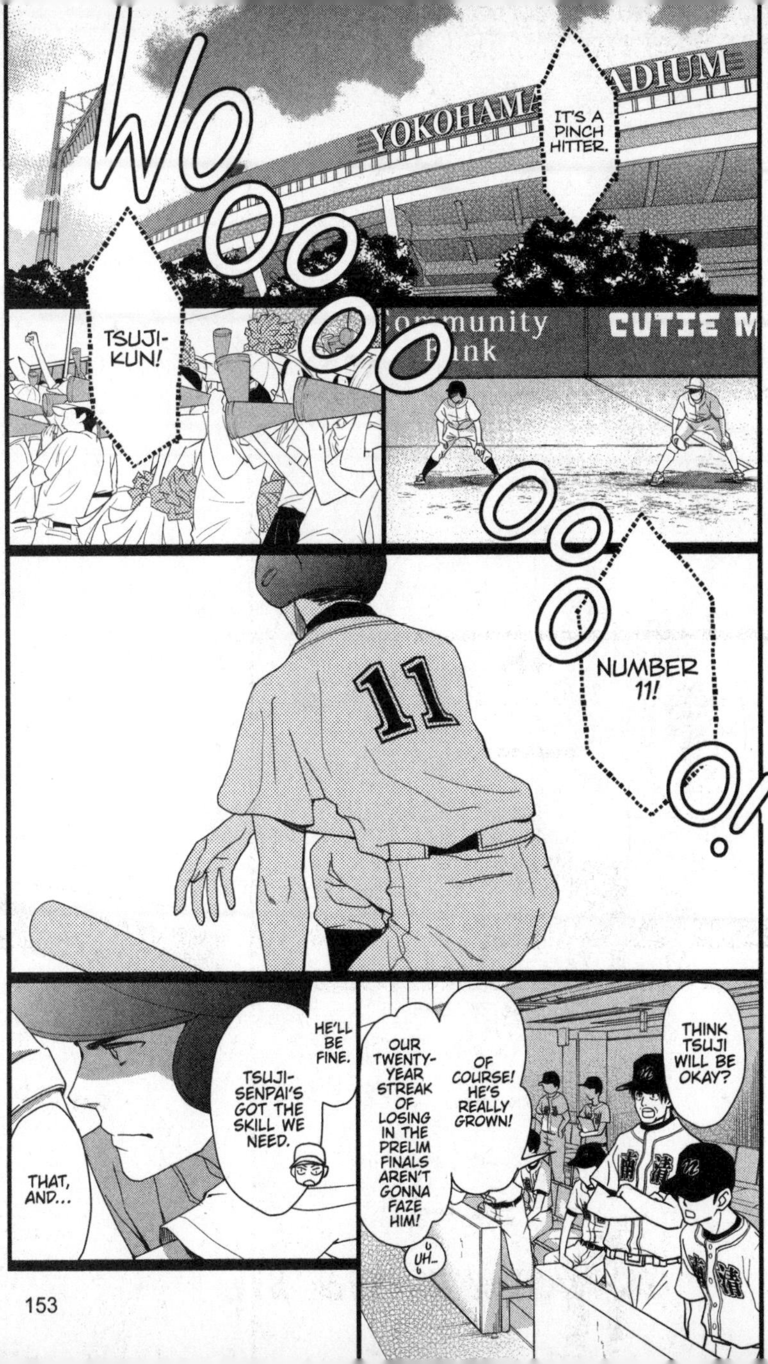
YOKOHAMA
ADIUM
IT'S A PINCH HITTER.
WOOOOOOOOOOO!
CUTIE M
TSUJI-KUN!
NUMBER 11!
THINK TSUJI WILL BE OKAY?
OF COURSE! HE'S REALLY GROWN!
OUR TWENTY-YEAR STREAK OF LOSING IN THE PRELIM FINALS AREN'T GONNA FAZE HIM!
UH...
HE'LL BE FINE.
TSUJI-SENPAI'S GOT THE SKILL WE NEED.
THAT, AND...

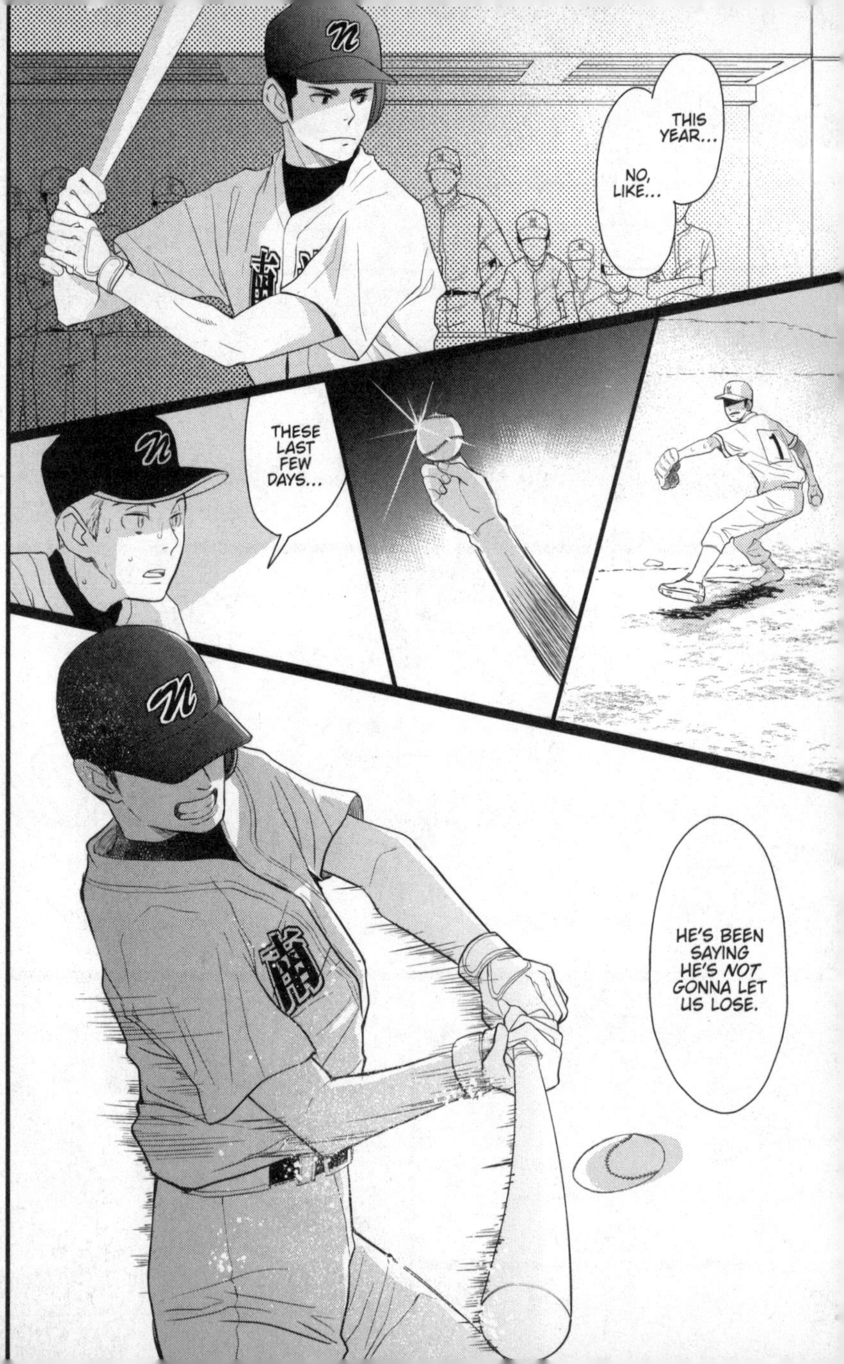
THIS YEAR...
NO, LIKE...
THESE LAST FEW DAYS...
HE'S BEEN SAYING HE'S *NOT* GONNA LET US LOSE.

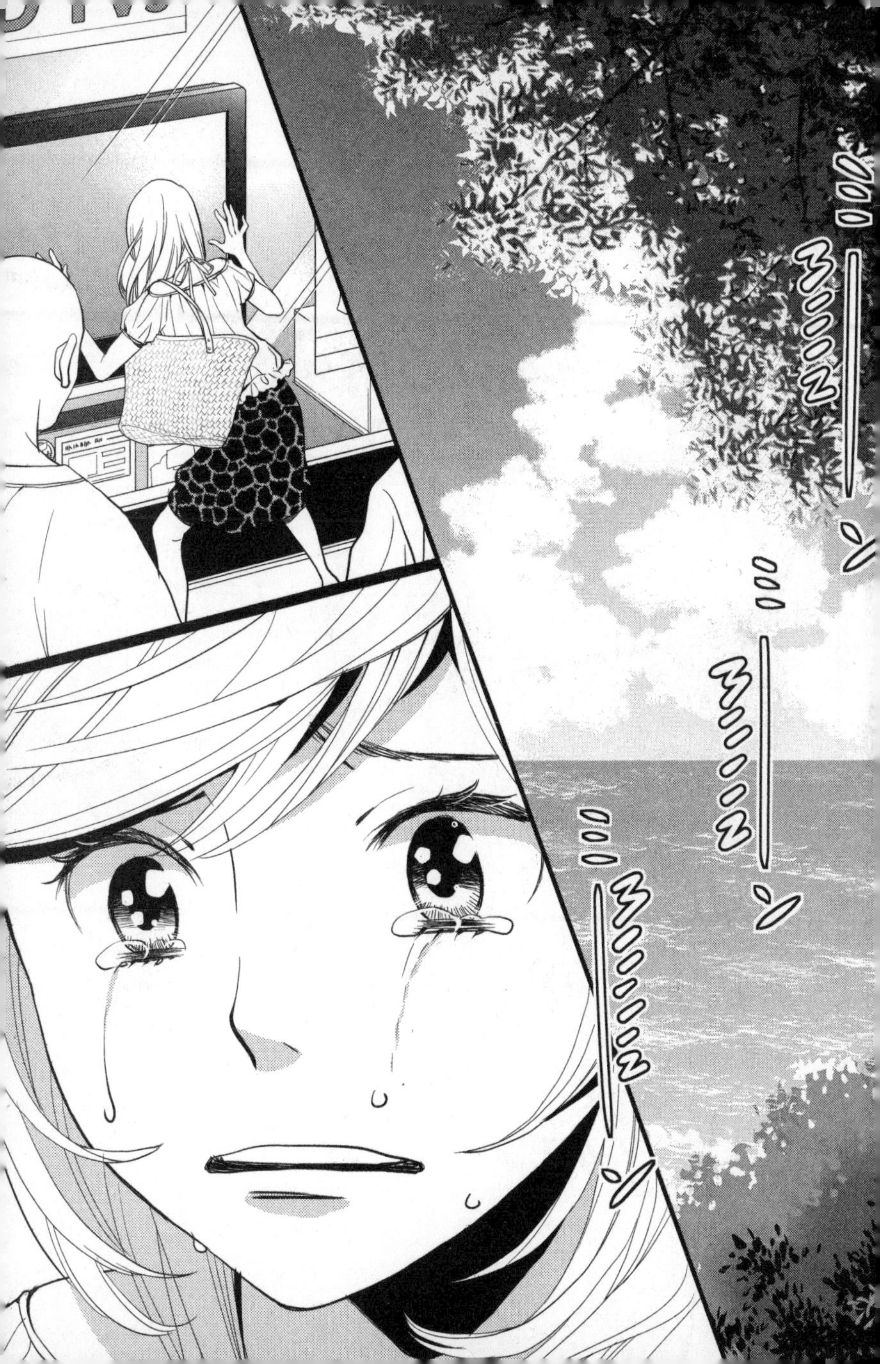
MOOON
MOOOOON
MOOOOOOON

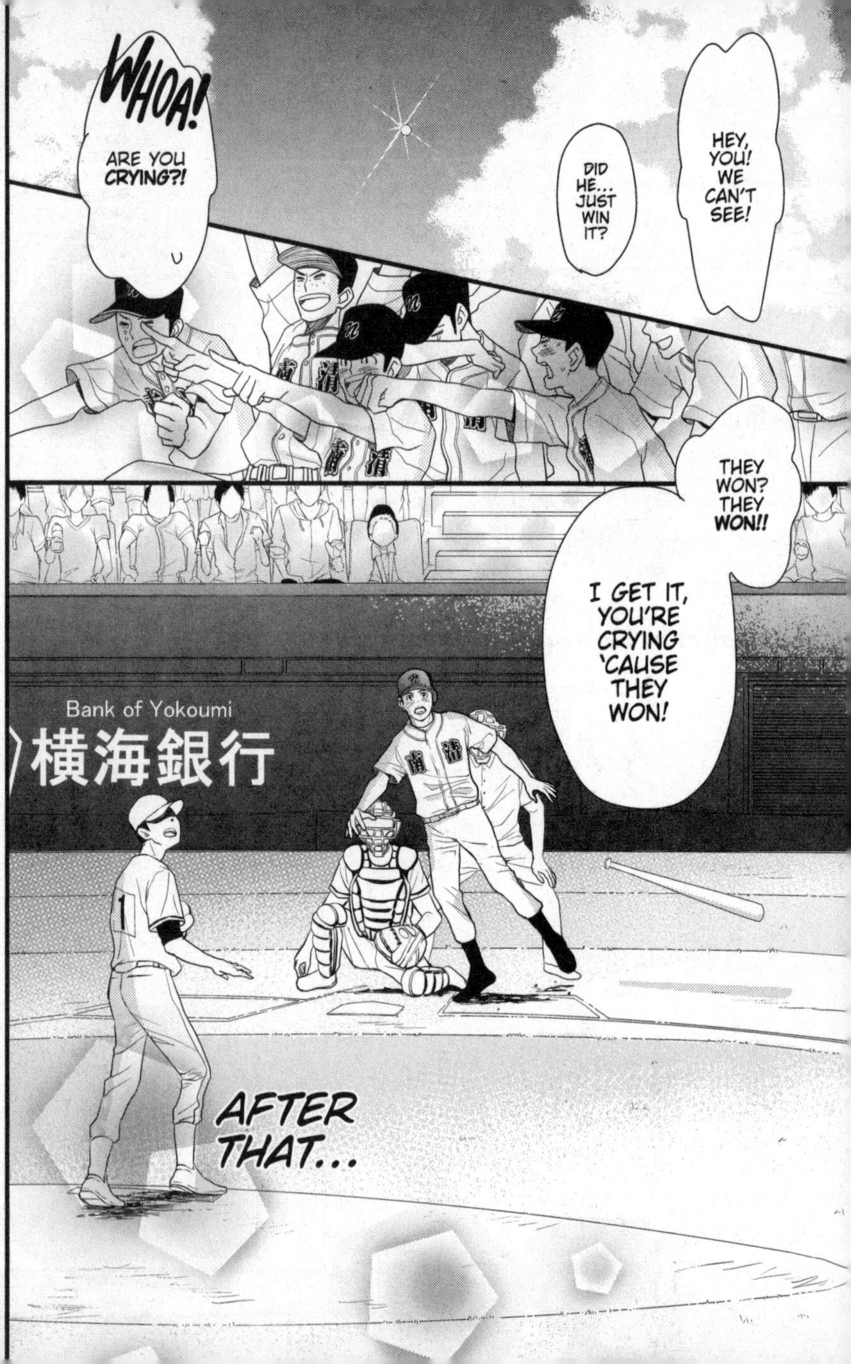
HEY, YOU! WE CAN'T SEE!
DID HE... JUST WIN IT?
WHOA!
ARE YOU CRYING?!
THEY WON? THEY WON!!
I GET IT, YOU'RE CRYING 'CAUSE THEY WON!
Bank of Yokoumi
横海銀行
AFTER THAT...

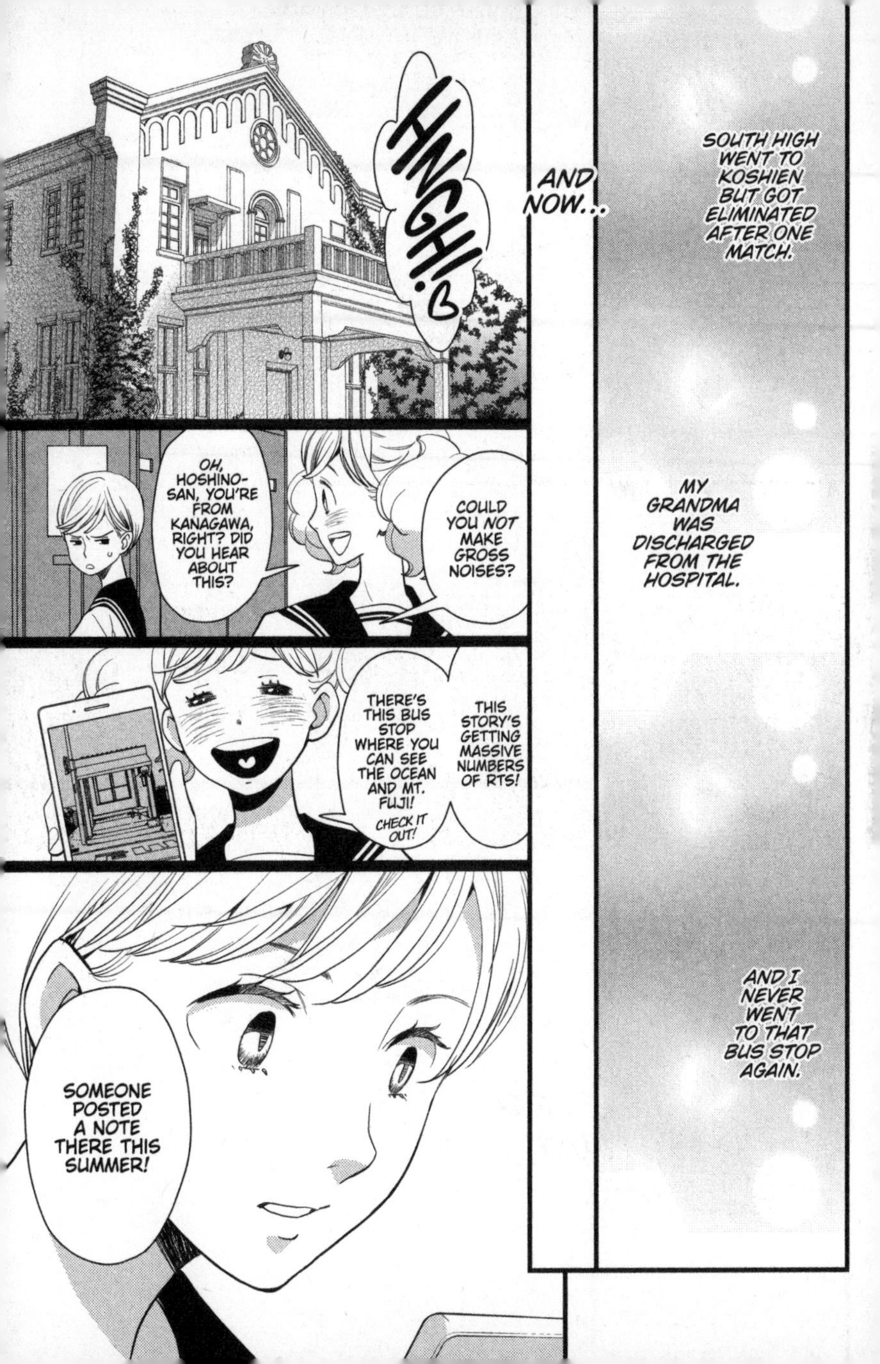
AND NOW...
SOUTH HIGH WENT TO KOSHIEN BUT GOT ELIMINATED AFTER ONE MATCH.
MY GRANDMA WAS DISCHARGED FROM THE HOSPITAL.
AND I NEVER WENT TO THAT BUS STOP AGAIN.
HNGH!♡
COULD YOU NOT MAKE GROSS NOISES?
OH, HOSHINO-SAN, YOU'RE FROM KANAGAWA, RIGHT? DID YOU HEAR ABOUT THIS?
THIS STORY'S GETTING MASSIVE NUMBERS OF RTS!
THERE'S THIS BUS STOP WHERE YOU CAN SEE THE OCEAN AND MT. FUJI!
CHECK IT OUT!
SOMEONE POSTED A NOTE THERE THIS SUMMER!

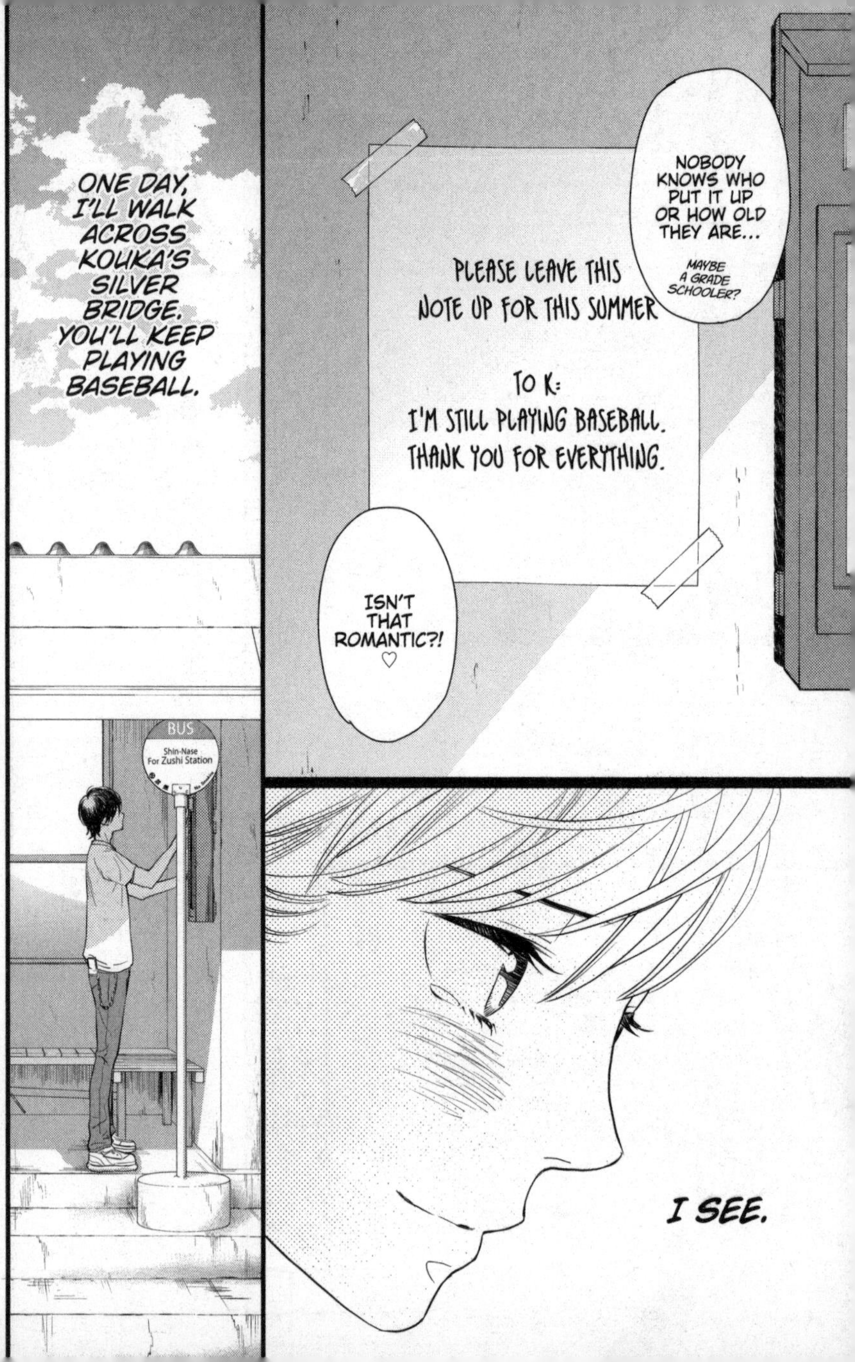
NOBODY KNOWS WHO PUT IT UP OR HOW OLD THEY ARE...
MAYBE A GRADE SCHOOLER?
PLEASE LEAVE THIS NOTE UP FOR THIS SUMMER
TO K: I'M STILL PLAYING BASEBALL. THANK YOU FOR EVERYTHING.
ISN'T THAT ROMANTIC?! ♡
I SEE.
ONE DAY, I'LL WALK ACROSS KOUKA'S SILVER BRIDGE. YOU'LL KEEP PLAYING BASEBALL.
BUS
Shin-Nase For Zushi Station

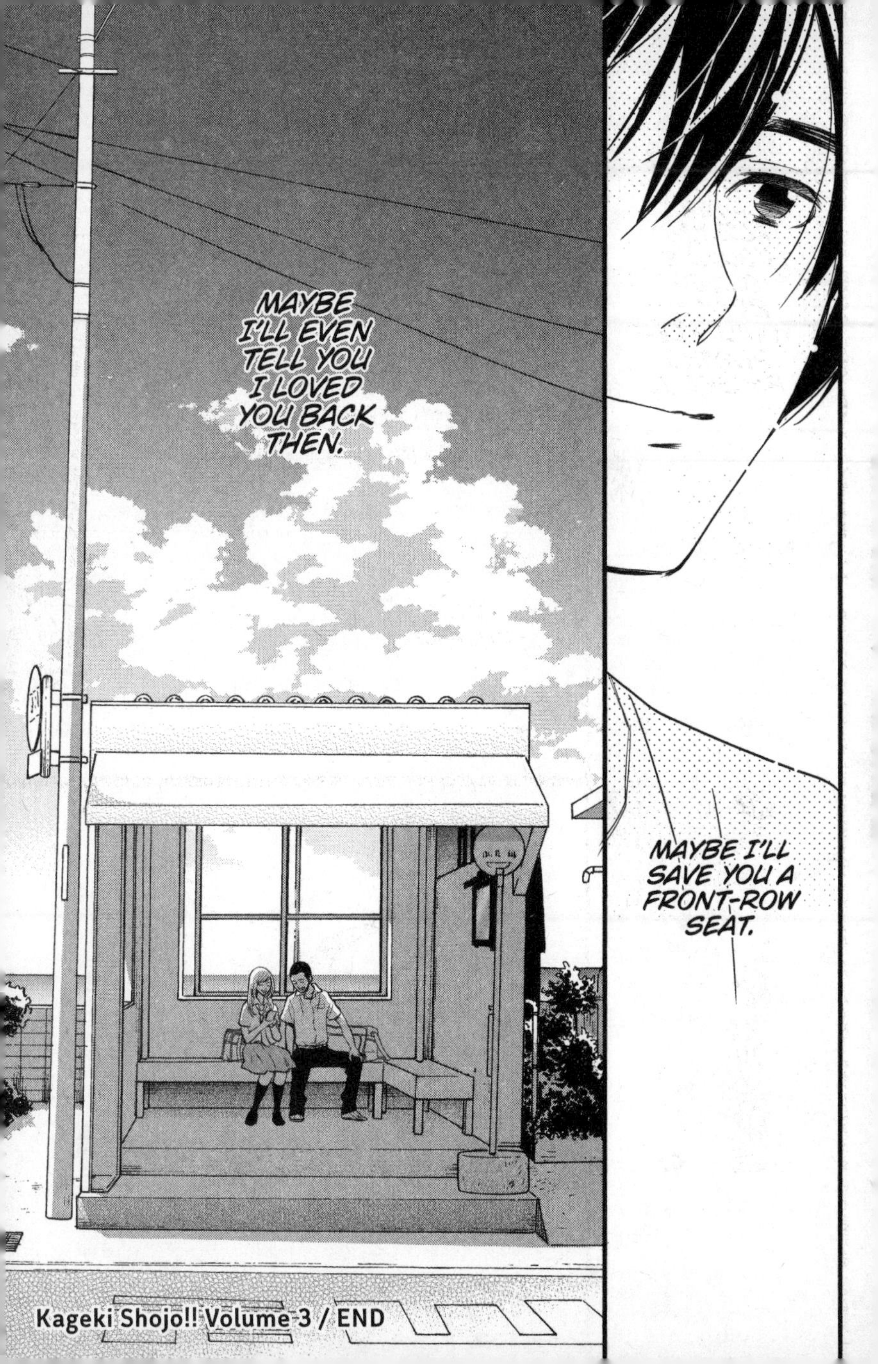
MAYBE I'LL SAVE YOU A FRONT-ROW SEAT.
MAYBE I'LL EVEN TELL YOU I LOVED YOU BACK THEN.
Kageki Shojo!! Volume 3 / END

SEVEN SEAS ENTERTAINMENT PRESENTS

KAGEKI SHOJO!!

story and art by KUMIKO SAIKI

VOLUME 3

TRANSLATION
Katrina Leonoudakis

LETTERING
Aila Nagamine

COVER DESIGN
Hanase Qi

LOGO DESIGN
Courtney Williams

PROOFREADER
Alyssa Honsowetz
B. Lillian Martin

EDITOR
Shannon Fay

PRINT MANAGER
Rhiannon Rasmussen-Silverstein

PRODUCTION ASSOCIATE
Christina McKenzie

PRODUCTION MANAGER
Lissa Pattillo

MANAGING EDITOR
Julie Davis

ASSOCIATE PUBLISHER
Adam Arnold

PUBLISHER
Jason DeAngelis

First published in Japan in 2016 by HAKUSENSHA, INC., Tokyo.
English language translation rights in U.S.A. arranged with HAKUSENSHA, INC., Tokyo through TOHAN CORPORATION, Tokyo.

Reference Material: The Rose of Versailles
© Ikeda Riyoko Production

Seven Seas press and purchase enquiries can be sent to Marketing Manager Lianne Sentar at press@gomanga.com. Information regarding the distribution and purchase of digital editions is available from Digital Manager CK Russell at digital@gomanga.com.

ISBN: 978-1-64827-634-7
Printed in Canada
First Printing: December 2021
10 9 8 7 6 5 4 3 2 1

READING DIRECTIONS

This book reads from ***right to left***, Japanese style. If this is your first time reading manga, you start reading from the top right panel on each page and take it from there. If you get lost, just follow the numbered diagram here. It may seem backwards at first, but you'll get the hang of it! Have fun!!

3
1
2
5
4
6
8
7
9

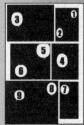

Follow us online: www.SevenSeasEntertainment.com